CW01496155

www.connectionsbooks.co.uk

STONES IN MY JAR

by

PAUL STUART

This edition first published in October 2017.

Paul Stuart asserts his right to be identified as the author of this work under the Copyright, Designs and Patents Act 1988.

ISBN: 978-0-244-93785-0

ALSO BY PAUL STUART

Connections 1 Who Did You Sit Next To Today?
Connections 2 Hell Has No Fury
Connections 3 That's None of Your Business
Connections 4 Which Room Did You Stay In?
Connections 5 I Need a Word
Connections 6 An Extraordinary Life
The Mobile and the Ring - The John Lomax Story
The Mobile and the Ring - The John Lomax Story (Hardcover)
Lomax and the Biker - The Complete Trilogy (Limited Edition Hardcover)
The Exmoor Trilogy – (Limited Edition Hardcover)

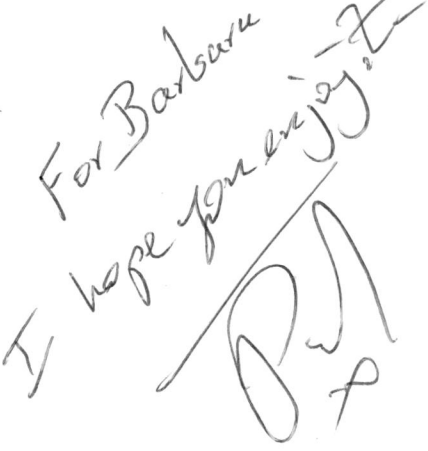

FOREWORD

A philosophy professor stood in front of his students, having already placed some items on the desk in front of him. He waited for the stragglers to sneak in sheepishly, looked around the room to make sure he had the attention of all, and proceeded to pick up a large jar and fill it with stones, each measuring about six centimetres in diameter. He then asked the last student to arrive, just for the sake of embarrassment, whether the jar was full. The red faced student whispered that it was.

The professor smiled, picked up a box of pebbles and poured them into the jar. He shook the jar lightly. The pebbles, of course, rolled into the open spaces between the stones. He asked another student, who appeared to be distracted by texting on her mobile phone, whether the jar was now full. The student, without paying much attention, said that it was.

The professor picked up a box of sand and poured it into the jar. By this time, he had the attention of the entire audience. The sand, naturally, filled up everything else.

"Now," said the professor, "I want you to recognise this is your life. The stones are the important things, your family, your partner, your health, your children, things that if everything else was lost and only they remained, your life would still be full. The pebbles are the other things that matter like your job, your house, your car. The sand is everything else. The small stuff. If you put the sand into the jar first, there would be no room for the pebbles or the stones.

The same goes for your life. If you spend all your time and energy on the small stuff, such as your mobile phone, you will never have room for the things that are important to you. Pay attention to the things that are critical to your happiness. Play with your children. Take care of your health, take your partner out dancing. There will always be time to go to work, clean the house, give a dinner party and deal with the rubbish. Take care of the stones first: the things that really matter. Set your priorities. The rest is just sand."

I think that professor was on to something. We all make excuses for not doing things. We erect barriers. We all have everyday things to deal with and we allow them to become too important. It is far too easy for the trivial to overtake the crucial. How many mothers have you seen with a child in a pushchair totally engrossed in her mobile phone instead of interacting with her infant?

It is also important that we actually do the things we really want to do. There isn't really an acceptable reason for putting off doing something you've always wanted to do. There are only excuses. If the desire is strong enough, if the burning is there, you make time; you find the space.

I found the time and space to write my first book, but I had to remove the clutter, the excuses. I had to assess and change priorities and most crucially of all, I have had to rely on the people who matter to me most.

My lovely wife, Jan, without whom I wouldn't have completed one book, let alone this, the seventh, and who has guided and supported me in all things. My Mum and Dad, more than just parents, more like carefully chosen friends. All three; the stones in my jar.

It would be invidious to try to name my other true friends as I am bound to leave somebody out and that would be embarrassing. They know who they are, I think.

Just to make you smile, one of the professor's students strolled to the front of the room, picked up the jar full of stones, pebbles and sand and proceeded to pour a can of beer into it. Of course, the beer soaked the sand and filled any remaining spaces within the jar, making it truly full. He turned to his fellow students and said, "no matter how full your life is, there is always room for beer."

I wonder whether life's experiences have changed his priorities?

PROLOGUE

OUT WITH THE OLD: IN WITH THE NEW.

Ray Quinn was a patient man, but even he had been sorely tested. He was looking for whatever Sandy Lane had left secretly hidden at The Exford White Horse Inn and he was convinced that Quentin Legard was involved in some way. The highest authority in the land had interrupted his quest by seeking his assistance on another issue. He had been given the highest possible clearance and complete freedom as to how he pursued the matter and he had delivered, in the face of enormous odds.

But it had stalled his quest and he knew he needed to complete his search for the file which had been secreted by his old foe, Sandy Lane. He had promised himself that he would pursue it as soon as he had completed his current task. He hadn't realised at the outset, of course, that it was all inextricably linked. Finally, Quentin Legard, before his unfortunate rendezvous with the Atlantic Ocean, had inadvertently led him to the file.

And so it was that Ray Quinn was able to hand all the material to the Prime Minister. He was relieved to be rid of the burden.

"Do you know what is in this?" asked the politician.

Before Quinn could frame a reply, the Prime Minister continued.

"Please don't answer that, Mr. Quinn. It would put you in an invidious position and you don't deserve that. If anybody wants to know, I'll tell them that I didn't ask you. Put it down to my oversight."

"I understand," Quinn affirmed.

He decided it was best not to say anything more at that moment, so he restricted himself to a knowing smile as he handed over the document. It contained a transcript from the listening device delivered by Books and the second section, the necessary adjunct to the document, which had been hidden by Sandy Lane in a secret place at The White Horse Inn at Exford, in the heart of Exmoor. The final pieces of the jigsaw. Lane had come into possession of the first section of the explosive document as a result of arresting a terrorist in an apparently unrelated operation. The arrested terrorist had stolen it from a well-known philanthropist, who was trusted by both sides and was acting as an intermediary between them. The document had been offered up to enable the terrorist and the members of his group to be given softer treatment by the British. It listed plans to co-ordinate attacks by various terrorist groups as a concerted effort. The heart of Exmoor had become the heart of existence of the country itself.

By itself, the first section was bad enough but the second section, together with the transcript, now also being held so carefully by the Prime Minister, confirmed details, descriptions, e-mail addresses, Facebook and Twitter information, other more secret information, even simple details such as phone numbers, and, most crucially, locations of the nation's most wanted terrorists and their sponsors. It also gave a list of future targets, both human and otherwise. Now complete, the document was, quite literally, dynamite on a world-wide scale. It possessed the power to unseat governments, send establishment figures to jail or their deaths, send nations and movements to war, cause massive and intractable political problems and much, much more. Quinn thought it could be so potent and could pose such a threat to stability that nobody would have the fortitude to use it for the common good.

The Prime Minister held the file with a surprising gentleness of touch, as if it would explode.

"Don't worry, Ray," the Prime Minister said, "I will use it appropriately. We cannot go on as we have."

Ray Quinn smiled again at the Prime Minister. Here, possibly, just possibly, at long last, was a leader who demanded respect, and Quinn recognized a kindred spirit. Once in a generation, maybe even less often than that, such a person came along. He shook hands with a firmness that both understood. There had grown a mutual respect between them. They held each other's eyes for a lingering moment, before Quinn turned and left the room, and the service of his country.

Her Majesty watched the exchange and smiled inwardly, still holding the ceremonial sword with which she had conferred Ray Quinn's knighthood in complete secrecy in a small room hidden from public view. She sighed with gratitude and pleasure at the poignancy of the moment. If only there were more like him, she mused to herself.

The only witnesses had been an extremely proud wife and an equally impressed Prime Minister.

Quinn realised he had, almost by osmosis, become more of a case manager than the man of action he preferred to be. It was time to walk away. He took comfort from, and indeed was proud of, the fact that he was leaving a legacy. He had established a team that was built in his image.

Sir Raymond Quinn took his new title and his long-suffering wife to what she hoped would be a quiet retirement. Her hopes and reality would be different, she knew. Quinn, bless him, could never fully withdraw. Men like him never do. All she could realistically expect was that the interruptions to her Utopia would be few and far between.

For his part, Frank, tried and tested friend, comrade in too many scrapes to recount, now took the reins of the ultra-secret unit and would only seek assistance from his old friend and mentor in extremis. He took responsibility for all Ray Quinn's legacies, which included John Lomax, his wife Leanne, and her son Billy, who was now living in Australia. They had been involved in an earlier case, but there were still connections to the present. Tenuous links, maybe; they were there, nevertheless. He didn't yet realise it, but they would now be needed. He would have to call in their debt and it would not be an easy assignment.

Frank's daughter, Emily, had already proved herself within the unit, and was now central to its success or failure. Complicated young woman though she undoubtedly was, she had a gift that training couldn't instill. She was a person who didn't think in straight lines. She had an uncanny ability to find the small things, the important minutiae that turned things around. Books, a recent addition to the team after their previous case, brought his own particular brand of street cunning and knowledge. He had graduated from being a young street pick pocket to a fast maturing, clever operator, with a toughness that Frank admired and needed in the team. His disposal of Quentin Legard over the Atlantic Ocean proved that.

All in all, a small and very effective elite team had been put together. It was about to be tested to its limits as body parts started springing up all over the place and the illegal arms trade exercised its insidious, far-reaching, secretive and deadly influence. Ray Quinn and Frank supervise from a distance as Emily's special gift is stretched to its limit and her fragility is exposed. Books must step up, but is he up to the task? And all the time the relationship between them develops. Love is in the air, just to complicate matters.

-1-

HM Prison, Dartmoor, Princetown, Devon.

"Welcome to my humble abode."

Jon Johnston opened his hands in what was intended as a spreading gesture, but they only got about eight inches apart, as if the ghosts of handcuffs were still in place.

"This is nice," said Emily, taking in her surroundings, "the latest in furniture design."

She was looking at Formica tables with metal legs and felt the heat of the overhead fluorescent lighting. No daylight penetrated that far into the prison. There were official notices on the wall and a couple of prison warders watched everything in a kind of bored detachment.

"How are you settling in?" she asked. "Are the neighbours friendly?

"Well, I haven't met the other six hundred and thirty- nine," Johnston replied. "I think I'll have to freshen things up a bit, maybe repaint, before I invite people to drop in. You know how it is."

"Will you manage it?" Emily asked, meaning the time rather than the paintwork.

Johnston had been handed a four-year sentence, every second of it deserved. She had been instrumental in putting him behind bars, but he didn't seem to bear a grudge. Jon Johnston was a bent ex-copper with a line in fraud and one or two worse things besides. She knew she shouldn't like him, but couldn't help herself. He wasn't nasty, or evil; just a chancer who had made too many mistakes.

"Four years, serve two. Yeah, I'll manage." His face went through a few different expressions before settling on something blandly generic. "In my first week here, a bloke in the same wing as me killed himself. Took a piece of broken glass." He made a gesture along the inside of both wrists. "They only noticed when there was blood leaking out from under the door." He shook his head instead of finishing, but Emily understood perfectly. "Idiot was only in for eighteen months and didn't even seem depressed, apparently."

She thought for a moment, but only recalled it vaguely, as so much had happened to her since. What she did remember was the arrest. It was a young father who worked for a precision engineering company. Nice lad, doing well. Everything going for him and he had a good future. Done for trying to import cocaine from southern Spain, in a shipment of steel tubing. He lost his job, his wife, his children and ended up in the loving embrace of Dartmoor Prison. Life over.

"You'll be okay, Jon," Emily tried reassurance.

"Yeah, once I get the place freshened up a bit, eh?"

They talked for another thirty minutes, which to both, for different reasons, felt like a century. When she left the building, she found she was almost running away from the high granite walls as they loomed over her, dominating that area of the moor, exuding menace and instilling fear with the legacy of their history.

They seemed to be reaching out for her, trying to gather her up to entomb her within, and add her to the broken lives they had already captured.

-2-

Prison time drags they say and Jon Johnston spent some of the early days of his sentence whiling away the hours reading about his new palace and its history. He quickly became something of an expert on the subject as he filled his mind with information that he knew he would have no cause to use unless he entered Mastermind and used it as his specialist subject. Nevertheless, he wrote down what he had found.

Dartmoor is a Category C men's prison, owned by the Duchy of Cornwall. It took three years to build and in 1809 took in its first prisoners. They were French captured during the Napoleonic War in 1805. They were joined in 1812 by American POWs taken in the war of 1812. At one time the prison population numbered almost 6,000. When both wars ended repatriation took place and it lay empty until 1850 when it was commissioned for convicts. It was closed again in 1917 and converted into a Work Centre for conscientious objectors. From 1920 its use was changed again and it housed some of Britain's most serious offenders.

The prison still has a reputation for being a high-security prison that is escape-proof, but it is no longer an accurate depiction. It now houses mainly non-violent offenders and also offers sex offender treatment programmes.

Dartmoor prison has also featured many times in popular culture. In John Galsworthy's play 'Escape' the hero escapes from the prison; Evelyn Waugh's 'Decline and Fall' makes thinly disguised references to it; Agatha Christie mentions it in 'The Thirteen Problems; Arthur Conan Doyle uses it in four stories between 1890 and 1903 and it features in 'The Hound of the Baskervilles'; Sherlock Holmes uses it in 'Dressed to Kill'. It features in

'The Tales of Old Dartmoor' episode of the Goons which was recorded in 1956; an episode of 'The Saint in 1966; the parody of 'The Smurf Song' by the Barron Knights. In 1988 the prison played host to Den Watts in 'Eastenders', as well as Nick Cotton. In the first episode of the second series of 'James May's Man Lab', May and Oz Clarke were demonstrating map reading skills by pretending to escape from the prison and cross Dartmoor to their escape car.

Whilst on the subject of escape, the 'Dartmoor Jailbreak' is a charity event which takes place every year, in which members of the public escape from the prison and attempt to travel as far as possible in four days without paying for transport. Some have managed incredible distances.

All of this he committed to memory purely to pass the time.

-3-

Her diary said it was an October Friday afternoon, but nature had other ideas. Abnormally high clouds scudded in from the Atlantic Ocean and were dragging plenty of sunshine with them. The last shreds of summer seemed reluctant to say goodbye, even though leaves were falling as they should at that time of year.

Emily was embedded, under cover, in an area police force. The aim was to target corruption within the force. It didn't matter what was involved, what rank or level, Emily had been inserted to identify and root out the cancers. She had been attached via 'promotion' from another force. All her paperwork had been meticulously prepared and her 'legend' invented so that it would withstand the most rigorous scrutiny.

It was, for her, an exciting assignment. She had earned it, Frank said, with her role in the capture of 'The Elegant Lady' in Ray Quinn's last case. It was his gift to her as reward. His use of the word 'gift' was deliberate, as he was referring not just to his reward to her but also to her own special talent; her 'gift.' Her ability to think and reason in different ways to normal people. Outside the box didn't cover it. There was more to it than that. She didn't think in straight lines, didn't use logic as others do, saw things that the majority of people miss. In short, she was unique. Or, at least, a rare talent. These qualities made her an invaluable member of his team. She just needed to be managed. Carefully and with discretion.

Books, another member of Frank's small, and highly secret team was similarly tasked. He had come a long way since his days of petty thieving and eking out a living in the seediest parts of London. The streets were definitely not paved with gold in his experience, but he had survived. His role in the demise of Quentin Legard, also in Ray Quinn's final case, had alerted Frank to his possibilities. Books understood the streets and how they worked. His background, together with an unusually ruthless streak nurtured in early manhood, were assets to be utilized. Books, too, just needed to be managed. Carefully and with discretion.

It meant that they could work together as much as possible, whilst retaining the capacity to carry out investigations alone where necessary. It also meant that their burgeoning affinity could flourish.

And then, just to complicate matters, love was most definitely in the air. Frank knew, of course. He didn't mind at all, as long as it didn't hinder their work. In fact, he recognized that it might have its advantages, if managed appropriately. Just another ball in the air to him. Just another management task requiring care and discretion.

Frank had learned from Ray Quinn. Understatement, detailed planning and flexibility were watchwords for them. There also had to be a mean, ruthless streak, which, if brought into play, was always hard and uncompromising. There could be no other way. Their lives had been saved by these maxims on many occasions. Together, of course, with total trust. Their time in the SAS had hammered that home.

Emily was in a patrol car with a PC Alan Conley, returning from wasting most of their day knocking on doors searching for information about a late night fight outside a dubious club. One young female, apparently drunk, displaying far too much flesh and provoking the bouncers with her foul language, had been injured. Two men, apparently vying for her company and her physical attractions, had also been hurt. One of them was in hospital with a fractured skull and, no doubt, with his pride severely dented. They had discovered nothing useful, but hadn't expected to. If the CCTV had been working across the road things would have been much easier, but it wasn't. They were thus reduced to knocking on doors, receiving little co-operation and less information. They were just showing willing, really; letting the locals know they were around, albeit some hours after the event and too late to make a difference. Ticking boxes in place of being on the beat as the public would prefer. Doing it because it was expected.

They were tired and drifting along, winding down as the end of their shift approached, preparing to return to the normality of whatever they each planned for their hours off duty. Conley's radio squawked and interrupted their pleasant reverie. Amidst the mushy interference it told of an incident not far away. Conley tweaked the control and established a slightly clearer reception. Someone had discovered something illegal in a house clearance and found it necessary to dial 999. They looked at each other. Both knew they could let it go and others would pick it up, but for different reasons complacency was not an option. Emily was alert to the possibilities the call might bring, while Conley was still at the honeymoon stage of his early career. Illegal rubbish didn't sound promising, but it would be a change from pounding the streets knocking on doors. It might just be an interesting end to the day.

Emily asked for the address as Conley turned the unmarked car around. The dispatcher's voice, almost whispering for some reason, pointed them in the direction of the reservoir. It wasn't the sort of address that generally gave trouble, being an area of tidy front gardens and net curtains. Neatly clipped privet hedges marked the boundaries between bungalows and Lladro china figures kept watch from window-sills.

The first thing they saw as they drew into the only remaining space on the drive was a blue van with its doors open, swinging in the strengthening autumnal wind. A cherry tree hung over them, its branches stripped bare of blossom.

The car stopped, but Emily didn't jump out immediately. She chose to take stock. Experience had already taught her the value of treading carefully. She knew the importance of preserving the scene. After all, they didn't yet know the nature of the 'illegal rubbish.' Conley stepped out of the car and introduced himself to the men from the clearance company. Emily waited until the handshaking was over before joining the group. She noticed that Conley failed to introduce her, even though she was, as far as outsider observers were concerned, the superior officer. She hid her feelings about the lack of manners and protocol, deciding to store it and come back to it later. She preferred to deal with the matter at hand first and stood back watching the clouds scoot along above her head.

She was close enough to hear the initial details as the clearance men told her colleague the reason for their call. They said the bungalow belonged to an old woman who had passed away a couple of months ago. Her nearest family were on the other side of the world in Australia.

Emily noticed their blue van was packed with old-lady furniture. She saw curved mahogany legs and green trim, beige cushions with pale blue tassels before the swinging doors prevented further viewing.

PC Alan Conley, in uniform, walked with the men in the direction of the garage. Emily, in plain clothes, followed. She took in the raised garage door with the half full skip in front. It contained a fair few pieces of old garden junk, some pots of paint with dried up drips down their sides, a couple of brooms without any bristles. Movement caught her eye and she saw a large spider, its carefully selected hiding place disturbed and about to be destroyed, crawling across a cobwebbed deckchair. She shuddered. She hadn't found much to be afraid of in her young life, but spiders, small and large, always seemed to give her the shivers. There were several pieces of garden furniture stacked neatly along one wall of the garage. Emily wondered who had put them there because the old lady died two months ago, which was just when the furniture should be outside being put to its intended use. Somebody must have moved them into the garage after she had passed, unless they had not been used all summer.

Emily was good at logic and she often spotted things that others missed. In fact, it had become something of a standing joke among her colleagues, who had learned to be careful when she was around, for fear of her spotting something embarrassing and storing it for future use. Somebody had once asked her the secret of how she did it, and she simply replied "it's a gift." It became her nickname thereafter.

She didn't need her sharpest skills to spot the chest freezer, residing along the back wall of the garage. Emily thought it was a few years old because the original brilliant whiteness of its casing had been greyed by dust and damp. It was large enough to feed a small army, she speculated, but was only about half full. Or half empty, depending on your outlook on life.

The other thing she noticed was the smell. The power to the garage had been switched off and the contents of the freezer had defrosted. The carefully wrapped packages of lamb and other meat had already begun to leak and the colour had turned to a greyish yellow. The frozen fruit was now just a sloppy mush. Somebody had placed a wheelie bin beside the freezer and the bags were put into it as they were lifted by thickly gloved hands.

Emily's eyes took it all in quickly. Then she noticed the reason for the 999 call. It was a polythene bag, more than a metre in length, which had been placed on the concrete floor in front of the other items. It had the same colour as the other decaying meat and sat in a similar puddle of leaking liquid. It had the same smell as well. The big difference was that it looked remarkably like a human leg. The big giveaway was that it was wearing a high-heeled shoe.

-4-

PC Alan Conley was the first to spot the leg and, although not a hugely experienced officer, he knew enough to rush out of the garage seconds before nature took over, with inevitable nausea. He managed to avoid ruining the crime scene but the flower bed was not quite as fortunate. Emily was a more resilient soul. She approached the bag and knelt to feel the flesh through the thick polythene. It felt to her much like an old, cold steak. She stayed knelt beside the victim's leg, trying to assimilate things. She felt she had an ability to empathise more than her colleagues. Conley, having completed his assignation with the flower bed, turned to see "The Gift" in action. He, however, wasn't yet ready to return to the gruesome scene.

Emily noticed the clearance men looking like silhouettes in the doorway of the garage, and, with one hand resting on the girl's thigh, used the other to make a phone call. She was a woman after all, and multi-skilling wasn't difficult. She was put through to Detective Inspector Rhoda Webster who happened to be the only ranking officer on duty. Cutbacks were biting deep. Emily outlined the main points of the affair and hoped she would not be usurped. She wanted this case. To hell with her plans for the weekend.

She gave the thigh a long, affectionate squeeze and stood up, trying to find out what was also in the freezer. It would be easier if she came across arms, head and the other leg. Bits of torso would help as well. But she drew a blank. There was nothing else there. The cupboard was bare, so to speak, apart from some squidgy fruit puree and bags of vegetables which were obviously now unusable. There was, much to her disappointment, nothing that even faintly resembled body parts.

The clearance men were by now beginning to realise the inconvenience that was coming their way. They had made a gruesome discovery and, as they knew they should, reported it. They had stopped work immediately, again as they knew they should, and waited for things to start happening. As soon as the police arrived things certainly started happening and now the plans for each of them for the evening were changing radically. They were not going to be allowed to leave without making separate and detailed statements and their van would be removed for examination. It was, quite literally, a lorry-load of evidence.

Back at the station things were also swinging into action and arrangements altered for the evening and for an unknown amount of time thereafter. The jungle drums were beating as word spread of the discovery, shift patterns were changing, people were bundled into cars and started to race around the area with blue lights flashing and sirens screaming. The general public gradually became aware of a significant event within their community and were puzzled.

Emily actually enjoyed the mayhem that these happenings caused. It invigorated her, but she was not quite ready for this one yet. She felt the need for a moment's pause, a moment to gather her thoughts. She noticed that Conley was still busy at the front and decided to enter the house through the garage door. She wanted to get a feel of it, to immerse herself, before the chaos of invasion took over. The Gift needed to be allowed to rise to the surface and she needed to feel it happening. The clocks hadn't gone back yet which ensured her plenty of light to work with. The house was more or less empty. The carpet was dented in places where heavy pieces of furniture once stood and there was a mantelpiece in the living room upon which some figures in photos stared back at her. The eyes of some of them seemed to follow her as she moved. It would have been disturbing and disconcerting to most people, but Emily's concentration was such that, although she was aware of it, it had no effect at all.

Emily's mind began to process the information her eyes were transmitting. She noticed there were not many photos and wondered whether that meant there wasn't much of a family. She saw a wedding picture which she assumed to be of the widow and her late husband. He was in army uniform. She recognized it as belonging to the Second World War and calculated that made the widow somewhere around her eighties or nineties, even if she had been a young bride. She was pretty and half-smiling, as if unsure whether to look at the camera or her new husband.

She moved on to look at another photo. It was of the same pair, older now and with a baby. Then the sequence continued with the same daughter as a teenager, and then a young woman, and, finally, as a bride herself. The last photo showed the widow's late husband in his late forties or early fifties with a cigarette in his hand. Emily spotted that there were no more photos of him; no proof that he lived into his sixties and she wondered whether he had smoked himself into his grave.

Emily's thinking returned to the dead girl and her left leg. The shoe that was still on it was pink suede, with a platform sole, skinny wedge heels and a round toe. There was also an ankle strap. It was not brand new she saw, but it was not very old either. She made a mental note to find out when such shoes were in fashion.

She finished her perusal with a summary to herself. Photos of a dead husband, a widow, a daughter and a murder victim who, at that moment in time, consisted only of a left leg and a specific taste in shoes. As she left the house and wandered outside she couldn't help smiling. She had something to get her teeth into and was loving every minute. The weekend had started very well; very well indeed.

-5-

Emily heard the mayhem approaching before she saw it. She knew it was about to take possession and its queen was Rhoda Webster. Webster The Badge. Rhoda Bloody Webster. The youngest woman ever to have ascended the greasy incline of promotion to the exulted rank of DI. The longest serving officer of that rank, she could, and certainly should, have been breathing even more rarified air by now, but she had 'issues.' The most obvious was her uncanny ability to make herself disliked by almost everybody who came across her. Many secretly hoped they would one day be investigating her own demise. There would certainly be a million plausible suspects.

It was typical that she should be the first to arrive, in a screech of brakes, sirens and flashing blue lights. Almost instantaneously there was an army of black-jacketed lackeys spreading out like a disease in her considerable wake. To a constant accompaniment of radio and phone mush, the crime scene was quickly taped out and neighbours were being talked to. The removal van didn't hang around for long and was soon being carted off to disclose whatever secrets it might hold. The removal men, having seen their van disappear, had statements taken separately for later comparison and inconsistency. They were not anticipating an evening of fun and laughter.

Emily was fiddling with her phone, keeping her head down. She heard Webster criticizing the SOCO team for being slow. There were probably other things she was having a go at as well. Perhaps lack of moral fibre; lack of attention to detail; maybe off centre trouser creases or even having had the audacity to smile at some time in their lives. She never missed an opportunity.

PC Conley also received the benefit. She was always consistent in her tongue-lashings. Nobody escaped. People were treated fairly. Emily couldn't hear why he deserved such equal treatment, but he stalked past her looking ashen. It must have been a good one, she thought to herself, as she braced for what was to come her way. Webster The Badge beckoned her with an imperious waft of her regal hand. She was dressed in a severe black suit with a crisp white shirt.

"Why did you enter the house?" She hadn't wasted time on civil niceties.

Emily treated her to a full on white toothed smile, quite prepared to play mind games with the officer and quite looking forward to it.

"We didn't know if there was further evidence inside the property, and if so whether that evidence was appropriately secured. I made it my business to check."

"The interior of the house is a crime scene and.."

"I touched nothing. I didn't want to confuse the picture for the SOCOs. I assume you noticed the shoe?"

DI Webster liked that. She liked it the way a snake would like it if a vole popped up to ask if anyone was hungry. Strike, swallow, digest.

She smiled at Emily, who smiled fearlessly back; sharing the joy.

"Did I notice the shoe?" Webster mulled it over, lingering in the moment. "Well, yes, I did take a look at the leg, and my twenty-eight years of experience in the CID helped me notice, even through the polythene, that.."

"Oh, sorry, I wasn't clear," Emily jumped in, unwilling to waste the opportunity, "that shoe is not a contemporary style." She showed her the phone and pictures she had just downloaded from the internet. "I've only had a few moments, but I'd place the shoe as being approximately 2001 or 2002. That suggests any crime could be almost twenty years old. I assume that you've got people back at the station searching for investigations where nobody was ever fully recovered. You might wish to direct those team members to focus their efforts on the first few years of the last decade."

Emily, enjoying herself by now, gave her the loveliest smile she could muster.

They were standing in the property's little forecourt and the last of the sun was going down in a boil of cloud to the northwest. Webster wanted to bite her head off, but she couldn't. Emily's standing, her position, and background stilled her tongue. Also, she was aware that Emily had connections, but didn't know how far they reached or how powerful they might be. That ignorance made her wary. Thus, for the time being at least she treated Emily differently to others. If Webster had been fully aware of her connections, she might well have been far more deferential all the time. Emily was immune; safe and thankful for it. Worse still, Webster had to stand there and let her watch as she called the station to relay her information.

Emily was aware that behind them there was an increase in activity. More cars were beginning to darken the street, whilst flash photography split the spaces between them. She thought to herself that the print media were normally first to events such as this one, but it could be big enough to attract a film crew before too long.

Webster was also aware of the media scrum. Like all people in senior posts, she couldn't ignore the increasingly chaotic attention. Emily could not be certain how Webster would react, but she already knew her well enough to know that she would not forget to be horrible to her.

"Thank you for the useful shoe information. I'm sure it will be significant." The words were whispered through clenched teeth and her lips barely moved. Icy words. "Since you are obviously alert to such detail, I suggest you go back to the station and join the research team there." More ice. Now in the eyes as well as the voice and face. "Perhaps you'd be so kind as to present me with a summary of your conclusions in the morning." Triumphant in the knowledge that Emily would need to work half the night, she turned away.

Emily smiled behind her back. She wanted to put in the hours. Her gift would see her through and find surprising things. She was certain of that. She moved away to find Conley and a lift into town. As she approached she could hear him placating the van driver about his vehicle and when he could get it back. He was doing a good job, handling it by the book. He appeared calm, but Emily could tell he was still shaken from his encounter with Webster.

"I'm sorry, but you'll get your van back when DI Webster tells us. Unfortunately, she can be difficult, so it could be a while." Conley smiled his gratitude for Emily's intervention, but he was surprised at her comment about a senior officer.

"Thanks for being straight," the van driver said. "It's unusual from a police officer." He laughed, nervously.

"When you found the leg, where was it stored, exactly? I mean, I know it was in the freezer, but where exactly was it lying? At the front? Deep down? On top?" Emily used her newly established rapport with the driver.

"Along the back wall of the freezer, not quite at the bottom, but almost." He was responding to Emily's charm, which gave her a warm feeling inside.

"Was it neatly packed or did it look like it had been dropped in a hurry? Emily pressed on.

He was surprised at her need for such detail. "Oh no, quite tidy. Like if..."

Emily thought he was turning green, but the ebbing daylight made it difficult to be sure.

"Don't worry," she told him, "you've been helpful. Let me have your number in case I think of something else." She gave him her best smile as he handed her his business card.

Emily told Conley to wait and ran back up to the house. Detail. She needed detail.

"Give me the dates from the packages still in the bottom of the freezer," she said to a SOCO photographer who was dressed in a white polypropylene suit. She noticed the elasticated hood and cuffs. Detail. Her gift.

She got no response and assumed it was because he was wrestling with her demands, deciding between them and the training manual which was telling him to do things in a different order. She ended his indecision for him.

"Do you want me to pass your professional reservations to DI Webster?" Harsh, but she was short of time.

The white suit made a wise decision and bent down into the freezer with a torch. Emily inspected the packages lying loose on the floor as he did so. She noted that not all of them were dated. Some were, however. There was a pile of thin little freezer bags of apple compote, dating from 2005, some butcher's packages dated 2006, 2007, 2008 and 2009. One package caught her particular attention as it was dated 1984, in such wavering handwriting that she was inclined to suspect the old lady's mind had wandered.

She finished her quick gathering of detail just as the SOCO pulled out of the freezer. Emily knew that despite the mask he wore, it must have stunk in there, but she had no sympathy. She didn't know why, but had no time to ponder the problem.

"I couldn't see them all," he said, "and I won't move anything until we're done with the imaging. But I could see that the oldest is 1996 and the newest is maybe 2002, possibly 2003. Difficult to tell. The ink has run. We'll know more once we start moving them and can get a proper look." He finished with a shrug, which was his way of indicating he had come to the end of his discourse.

The quirk made Emily smile as she took some pictures of the dead girl's shoes on her phone. She asked for better quality images and left the white suit to its grim task.

-6-

Conley took Emily home. She wanted to prepare for a long weekend of work and paid attention to making sure she was thoroughly ready. She swapped her skirt for jeans and opted for her most comfortable pair of boots. A jumper completed the transformation. She packed a toothbrush and toothpaste as well as a change of underwear. As she moved around the house the streetlamps threw a light of sorts through her windows, so she didn't bother to switch on the house lights. It helped her concentrate on the things that were known.

She mentally listed the facts. Somebody cut a young woman into pieces and put her left leg into a suburban freezer. It was probably a man, but that wasn't certain.

Her mind wandered. Up by the reservoir it was as dark as it was outside her house. The voles, snakes, toads and bats were either going to bed or coming out to hunt. She recognized the parallel. She was coming out to hunt as well, alongside Webster and the might of the local force. For her, it was not only about finding the killers, but also about giving peace to the dead and their loved ones. It was primarily a question of justice, but the dead don't care about that. The murder investigation, arrest and conviction were just part of the funeral rite, the final acts of completion. They were gifts she brought the dead in exchange for the peace they gave her. The peace of the dead, which passeth all understanding.

Emily moved slowly for no reason that she could discern. She felt she was waiting for her energy levels to rise and when they did she jumped in her car and headed for the station. However, as soon as she arrived something made her carry on past. Driving slowly, she found herself in an area populated by large Victorian houses with ornaments in their gardens. She thought they would be high ceilinged and respectable inside. Tidy and organized. She pulled up at a house, which was the home of Jordan Sharman, MP. She remembered that he also had a house in Kensington and a bolt hole in France. There were lights on inside the house and the curtains were drawn.

She recognized his car. She thought the silver Aston Martin entirely appropriate, being an accurate reflection of his personality. His wife's car, a mini, suited her too. She walked up and down the road, making a note of number plates as she had done several times before. You never know when such detail might come in handy. She noted that some of the cars were new, but she recognized most of them from earlier visits. She tried to connect the new ones to particular houses, but most were not parked closely enough. This annoyed her, as she was trying to link any of the new ones to Sharman's house.

Eventually she found herself in her car, making her way towards the next target's home. He had made a pile of money in the insurance business. She corrected herself as she recalled that he had sold his business to a private equity buyer and had since become a constant nuisance to the authorities. There was nothing that could have him prosecuted, but he sailed very close to the edge all the time. Actually, that was what Emily thought about him even though she had never met him.

All she was doing was fishing. She had done this before and her patience had been rewarded with little nuggets of detail, but it took patience. In the end she decided not to carry on. She often acted upon a whim and she had learned to trust her instincts. It was part of her gift.

She sent a text to Books, her boyfriend, letting him know where she was. She smiled as she thought about the word, which seemed so old-fashioned but so appropriate. She also thought about the fact that people carried on with their lives before the communications revolution, without feeling the need to let others know where they were all the time. Progress? She doubted it.

She drove quickly back to the station, ready for a long night hunting corpses.

-7-

She discovered her corpse during the early hours of that night.

Rose Flowers had disappeared in August 2005. She was a twenty-two year old student at Bristol University. There had been a media frenzy when she had gone missing, but it had gradually died down as time passed and there was no progress in the investigation. The case was never closed. Emily noticed that, coincidentally, Webster had been in charge of that case too.

Emily knew Flowers was the corpse because one of the photos showed her at a party. She looked slightly plump, wore a short dress and had blonde hair. Emily asked herself why girls wore short skirts when they are even slightly plump. They were either oblivious to how they looked, or were determined to brazen it out. Her thoughts were trundling along slowly with this thought when they were interrupted by the shoes. They were pink suede with round toes and narrow wedge heels. Emily thought that Rose would have bought them a couple of years before she died, and liked them so much that she wore them all the time. So much so that they had come back into fashion again. Emily had the grim thought that Rose was wearing them still, in death and beyond; in a stinking freezer and by an empty reservoir.

She realised she was the last person left in the office. The others in the research team had left around midnight. They had worked it so that even Webster, in her inimitably unique way, couldn't reprimand them for slacking. The ceiling lights were off, which increased Emily's awareness of her being alone. The tiny rectangular lights of phones and printers glimmered like fireflies in the dark.

Emily knew she should tell somebody about Flowers, but she wanted to find out more detail first. She flipped rapidly through the file and saw an MA in English Literature, with a dissertation on T. S. Eliot. Bright girl. Rose's parents lived in Bath. Father was a solicitor and Mum was a charity worker. She had a brother and a sister. There was nothing untoward, unless you took a dim view of a bit of dope found in her student room. She seemed to have had some boyfriends, but the number didn't appear unusual. Her grades were not brilliant, but good enough. She was thinking about a career in publishing, but there was nothing definite. She was just an ordinary girl who liked shoes. Emily had never been besotted by shoes, so didn't understand what it was about women and shoes.

She spotted one detail that was out of place. The file and the notes from the current investigation stated that Rose Flowers supported herself as a student as an 'exotic dancer.' Emily thought the phrase was stupid. For one thing, the word 'exotic' was hardly an accurate description of a slightly plump English girl cavorting around a scaffolding pole. For another, it's not about dancing. It's about flesh, men and money. The file included photos of her as a dancer, wearing a tiny spangled mini skirt in one picture and a sequined bikini in another. She had a grin on her face in both pictures, which was more schoolgirl than sexy.

For Emily it was a nightmare scenario; the one thing she hoped would never happen. She actually thought it would never happen and consequently didn't know how to deal with it now that it had. She wanted to get up and leave, go for a drive, give herself time to think. But time was something she didn't have. If she had been at home she would have raided the fridge for some comforting chocolate; something dark and indulgent that gradually melts and coats the teeth. Even better, she would have taken Books to bed and found a much more satisfying comfort that way.

She tried to convince herself that there probably wasn't a problem, but couldn't shake off the feeling that there possibly was. She tried not to think of its magnitude, as she found herself picking up the phone, much against her better judgement.

When Emily was younger and teenager nosey, her Father told her stories about a man called John Lomax. She was told that Frank, her Father, and Ray Quinn had helped Lomax and the last she had heard of him was that he was running a jewellery business, which had now been taken on by his son, Billy. Apparently Lomax was fundamentally harmless, but had his fingers in many pies. One of these was 'adult entertainment.' He was, by all accounts, only just on the right side of the law and had contacts that could get almost anything done for the right price. It was thanks to Ray Quinn and Dad that Lomax had tiptoed his way through the maze of life and come through, so far at least, relatively unscathed.

Her Father answered her call and she told him the story so far. He already knew it all, of course, but he listened patiently. Emily could not have known that Frank and Ray Quinn had set Lomax up in that particular business for one purpose. It was a front, a lure. It was designed to attract corrupt police officers and others who deserved to be the object of the team's particular style of attention. One victim, Jon Johnston, was already languishing in Dartmoor Prison for his sins.

Emily had not been told of the facts because they wanted her to behave normally and to follow what she found. She was being managed; carefully and with discretion.

"The dead girl was Rose Flowers," said Emily. She left a pause in case he wanted to say anything, but he did not respond. "She disappeared in August 2005. She was a pole dancer. Well, no, that's not strictly true. She was a student who did some pole dancing to earn extra money."

"Poor girl," Frank replied, eventually. "Awful that sort of thing, isn't it? I mean, she had her whole life in front of her. Her poor parents."

"I need to find out if she danced at one of John Lomax's clubs," Emily continued. She was asking for information that she thought he may not have to hand, or which he may not want to find out. "Can you let me have his contact details? I'm sorry if it seems to break any confidence arrangements you have with him, but I'm sure he'd prefer to deal with me than somebody actually in the police force." She was thinking of DI Rhoda Webster.

A few moments later she had the phone number accompanied by a warning from Frank to tread carefully with John Lomax, as he had been given certain guarantees by powerful people in high places. One of these was Ray Quinn. Even though he was officially retired, Emily knew that if he was involved she needed to tread very carefully indeed. People like him never actually switch off. Besides, Emily knew him and liked him.

"Give me a minute and I'll get him to ring you. I'll let him know what you need."

Emily realised, of course, that he would brief Lomax as to how to deal with this unfortunate intrusion. Five minutes later her mobile buzzed and vibrated.

"Emily?"

"Yes. John Lomax, I assume."

"It is. Your father has asked me to contact you. I'll help you as much as I can, but I hope he's told you that there has to be limits as to how far I can go."

"Don't worry, Mr. Lomax, I understand the position. I'll ask the questions and you tell me if there's anything you can't or are prevented from answering." Emily was treading carefully. She wanted answers, but also needed to respect her father and Ray. She waited politely for a reply, but answer came there none.

"Rose Flowers?" she prompted.

"Ah, yes," John Lomax said and then stopped as if he wasn't going to say anything more. After what seemed like an eternity, but was actually a mere second or two, he continued. "We've had so many dancers here. I couldn't possibly remember each one. I've got some records of course. I'll look at them if you think it would help. If you think it's important."

The implicit message was that he'd prefer not to have to go the trouble. Emily took the hint.

"No, it's fine. I'll get back to you if I need to. Thanks from calling me back. I've got your number now, if there's anything I need. Bye."

She let her brain run riot. She'd alerted a potential witness, or a possible suspect, about the investigation. She'd given him information, which may not have been a good idea. On the other hand, she reasoned to herself, there has to be compromises sometimes. Also, she knew her father trusted him. If she got herself into trouble he would sort it out. It was comforting to have such powerful back up, but her father was not a man to annoy. He was a fantastically loyal father, but she would have to tread carefully from then on.

She spent a moment or two on a well- used exercise. She tried to tune in to her heartbeat; her breathing. She was finding her body, searching for her self. She pressed her knuckles down on the wooden desk until she felt pain. She couldn't quite feel her feet, but that wasn't unusual for her. Also, she had, after all, been awake for almost twenty-four hours. She realised that her tiredness was a good feeling, appropriate, normal. She took off her boots, bundled her papers together and took the lift up to Webster's office. She opened the door, ready to leave everything on her desk with a note. Emily didn't put any lights on because she preferred the dark at that time of night and it served to emphasise the pool light from the desk lamp. Behind the desk, Webster was asleep in her chair, looking more like a grandmother than the ferocious Queen Bitch of the station.

As Emily was wondering how best to wake her, she did so of her own accord. Her gaze struggled to focus as she took some time to remember where she was, who was standing in front of her and why she may be there. Her short grey hair was a mess and her suit was rumpled. It wasn't really the kind of clothing designed to look good after being worn all day and slept in half the night.

Emily waved the file. "Rose Flowers. Our victim. I've matched the shoes."

She gave her the file, pulling out the shoe photo and showing that first, matching it against her own photos of the murder scene. Webster, newly awoken, looked carefully at the pictures, then very briefly at the file, before saying, "Good. Look, just give me a moment."

She rubbed her face and groped around under her desk for her shoes, which weren't there because they were set neatly beside each other to her right. She yawned, stood up, and grimaced at Emily with a kind of 'good job, stay for a moment' kind of face and left the room. Emily was struck by the contrast between the slowness with which Webster gathered herself and her father's process. He always came alert in an instant. She wondered whether Webster and her father were on opposite sides of the investigation or whether they had nothing to do with each other. She hoped it would prove to be the latter.

Webster returned, poking her head around the door. "I'm getting coffee; do you want some?"

"Yes, please," Emily replied, shocked by this outward sign of civility.

She sat, making herself at home, as much as possible in an office that wasn't her own. She was considering moving the chairs, just to see the effect, when Webster came back with two steaming mugs of coffee. The mugs were obviously used by one and all in the office and Emily hoped they had been washed properly. She tried to put it to the back of her mind. She didn't wish to be struck down with some rare illness just because somebody hadn't bothered to wash the crockery. Things like that mattered to her.

Webster studied the file for a few minutes. The silence was deafening and Emily was on the point of fidgeting when Webster called the lab. Normally the lab didn't work through the night, but it seemed Webster had been able to work some magic, probably by frightening some poor soul about the imminent stalling of his or her career. Most murders are solved within a couple of days and if not, then they are not solved at all. That means there was a degree of urgency and Webster treated whoever was on the other end of the line to her special style of management. Not for her the benefits of care and discretion.

"I need the results within an hour," She demanded. She listened a moment to the reply and stormed in. "I don't care what else you're doing. Drop it. I'll have those results in an hour and you can deliver them here, to my office. Be here, but don't come empty handed, or your next steps will be through the exit door."

She slammed the phone down with a force that probably rendered it useless from that moment on.

"I think we've identified the murder victim. We have Rose Flowers' DNA on file from the previous investigation, so it will be a swift business making the match. It shouldn't take them long." Webster said this more for her own benefit than Emily's.

Emily knew the lab would have solved it anyway, but she hoped her night's work would have saved a few hours, if nothing else.

"When did you start this morning?" Webster asked.

"Yesterday morning, actually," Emily replied.

"You need some sleep. Go home." Webster was still in authority mode and enjoying it.

Emily ignored it and said, "so, you'll be seeing the parents, then?" She didn't intend it to be a question.

There was a pause as Webster considered her response. Emily wasn't sure whether that was because she was angry at her or because she hadn't thought ahead to the business of informing the next of kin. Most DIs don't do the next of kin bit themselves and Emily was surprised when Webster said that she intended to do it.

"I'd like to come," said Emily.

"Even though you've been working all week? Monday to Friday?"

"Actually, it's because I've been working all week. Think of it as finishing off a certain stage of the case." Emily was not going to back down.

There was a pause and then, "okay. We'll leave as soon as the lab comes back with the confirmation." Webster rooted around in a cupboard and came out with a tartan picnic blanket. Emily had a quick bet with herself that it was one of the itchy variety.

"There's a sofa in the office next door. You can use that. Take a nap while we wait." She ended the order with a nod to indicate that the discussion was at an end and Emily should leave.

Emily said nothing, despite thinking that 'thank you' would have been nice to hear because Webster had gone to sleep without a victim identification and awoken with one. She bit her tongue, took the blanket and the coffee in the suspect mug and took herself off to the office next door and its sofa. It was fake black leather, sticky and synthetic, and the blanket was decidedly itchy.

Through the thin office walls Emily could hear Webster starting to make calls. She was alerting people to come in early, starting to hand out assignments, checking with the lab as if she hadn't applied enough pressure there already. She was getting the machinery of investigation ready for its next clanking, ungainly advance.

It took Emily twenty minutes or more, but then sleep came to her like night over the reservoir. Swift, silent and total. A snake, vanishing under rocks. Unusually for her she didn't dream, or at least she didn't remember it if she did.

-8-

When Emily awoke she was pleasantly surprised to find Fiona Archibald opening the door, balancing a cup and saucer in one hand and a look of anxiety on her face. The aroma of peppermint tea drifted pleasantly and hung in the air.

"Thanks, you're a gem," Emily yawned and stretched both arms towards the ceiling.

"Were you here all night?" Fiona asked.

Emily glanced at her watch and saw seven thirty-five. She felt instantly sorry for the lab technician who was supposed to have delivered the result within an hour of having been given it by the ever forgiving Webster. His future did not look too bright.

"I've been asked to let you know that the results are now expected at eight this morning," Fiona intoned.

Emily wondered whether Webster would be satisfied with the removal of only one of the technician's testicles. Fiona the messenger added that Webster would leave without her if she wasn't ready. She sent Fiona to scavenge something to eat while she set about getting her morning routine done in about half an hour less time than normal. She dashed to the Ladies, brushed her teeth and changed her underwear. She finished by washing her face in barely warm water using that pink liquid soap that never rinses off properly. She grabbed handfuls of paper towels and dabbed and rubbed until her face was almost as pink as the soap she was trying to remove. She didn't feel properly clean, but what can you do in such a short time? At least she was slightly fragranced with whatever scent had been put into the soap. Fiona returned with a chicken sandwich, which Emily thought looked extremely unappetizing, but was good mannered enough not to say so. She found her boots where she had left them the previous evening and looked at her watch again. Seven fifty-two. She concentrated on forcing herself to eat the sandwich. At least the tea was better than passable.

"I was always told not to rush my food!" Fiona smiled and moved to the door for safety.

"No trouble," she said. "Time to spare."

Seven Fifty-nine.

Eight minutes later she found herself in a car heading out of town. It was Webster's BMW and it was being driven, carefully, by a uniformed driver because Webster had said that she didn't trust Emily to drive and she also needed to make some calls. Emily continued to eat her chicken and swallowed the insult at the same time. The lab had confirmed Rose Flowers' identification. The technician had phone the result through rather than risk his manhood by facing Webster in person.

Emily read the papers she had printed. The widow was called Jean Church. She died following a stroke at the age of eighty-five and had been five foot three. Her medical records showed a succession of minor health problems; arthritis, high cholesterol, difficulty sleeping. Her husband died twenty years before her with lung cancer. Emily thought that was a reasonable alibi. They had a daughter, Kathleen Harvey, who now lived in Australia and had an Australian husband whose job was in food processing. They seemed to have visited Jean Church every summer, staying for two or three weeks each time. The family appeared closely knit and supportive. Regular phone calls, and Skype, almost made up for the distance they were apart. The old lady's pension was topped up by the Australian end and this paid for her conservatory. There was nothing to indicate whether they had been in the country for the relevant dates, but there was a good chance, Emily thought.

The file contained an inventory of items found in the house, but it was incomplete. It included everything that might be needed to dismember a corpse. A small electric saw, a handsaw and various knives. Emily knew that most houses kept the same tools, so there could be no conclusions drawn. Numerous stains, including probable biological stains, had been found in the garage and the house. These were still being analysed. No other body parts had yet come to light.

Research on neighbours showed no known criminals or sex offenders and Emily was struck by just how unusually law abiding they all were. The file told of Jean Church having a number of petty quarrels with neighbours. She seemed to have been against cats and dogs, anti-music, anti-children on bikes, skateboards or anything else and anti those who didn't wear shirts. She did have an official caution on her record, having jammed her walking stick into the spokes of a child's bike while he was riding it. The boy had fallen and started to cry and some sort of altercation had followed. The upshot was that the boy's mother was warned for using foul and abusive language to a police officer and the same officer issued an official caution to Mrs. Church. The incident took place in 2007 and didn't appear to have any direct link to Rose Flowers' leg, except in so far as the episode shed light upon Mrs. Church's general character and outlook, which, Emily thought, was not particularly sunny.

There was also nothing obvious to link anyone in the area to the murder victim, whose excursion into exotic dancing seemed to have been temporary. Her first encounter with the industry was Easter 2004 and it had more or less ended by early 2005, several months before her death. Thus, it looked doubtful that there was a connection.

Emily finished her reading and let the countryside slip by. It was wet and the wipers were going all the time. The police driver kept the car at a precise seventy miles an hour, moving out from the slow lane when he needed to overtake and moving back again as soon as he could. The indicators were correctly used every time. In short, he was a boring perfectionist and Emily wondered if he did everything in his life with as much precision. She hoped not for the sake of his partner, if he had one.

Webster was on her mobile being important and loving it. Making calls, checking and sending e-mails, handling the media, forensics, neighbourhood enquiries, public information appeals, progress reports to her superior officer, Interpol liaison due to the Australian angle, getting updates on anyone whose names cropped up in the early phase of the investigation. She was at the centre of a veritable communications blizzard and was born for it.

Webster eventually completed her media campaign and looked with disapproval at Emily's attire, which obviously did not compare favourably with her own grey suit that must have been stored in her office for such occasions.

"The leg was at the back of the freezer," Emily offered, more to break the ice than anything else. When Webster showed no sign of responding she continued. "Mrs. Church was not tall and arthritic. The freezer was almost a metre high and only two feet deep. If I had to bundle a leg in there, I could probably manage it, but I don't think I could have laid it neatly along the bottom of the back wall unless I virtually climbed into the thing, and she was shorter than me."

"No."

"And the polythene didn't match any of the other packages."

"I don't think Jean Church is our killer."

"Do we know if she left her garage unlocked? Or if any of the neighbours had a key?"

Webster seemed to acknowledge the questions, but didn't indicate whether they were on her list of things to look at or not.

They continued their journey, off the motorway, and were now surrounded by hills. Farmhouses and villages glimmered in the rain as the car went over the top and began to plunge downhill into the city. The driver relied on the satnav to guide them to the required address, which was amongst ordinary, pleasant streets. The car drew to a halt and they braced themselves for the brutal moment.

Webster did not indicate how she wanted the interview to be conducted, but was first out of the car and part way to the front door, making Emily hurry to keep up. She rang the doorbell. There were lights on inside the house and they could hear noise as a shape moved behind the door.

A woman opened it and stood before them. Rose Flowers' mother had dark hair and wore jeans and a rugby top. Her face was composed, asking wordlessly "can I help you?" The look lasted for a fleeting moment before she recognized Webster.

"Oh." Nothing else. Just "Oh."

She turned and took her visitors through to the kitchen. Her husband looked up from his chair and his face collapsed.

Webster wasted no time and simply launched straight into it. "I'm sorry. Yesterday evening one of my officers was called to a house in the city. We found some human remains. Your daughter. We've been able to identify her from her clothing and DNA. I'm very sorry."

Mr. Flowers had that numbed look where you're only partly present in the room, where feelings and sounds and sensations all feel deadened, as if they were being glimpsed through a glass wall. His wife was different. She was crying without a sound; tears falling like sand. She seemed to want to be civil and offer a drink, but didn't quite get there. After what seemed an eternity to all concerned, Emily took a decision and put the kettle on. She then stood behind Rose's mother and rested her hands on her shoulders, trying to transmit feelings of comfort. Mrs. Flowers sat and sobbed noisy, juddering sobs as Emily stayed behind her giving support. Webster and Mr. Flowers made the tea.

Emily knew the rest of the information had to be given and was grateful that the task fell to Webster. She drew breath and told the truth.

"There's no way of avoiding this, so I'll just give you the facts so far. We have a leg, but we don't have a complete daughter. We cannot say how she died. We can't offer any comfort or close off any possibilities, however awful they may be. We can say that the worst of those possibilities are all too likely."

She let out a long breath, pleased to have finished. She hadn't told the whole truth, of course. She hadn't said that there may be some sexual, sadistic, long drawn out weirdness with a macabre ending. She hadn't said those things, but they were there, present in the room, and as real as the rain pattering on the windows.

Mrs. Flowers gradually managed to force the tears into submission and, through gritted teeth, said, "We've never really given up, you know. We always hoped. Her room is still there, just as the day she left it." It was all she could manage before the flood came and her shoulders rocked uncontrollably.

"I'm sorry to ask this," Emily whispered, "but may I take a look at it."

The request took Mrs. Flowers by surprise, but she was so upset that she agreed almost without thought, and also because there was no reason to refuse. Emily followed her upstairs, treading carefully on the recently hoovered beige carpet and taking in the willow tree beyond the landing window. Standing at Rose's bedroom door she saw immediately how scrupulously tidy it was. Student books lined shelves, a revision chart told of her plans and a poster with a Dylan Thomas poem adorned the wall above her bed. Emily sat on the bed, trying not to crease the duvet. Mrs. Flowers placed herself gingerly on the desk chair.

"I'm really sorry, Mrs. Flowers."

"Call me Rose, please. At least I've got her name to hold onto."

"I'm Emily."

"Is this how her room was? This tidy? When she left it?"

"Oh, she was always tidy," Mrs. Flowers affirmed.

"May I?" Emily asked, approaching the wardrobe and beginning to open a door. There was a nod in response as Mrs. Flowers turned away, not wishing to look at what it contained. Emily took in Rose's clothes. They were normal student wear. If anything, her taste seemed a bit dark, Emily thought. Definitely no sign of anything spangly which might be worn at a night club. No mini skirt either.

"Sorry, is it ok to look around? It often helps to get the feel of someone."

Mrs. Flowers nodded her assent and added, almost excusing what Emily was seeing, "I know it looks strange, keeping things like this. But we're not...I mean we use it as a spare room too. It's just nice keeping her things around."

Emily knew there was more to it than that, but said nothing. There were photos on the desk: a family shot, a formal school picture, Rose on a pony, Rose playing hockey, red-faced chasing an invisible ball. There was no photo of anyone pole dancing. They sat quietly for a while as Emily tried to imagine herself as Rose Flowers with Rose as her mother. She was about the appropriate age, but hockey and Dylan Thomas didn't sit easily with her.

"Will you be ok?" Emily asked, and regretted it instantly. She cursed herself for asking such a crass question, but couldn't find anything else to say.

"You know, I don't think it will ever leave us," Mrs. Flowers replied, slightly irked by Emily's embarrassing question. "But we know life has to go on. We have two others, a boy and a girl. I'll show you their rooms."

"There's no need," Emily replied quickly. She wasn't interested, but tried to deflect the direction of the conversation. "DI Webster is very good, you know. She's a bit scary, but she's the best investigator for miles around." Emily was trying to end on a positive note.

"That's nice to know, actually. Thank you."

They sat quietly for some moments before, by silent mutual agreement, they rose together and made their way downstairs. A polite departure was effected and the two investigators settled onto the back seat of their car.

"She needed a hug. I thought she might be better off doing that one to one. She had a good cry. I think it made her feel better."

Emily thought she shouldn't need to explain herself, but did so anyway.   Webster was not a happy officer. Emily could tell because she was treated to one of her speciality looks; storm clouds over glaciers. No words accompanied it; none were necessary.

The driver retraced their earlier journey, still sticking precisely to the rules of the road. Emily smiled inwardly as her earlier thought about his metronomic habits returned. She was beginning to feel sorry for his partner. Webster was also back in her earlier routine of binge use of her mobile phone.

"They've found a hand," she announced to nobody in particular, waving the phone in the air like an Olympic torch. "A right hand. Three hundred yards from the house. On the banks of the reservoir." Webster actually appeared to be enjoying herself, immersing herself in the carnage that was unfolding.

Emily thought the discovery should be good news. Important, as it was a step forward. She nodded, hoping the grim look on her face would resonate with Webster and reign in her jubilation. It didn't.

"It's a man's hand. Dark skinned, Arab, Mediterranean, or something like that. It's fresh. It's completely fresh."

-9-

Webster insisted on having her driver take Emily home, despite the latter's protests, and leaving her at her door with a parting shot.

"If you want to investigate a bedroom, then just do it, but don't lie to me about hugging the woman."

Emily nodded, wondering how the dragon knew. She didn't care, though. Webster would have to be a good deal nastier than that to get under her skin. "Does she still have that poster?" Webster asked.

"The Dylan Thomas one?" Emily replied. "'The force that through the green fuse drives the flower.' Yes, it's still there."

"Weird poem," Webster concluded.

Emily shrugged. She didn't know whether the poem is weird or not and she cared even less. Before she could respond, Webster slammed the car door shut and was gone.

Emily was tired, but found it difficult to sleep in daylight. She ran a bath and pondered whether to have a smoke to help with relaxation. She had been indulging in the habit since Ray Quinn concluded his final case and Frank, her father, took over the team. She decided it was because they both expected so much of her and she was feeling the pressure. She didn't think they knew about her having the occasional joint, but nothing would surprise her about both of them. Extraordinary men, both. She was also trying to kick the habit for the sake of Books.

She made herself some peppermint tea and drank slowly, allowing Books to fill her mind while watching the rain fall. She had always enjoyed the rain and often went outside just to get wet. She found it restorative. Eventually, she finished her tea, had her bath and managed to sleep for a couple of hours. It was not sound sleep, however, as it was filled by body parts falling like rain. A hand, a leg, an ear or two. A drizzle of humanity.

When she woke she felt worse than she had before. She made more tea, looked out at the rain and decided to call Books rather than smoke.

"Hi, Em. Had a nice time with Webster?" It was a question that didn't require an answer, so she listened as he brought her up to speed on the investigation. He told her about another hand being found, as well as a foot and a forearm, which all belonged to the same dark skinned male body as the original hand. "Better fresh than frozen, eh?"

"On public land, or in the gardens, or where?" Emily asked.

"One of the hands and the foot were in that little bit of wood just down from the house. Public access land. The other hand and forearm in back gardens no more than three hundred yards away from the house. The hand could have been thrown in there from the open land behind the garden. The forearm looked placed rather than thrown," Books said.

"Any ideas yet?" Emily pursued.

"Nothing. Not a clue. It's too early for DNA but we might have something by this evening. Nobody on the missing persons register who looks likely. No one local, anyway."

Emily knew what he meant. At a national level, the missing persons register is always well stocked, not least with Londoners of every possible ethnic background. Emily knew, however, that it wouldn't be clever to chase every Arab-Londoner, Mediterranean-Londoner, or whoever. She hoped the DNA would reveal more. Their chat lasted a few minutes more, but Emily found it difficult to move away from the details he had given. In her mind she was already walking across the sodden slopes, examining every tussock of grass, always hoping to find something like a foot, an ear, a pair of fingers shining in the mud like an autumn mushroom. They ended the call with both knowing it would be easier when they could spend some time together. She wished she was better at those little intimacies and was thankful that Books was a patient man.

A thumping noise intruded on her thoughts as a helicopter flew overhead looking for changes in the vegetation or discolouration in the soil. Shallow graves are more difficult to locate because the earth is not disturbed enough. In a drought, perhaps, a corpse could be revealed by the moisture it holds, but Emily knew that to be unlikely at the end of a wet October. She also knew that the helicopter was there as a warning to the area and any criminals around, saying to the whole area that the police were watching. Be good.

Emily went upstairs to the spare room, which Books preferred to call 'the operations room.' She looked at the desk, the table and the cupboard, which were all flat packs not very well put together. There was also a bed, covered by a sheet of plywood, and a felt covered corkboard on the wall. The room also held papers, photos, files, lists, a laptop, a printer, a wi-fi router. The electrical items, supplied by Frank, had all been connected correctly, but not by Emily. Books had surprised her with his hitherto latent talent. Was there no end to it, she wondered?

The room served as the team's operations centre for this case. From there they could access the Police National Computer and almost anything else they wanted thanks to Ray Quinn and Frank's clearance. It gave

Emily enormous power. She kept the extent of that power under wraps, for she knew that it was always a sound idea to let other people underestimate her. It was something she had learned from Ray Quinn, and her father, Frank. Books had told her many times that it was a good idea to keep people guessing, keep something in reserve. Emily believed his philosophy must have come from his ingrained street cunning.

Emily stood in the room and recalled a recent success enjoyed by the small, elite team. They had recently broken a case of slavery, which involved girls being trafficked by some charming gentlemen from a place in Eastern Europe. The main character was known by the name Hellman, whose body had been disposed of at sea. Emily's main concern was that he had friends, who would fill his boots and take over the conveyor belt he had established. She needed to find out who those friends were, as, in her eyes, they were equally as guilty. She was in no mood to deal with them lightly.

She sat at the desk and began to type. She entered the latest list of number plates. She hadn't been able to track everyone who knew Hellman, so she limited herself to his closest associates. Those connected to him in multiple ways: company directorships, racing syndicates, dining clubs, yachting holidays, weddings, investment partnerships, charitable boards, political donations. She picked six names, local ones, so that she could give them proper focus.

Name 1: He mostly seemed to hang out with other wealthy, politically connected people and spent most of his time in London. She hadn't yet been able to connect him to anybody obviously suspicious. No drug, pimp or prostitution connections, and no strange patterns of movement.

Name 2: He was reputed to be worth at least fifty million pounds. He was a playboy. The number plates of visiting cars showed them as belonging younger women, but only a couple of them had minor possession offences. Trivial. It was hard to detect any pattern to his movements. He went wherever he wanted.

There were four other names on her list.

She had a 'B' list as well. A list of people who knew Hellman fairly well, but whose links weren't quite as close. She was willing to bet that a number of the people on that list, possibly twelve in number, knew at least something about Hellman's proclivities, which made them culpable too. The latest batch of number plates, collected for Name 1, didn't yield anything new. She had a new one for Name 2, which she intended to check later. She carried on logging information and searching the internet for information. She checked some of the other databases and logged whatever she found. It wasn't much, but she knew that what she thought of as her 'gift' would come out to play and point the way. She would eventually notice something, she knew, and then find a way to use it. Use the gift.

She rubbed her eyes and looked around her spare room. Her gaze stopped at a small, pink dress with a white bow which was hanging on the back if the door. Her eyes continued to roam and took in the shiny black shoes on a shelf, a hair grip and a camera. There was also a photo of her in the dress. She would have been about two years old, she thought. It was her earliest recollection and it always made her feel weak at the knees.

She knew she needed to break the spell and walked into her bedroom. She lay on her back and before long her imagination turned to Books, and everything they had done together on that very bed. She had no trouble at all in remembering each and every tender and passionate moment and she allowed herself to wallow in the feelings that washed over her entire body. He always made her feel like this. She thought of it as his 'gift.' If she had a gift, then so did he, and she preferred his.

Her gift eventually asserted itself and, without really understanding why, she suddenly got up, made her way quickly to her car and drove rapidly out into the rain.

The ironing would have to wait.

-9-

She needed to do something practical, something active. Thus, she found herself in the field and woods by the reservoir inching forward in a line of uniformed officers. It wasn't really her job to do, but she felt that she was doing something really useful. The pace was slow, and her back ached, but she didn't mind. It was therapy for her. She liked the practical side of things and it made her recall earlier investigations when Ray Quinn directed his fledgling, elite team. He taught her skills that she would never forget, about detail and lateral thinking and instinct, and, above all, never failing. His closest friend, her father, had also learned the same lessons from the great man, and now, here she was, continuing the line. Ensuring the future of their team, carrying on their legacy. She knew also that Books was learning these things at the same time. A journey for them both, to be taken willingly, while their love for each other grew as well. It made her feel warm and glowing. And moist, she noticed with a smile.

The haul of body parts grew. There was nothing more of Rose Flowers, but the male corpse had now yielded a harvest of both hands, both feet, a forearm, a liver, a calf and a thigh. A Labrador was spotted with the liver in its mouth half a mile away, towards the reservoir, so the search was now covering an area at least a mile square, and possibly much more.

It wasn't only parts of corpse that was being hunted. The forensic team wanted everything of possible interest marked, be it a straggle of fibre, a boot print or even a single hair. She couldn't help thinking that Ray and her father would have approved. The whole area was now tagged with a small forest of bamboo wands, marked with luminous paint. The space suited beings were travelling from wand to wand, photographing, bagging, collecting.

The public land was the easiest part, even when it was overgrown. The gardens that backed onto the reservoir made it a more difficult search. Flower beds, sheds, greenhouses, garages. Complicated spaces that were accompanied by complicated owners, fretting, watching, asking and needing.

Emily worked with a team of three uniformed officers. They searched five gardens. They were asked seven times whether they wanted tea and were told at least six times to be careful of various tedious looking plants. Emily made a point of standing on them when she felt nobody was looking. The rain was intermittent now, but water still flashed from every hard surface, and still filled every boot print with a curl of silver. She was finding her temporary colleagues as annoying as the owners, and when they arrived at the next couple of properties, two newly built brick houses with bland lawns and new brickwork, she told them she would make a start on the next one and hopped over the fence.

She was in garden eight. It was a proper old fashioned plot, framed by a lattice of espaliered fruit trees. Within, there was a patchwork of vegetable beds. There were pegs, strings, bean sticks, marrows going over and the leeks just coming, runner beans and some unhappy looking spinach which had been defeated by the turning weather. There was a tiny greenhouse, a wooden compost bin and a shed. There was a definite aroma of sodden wood, wet leaves and creosote.

The owner emerged and introduced himself as Neville Brown. He was an old man and was dressed in a soft grey suit and tie. Emily thought he definitely belonged to the National Service generation. He invited

Emily to check everything, and then hurried back inside the house, showing that he didn't intend to interfere.

"Shout if you need me," he called.

Emily was grateful that she could work on her own, but was slightly suspicious of the man's real motive for disappearing so rapidly. The light was fading, leaving a violent orange sunset tangled in trees. A flock of geese, V shaped like a squadron of bombers, made its noisy descent towards the reservoir mud. The helicopter had returned to base.

She decided to look at the shed first, in order to use what little light was left. She had a torch with her, ready for later use. She pushed the door open, walked inside and stood still. It was her way. She was letting the silence settle while she acclimatized. If the Gift was going to appear she had to give it the opportunity. She realised, as she stood there, that she had been searching in a systematic and disciplined way. It was the police way, not hers. She needed to allow things to happen, to seep into her consciousness. The corpses had to be facilitated, helped to talk to her.

She saw balls of green and undyed twine, forks and spades hanging from nails. There was a hoe, a lawn mower, some garden chemicals, bags of compost and sharp sand. She recognized old fashioned items like griddles and pruning saws. There was also a pair of shears, its wooden handles shiny and polished from use. She also sensed the peace. Far too much peace, she thought.

She leaned against the workbench, melting into the moment as the geese flew overhead and her colleagues worked shoulder to shoulder outside. In the corner she saw the bottom half of a plastic barrel which was filled with a dark liquid. Her first thought was that it was water, but it wasn't. It smelled of oil, presumably for the mower. But the oil was old, collected year after year along with the cobwebs and dead wasps and its surface was covered with scum.   She wondered how many summers' worth of oil was in the barrel.

She smiled. Her gift was at work. She felt the signs. She knelt down by the barrel and thrust both hands deep into the darkness. When her hands came out, they gripped the blonde and dripping head of Rose Flowers.

-10-

A week of mayhem ended, after more searching, in weather which had turned windy as well as wet. There was an ever increasing collection of body parts and media interest which had turned so intense that cameras and microphones seemed to be at the end of every road and on every corner.

More information appeared during the weekend. The male corpse had been identified as Aftab Khaled who was a lecturer at a local college. His lung had been discovered, bobbing like a clumsy grey balloon half filled with water, on the leeward side of the reservoir. Rose Flowers' arms, bound together with duct tape and bagged up in polythene, were found amongst some loose timber and sheets of fibreboard that Dick Hertford, a plumbers' merchant, stored in his garage roof.

Just to add to the confusion, PC Jackie Mountford was taken to hospital with a suspected case of hypothermia after getting too wet during the search. Lastly, but no less important to the unfortunate recipient, Webster publicly shouted at a DI for a scheduling muddle.

All in all, the investigation accumulated ever more information and ever less direction. A white board was set up listing fourteen properties where body parts were found. Thirty-eight people lived in those properties. If the extended families were included, there were at least seventy-one people who could have been counted as implicated. Then, with the addition of close friends or colleagues the number in the circle of suspects was over one hundred. Pieces of corpse were still being found, so the total constantly grew. Nobody the investigation had so far looked at had been involved in any meaningful way with the police or had any serious indicator of potential for sexual violence.

Anybody living locally who had any kind of record for sexual assault, violence, or child sex offences was scrutinized. There were a few such people, of course, but anything more than a basic look at them took too much time. The reservoir was a well- used beauty spot and dog walking area and therefore all the local villages, towns and surrounding areas became relevant to the investigation. In total, including the nearest city, there were a million suspects and two corpses.

Books and Emily both worked with different teams of officers. That had been done because they hoped they could gather more information that way. It had, of course, been arranged behind the scenes by Frank.

They spent as much time together as possible, both to exchange details and for their own purposes. Usually they stayed at Books' apartment. Sunday became a regular time for going through notes, cooking, eating, sharing a few drinks and enjoying each other's bodies as much as tiredness allowed. They were determined not to allow fatigue to interfere with their lovemaking, which they considered to be of extreme importance. They guarded those times preciously and often fell asleep in each other's arms afterwards. Tired though it made them, it was also a means of refreshment for both. Bacon and eggs was favourite, mainly because neither was particularly skilled in the kitchen. At least, not when it came to cooking.

They often started by watching a film, only to end up talking through it and nipping off to the bedroom to make love, while George Clooney was being a funny man in the living room. Afterwards, a tired but satisfied Emily would drag herself to the shower, then fall back into bed, while Books turned George Clooney off in the living room. She often dreamed during these nights, but it wasn't about geese flying in formation or anything to do with the investigation.

On Monday morning the white board became the altar at which all would worship as the scattered fragments were welded together by Webster. She was introduced by somebody else, but there was no doubt as to who was running the show. The incident room was packed full of exhausted faces and strong coffee. There was a thick stew of conversation. Webster had given the operation a properly formal code name. Operation Algernon, for some obscure reason. Everybody else dubbed it Takeaway, but it wasn't ever said to her face or in her company.

People came in late, but Webster called the room to order with nothing more than a look. She stood at the front. She had no podium or notes. She wore low-heeled black shoes, a grey suit and was totally devoid of humour. She wasted no words and summarized the state of the investigation.

She dealt with Aftab Khaled first. It was a week since he was last seen at work, at a seminar for graduate students in materials science. Owing to the mysteries of the college timetable, his workload this last week was very light, so although his absence was noted, no one was particularly worried. He travelled fairly extensively anyway and it was assumed he'd simply turn up when required. When an Arab looking corpse was reported, the college called with their concerns. They collected DNA from his office and a match was made.

"From what we know," said Webster, "Khaled had no wife, no partner. We've spoken with his department head and one or two others, but we need much more.

What connection did he have to Rose Flowers? Who might have wanted him dead and why?"

Next, Flowers became the subject. Needless to say, you can't find large chunks of human remains in someone's shed or garage without pulling those people in for questioning. So on Saturday night the old man who owned the barrel from which a head had been plucked found himself sat in a most unwelcoming room waiting for something to begin. The interview plan had been to let him sweat for an hour or so, not quite accusing the old man, but almost, and seeing if any cracks emerged. In fact, the old man was so open, so soldier-like, flirtatious and charming that after twenty minutes the interview was suspended for a behind the scenes consultation. A decision was made to run the whole thing differently. Someone went out to get chips, and the rest of the interview was conducted over mugs of tea and plates of chips with brown sauce, with the old man doing his gallant best to assist.

The interrogation revealed no grounds for suspicion. His garden was easily accessed from the land to the rear of his property. He reported a minor squabble with the old lady who didn't like children and their noise, as she also didn't like him burning garden clippings. Her dislike list was growing. He called her an 'old harpie,' but there was no real contact. The Ice Queen didn't say it, but that old lady could have picked an argument with an empty room.

"And in any case," Webster went on to say, "there doesn't seem to be any connection between any of the names we have so far come up with. Also, we have found no connections with tradesmen, friends, family or anybody else who has access to the property. We are currently cross-checking those lists against address books and phone records, but so far we have found no significant overlap."

Webster grimaced at the lack of correlations. As though it was someone's fault. All heads were studiously down, ostensibly consulting their notes, but in reality avoiding eye contact and thus the possibility of blame.

"Causes of death," she announced.

There was laughter at that. It sounded stupid, because people do not tend to live long and healthy lives when they've been divided into dozens of pieces and distributed to all points of the compass. But Webster was right: they didn't actually know what killed either Flowers or Khaled. Were they cut up whilst still alive? If so, why? If not, then when?

There were more questions than answers. The corpses seemed to have been butchered reasonably proficiently, "but a garden saw or kitchen knives could not have done the job adequately. We've got no evidence so far of slashing, hacking, or even signs of a struggle. So, quite likely a clean death, with butchery taking place thereafter."

There was then some complex and uncertain forensic material, which Webster summarized in her usual brusque, take-no-prisoners way.

The biggest curiosity was the condition of Rose Flowers. The leg found in the freezer was, according to the guesstimates they had thus far, in roughly the condition you'd expect from a leg that had been frozen for five years, then left to rot in a wet freezer with the power off. The arms and the head were in worse condition, but probably not five years worse. It seemed that forensic science didn't have a great deal of statistical data on how rapidly a head decomposes when submerged in a barrel of old lawn mower oil. Various tests were carried out to explore how far the oil had penetrated the bone and soft tissues, but were unlikely to provide a firm idea of the timing. may or may not give them something more definite, but we're never likely to get a firm fix on the timing.

"Best estimate," said Webster, "the head was in that barrel for one to three years. Maybe more, maybe less."

A stone had been left in the mouth to keep the head below the surface. It had fallen out with a little oily plop, when Emily had lifted the head. In ancient Greece, corpses were buried with a coin in their mouths, so the newly dead had something with which to pay for their passage into the underworld. That falling pebble felt like Rose Flowers finally making payment. Her spirit finally exiting this world.

"With the arms, it's a little clearer," Webster continued. "If those arms were consistently stored at ambient temperature, the extent of the decomposition is consistent with something between two and four years. I'm told that, in the opinion of our forensics team, it is highly unlikely that the arms were stored in someone's roof for five years."

She emphasized those words: *highly unlikely.* Emily realised that nearly everyone was writing notes in their little notebooks, but she wasn't. She preferred to look keen instead.

Webster found a psychologist from somewhere to give a psych briefing. Emily hated those. She found them to be mind-numbingly stupid, amounting to little more than 'I think your killer may not be quite right in the head.' A tedious message wrapped up in half-baked jargon and faux-scientific references. The tarot of modern criminal investigations.

This time, however, the tired looking little psychologist had a little more to offer. He noted that the Flowers killing was odd, for at least three reasons. One, the dismemberment. Two, the very wide distribution of body parts. Three, the apparent efforts made to preserve the body parts (the freezer, the barrel of oil, the airtight wrapping of the arms) could suggest some novel type of disorder or obsession.

"Naturally, it's possible," said the psychologist, "that the killer distributed the body parts in order to confuse and deflect criminal investigation. That could be a rational behaviour under the circumstances. But there are other ways to deflect attention and of course disposing of the corpse so that it isn't found at all might have been an even more rational course of action." He paused, then said, "What I would say is that dismembering of corpses has been strongly associated in the past with offenders suffering from various personality disorders, often with possible schizoid features. I'd suggest it's reasonably probable that the killer chose to retain at least one item for himself as a kind of memento. That kind of retentiveness is common in some offenders. Think of it as trophy hunting, if you will. But the obsession with preserving the corpse is a new one on me. It's as though there's a splash of compulsive hoarding in there. A refusal to give things up. A desire to retain control. I don't want to pretend there's much science I can offer here, but if you want my gut feeling, I'd say we were looking for a man who likes to hold on to things. Possibly a hoarder. At very high risk of being a repeat offender."

One colleague asked whether the Flowers killer and the Khaled killer were likely to be the same person. The psychologist thought maybe not, though he, and everyone else there, thought the killings were certainly linked.

A discussion, led by Webster, ensued, but the energy which filled the room at the start, that bristling energy that had stalked the room like some giant beast, was pretty much dead by then. Times like this showed Webster at her best and worse. At her worst, because she was so taut, so devoid of humour or sympathy, she was like an order-issuing robot: rapid, precise, disapproving, relentless. And at her best, for the same reason, an order-issuing robot was just what was needed. There were search teams for the city, search teams for the reservoir, teams for database research, and teams for the Khaled interviews. She spat orders like something ejecting nails.

Emily thought about Rose Flowers. She was a red-cheeked English girl who chased a hockey ball and found her death. When you have a dead girl's head in your hands, a head that can't help but stare at you with sightless eyes even as it spits its black penny out, you have a connection. Like it or not, you're joined. Whilst people scribbled notes, she remembered Rose. The weight of her head. The slipperiness. That feel of bone.

"How did you die, Rose?" she asked her. She didn't get a reply, but it was early days.

Eventually, forty minutes after starting, Webster finally fell silent. Emily had a ringing in her ears. Her voice, those commands, that tone. She thought everyone felt the same way.

Emily was assigned to the Khaled team, which disappointed her. She had assumed she'd be on the Flowers team, and she thought about asking to be switched. She didn't ask because it was Webster and restricted herself to walking grumpily upstairs to a smaller conference room where the team were assembling.

Against the wall, there was a table laid out with ID photos, known facts, basic biography. Born Moroccan, but a longtime British resident, here since he was a student. Born Muslim, but non-practicing, non-religious. Family in North Africa, but limited contacts with them. The intelligence databases were closed to the team, but they were able to send in queries and received a clean bill of health in return. There were no known terrorist links and no hints of religious fundamentalism. Emily could have told them that if they had bothered to ask as her own connections, far more far reaching and efficient, had already given her the edge in detailed information. She let them believe it was some sort of strange gift and that legend grew. It suited her.

The team started taking what they needed: photos, fact sheets. Khaled had a thin brown face. Forty-something. Neat dark hair. A kind of fussy precision in his suit, his narrow tie and white shirt. But there was something else too, something that scampered away from her before she could define it. His face wasn't static. It was in motion, half looking away from the camera, with his mouth opening into a laugh. Or perhaps opening to say something. But there was a disconnect between the eyes and the mouth. It was like the eyes were saying one thing and the mouth was about to say another.

Emily was deep in concentration. The photograph eluded her. Rose Flowers' photos were as plain as toast. A cow-toothed English girl who played hockey. When Emily found her head, her flesh was in a pretty decayed state, but the cow teeth were still there. Somewhere in her eyeless stare, the clack of a hockey ball, the smell of riding tackle, were still there.

Emily's annoyance at being on the Khaled team instead of on the other team was already beginning to dissolve.

Who were you, Mr. Khaled? And what did you have to do with Rose Flowers?

They were about to find out.

-11-

The Engineering Faculty was a short walk from the station. She had never been there before. They arrived at ten. Three DCs, Emily and DS Jamie Donaldson, who loved and adored her. The feeling was mutual and they expressed their love and adoration by never talking to each other and by making snide comments through third parties whenever they got the chance.

They were greeted by Virginia Platt, the Head of School's assistant. She offered three platitudes about the 'terrible tragedy.' Then gave them a list of Khaled's students and a list of his faculty colleagues. She showed them to an 'interview space,' an under-heated room with old carpet, big windows, and some books behind glass cupboards.

"Refreshments for you there," she said, pointing to a tray of thermos flasks, as though they wouldn't be able to recognize them without assistance. Why is it that organisations insist on providing third rate, almost undrinkable, coffee, kept warm in flasks, to their guests? To Emily, it indicated minimal respect and a view that only the really high-up worthies are held in sufficient esteem to be served proper coffee in porcelain crockery. She took it as a slight and it always rankled.

"We've drawn up an interview schedule to help get things organized. Obviously if you need longer with anyone, that can be arranged. All the students have been notified and they know it's okay for them to skip a lecture if they have to." The assistant completed her speech.

How innocent can you be? Doesn't she know that students do not need permission to miss a lecture or two. In fact, it's an unusual student who attends more than the bare minimum required to achieve staying on the course and, therefore, continuing a life of indolence.

The assistant gave a little smile. One of those 'hospitality smiles.' The sort which says, 'I'm professionally dressed in an inoffensive blue suit, I've put tea bags in individual sachets out on a small china saucer, I've made you some lists which are all neatly stapled, and look – I'm smiling.' Small white efficient teeth.

Through the glass pane in the door, Emily could see the first students assembling. It was a well-organized setup and they needed to interview these people, but she hated the sense of being managed. She knew that Ray and Frank managed her, but she accepted them; trusted them with her life. Books was almost in that category too, she reminded herself with a familiar warm feeling in her lower torso as an added bonus.

Donaldson started grumbling about the tables, and privacy issues. Hospitality Platt held her hands in front of her like a supplicant at some Catholic shrine. She told Donaldson that she would arrange for some other rooms. He grumbled some more and she did prayer hands. He grumbled once more about the coffee, then dropped it.   It saved Emily from making the point, though.

The first students came in and Emily interviewed three of them. Three people, not much younger than her. It seemed Khaled was a reasonably popular lecturer as well as being an expert in materials science and mechanical engineering.

The third of her students, Katie, was a mouse-haired girl who sat opposite Emily wearing a long gauzy scarf and pulled at it as if she was dying to perform experiments in self-strangulation. She bored Emily.

"Did he ever make a pass at you?"

"A pass? No. No." she looked shocked by the idea.

"Did he have a fling with any of your fellow students? A one-night stand? Late-night snog? Anything like that. Anything at all?"

"No."

It was poor interview technique, but Emily was bored and felt uppity. She didn't want her lovely little murder case to turn dull. She felt angry at these girls for being alive, when Rose Flowers was dead.

"Sexual relationships with other lecturers? Drugs? Global jihad? Bondage games?"

"No."

"Fine," said Emily. "Could you look through these questions and note down anything that might be relevant? Thanks."

She left her with pen and paper going through their list of interview questions. She walked out of the room and let the door bang shut behind her. It was all far too formulaic, there was no intuition being used. It needed a touch of 'the gift.'

Emily was in a bland official corridor, with blue carpets and student posters and notices tacked to the wall. It was academic earnestness and hippiness trying too hard. Where do you hide a leaf? In a forest. How do you conceal a secret? With openness. Prayer hands and efficient teeth. She started to prowl, unsure of where she was going. She was not overly surprised when she found herself up on the management floor. Same blue carpet; no student posters.

She found her way to the Head of Faculty's office. The polished steel name plate on the door left no doubt as to who lay in wait inside: Kelvin Macintosh. Outside his office, moored like a motorboat and freighted with an impressive amount of office hardware, was a PA's station, complete with a blonde, fragile PA. Her nameplate was plastic and gave her name as Cara. On the wall behind her were some photos. Prize awards for some student projects. The Head of Faculty with donors and grandees. The local MP was among them.

"Hi."

She gave her best smile, trying to impress with her good teeth, all brushed and shiny white.

"Hello?"

She clearly didn't know who Emily was or why she was there.

"I need to see Mr. Macintosh," Emily said and walked into the office without slowing or knocking. Obviously being a guard for her boss was not one of her strengths. Perhaps she had other talents of which he was fond.

Macintosh looked up, surprised and a tad annoyed. His appearance was as Emily expected: half engineer, half beaurocrat, grey suit, grey curly hair. He was solid looking and slabby, as though inexpensively manufactured from some durable sheer material.

"Mr. Macintosh, your guardian out there," she said, at the same time as pointing towards the ineffective woman through the open door, "told me you were free. I'm Emily and I'm part of an ongoing police investigation. I wonder if I could have a few minutes of your time."

He didn't look pleased about it, but waved a hand towards the seating area in the corner. A boxy armchair, boxy sofa, glass table. She chose the sofa, just because she knew it was his normal spot. Macintosh did a momentary double take, then sat in the armchair. A red tag dangled from the arm, giving details of fire regulations.

"Flame retardant," Emily said. "Nice."

"You all right downstairs?"

"Yes."

She didn't say anything more and neither did he. He was waiting for her to start things off, which suited her. She preferred that and sat there in silence because silence is uncomfortable if you're not in control of it.

Eventually she said, "why was Khaled killed?"

"Why? I have no idea."

Emily nodded, as if he'd said something sensible. She wrote it in her notebook. Slowly.

It wasn't the obvious things, was it?" she said. "Sex, drugs, honour killings. None of the above."

"Isn't that your job? To find out?"

She nodded again and wrote once more. She wrote slowly, deliberately slowly. She knew she was annoying him.

"Yes. Yes, it is my job. So why was your colleague, Aftab Khaled, murdered? In your opinion."

"I don't have an opinion."

"Yes, you do. You think it wasn't sex, drugs or honour killings."

"I didn't say that."

"Sorry, so you think it was one of those things?"

Macintosh sighed. "Look, Aftab was a diligent member of the department. We certainly weren't aware of any..."

"No. I know you weren't."

She paused again. Not a tactical silence this time, a real one. There was an emptiness in the room, a withholding, that shouldn't have been there. If Macintosh really had nothing to hide, he'd have been more talkative. She knew she was being a total pain in the arse, but she reasoned that people are inclined to talk more under those circumstances or at least to get angry. Macintosh was being too controlled. She didn't think he murdered

Khaled or even that he knew why Khaled was killed, but there was something that he didn't want her to know, which made her want to know it twice over.

She tried the sex angle first.

"Obviously, he was a single man," she said.

"Yes, and Mr Khaled liked to have fun. But look, we aren't here to judge our staff's private lives. What Aftab did or didn't do..."

He continued, but he began to relax as he talked. Whatever made him come over all controlled, it wasn't this. Emily's guess was that Khaled was a bit of a womanizer. He was too smart to risk his job by playing fast and loose with the students. The rest of the city would have been a different matter, however. The conversation was shifting away from whatever Mr. Macintosh was trying to guard. She wanted to get him back to the emptiness, the withholding.

"Materials science; tell me about it."

Macintosh nodded. This was home ground for him. "That was Aftab's speciality. Materials science has to do with the fundamental properties of various materials. It's at the confluence of physics, chemistry and engineering. Nanotechnologies as well now, of course. Aftab was extremely good with various types of steels. Some polymers, high-modulus polyethylenes. Engineering plastics. That kind of thing."

Emily nodded, jotting down some of the terms, needing to be slow this time. As she did, he went on talking.

"You know, because we're out here, not a big name university, people tend to think of us as somehow second rate. They assume we can't compete with the big boys. But, you know, we've got one of the best engineering schools in the entire country here. And in our chosen fields, Aftab's for one, we're as good as anyone. He's going to be tough to replace. We'll miss him."

She nodded again, wondering how to use the flow. That's the thing about secrets, people want to talk about them. They can't help themselves.

"You'll miss him in other ways too," she said, opting to stick with the positive.

"Yes. I wouldn't say he was the most, I don't know, popular member of the faculty. I'm not saying the opposite; just that he was happy enough to work hard, he didn't need to come to every summer barbecue. On the other hand, when it came to helping the faculty; you know, donors, tie-ups with businesses, getting students into real engineering positions, those sort of things, he was first class. Dedicated."

Emily nodded yet again. She couldn't see that she'd got what she had come for, but she wasn't sure how she could get it. Or even what it was. Her pencil hesitated over the page.

"I'll put that he was helpful, shall I?"

Macintosh smirked patronizingly. "Yes, you can put that."

The air had cleared up now, as if the emptiness wasn't there, or was sealed off, if it was. She insisted on talking a bit more, but only to be annoying. She didn't think she could get anything more. As she got up to leave, she said, "donors. What kind of money are we talking about?"

"This is an engineering faculty. It's not one of the arts, where some donor agrees to host a poetry evening or a wine and cheese party."

Emily nodded once more, encouraging more of the same.

"Look, I've got an invoice here for a new universal electromechanical testing machine. Nothing fancy. Not one of our priciest bits of kit. But you take into account data acquisition software, installation, everything else, and we'll have no change from forty to forty-five thousand pounds. We don't get kit like that on government budgets. It's all private sector money. Research, collaborations, product development, partnerships, licensing agreements. We're all going to miss Aftab. He was bloody good at that."

Macintosh hovered over her, shuffling her towards the door. She allowed herself to be shuffled, reflecting inwardly that the man didn't know what a dangerous act it was.

"I've put down that he was helpful," she said, giving him and his guardian angel who had magically re-appeared, a final smile. "Very helpful."

And that was that. It really was, except that as she went downstairs from one blue-carpeted floor to another, it didn't feel that way at all. She was on the stairs, walking down, facing the light of the window. She was deep in thought about Macintosh and whether there was anything awry in his answers. She was also thinking that her absence must have been noticed. Suddenly, her leg twisted and her ankle couldn't support her. She would have fallen were it not for the bannister, which she grabbed for support. As this was happening, she twisted around, as though someone had come from behind and forcibly moved her.

She assumed that she had been moved violently by another person, as though helping her to avoid something. But there was nothing which could have harmed her and there was no other person anywhere around. She was alone on the stairs. She sat down, assuming she had just fainted, even though that would be unusual for her. It had to be her knee or ankle. She tried standing, cautiously, a hand still out on the bannister, but her legs were fine. She knew she was young healthy adult and there was nothing wrong with her. She could feel her feet and hands normally and her breathing was a little flustered but basically ok. She stamped feeling down into her feet, clenched and unclenched her hands to get the senses moving there too.

Then she wondered whether it could be morning sickness. She was on the pill, but was wise enough to know that accidents can happen. For a panicked moment she considered the possibility. She knew Books would take it in his stride, but she was certainly not ready yet. It couldn't be; it mustn't be.

-12-

That evening she was with Books at his apartment. There were pictures on the wall, cushions on the sofa, photos on the shelves and candles on the table. Every time she had dinner with him she had a slightly spacy, buzzy feeling as she sat opposite her handsome and capable young man who moved around the room setting food on the table, dimming lights, lighting candles and arranging glasses. He was now a long way from the street wise illiterate that he once was. She had taught him to read and it had unlocked his potential. She thought that there may be nothing of which he wasn't capable. She was thrilled by the adventure and her part in it. So thrilled, excited and warmed in certain private places that she found herself forgetting things. She forgot to light candles, so he had to, she forgot to put out the cloth napkins rather than the paper ones. And she sat at the table before they were ready. Little things.

Books was never impatient with her, but she sometimes found his goodness a little hard to deal with. Could he possibly be the world's nicest man? He was certainly good to her. She always returned to the fact that he was not naïve at all when it came to survival and knowing how to deal with people. He had an inbuilt assurance, a steel, that made her feel comfortable and secure. She also knew he was not a man to be crossed and made an enemy. He was becoming much like Ray Quinn and her father rolled into one. She knew she was a lucky young woman, and wondered whether she was gradually working her way around to a description of love. She hoped so.

"Well, Em," Books said. He didn't finish the sentence, preferring instead to look into her eyes and chink glasses.

Emily wanted to discuss the investigation, but Books had rules about not allowing work to intrude into their private moments. They talked about other things. Books had recently started to play hockey, which Emily initially believed to be a girl's game. That belief was changed the instant she went to see him play and was shocked by the aggression and speed. She felt sorry for his opponents, for he seemed to simply run past or through them with impunity. She learned later that the game is taken seriously and there are leagues with relegation and promotion. She kept her disbelief to herself and tried to follow the game's intricacies as best she could. She hated it when she was at school and avoided it as much as possible, as well as the pointless cross-country. Nevertheless, she said the right things, the things she thought he wanted to hear.

"Rose Flowers played hockey. She had a photo in her room." She couldn't help herself.

Books treated her to a sharp look and then laughed.

"Okay, Em. I give in. Let's talk about murder."

"Do you think it was a sex killing?" Emily began.

"Which one?"

"Either."

"I'd say it was almost certain in the case of Rose Flowers," he said. "Logic says that if it wasn't close family or a dodgy boyfriend, and Webster would have caught any of those if they'd been the killer, then it has to be a sex related thing. Partly because Flowers was a twenty-something girl. Partly because of what she did, or had done, for a living. Put those two things together and the stars say it has to be a sex crime."

"And Khaled?"

"Don't know."

Emily said, "I was with his students today. His boring, boring students. No frisson from them. If he was some lecherous professor type, I reckon we'd have picked it up."

"Right, but sex doesn't have to be like that, does it? I mean, maybe Khaled was a perfect professional at work. Then maybe not even that often, once or twice a month maybe, he goes down to a club, sinks a few, loses control and gets involved in something he can't handle. They've been going through his bank records and it seems that he's been well up for a party in his time. A bit of a bad boy on occasion."

"OK," she nodded. "Let's assume that's right. That doesn't mean there's any connection at all with Rose Flowers. She was a twenty-something girl who died five years ago. He's a late-thirties man who died on Friday."

"True, but…"

Again, Books did not trace the logic all the way through, but he knew Emily was aware what he was thinking, which was that this isn't Mexico City or a Brazilian favela. Bodies just don't get chopped up like a takeaway and scattered all over town. If it does happen, it's weird, a once in a century thing. If it happens twice, and in the same part of town, there must be a connection. That connection will suggest an avenue for investigation. Find the connection and investigate hard, get a break, get the killer.

"It could be copycatting. Could be. I mean, I know the timing's not helpful."

"Not helpful? Honestly, what are the chances? You're a murderer. You hear about the Flowers find on the radio, so you think, "that sounds fun," and quick as anything, you grab a victim, bump him off, and scatter his body parts. You do all that the very same night that you hear the first radio or TV broadcast. Within hours, probably."

"Or, more likely, you've already got a victim and have been wondering what to do with him."

"Same thing, though. I mean, what are the chances? It's hardly likely, is it?"

"That's true. But the coincidences cut both ways. The Flowers body parts waited seven years to be found. Even if both victims did have the same killer, how did that person know to kill Khaled at essentially the same time that the first piece of Rose Flowers was discovered? Whichever way you look at it, something improbable happened."

Emily wanted to go on talking about it, but Books had other ideas. He had already switched off because he wasn't interested in speculation. He started to ask Emily about her day.

"It was boring. Tedious. The students were dead from the neck up. Plus, I think the whole process is over managed. We're ticking boxes and that won't break the case. We should think in a different way."

"I was told you went AWOL," Books said.

"Women's troubles," replied Emily.

"Bullshit." A friendly bullshit, not a mean one. But a bullshit nevertheless.

"OK. I went to interview the Head of Faculty. He was quite boring too. He didn't tell me anything, though."

Emily was about to tell Books about the thing that happened on the stairs. The moment when her knee buckled and her panic about a possible pregnancy. Then she realised she couldn't tell him a thing. If she said she might be pregnant, he wouldn't treat that as some awful drama. He'd be pleased, calming, treating it as an opportunity. She didn't think he was about to propose exactly, but she knew that, if everything worked out between them, Books saw marriage as the ultimate destination. It was what this whole thing was about; the candlesticks, the glassware, the patience.

Emily felt more panicked than she had on the stairs, and Books saw it.

"Are you ok, love?"

Emily nodded. "Yes. Yes, I'm ok." In fact, she thought, I'm very much ok. I have a wonderful man who loves me, who is committed to me and is patient and kind and will look after me. To her, it was actually a scary feeling. She looked at Books and could tell he wanted to make love, but was concerned about what could have made her fall. She mumbled her way out of the situation and the evening moved away from the inevitable ending. They finished their meal, cuddled on the sofa and Emily eventually made her move to leave.

Outside she found herself on a wet, cold autumnal street. She actually enjoyed such hostile weather. The town was modern, functional, well designed and yet devoid of life. In times gone by it was a warren of rusting docks, narrow streets, and dark, secretive little pubs. The people were different too. A stew of foreign sailors, home town prostitutes and Somalian, Norwegian, Yemeni and Caribbean immigrants with their maze of accents and unknowable intrigues. It was where her father came from, the place that gave him his beginning. What developed him, made him what he became, was the Army. What put the finishing touches was the SAS and his friend and mentor, Ray Quinn.

Emily had emerged from that world and was forever grateful for the grounding they gave her. He and Ray Quinn shaped her life and it was a constant cause of strength.

She started to drive home. No music played and she did not speed. She took her time, mulling over recent events. She was almost there when she decided to keep going rather than turn off for home. She kept going, unsure where she was headed, hoping to navigate from old memories, sepia-tinted prints up in the attic of her mind. She lost herself in the old cul-de-sacs, swore a bit and wondered if it was a good idea. Then, suddenly, she was there. Her headlights shone on hooped iron railings. The lawn, the circular flower bed, rosebushes cropped against the weather.

The house was dark. She looked at the dashboard clock which told her it was 11pm and too late to knock. But she saw a light come on downstairs and took it as a sign. She knocked.

-13-

Trevor Johnston didn't seem to have aged. Not that he was old, even. Sixty, sixty-five. White haired and courteous. A bit slow, but he was always slow.

Emily wanted to sit with him in his yellow walled kitchen and ask some questions, but that was all too fast for him. He took his time taking her coat, shaking it out, hanging it on a peg by the front door, obviously buying some thinking time.

They exchanged comments about the weather, while they walked to the kitchen and tea and biscuits were organised.

"You've grown, haven't you? A bit, anyway."

Emily avoided the small talk. "I saw the light on," she explained for the second time.

"Oh, that's all right, dear. I don't sleep as much as I used to."

"You know – well, you know that I'm a detective now."

It was a stupid question. Trevor and her father were old friends. She fell to silence and Trevor waited. Eventually she decided to say, "There was this girl, Rose Flowers. You'll have heard about her. The girl whose body parts keep popping up all over the place."

Trevor nodded but still said nothing.

"She was a lap dancer. Pole dancer. According to records she worked for various clubs, but never for John Lomax. Never for his Unicorn Club."

The Unicorn was Lomax's first club, but not his first business venture. He still had his jeweller's shop, which was managed by Leanne, his wife. He had an amazing knack of making money whatever he turned his attention to. The Unicorn was the source of the vast majority of his fortune, though.

"I don't know," murmured Trevor. "It must have been checked at the time, but..."

"Oh, I'm sure she was never on the payroll or we'd have known about it. But most of these girls dance for cash. If emergency cover was needed one night and a girl was found willing to do it for tips alone, someone might have agreed to it. I'm not saying that's how things were normally done, or that anybody wanted to do things that way, but the manager may have made his own decision." She was fishing.

There was no way John Lomax would ever admit anything to a police officer. He had good cause to be wary of them and Trevor was the same. He was cut from the same cloth, hacked from the same block. Nevertheless, he tilted his head in a way that didn't specifically deny what had just been said.

"And maybe if some of those managers were asked again about Flowers, on the strict understanding that there'd be no comeback, they might remember things differently from the first time around. Especially if, let's say, it wasn't me asking, if there was no official interest at all, if it was just you asking people what they could remember." Emily was fishing in deeper waters now.

Trevor said nothing at all, but by the same token he wasn't moving her onto neutral conversational territory.

"And then there's this other man, Aftab Khaled. His is the other body that's keeping us busy. My colleagues are very keen to connect him to Rose Flowers. Trying to see if he knew her when she was still alive. And let's just say that you've got credit card receipts or CCTV footage that places Khaled in the club on one of those nights – well, wouldn't that be interesting?"

Trevor had become very still and now and had to shake himself alert.

"No CCTV," he said. "We wouldn't have that. Not that far back."

"I haven't come here. I haven't asked you anything. I won't push for any answer at all. I don't need to know anything. Just if certain things turned out to be true, they might be interesting."

Trevor nodded, but didn't say yes or no, or even acknowledge anything she had said. She let the conversation shift off to other places. It was nice being with Trevor; she had always liked him. Then he yawned, got up and walked back to the living room to readjust the heating. Emily followed.

The living room was pretty much as she remembered. The Cluedo set was still there, as was the Monopoly. There was a photo of Trevor and her father, both looking younger, Trevor in a black shirt with the top three buttons undone and a spark of gold from a large signet ring. He always had that bit of flash to him, a whiff of the gangster. She picked up the photo and stared at it closely because it was the same kind of angle, the same kind of sunny street; a road filled with sunshine and secrets.

"Trevor can I borrow this? I'll give it back,"

"You want to borrow it. Of course you can."

She thanked him and held on to the photo.

"It'd be nice to spend some time together sometime, Trevor," she said. "A bit less last minute."

He agreed and seemed quite pleased. They promised to make a date and meant it. As she drove away, her thoughts were with her sunny street.

She did not drive home immediately, choosing instead to make her way to the reservoir. It was a thumbprint of darkness pressed down on a neon city; muddy grass, inky trees, and that dark, aquatic mud.

Flowers was at a party on the other side of the railway line. She'd left it early, before it was properly dark. The initial investigation was unable to find out whether she had ever boarded a train, so the inquiry was unable to restrict itself to a single geographical focus. It had, however, been assumed that any abduction would either have taken place in the city centre, which was her intended destination, or on the streets directly connecting the party address with the railway station.

But maybe not.

Some people like twilight. Maybe the reservoir called her, drew her away from those lighted, populated streets. There was something creepily welcoming about the place, the way it was unlike everything else.

Would you come here in a party dress? In party shoes, and at twilight? Emily wouldn't and she liked darkness. But she wasn't sure about Rose Flowers. Maybe on an August evening at a bad party, she came out there to clear her head, or smoke or pop a pill. It was only a few hundred yards from the station. Why not?

Emily didn't know, so she drove home.

In the bathroom, she checked her little disc containing her contraceptive pills and confirmed that she hadn't missed a day. And the pill is better than 99 percent safe if you take it right. So she didn't know what it was, that moment on the stairs.

-14-

Days went by, short blustery days, with long nights and no progress. Webster continued to hold well-attended briefings at the start of every working day. It was Webster's show and everyone knew it. Information accumulated, but not much wisdom.

They couldn't find evidence that Khaled ever met Rose Flowers. On the morning of his death, Khaled withdrew two hundred pounds from a cash machine in the centre of town at 9.43am. CCTV showed him entering a coffee shop immediately thereafter. He stayed nineteen minutes, then left. CCTV had him walking out of shot. Not hurried, not scared, not furtive, not anything. Just a man walking calmly to his death. He made one phone call that morning; to a midlands machine tool company about some piece of research they were both involved in.

The coffee shop staff had been interviewed as well as the machine tools people. There were no reports of anything interesting. Emily interviewed more students, more faculty staff. On the downside, they were all still boring, but on the upside, she had no more episodes on the stairs and was thus certain that she wasn't pregnant.

They were no longer searching for bits of Khaled. They had recovered about 60 percent of his corpse, and assumed that dogs, crows and foxes would by then have taken the rest. All of Khaled's parts were found in open land, or in gardens or unlocked outbuildings backing onto open land.

They had found about 50 percent of Rose Flowers. Emily herself found a leg and a head, which put her ahead of the Flowers' Collectors League. Weirdly, and disturbingly, they found chunks of her thigh, sawn up and skin removed, wrapped in an unlabelled plastic bag in somebody's garage freezer. Because of the way the chunk was packaged, it looked more or less like a joint of pork.

There was some debate about whether such packages would be noticed. The theory was that with smaller, kitchen freezers, people tended to know what was in them with reasonable accuracy. With larger chest type cabinets, the sort that are kept in an outbuilding or garage, or at any rate away from the main living areas, it seemed no one really kept accurate tabs on things. Garden vegetables were put in there in season. Ditto leftovers, ditto soft fruits, ditto any cuts of meat that were on special offer locally. Sometimes these things were properly labelled, but often enough they were not, or the labels fell off, or become illegible.

No one quite wanted to say it, but it was pretty clear that, for a proportion of people at any rate, there was a fair risk that mistakes could have been made; that pieces of Rose Flowers could have been mistaken for something else. Mistaken, cooked and eaten. That was not information they were about to spread too widely, but the press was already full of snickering innuendo. The City Cannibals.

The police had, of course, interviewed the lady in whose freezer the pork was found. She knew who Elsie Williams was, but had never spoken to her. Her husband, now deceased, had a driveway cleaning business; operating a pressure washer to remove bird poo as far as Emily could make out, so he knew plenty of people in the area, and indeed all of the city. They could find no connection to Rose Flowers. There was also the fact that the freezer was kept in their garage, which was left unlocked most of the summer months. So, in short, anyone at all could have placed the item in there.

One wall of the incident room was completely given over to 'People of Interest.' These were people in whose homes bits of Flowers or Khaled were found, plus immediate family and close associates; also anyone living in the area with a history of sex offences or violence. They now had 167 such people. Someone, for a joke, had pinned the local phone directory to the noticeboard. The directory was removed, but the point echoed.

Emily felt that the investigation lacked a centre. Her view was that they didn't know where they ought to be looking. Pressure was also being applied by people higher up the chain of command to cut back on the number involved in the investigation. Burglaries and attempted rapes required attention and staff began to be re-assigned. Overtime was curbed and leave returned to normality. Webster, however, was determined to maintain the pressure. She stomped around the building, with her short iron-grey hair and dark, manly suits, asking for lists, questioning facts, demanding notes. She distributed happiness the way a storm cloud distributes sunshine. Emily liked working for her, even though the truth was that Emily was working with her and had the power to bury her whenever she fancied. Yet there was something about her bad-tempered relentlessness which appealed to Emily.

Webster had been told by somebody about Emily's episode with the Head of Faculty, and she dragged her into her office.

"He wasn't on the interview list, but you went up anyway."

"Yes, I did."

"Why?"

"Khaled was killed because of sex or money. If it was sex, we're already covering every possible angle. If it was money, then that Head of Faculty is the only person we know who's both connected to Khaled and has control of large sums of cash.

"Him?"

Emily told Webster what he told her about the engineering budgets, and what she'd been able to glean from public accounts, as well as the public accounts of those companies with whom Khaled struck partnership deals. The smallest of them had a turnover of twenty million pounds. The largest had revenues of more than one billion. His contacts ranged much further still.

Webster listened without comment. "Where and when were you going to tell me any of this?"

"It's in my notes." Which it was, even if presented in a way that hardly drew attention to the issue.

Webster glared at Emily, or, rather, scrutinized her, the way an entomologist looks at a pinned butterfly. It didn't upset her, though, because she liked directness.

"Go on."

"These two deaths are weird. Because Flowers was who she was, we assume we're looking for something sexual. But it's possible we're looking in the wrong direction. Those two aren't the only violent deaths there have been recently. And Khaled's death has some clear connections with one of the others."

Webster's eyebrows were high now. Her face was angry, or Emily thought it was.

She continued, "In early September, a prisoner in the city prison, Mark Mortimer, committed suicide. Slashed both wrists with broken glass. He worked for a precision engineering company near here. His firm had an ongoing development project with the university."

"Any money involved?"

"No. I mean yes, some money. But peanuts. Not slash-your-wrists-and-chop-lecturers-into-pieces-money."

Webster treated Emily to her best laser eyes treatment to show how much she appreciated her turn of phrase and then tapped on her computer keys. She said nothing as she tapped away, so Emily just stood there. She couldn't see the screen, but thought she ought to be looking at the notes and details of the Mortimer inquest. Emily had already studied the inquest files, which concluded what she expected. In summary: a promising young man screwed up his career with a stupid drug deal. He lost his job, rendered himself unemployable, saw his wife and kids bugger off back to her mum's house in the West Midlands. He couldn't take the mess he'd made of his own life and chose to end it.

Emily decided that she'd had enough of just standing there waiting. "Would you like some coffee?"

She glowered at Emily. "Black. No sugar."

Emily made treacle for her, peppermint tea for herself. Shona, who managed the office and shared her addiction for peppermint tea, was in the kitchenette too. They chatted. Shona was the queen of office gossip and Emily spent the time gathering the latest, before telling her that she was in the middle of being bollocked by Rhoda Webster and better make a move.

"Oh my God, that woman."

Emily shrugged. "Someone complained about me."

Shona wanted to know more and Emily told her what she wanted the office to know.

"I was having my period, cramping up, having problems." She knew that telling that stuff to Shona was like broadcasting it on some in-house Twitter service. "And that man who complained? No names, no packdrill. His breath really stank that day. Do you think he drinks, maybe? He seemed, I don't know, unsteady or something."

Emily left her with that thought, and went back upstairs with the mugs, entering Webster's room without knocking. She didn't say thank you, just "The Mortimer suicide seems straightforward. And we haven't found drug traces in Khaled's flat or anywhere else."

"He's a plastics man."

Webster wasn't as interested in the various uses of industrial plastics as Emily and just glared, which she took as an invitation to educate her.

"One of his areas of expertise was high modulus polyethylenes. That's the stuff you use to make plastic shopping bags, only far tougher. The super high density stuff, Khaled's speciality, can be used as glide rails in industrial equipment, docking gear, that kind of thing. The high, but not super high, density plastics are what you make buckets out of, water pipes, plastic milk bottles, stuff like that."

"Packaging. You think he created packaging systems for drugs shipments? No smell. No leakage. Shockproof. Completely sealed."

"It's possible. Mortimer and Khaled probably knew each other. Khaled worked with Mortimer's company, which had only ninety people on its payroll, and Mortimer was one of only six mechanical engineers there.

Mortimer was busted because his packaging was amateurish. He had the stuff put in a steel tube and had the ends welded up. Khaled was probably the go-to man around these parts, maybe in all of the country, for plastics expertise. The university didn't have the manufacturing facilities as such, but Khaled would have known precisely where to go for that. He was the department's networker."

Webster pondered all this. Nothing that Emily said could be considered as evidence. She was merely exploring possibilities. But then again, they didn't have any evidence of any sexual link to Flowers, so that was all speculative too.

"Why didn't you tell me all this earlier?"

"It's in my notes."

"It's not in your notes. I've just looked. Not properly."

"I wanted to look further before bothering you. I wanted something tangible."

"What does that mean? Look further? You think you can go it alone? You think you can conduct private investigations?"

"No."

"You carry out your designated tasks. You report when they're completed. Then you're given further tasks."

"I have carried out my designated tasks."

"You didn't answer my question."

"I know one of the inmates in the city prison. I'm seeing him on Saturday."

Webster shook her head. "You won't get anything."

"Jon Johnston. He's a former police office. A good one. Good apart from being an embezzler, I mean."

"And you'll do what?

"Ask him for gossip about Mortimer's suicide. See what he can find out."

Webster thought for a while and her jaw moved as if she was masticating something chewy or cartilaginous. If she had been a man, she'd have been clamping her jaw muscles.

"Jamie Donaldson is an idiot," she said eventually. "You are not an idiot. But Jim is part of a team and you are no use to me if you can't play with the team."

Emily took her time as she considered the situation. She knew that the most useful things she'd done so far had nothing to do with team play, and all the most boring things were because some idiot like Jamie Donaldson asked her to do them. It seemed to her that the evidence strongly suggested she was vastly more useful to Webster working the way she preferred to work and, in any case, she'd hardly been working off-piste at all. Not by her standards.

But Webster was still doing that thing with her jaw, so Emily restricted herself to an acquiescent "Yes," and looked at her hands. Webster stopped her lecture.

Emily wanted to depart on a better note, so she asked, "Sorry, do you mind? Can I ask where you got your suit? I just think it really works on you." She followed this with a beatific smile and walked out of her office.

-15-

She visited Johnston again. He was in the same room, with the same lighting and the same paintwork. He hadn't improved the place as he said he would when she last saw him. He had the same guards too. He was in a better mood this time. She thought it was too good; over energetic the way a four-year-old is before a sugar crash.

"Bloody hell," he started with a rush. "You spend a lifetime in the police force, but it's only when you get in here you understand what's really going on. Some of the stories I've heard…"

He started to tell some of them, waving his hands and laughing out loud. The tales he told didn't seem credible to her and she expected them to sound the same to him when he calmed down. She reminded him that he still had two years to serve and he needed to view things more rationally.

"Can I ask a favour?" She asked.

She told him the picture as she saw it. Two murders, one suicide. "Everyone thinks that Khaled must somehow be linked to the Flowers' death, but it seems to me we ought to be looking hard at the Mortimer death too."

Johnston asked a few questions in quick succession, getting himself up to speed. His assessment of the case was rapid and decisive. She realised she was seeing him in police mode, the way he was before his career went off the rails.

"This is real, Emily, is it? You're not just…..?"

"Trying to cheer you up? No. It's real. I mean, it is from my point of view. Webster thinks it might be worth looking at. Everyone else thinks I'm barking mad."

"Good enough." He rubbed his face with both hands. When he removed them he looked older, more like himself, actually, minus the sugar high. "What's your hypothesis?"

"Don't have one. But here are the pieces. Mortimer was involved in drugs, but an idiot when it came to bringing them into the country. Khaled had expertise in materials and access to an enormous amount of manufacturing knowhow. Plastics certainly, but general engineering too. The two men very likely knew each other. If Khaled did something that pissed off some big-league drug dealer, then maybe Mortimer was in the firing line as well. Obviously, no one snuck into Mortimer's cell to bump him off, but maybe he got a message saying that unless he killed himself his family will be murdered. Or whatever."

Emily stopped. She knew it all sounded highly unlikely but, then again, there were three corpses to be explained.

"Got it," said Johnston. "I'll see what I can do."

They talked about nothing in particular for another ten minutes. They were uncomfortable minutes because she was aware of the guards, the other prisoners, the atmosphere of poverty and limits. And, of course, the walls. She left as soon as she reasonably could.

Standing outside Dartmoor Prison she was overcome by a new, strange and worrying feeling. At first she couldn't even describe it to herself, so shocked was she, but eventually she found the vocabulary. She was experiencing feelings of wanting to self -harm. This was the first time in her entire life that she had felt that way. She had seen it in others, of course, but never associated herself with it. It was like fog patches forming in the beam of car headlights. The prison and the moor. Were they playing a part? Or was something more serious and sinister rearing its ugly head? She couldn't be sure, and it frightened her. She remembered as a child she used to like pressing kitchen knives against her forearms to see how much she could feel. The usual answer was almost nothing. She even drew blood occasionally, but they were accidental moments, she thought. Now she wasn't so certain.

Now, standing on the road outside Dartmoor Prison, she felt that long buried impulse again. To press some cold steel against her exposed arm. To study the blade as it whitened her skin, hoping to feel something and terrified she would not. She wanted to roll up her sleeve so that she could look at her white skin and blue veins. She knew the thoughts; the impulses were not good; a flight of stairs leading down.

She had a plastic bag of ready-rolled joints in the boot of her car, concealed under the tyre lever and spare wheel, along with a cigarette lighter and a bar of chocolate. She had an impulse to stand and smoke a joint, right there outside the jail, in broad daylight. Books was tediously traditional on issues like whether or not it's ok for officers of the law, or anybody, to smoke weed, so Emily hadn't told him that she did it. He didn't yet know that she grew it in her garden shed and she was certain he would demand she stopped immediately. She knew he would find a way to make her stop, but he wouldn't tell anybody either. He'd just solve the problem himself. He could be very resourceful. She decided not to give in to her irrational need, so she stamped feeling into her legs, jumped up and down and ran just far enough to feel out of breath and for one of her feet to start blistering.

She limped back to her car, wondering how long it would take to get to Solihull.

-16-

Two and a half hours was the answer. There was an accident just south of Worcester which blocked two lanes and she spent an hour in almost stationary traffic, watching long curtains of rain sweep across from the Malvern Hills. She switched stations on the radio, trying and failing to find music that didn't annoy her. She dismissed her memory stick or cd player because she knew all the tracks by heart. In the end she settled for exhaust fumes and silence. She texted Books to let him know she'd be late and just that simple act caused her body to glow with a warmth she loved but couldn't explain.

The farther she got from Dartmoor Prison, the less sure she was of what she was doing. She wasn't worried about another Webster ear bashing, so she stopped the car and called her. She answered it in her normal snappish way, but Emily ignored that and told her what she wanted to do and where she was.

"Solihull?"

"Mortimer's wife and kids moved back here when he went to prison."

"And you're there why?"

"I've been visiting a friend," she lied. "So I'm in the area."

There was a pause down the end of the line. Emily couldn't hear anything, but could see her doing that thing with her jaw. Then, "OK."

"OK as in 'yes please go ahead and interview Stephanie Mortimer?' I don't have to."

"It's fine. You might as well, since you're there."

It was hardly a massive vote of confidence, but it was good enough. "Let me know what you get from

Mortimer." She cut the line before Emily had time to say goodbye.

Emily drove slowly to Mortimer's house. The house was at the end of a short cul-de-sac. Pleasant and unremarkable. There were patches of lawn in front of every house, with few shrubs. She summarized it in her head as tidy, clean. There were lights on in the house and she rang the bell. No response came, so she tried again. Still nothing. She was about to ring for the third time when the door opened. A woman stood before her who was younger than she expected. She looked to be in her mid-thirties, and she was pretty and slim. Her blonde hair fell more than shoulder length and there was a kind of natural sulkiness around her mouth. She wore skinny jeans, a floral print top in dark grey and lilac and a black biker jacket.

"Mrs Mortimer?"

"Not anymore. I don't use that name anymore. I'm Stephanie West now."

Emily introduced herself, showed her warrant card and asked for twenty minutes of her time. She opened the door with a marked reluctance and took Emily through to the kitchen. The room was tired, in need of decoration, or perhaps, modernizing. It was stuck in the 1980's with country-style cabinets with limed oak doors and tiled countertops. Emily thought the look would probably come back one day, much like flared jeans and trousers. If you waited long enough everything comes back to you. She also couldn't match the kitchen with this woman. There something incongruous, out of place, but then she remembered she was in the mother's house.

Emily sat down, but Stephanie West remained standing, trying to convey that she had other, more important, things to do. She also kept her jacket on to reinforce the lack of time. There was an atmosphere in the room which Emily was struggling to explain. It was more than the natural reticence about dealing with the police which can be exhibited by the public. Not something she expected in such a nice little cul-de-sac in Solihull.

Emily introduced herself and said, "We're investigating a couple of serious crimes. One of the victims knew your husband. I just want to check if there's anything we need to explore."

Stephanie West sat down on a stool at the breakfast bar, but there was something provisional in the way she sat, one long leg sloping all the way to the floor, as though showing that she could get up and walk out at a moment's notice.

"Have you ever heard of a man named Aftab Khaled?" Emily began. "He was an engineering lecturer at the university."

"Never heard of him." Her response was instant, but followed by a hesitation. She amended her answer. "A Middle Eastern man?"

"Yes, North African."

"Met him at an office party, maybe. I didn't talk to him."

Her leg moved as she said this. Her toes came in under her centre of gravity, so she was even closer to standing up than she was before.

"We found him cut into about fifteen different pieces around the reservoir. He used to work with your ex."

West's colour rose, and she searched for her phone and fiddled with it.

"We found his lung bobbing around in the water."

Her colour hardened but something else did too.

"Look, I don't know that person. I don't want to sound insensitive. I'm very sorry and everything, but..." she shrugged. "What was your question?"

"Do you know why your husband, sorry, your ex-husband, killed himself?"

"Because he was an idiot."

"Did anyone ever threaten you? You or your children? Did your ex-husband ever receive threats that he told you about?"

The question didn't get anything much more than a snort, which was half laugh and half dismissal.

"No," she said, beginning to stand up, and reaching for her phone and car key on the worktop. Her colour was still high, still too bright, but there was a kind of armouring now which Emily doubted she could penetrate.

"Why did you leave him?"

"Why did I leave him? He was a drug dealer. He had this Saint Mark thing going. Butter wouldn't melt, and all that. Then what is he, really? A drug dealer who was busted and sent to jail. And we had two children together."

There were tears in her eyes, but the armour was still present, still shone.

"Your ex wasn't a dealer. Not really. He was some sort of middleman who screwed up. The person who killed Khaled is the sort of person who would be happy to threaten wives and children too. We can't protect you if you don't tell us stuff. Stephanie, have you been threatened? You or the kids? Now or in the past?"

"No." She ran her hand hard through her hair, shaking it out. There was anger and defiance there.

"Or any recent contacts which struck you as odd?"

There were other questions which needed asking, but Emily knew she had lost the attention of her witness. Stephanie West was elsewhere, in a space which was calling her and wanting Emily to leave.

"I'm going to leave you my phone number. If you need any kind of help, let me know. We *can* help, we just need you to ask."

She nodded as Emily wrote her name and number, tore out the sheet from her notebook, and pushed it over the counter to her. As she did so, they heard a car outside, followed by doors being slammed and the sound of children's voices. The piece of paper was ignored and left on the worktop. They walked to the front door. The strange atmosphere was still with them, but Emily didn't understand it.

West went out to get her kids. Emily hung back, because she didn't know what she was supposed to do. She knew West had said something about her, because she saw her gesture in her direction. The kids spilled out of the car. Tristan and Althea, six and five. Althea must have been in some kind of ballet costume and wanted to show her mother her pirouette. The friend drove away with a wave.

Emily said, "Thank you, Stephanie. I'll get going."

West gave Emily a look that said she couldn't leave soon enough for her, then, abruptly, as she had her hand on the door of her car, said, "Actually, look, I have to go out. It would be easier if I didn't have them. Can you look after them for ten minutes? My mum should be back soon. She should be here any moment."

West looked at Emily with a fierceness that was almost physical. Emily thought she was trying to let her know that she had high child care standards, and she was seeking to determine if she met those tests. Emily reassured her with her best child care face.

"OK." She nodded and took Emily and the children into the house. She got orange juice for Tristan and put the TV on. She said, "It'll be five minutes, literally."

Emily didn't believe her. She thought Stephanie was the kind of person who took the path of least resistance in most situations. That she did whatever was most pleasant and most convenient and simply rearranged her mental furniture to make her own behaviour seem acceptable. She wondered whether everybody did the same thing, if not quite on West's scale.

West gave Emily the hard stare one last time, then whirled off. Tristan was in front of the TV already, watching an American cartoon. Things being whacked, splatted and chased.

She said to Althea, "I'm Emily, a friend of your mum's. You're Althea, aren't you?"

Althea nodded. Her eyes were wide and serious. "Are you a policewoman?"

"Yes"

Althea frowned at the answer, but Emily didn't know why.

"I'm a detective, so I don't get to wear a uniform."

Tristan was watching now, or, more accurately, half watching because the cartoon on the TV also held part of his attention.

"That's why I don't have a police car either. Detectives aren't usually allowed them."

"Do you have a gun?" Tristan asked the boy's question.

"No, they don't let us have guns," but she showed him her warrant card, and he liked that.

"My daddy went to prison," Tristan continued and Althea's eyes travelled to a photo on the windowsill of Mark Mortimer, with his family. Emily had not noticed any other photos of him anywhere. She muted the TV and, acknowledging Althea's look, said, "that's your daddy there, is it? He looks nice."

Althea nodded as if she understood. Wise beyond her years. Emily picked up the photo and sat on the floor with her back against the sofa and the children sat either side. Althea was quite close, almost cuddled in, but Tristan kept his distance. "Tell me about your daddy," Emily said. "Anything you remember."

They didn't say much at first, but then Althea volunteered something. "He was really tall". And then Tristan joined in and they were both talking. They weren't crying exactly, but tears were not far away. Emily listened, allowing them to keep talking. She wasn't in police mode because the children couldn't possibly have had any useful evidence, but it seemed fair to let them remember their father, in their own way, at their pace. Whatever Mortimer did or didn't do, his children did not deserve to have him airbrushed from their lives.

Then Tristan said, "why did he go to prison?"

Althea, who had been saying something, shut up completely.

"If you're in the police," added Tristan, pushing.

"I don't know," Emily whispered. "I know what they say he did, but I don't really know. The real reason, I mean."

"Was it a mistake?"

It was a very good question, Emily thought. *Was* it a mistake? Nothing about Mortimer shouted drug smuggler, or at least, nothing beyond a steel tube packed full of cocaine.

"Maybe," she said to Tristan. "I don't know. We're trying to find out."

"Is that why you're here?"

"Sort of, yes."

And, unexpectedly, she felt she was telling the truth. Two other corpses brought her there, but Mortimer's corpse mattered too, and so did his children. She felt their questioning plucking at her, demanding something. Tristan was a good interrogator. Like many children he could extract truths and insights, that the subject had no intention of disclosing.

Time passed and the children switched their attention to other things with the alarming ease of the very young. The TV came back in a storm of car chases and shouting. There was no sign of Stephanie West or of her mum. Emily didn't mind, but she had been there twenty minutes, not the promised five. Eventually they heard a car stopping outside and West's mother arrived. Emily went to meet her, explain who she was and why she, a complete stranger, was looking after her grandchildren. She didn't seem surprised to find a stranger looking after her daughter's children.

Emily said, "they seem lovely. Must be so hard for them after losing their father."

West's mother, Geraldine, tutted at that and scowled. Emily bent down to the kids. "I'll do my best. To find out if it was a mistake."

Tristan nodded, as though he was swearing some sort of sacred oath. Althea was wearing a little bracelet: seashells on a piece of elastic. She took it off and held it out to me. "For you."

"Thank you, Althea. Thank you sweetheart."

Emily left and their grandmother shuffled them inside. She walked to her car, opened the boot, and rooted around until she found a joint and a lighter. Smoking outside the prison would have been against her rules, because it would have been a bad response to a temporary emergency.

She was about halfway through, when Stephanie West's red Mini swept down the cul-de-sac. She got out, with something liquid in her eyes and Emily wondered if whatever she'd been out doing involved a glass or two of white wine.

"You're still here."

"Just leaving. The kids are terrific. Your mum's in there with them now."

She nodded brusquely.

"Stephanie, that office party where you met Khaled: who threw it? Mark's firm? The university? Or what?"

"I don't know. Some engineering things. Local organization of engineers or something."

"Okay. And if you remember anything else, you have my number."

West nodded and headed inside. Emily decided she didn't want the rest of her joint and threw it down a drain, wondering whether it was progress. She also wondered whether Stephanie West was annoyed with her because she didn't want to be reminded of her troublesome former husband? Pissed off because she had been threatened and didn't want to risk any police involvement? Pissed off because she resented the police for jailing her husband? Or was she just a spoiled pretty girl whose life wasn't running the way she'd intended and who was perfectly ready to let her bad mood spill out onto anyone who got in its way?

She saw Stephanie West glowering from the kitchen window as she drove away. She waved at her and headed home with her new shell bracelet on her wrist.

-17-

For the next few days Emily worked on the routine issues, coming in on time, making worthless calls, writing stupid lists, checking bits of paper, writing up notes and listening to briefings. None of which excited her at all. The incident room board listing their people of interest now showed a tally of 221. That was not a sign of progress, but one of failure.

She worked on Khaled's bank records, which placed him at two lap dancing clubs, but it wasn't enough. It was tantalizing. She also worked on what she considered more interesting. The six names: Ivor Harris, Galton Evans, Trevor Yergin, Huw Allsop, Ben Rossiter, David Marr. She added another, Idris Khan, transferring him from the Championship to the Premier League. He and Ivor Harris both had their thumbprints somewhere near this case. Ivor Harris had quite a lot to do with the university, including the engineering faculty, but that would be expected from a busy local MP. Not much of a thumbprint.

Idris Khan interested her much more. He was a business associate of Rattigan's. More than a friend, which is why he was on the B list, not the A-team. But Khan had a variety of venture capital type investments in local businesses, including the outright ownership of the late Mark Mortimer's firm, Precision Tools. Emily couldn't see how a financial investment in a firm that once employed a not very competent drug smuggler tied Khan into anything much, and still less did it suggest that he was part of Rattigan's circle. She was determined to investigate that as well as to scratch away at that Mark Mortimer itch. In an ideal world she wanted to look at these things on her own, but she consulted Webster for the sake of a quiet life.   She gave her the notes on her interview with West and told her there was something strange in the widow's manner. A strangeness that suggested something being withheld. Webster didn't like the possibility of a Mortimer-Khaled connection, but she couldn't ignore it, and without a better alternative she gave Emily the go ahead. She set parameters, though, which irked Emily. Every call, each interview had to be sanctioned.

Emily phoned Mortimer's ex-colleagues, his university connections, as well as his brother and sister. She didn't unearth anything tangible, but she also didn't get the sense that she was looking at a drug dealer. He just didn't have that smell about him. He seemed to have been a scrupulous employee, never late, seldom absent. Then, too, there was that 'Saint Mark' comment of Stephanie West's. Emily had found nothing that would count for anything in court; nothing even to justify a shift in investigative resources and yet she still felt strongly that something was not quite right. Something was awry.

Webster only half agreed, but half was enough for now. Nevertheless, there was a growing feeling that the investigation was going nowhere. They didn't have a single useful lead on Rose Flowers and Khaled was another dead end. They knew about a few sexual liaisons for the man was no hermit, but there was nothing to connect with Flowers, nothing to suggest a motive for his murder. The Mortimer-Khaled link and Stephanie West's odd evasion was as good as anything else they had. Emily had nothing tangible to show for her efforts yet, but some flowers bloom slowly. She remembered once watching a moody cow, a big Hereford heifer, starting to lean against a post and rail fence on a farm. She pushed and the fence resisted. But the cow didn't give up. She just kept at it, shifting her position from time to time while making sure that nine-hundred-pound weight was always hard against the upper rail. In the end, of course, the rail broke, snapping into two jagged timber lances. The cow studied her work, then backed away peacefully, happy to start munching again. Emily remembered that lesson. Apply pressure, keep going and things can snap even when they seem to be their most static and immovable. If there's a line of weakness, sooner or later something will fracture.

And it did.

The engineering group at whose party Stephanie West once met Khaled was called, rather pretentiously, the Circle of Engineering Excellence. Its chairman was a retired engineer, Barney Adams. Emily hesitated briefly before calling him. She knew that she had already told Webster she'd call Adams, not visit him, but she reasoned that even Webster surely couldn't care if she did little more than promised. Also, Emily had grown tired of desks and offices and overhead lamps.

His house, when she got there, turned out to be right by the shore, overlooking the sea with picture windows that framed a strip of grass, a band of scrub, then a line of grey sea and a mountain scape of grey cloud.

He offered her tea. Emily refused, but asked, "What is it like all day, looking out at this?"

He gave the usual answers extolling the virtues of the light, the movement and the ceaseless change. Emily believed that the view never changed. It was a vision of eternity, sometimes sunlit, sometimes furious, but always there. Gazing at you gazing at it.   She verbalized her thoughts and Adams said, "You could be right." He didn't put the lights on, so they were just there watching the light fail over water. There would be rain before long.

Emily outlined the reason for her visit, letting him know it was a routine enquiry, pursuant to the murder of Aftab Khaled. She started asking questions, and Adams proved to be a helpful witness who was good on names and dates with a swift recall, documentary records and precise answers.

"Aftab and Mark knew each other. They were both Circle regulars. I've often seen them chatting together. I got the impression they knew each other outside these meetings too."

"How far did their connection go back?"

Adams consulted his attendance records. He had to put the lights on for this, and the sea beyond the windows receded into the darkness. "I've only got records for the last four years," he said, "but they were both booked to attend a meeting in July 2006. If it helps, I could talk to my predecessor and go further back."

Emily shook her head and poked away at the nature of their connection. "What were their shared interests? What did they talk about?"

"I'm not sure. Aftab's passion was industrial plastics which Mark wouldn't have had much to do with. But Aftab was a university man, of course. He needed to keep abreast of the literature, especially highly engineered steels. If you needed a specific part with some demanding specifications such as shock resistance, heat resistance, very narrow design tolerances and so on, then Mark's outfit would take care of that. Aftab didn't have a research interest in that kind of area, but he was still very well versed in it. And, of course, Aftab was amazingly well connected. If you had a problem that Aftab couldn't solve, he'd know somebody who could. In a way, that was his real expertise. Aftab knew everyone."

"What about geography?" Emily asked, and then explained what she meant. "One of the things that has niggled at me was that Khaled was of Moroccan extraction. Mortimer tried to bring in his drugs via southern Spain, just north of Gibraltar. Now, in itself, there's nothing odd about Spain as an import route. Most cocaine enters the UK via Spain or Holland. Spain because of its Latin American connections, Holland because of Rotterdam's importance as a logistics hub. On the other hand, it's possible in this instance that there's more to Mortimer's import route than mere probabilities. Khaled still had family in Morocco and the Spanish supplier whose steel tubing Mortimer had tried to use did business all over North Africa. It's one of those tantalizing almost-connections which might or might not prove significant."

Adams couldn't help. "Khaled still kept current with things in North Africa. We've heard the same from other sources and his bank records show that he travelled as far afield as Dubai and Jordan, but I can't say whether Mortimer had any professional interest in the area."

They talked for a while. Adams was amazed that Mortimer turned out to have an involvement with drugs. He seemed somewhat less amazed that someone chose to chop Khaled into several dozen pieces. He had no tangible suspicion or anything like that, just less amazement, and no knowledge whatsoever of Rose Flowers.

She left Adams's house unsure how to proceed. His grey sea had leaked into a dark night; dark and rain swept.

Emily started walking as she was in a mood to think, and because she wasn't far away, she decided to drop by Idris Khan's home and have a snoop. Khan: the owner of the place where Mark Mortimer worked and the business buddy of Brendan Rattigan.

She walked the six or seven minutes to Marine Parade, Khan's street. She had already scanned the vehicles parked in his front drive, and was checking the rest of the street for the sake of completeness. It wasn't a good night for it; rain mixed with sleet and worse weather promised.

She was wearing gloves and had to write in felt tip pen, because it was the only thing that marked the wet pages of her notebook. She tried to make notes, keep the notebook vaguely dry, and avoid getting too soaked herself. Concentrating on juggling meant that she was slow to notice a couple of men on the street. They wore dark coats, scarves. One had a woolen hat, one not. The bare headed one had close cropped hair. They saw her, began to move again, but then stopped and walked back.

Emily finished putting a registration number in her book, her senses on alert, then looked up, making proper eye contact.

"Hi," she said.

"You might not want to do that. People can be a bit funny about their privacy." This from the one with the beard who looked to be in his thirties.

Emily simply levelled a glare at him. "Oh, I think I'll just carry on," she said.

The taller man, who had been silent, enjoyed her response. He smiled involuntarily and raised a hand to cover his mouth as though there was a law against smiling.

"Let me see that," said the other man, gesturing at her notebook. He had a Scottish accent.

"No. I've got work to do," Emily smiled and continued with her glare. She turned her back on them, and took a few steps down the road to the next car. She was ready to carry on and turned.

The street was lit and was a reasonably well populated residential street, but there was no one around, not even much traffic. Just the two men. Houses were set back from the road. They might as well have been in a dark wood or deserted inner city alley for all the protection she had.

She could hear Webster's voice in her head, telling her to step away, not to seek confrontation. 'Step away now.' She could hear Lenny too, telling her 'to choose the fight you want, not the one they want. If you can't win, don't start. It's ok to say no; sometimes it's the only smart thing to do.' And he was right. He always was. Lenny: her martial arts instructor, if you could call him that, though the term diminished him. He wasn't a man who believed in fighting for relaxation or pure exercise. To him, that was a waste of time and energy. He was ex Spetsnaz and one of Frank and Ray's team. An operative who worked in the shadows and had taught her well.

She took a pace or two backwards and the men took a pace or two forward. They exchanged glances; some hidden exchange of communication, but she couldn't guess what about. She continued to back away and shoved her book into her shoulder bag. Something fell from her bag and splashed onto the wet concrete. She didn't look down. She didn't want to make herself vulnerable. Emily backed away another step, but hesitated, as though reluctant to part with whatever it was she'd dropped.

The taller man, who had been silent, whispered something to his companion, and the mood seemed to shift. Any threat seemed to be vanishing. The shorter man bent to pick up her energy bar.

'Choose the fight you want, not the one they want. If you can't win, don't start.'

Lenny's words. Wise words.

She shifted her body so that the weight fell over the ball of her leading foot, the left one. Her heel came off the ground, but the men didn't notice. Then she moved. She brought her right leg around hard, lashing at the man's jaw and made contact with the toe of her right foot. She was wearing chunky winter boots which were designed for fashion but proved to be effective for combat. Her toe struck his jawline almost dead centre, smashing through bone. She felt as much as saw the man's head jerk back with the whiplash and then she saw the bone broken, the jaw sagging loose and useless from its socket. His beard could not hide the damage she had inflicted.

The man sprawled backward on the tarmac, disbelieving eyes raised to the pelting rain. His companion gawped at the fallen man and then gawped at Emily. Nobody said anything and nobody cared about her energy bar now. She reached into her bag, grabbed something and held it up in the feeble orange glow of the streetlights.

"This is a rape alarm. If you take one step closer, I'm going to let this off and tell everyone you tried to assault me."

She moved backwards as she gave her warning, partly to put more distance between them but also because she didn't want them to notice that it was not a rape alarm she was holding, but a tube of deodorant.

The man whose jaw she'd broken was staggering to his feet. Part of him was nakedly furious, wanting to finish this fight, but the other part was bewildered. He kept putting his hand to his jaw as though he could just slot it back into place, but pain drove his hand away. His face looked unmade; a waxwork in the process of collapse. The taller man restrained him, stopping him doing anything, and already the energy was bleeding from the situation. Emily was calm and feeling safer already.

"Just so you know," she said, "I've been parking here and twice now someone has keyed my car. I wanted to know who, that's why I was looking at number plates. I don't know who you are. I don't care who you are. Now I'm going to walk away and if either of you comes after me, I will let off this alarm and press charges for assault."

She backed away, until twenty yards separated them, then she turned and walked normally, but kept constant watch over my shoulder. The two men stayed where they were, until they too started walking, but away from her, rather than towards her. She turned at the street corner. There was nothing now ahead of her but sleet and parked cars and the sigh of the sea beyond.

She realised that she was shaking. Huge waves started in the soles of her feet and rose up through her. She bobbed on their surface like a boat at anchor. Her car was parked in the other direction but she decided against going back to get it. She'd get Books to come with her tomorrow.

She found her way to a bus stop where a figure was sheltering from the rain and she stood next to him, because it felt safer. She was still shaking, but the waves had gone inside now and were not visible. When she got home, she started to run a bath and fetched a joint from the shed. While the bath was still running, she called the

A&E department of the nearest hospital. She told them she was a police officer looking for two men, one of whom had sustained a broken jaw in an altercation. She used the word deliberately, wondering whether it was only kept alive by the police. They said that there hadn't been anybody in like that yet and she left her number.

She turned off the tap, lit her joint and eased herself into the warm water. She called all the hospitals she could think of, but came up with blanks from them all. Nothing; nothing at all. Her shaking had become no more than a memory. She discovered a bruise on her forehead but could not remember how that had happened. She felt a darkening circle of pain when she pressed it with her finger.

As the last of the bathwater drained away, she finally got a call back. Two men had entered hospital A&E in Bristol. One had a serious compound fracture to the jaw and was seen to immediately. A nurse and junior doctor corrected the dislocation by simply thumbing the bone back into place, but prepared the patient for immediate surgery on the fracture. They placed a temporary bandage over the jaw to limit movement, then left to arrange the operation. When the nurse returned with the necessary consent paperwork, both men had vanished.

The patient had given his name, which she knew would undoubtedly prove to be false, as would the address.

Emily was pleased with the way she had handled things. She chose the fight she wanted, not the one they offered. Her kick was good and her actions afterward rapid and well planned. Except for one thing. She'd assumed she'd be able to get at her targets in hospital. She'd assumed she'd be able to get a pair of handcuffs on her man in the post-op recovery room and interview him under caution. She would have threatened him with a charge of threatening a police officer, which she knew she wouldn't have been able to sustain, but wouldn't have needed to. She'd have done enough to secure a verifiable identification, DNA, a car registration, phone numbers and address. Not merely the man she kicked but, quite possibly, his mate too. It simply had not occurred to her that the injured man would simply walk into hospital, get bandaged up, and walk out again. How on earth was he going to eat? She wondered.

She called Bristol again and asked to speak to the relevant nurse and to get her to look for any paper towels or bed coverings that might have gleaned a drop or two of blood. She promised to do what she could, but her voice told Emily that she'd get nothing. She would be able to secure the CCTV footage from the admissions area, but she doubted if the images would be clear enough to secure a proper ID.

It all sounded uncomfortably like a dead end, a tree without fruit, but somehow it didn't feel that way. She remembered the cow, the leaning, the break, and jagged timber lances flashing in the sun.

-18-

She decided not to tell anybody about her jaw crunching exercise because she felt it wouldn't be viewed well. She did some anatomical research on the Web and found that fixing a complex fracture of the jaw is a difficult business. Elastics are used to hold any loose teeth in place. Jaw wires are extended from the fractured bone to the line of teeth opposite, to provide stability. The patient can eat only fluids and very soft foods for six to eight weeks following surgery. In days gone by, a broken jaw could often prove lethal because you can't chew with a fractured jawbone.

The two men last night may not have been experts on these matters, but it was telling that they chose to drive an hour to get medical attention, when the nearest hospital was just a few minutes away. Telling that they gave false ID. Telling also that her victim chose to walk out of the hospital with nothing more than a bandage and a couple of paracetamol.

Emily was unsure of what she should do next. She saw their faces, of course, but not for long and not in good light. Experience with recognition technology places day-after accuracy at worse than twenty per cent. And in any case, those technologies work when you have a suspect whose identity needs confirmation. Emily had nothing; no name, no phone, no address.

She tried looking at the various car number plates she'd collected, but that failed to produce anything. One car, a Mercedes, was rented by an Egyptian man, at Heathrow Airport. Given the vague North African connections in the case so far, his nationality rang some kind of bell, but it wasn't loud. After all, it's two thousand miles from Cairo to Casablanca. Emily recalled that Khan owned Precision Tools, which sold to North Africa, which would possibly account for the Egyptian man's presence. She felt that she was more ignorant than knowledgeable. She didn't even know why the men had been interested in her. Because she'd been talking to Adams? To Stephanie West? Or because she was on Khan's street, looking into his front garden and collecting vehicle registrations? Or none of the above? She was at a loss.

She thought that her ignorance was actually a rich unknowing, not a poor one. Webster's investigation had gathered lots of facts, but increasingly her orchard seemed a barren one. It had neither buds nor flowers.

For example: Two more pieces of Flowers had been found. A small plastic-wrapped bit of calf was found in yet another outbuilding. It was only found because the mother of the family concerned became worried about the stories in the press, and organized a major clear-out of her garden shed and bike store. She found the Tupperware box, hidden out of sight in the sloping roof of the shed. The box was filled with table salt, turned pink with blood, and a chunk of Rose Flowers, about the size of two fists placed end to end.

The woman, Susan Lee, used to be a primary school teacher, but now, with four active kids under fifteen, was a full-time parent who worked as a churchwarden at the local church. Her husband, Karl, worked in local government finance. Neither of them seemed like the slice-up-a-dancer type. Neither knew Elsie Williams, Ryan Humphries, Arthur Price or any of the tremendously non-suspicious suspects. There were no connections with Flowers either. The shed had no doors and was just a step or two away from the street, so anyone could have had access to it.

More weirdly still, a jam jar was found tucked into the spare tyre compartment of a VW Passat. The jam jar, which according to its label once held 454 grams of honey, was now found to hold only vegetable oil and a thumb, speedily identified as Flowers's. The Passat belonged to a garage mechanic, George Johnston. Johnston was Ryan Humphreys' regular garage man, but the two men played in the same pub football team, declared themselves to be friends and didn't come across as members of some body-part swap club. Johnston may have once handled an MOT on a car belonging to Elsie Williams, but only may have done. It would have been only the once, and the total fee was fifty pounds, which hardly suggested a transaction of any great moment to either party. Johnston also once fixed Arthur Price's lawnmower, or thought he had. There was no known connection to Flowers.

The investigation didn't seem to have a focal point and the incident room wall now had 268 'people of interest.' The phone directory had returned as well, not as a joke, but as a practical resource. Operation Takeaway now had not one but two full time data managers. To Emily, the investigation felt as if it was teetering on the brink of failure. Webster's anger was visible to all. She was like a volcano in some Nordic myth; wreathed in smoke and spitting fire. Dragons on the horizon.

Emily was busy with these thoughts when the phone rang.

"Hello," he bellowed.

"Hello, Dad."

"Morning. I've probably interrupted you in the middle of something important. Have I? I expect you're applying the thumbscrews to some poor bugger right now."

Her father was sometimes like that. Too loud, too jokey, probably because he knew the phone lines were almost certainly monitored. It was his way of managing that. Old habits, learned the hard way, which he called into play as necessary.

He was calling to invite Emily and Books to view his latest project, which was a city bar. He could not admit that it was a front for his state sponsored activities targeting criminals, of course. Deliberately placed there to attract and entice them to congregate and so be a source of information and, where and when necessary, elimination. Ray Quinn's protégé moving with the times. He deliberately gave some details for the benefit of those listening to their conversation.

"No pole dancers, Emily. That market is saturated. It's a 1920's themed bar. The recession is used to take short leases on good quality properties at ridiculously low rates. Then we import some cheap junk from across the Atlantic Ocean, and, under low lighting, the place looks great. Works a treat. Can't fail."

Emily told him they'd be at the door at six that evening. She then got down to the boring work, pestering the hospital until they produced some CCTV footage, printing the best photos she could from that. It wasn't a great harvest, but possibly better than nothing. A memo was circulated asking if anyone was interested in going on a course about undercover work. Emily signed it, even though she could have run it herself. She smiled at the irony of being undercover and then signing up for a course on basic undercover work. If only they knew.

At five-thirty Books arrived at her desk.

"Ready?" he asked brightly, wanting her to be ready and waiting for him, even though that would have been most unusual.

"Almost," she said.

She finished an e-mail, looked at the paper on her desk and shoved it into a drawer, before going to the Ladies to 'freshen up.' She never really did much there, but Books was of the opinion that women needed to undergo some mysterious completion process before they could go out for the evening, and she didn't like to disappoint him. She stared at her face in the mirror for a minute or two, wondering if it felt like hers. In Bram Stoker's Dracula, the dark count is invisible in mirrors and Emily often felt something similar was true of her too. She couldn't feel any deep relationship between the face that was hers and the person she was. It was like they were two different things. She wondered if everybody felt that.

She went through the ritual of freshening up: mascara, lipstick, face cream, something for the eyelashes and so on. She finished by putting her hands on her hair and moving it around a little. Then she lost time and simply stood there doing nothing. It was only when someone came in that she remembered what she was supposed to be doing. It was 5.55 pm when she emerged.

He asked, "Done?"

"Done."

Books gave her one of those male expressions which said simultaneously: (a) you look great and it's going to be an immense pleasure to be with you this evening, and (b) what in God's name took you so long? Emily responded with a mysterious feminine smile of her own devising.

The bar was only a twenty-minute walk away and parking was difficult, so they walked. After a couple of minutes, Books put his arm around Emily and squeezed her in closer. It was a gesture that moved her every time, as if she was not just being hooked in close to one male body, but was actually being gathered back into the world of the living and protected.

It made her think of those astronauts dangling in space on the end of their tethering ropes. You think that those ropes are pipes feeding air to the space suit, but they're not. They're just ropes. If someone cut the rope or unhitched it from the spacecraft, the astronaut would be left dangling forever, hanging a thousand miles above the Earth, waiting to die. Books' enfolding arm brought her in from the void, through the airlock, back to the community of the human race.

She felt herself becoming more feminine and affectionate as his whole being protected her from the cruel world. She also felt the familiar glow which gradually worked its magical way through her body.

The streets were dark. The shopping scrums had finished and the drinking scrums were yet to form. There was no rain. Books kept on hugging her, shortening his steps so she didn't have to gallop.

"Only twenty minutes late," he said, as they arrived.

"Dad will be late, anyway," Emily said. She was concentrating more on her hand being inside Books' jacket, feeling the flex of his pectorals.

Frank was already there, much to his daughter's surprise, and he didn't notice them straight away. The grand opening was due in three days' time and the place was still a blizzard of sawdust and power tools. There were five workmen still on site, and the place looked a long way from being ready. They stood and watched. The place was smaller than Emily had envisaged and felt classy, small and intimate.

Frank saw them eventually and broke into a huge smile. He introduced them to everyone, shouting and charming, whilst making sure everyone knew Books and what he did. He noticeably avoided giving Emily the same publicity. It was, she thought, quite a performance. They spent forty minutes admiring the place, which actually looked a mess, but they could can see how nice it would become. They ended up in a room upstairs, furnished like an ordinary office, drinking beer from the bottle. Or rather Frank and Books did. Emily just fooled around with her bottle and sipped tiny bits of foam.

"Keeping busy? That Rose Flowers business, no further ahead on that are you? What a horrible business, eh? Imagine that, if it was your daughter, imagine how you'd feel."

Emily saw it for what it was. Frank was managing them, subtly guiding them. Anybody listening would never have guessed, but they knew. He had manufactured a situation, so that he could gather information and dole out advice. Also, the new club was different. It was being built purely to attract a certain clientele. Frank was making sure that if his team couldn't find the people they sought, then those people would come to him. Moths to light. It was much easier to control and destroy criminals if you had them gathered together. He was working towards dealing the criminal underworld a massive and lasting blow. His was the overall strategy whilst Emily and Books played their parts dealing with certain smaller, but nevertheless significant, issues.

Emily talked about going to see Flowers's parents. She'd already told Books, of course, but in a different way. She told how both the mother and father cried.

"You know I've always thought it was funny how we never came across the girl. I mean, a girl like that in a place like this, you'd think she'd have shown up once or twice." Emily ventured.

Books added, "We interviewed your managers at the time. Inspected payrolls records and so on." He was referring to the managers of the other establishments, particularly John Lomax and Leanne.

Dad said, "Payroll! Trouble is, when you're the boss, you want everything to be done just right, but then, you know how it is, the minute your back is turned. A girl doesn't turn up when she's meant to. Someone has flu. The night manager is short-handed. What's he going to do? Probably make a few calls and pay someone under the table. I said all that to John, in fact. Told him to ask around. They'll tell him stuff they'd never tell me." He was making sure anybody listening in would hear the expected reaction. "In fact, sod that, I'll call John now. Think of that poor girl in someone's bloody freezer!"

He pulled out his phone and stomped off. It was an impressive display and Emily smiled knowingly at Books, who didn't know how to read it all. Was this Frank being genuine? Or was this all prearranged? He tried to get a clue from her expression, but was met with a smooth, clear wall of nothing. After a few moments, Dad came back in. "Do you have photos? Of the girl? Rose?"

They had, but not with them, and promised to call them up from anywhere with internet access. Dad left again. Books and Emily chatted about the bar downstairs for a couple of minutes, until he came back. "Let's go," was all he said.

In his Range Rover Books sat in the front alongside Frank, whilst Emily was relegated to the back.

Sitting in the back made her feel about eight years old, with her heels swinging on the way to the beach, while the grown-ups talked about grown up things in the front.

The city moved past the window. The rain had returned, but was only a few speckles on the windscreen now. They left town and arrived in a village which just about remained that rather than having expanded to become a mere suburb. The car was parked outside one of the houses. It was white stucco, modern and had a decent garden.

"Rhys Jordan, one of my managers," Dad informed them, as they got out of the car.

The rain softened the air and Emily liked the feel of it on her face.

Frank banged on the door, rang the doorbell and shouted, "Hello Rhys?" He started to tell them that Jordan probably wasn't at home, although there were lights on inside and only a matter of seconds had passed since he started banging, ringing and shouting. Then a shape came into view behind the glass, and the door opened. He looked to be in his mid-forties with black hair which was thinning on top. He was disheveled in a way that inclined towards handsome rather than repellent. Rhys Jordan seemed sleepy, but Emily suspected that was all part of the look.

He saw Dad and said, "Oh, Frank. Okay, do you want to...." but Emily's father didn't need to be invited into places; an open door was sufficient. They were inside in an instant, moving through the hall and into the living room. It was larger than Emily expected and looked early seventies, with a big, curvy orange sofa, a fake zebra skin, a gas fire and a couple of lava lamps.

There was a woman on the sofa. She had pale skin. Her long black hair was immaculately smooth, the way some hair gets only with straighteners. She wore a black sweater over black jeans and there was plenty of jewellery and red nails.

"Corrinne, isn't it?" Frank said. It wasn't a question as he never got a name wrong.

Corrine swayed gracefully up from the sofa. She was about to go upstairs but a quick conference with hubby in the hall sent her out into the night. They watched her vanish down the garden path in a long coat, her hair wound up inside a woolen hat.

Dad looked at Jordan, who looked at Books first, then Dad. Emily didn't exist in this duel of glances.

Dad said, "John has spoken to you, has he?"

Jordan replied, "Yes."

Then Dad exploded. "Bloody hell, man. Why didn't you come clean? Years back. There's a dead girl involved here."

"Look, we gave the police..."

"Don't give me that crap. I never take crap." Dad's eyes blazed. He was either genuinely angry or giving a master class in how to act. Emily couldn't tell.   But Jordan was scared; not pretending, the real thing.

Emily knew what he wanted without him saying. There was a laptop closed up beside the sofa. Emily booted it up and waited for a connection. The computer processed slowly, while Books watched the scene silently with a vaguely amused look on his face. The connection was eventually made and Jordan had no choice but to give the password. Emily logged into the police portal and brought up the photos of Rose Flowers. Emily was tempted to bring up the photos of her dead: the leg, the head, the other bits and pieces, and especially the head, but her better instincts prevailed and she showed the other pictures.

They were of Rose Flowers playing hockey. Flowers graduating. There was a family photo and the one of her at the party wearing her Shoes of Death.

Jordan nodded. "Yes," he said. His voice was husky on his first attempt, and he cleared his throat and repeated the word.

Books said, "Are you able to identify this girl as a dancer at your club?"

"Yes. Or no. I'm not sure. Waitress probably."

Dad nodded, a micro-nod not intended for general consumption. Emily suspected he thought Flowers didn't have the physique required for a dancer in one of his clubs.

Books returned to his question. "Can you confirm that you employed this girl, Rose Flowers, in some capacity at your club?"

"Yes. She wasn't employed, exactly. She was never on the payroll. But she was on our list of phone numbers to call if we were shorthanded. And...."

And?

Books ran through the inevitable follow-up questions and Emily took notes.

How often would Flowers have been employed on that basis? A couple of times a month, probably. She had a reputation for being a steady worker. Under pressure from Books, it changed to "pretty often, I suppose."

How was she paid? In cash, from the till. Payments weren't large, because waitresses could make up to £120 an evening in tips. On busy evenings, waitresses would be expected to work for tips alone.

Why was this information not disclosed to the police at the time of the original investigation? Because the payments were under the table. Jordan was worried about the taxman. A dead girl and he was worried about the taxman!

Back to Books. Over what period of time was Flowers employed? Jordan offered one answer – a few – months – then corrected that to more like six – then said he didn't know.

Dad asked him how he could find out. Jordan said he wasn't sure, then admitted there would probably be a cashbook somewhere, so till takings could be reconciled with the electronic cash register. Then he said he wasn't sure if a book would still be around from so many years back. Dad got antsy again and made Jordan phone someone called Colin at the club. The person called Colin said he'd get straight back.

The room was quiet. Frank was still fuming and Books let him fume. Much safer. Outside, Emily saw Corrine coming back, a dark shape gliding up to her own front door. She went to intercept her and they stood outside together.

"Is there a problem?" She asked.

"Not really. Rhys withheld some information from a murder investigation and we may want to give him a bollocking, but that's about the limit of it."

She smiled; all white teeth and red lips. The phone rang inside the house and they could hear a conversation. There was a crashing sound behind us and Frank was yelling. Corrine and Emily were suddenly keenly aware that her father was furious and there was an awkward silence. He was not a man you'd want to upset.

Corrine said, "They say it's going to get a lot colder soon. Freezing apparently."

She could not have said a truer word if she had stayed there and tried for a hundred years.

Eventually the fracas subsided and Rhys came to the door and let them in. Dad was rolling his shoulders, eyes smouldering. Books stood aside, watching everything. They said goodbye, and got into the Range Rover.

"Where can I drop you?" said Dad. The first words since they left.

Books and Emily exchanged looks. The three main choices: Book's flat, police station, or Dad's club. But there was no choice really.

"We'd better go to the Unicorn, interview people there. Sorry Dad."

"No sorries. You two have got a job to do." He drove in silence. The rain was back again, but more heavy now. "Bloody traffic," he muttered a little later as they arrived at the Unicorn. Books and Emily got out and said goodbye to Dad. He apologized again and drove off with a fierce spray-back from his rear tyres. Emily's mind was already inside the club, with its girls, its cashbooks and its secrets.

-19-

The rain had gone and skies were clearing when Books and Emily left the club at about ten thirty. Only then was it starting to get busy. On the stage behind them, the first breasts and thighs were starting to appear, like stars emerging overhead.

Webster was waiting with her silver-grey BMW, sleekly parked, sidelights on. The Ice Queen's face expressed no sign of her having seen them, but the car purred into life and the sidelights switched to headlights.

Books claimed the front and Emily got in the back again. The child's seat; swinging her feet and thinking about ice-cream. There was not much talk as they drove to the station. They had already briefed Webster by phone, but were looking forward to a proper one in her office. When they arrived, Books, being a man, had to go and pee. Konchesky, who was to join them, hadn't yet arrived. Emily found herself going to the kitchenette with Webster to make coffee. While they were waiting for the kettle to boil, she put her hand out to feel the fabric of Webster's suit sleeve.

"Sorry," she said. "Do you mind? It's lovely."

If she did mind, it was too late, but there was no eruption because the kettle boiled at exactly the appropriate moment. Three coffees for everyone else and peppermint tea for Emily. There was a stupid moment of awkwardness at the door as they sorted out who picked up which mug and how they could get out of the door without pouring boiling fluids over each other. Emily was pleased because she had made Webster nervous. A minor triumph, but significant.

They were in Webster's office, with mugs still luckily full. Books arrived, his bladder nicely empty. Konchesky was there as well, nervously clutching paperwork. All the lights were on. The room felt wrong to Emily, but she couldn't explain it. She settled for blaming the ceiling tiles and that unblinking fluorescent glare. It was unsettling.

Webster began proceedings. "Okay, from the beginning," she ordered, looking at Books.

He reported everything that happened. Or rather, he took a series of life events and translated them into police jargon. It was designed to give it an official, important air, but Emily thought it just made them sound stupid. As if they couldn't say anything in a normal way that normal people would understand.

"The witness confirmed his identity as Rhys Jordan and that he has been employed as manager at the Virgin and Unicorn for a total of nine years."

He was talking like a training manual and Emily found it hard to suppress a smile.

"When we got to the club, we spoke to Colin Jones, who produced the cashbooks. We have them with us now. In the eight months before her death, Rose Flowers received cash payments from the Unicorn on fifteen different occasions. Amounts ranging from twenty to eighty pounds."

"Dates."

Emily had a list of the dates in her notebook and passed them over.

"Susan?"

Konchesky had been doing a lot of the basic groundwork on Khaled, going back through his bank records for a full nine years. He was no saint, and he had been more abstemious in recent years, but further back he appeared to have been out on the town most Friday and Saturday nights. She had the dates when Khaled used his card in the Unicorn, but none matched the Flowers' ones.

Khaled also used plenty of cash. He used to withdraw four hundred pounds at a time and spend it fairly rapidly and therefore could have been in the Unicorn on one of those Flowers nights, but spending cash. No suggestion that he was trying to keep himself invisible, just that he liked to use cash.

Webster, Books and Konchesky bent over the various lists and printouts trying to find a match. Emily leaned away, wondering if it would be okay to turn off the overhead lights and just rely on the desk lamp. The brightness was bothering her. The other three muttered to each other as they compared lists.

Emily said, "Cash payments to Flowers all fell on Tuesdays, Wednesdays and Thursdays. The Thursday payment tended to be lower. According to Jordan, the girls made most of their money from tips. I imagine waitresses worked for tips only on Fridays and Saturdays."

They all looked again at the lists. Flowers drew no payments from late November to early January either, although she'd worked the autumn before and in the months immediately after.

"Christmas," Emily pressed on. "More trade, bigger tips."

Webster looked up from the desk, staring at her and Emily held her gaze.

She said, "So, your hypothesis is that Flowers was working for tips only on some of the nights that Khaled was there?"

There was a prickling feeling in the room. A sense of movement or hidden life.

"Yes," She confirmed.

Three heads bent back over the lists, but Emily remained apart, trying to work out what the prickling sensation was, trying to comprehend the feeling. She was not getting anywhere.

"Flowers called her mother most nights." Emily said, just to keep awareness of her thoughts alive and kicking in the room, and, more importantly, in the three heads of the others. "It's a gift," she offered in response to the unspoken question.

Webster glared at her and couldn't prevent herself grinding her jaw. She pulled the phone records away from Susan Konchesky. This listed dates and times of calls. Flowers used to call her mother briefly and her mother would call back to save on the phone bill. Those calls were usually at around 9 or 10pm. On nights when Flowers was working, she called much earlier, at around 6 or 7pm, and spoke for a shorter time. There were a number of Fridays and Saturdays over the right period when Khaled was in the Unicorn and Flowers called her mother early. Webster and the others had a quick discussion about this. Flowers was a student, so if she wasn't working on a Friday or Saturday, she was probably going out for the evening anyway.

Books said, "Yes, but she wouldn't go out that early. These days, people seem to be going out just as I'm ready to go to bed. A girl like that wouldn't go out on the town until after nine o'clock, probably later. It isn't 'cool', or whatever the current word is."

Emily smiled at the idea of Books being 'cool'. She thought he was about as 'cool' as a lump of coal. Konchesky was a mother of two who worked part-time and hardly had her finger on the pulse either, but she agreed with Books. Emily had noticed that happening a lot lately.

Webster grabbed all the paperwork now and bent over it, leaving nothing for the others, except a view they could have all done without. Emily was fed up with the over-lit room and turned all the lights off, except the spot where Webster had now planted herself firmly in her chair. When she glared at Emily, she said, "Sorry," but made no move to put the lights back on. It felt better now. The prickling feeling was still there, but not in a bad way.

"Isn't this nice?" Emily said to no one in particular. Everyone stared at her, but no one said anything.

Then Webster finished. It seemed probable, but not certain, that Khaled knew Flowers. Webster said she would arrange a full set of interviews in the morning and officers would be sent to talk to Flowers's former colleagues at the Unicorn to see if any of them could connect Flowers to Khaled.

The meeting broke up. Webster said to Books and Emily, "Good work. Well done."

Books said something and Emily nodded and tried to look like a keen young thing.

In the street outside she asked, "Are you Okay?"

"Yes."

"You'll be okay driving?"

"Yes."

"Not too fast, all right?"

"All right," she conceded.

"Back to mine?" It wasn't a question, really.

"Yes."

She drove back to his place without speeding and parked neatly. Books poured wine and Emily walked around the flat fiddling with light switches and being annoying. It was something she was quite good at. Books tolerated it for a few minutes before lifting her up and carrying her to the bedroom. She wasn't really in the mood, but pretended. She faked the moves and the noises and was pleased with putting on a reasonable performance, until the fakery ceased at some point and the real thing kicked in. The acting fell away as the hormones took over and she started to feel things properly.

"Mmm. Thank you."

"You're very welcome," he replied. He was pleased with his sexual performance.

"Do you think your Dad was for real, earlier?" he asked, after what he considered a suitable interval.

"I assume so. He seemed pretty angry."

"I thought he was going to rip Jordan's head off."

"Yes, well. He could easily have done that. Believe me, he could." She said this even though she thought the whole thing was a show.

She thought Frank knew from the beginning of the original investigation that Flowers had worked in his club. When the leg appeared he was aware of the possibility that it would turn out to be hers. Emily didn't think he had anything to hide, but he would have known about any risks to business long before Webster did. As it was, she assumed John had spoken to her father. They had both spoken to Jordan, checking the cash books with Colin, discussing possible risks to the business and deciding whether any risks could be controlled, putting on the entire play for their benefit. Of course, there might have been some minor tax issues arising from the way the business was run, but police on a murder enquiry are hardly tax specialists and usually turn a blind eye to minor misadventures for the sake of the central issue.

Emily actually knew it was all a show, designed to help the investigation in general and her in particular.

Once again, she was awed by his competence; his ability to work on many levels at the same time. It was dangerous to his enemies, but comforting for her.

She didn't verbalise any of these thoughts, however, but Books teased her for her Mortimer ideas.

He said, "Looks like that one might get laid to rest."

Emily didn't feel like talking about that, and said, "Did you say "get laid?" and she ran her hand down his stomach until she ran out of stomach. He kept her hand where it was and they fell asleep like that, with the lights off, listening to the city being the city.

But she could still feel that prickling sensation from before. That sense of something being hidden.

She ran things through her memory, and recalled that when she started to investigate Mark Mortimer, two men had become over interested in where she was and what she was doing. When she put one of them in hospital, he gave a false name and address and walked out as soon as he could. As far as she was concerned, the Mortimer connection was still live.

-20-

Emily slept until Books woke her in the morning. He was back from a run, sweaty T-shirt off, shorts still on. To her he looked gorgeous in a rough and tumble kind of way. She watched him getting into the shower, then watched him more as he got out. He knew she was watching and made the most of it. He sat on the bed naked and let her bite him on the back of his neck, which was both salty and soapy.

When they finished fooling around, he told her that there was fresh juice, bacon, eggs, everything in the fridge. He'd already eaten.

"You're off already?" She remembered he had other duties, but had assumed they weren't until later.

He gave her a crooked smile. "Webster. She wants to work this angle. She's got me, Konchesky and a couple of others coming in today."

The news both surprised and bothered Emily. As far as Webster was concerned, the glory of the Rhys Jordan breakthrough belonged equally to her and Books. As far as reality was concerned, of course, the glory was shared between a triumvirate of Emily, John and her father. But by ordinary common decency and fairness, Webster ought at least to have offered her the chance to join the inner team.

Emily knew why she was being ditched. Webster had an icily tedious adherence to the rules and Emily's father owned the club where Rose Flowers might or might not have met Aftab Khaled in the months before her death. If that connection turned out to have a bearing on the case, she may be called to appear as a witness in court. A defence lawyer could make merry play of some potential conflicts of interest between Emily, her father, and the police investigation, so Webster was keeping her well away from the centre of the investigation. Emily thought it wildly unfair, even though it was correct. Also, Webster thought in straight lines and Emily didn't. She had an eye for hidden detail and Webster didn't. Emily had talents that Webster didn't possess and it obviously irked her. She hadn't yet learned how best to use Emily's gift. She resided at the jealousy stage and it stung her.

"Lucky you," Emily said, trying not to let her feelings show. "A Saturday love-in with Webster. Every girl's dream."

"What have you got on, today?"

She blinked at him, instead of answering. She didn't don't know what to say. Books made a face which was hard to interpret exactly, but was his way of nudging her to give an answer that was more complete than just blinking.

"I'm over to my family for a late brunch, then probably go shopping with Kay."

He said, "Brilliant. That sounds really nice."

Most men saying this would sound sarcastic, but Books just sounded like Books. He waited for her to get out of bed, so she could kiss him off at the door, then he realised that she was not getting of bed, so he kissed her where she was.

"Have a good day," Emily said. "Don't let Webster pinch your bum."

He left and she immediately felt the emptiness of his flat. She was missing him already. She decided to raise herself and fidgeted around, getting dressed slowly. She swung open the fridge door and was confronted with a stock of lovely food, very little of which she had any hand in acquiring and almost none of which was covered in interesting colours of mould. She didn't eat anything, just poked the packet of bacon, then swung the door shut again.

There was no mantelpiece, because the flat was too modern to have a fireplace, but there was a cupboard cum-display-unit which could probably bear the weight of an interesting china ornament. Books had some framed photos there. A couple were of the pair of them and some were of people she didn't recognize. She shifted them around a bit and then moved them back again.

When she was dressed, she left the flat and drove to her father's. She had no reason for doing so, except that it was what she had said to Books she would do, so doing it seemed easier than anything else. When she arrived, not long after nine, Mum was already up, dressed, hair done, fussing. Her younger sister, Ant, short-for-Antonia, was hanging over the kitchen counter protesting against some familial injustice or other. Frank was still sleeping. Kay hadn't got downstairs by that time, but Emily could hear her padding upstairs and she yelled down a greeting.

Emily arbitrated the dispute, by telling her mother that it was a special occasion because she was there, so Ant should be allowed to have her way. Ant accepted that gleefully and Emily got a special hug. Her mother accepted it with a sigh and a headshake.

She asked Emily if she had eaten and, without waiting for a reply, only gave her an orange juice and a croissant, taken from a packet and heated in a microwave. Ant told her about school. Kay came downstairs and got breakfast. She was tall and skinny and had a way of dressing that looked completely casual but hopelessly sexy. Today, a chunky jumper over leggings and boots, which doesn't sound much, but it was the way she wore it.

She asked Emily what she was up to and Emily offered to go shopping with her. Ant asked to come too and was rebuffed quickly and not too nicely. There was a bit more hubbub. Clamorous, intimate family stuff. Somewhere along the way, her father was woken up and came downstairs in his dressing gown, looking like a bear with its hair fluffed up. Emily gave him a kiss and fluffed his hair some more.

Tea, coffee, more juice, more croissants. Bacon and egg for her father. Everyone was talking and everyone at least half-listened.

Dad said, "Was it all okay yesterday?"

Emily said, "Yes, there'll be more interviewing today, but non one's worried about a few cash payments here and there."

Frank nodded and changed the subject.

Then Kay and Emily went shopping.

"Where do you want to go?" Kay asked.

"I don't know," Emily said, "Maybe Gap." She always said either Gap or Next, or, if she was feeling unsure of herself, she'd plump for M&S.

She made a face at Emily, but they toddled off to Gap. Emily stood in the middle of the floor surrounded by beige things and she thought of Rose Flowers's head. The feel of it in her hands. The look of it, as if Rose was grinning from the oil barrel with the large round pebble in its mouth. She heard the sound of that pebble as it moved against Flowers's teeth: an oily clacking.

"What do you want?" Asked Kay. Emily wouldn't say that she was patient exactly, but at least she was tolerant.

"I don't know. Not this anyway."

"What kind of things? Office wear? Casual? Or, you know it's going to be Christmas soon, do you even have any party dresses?" Emily thought of Khaled's grey lung bobbing on the last puddles of the reservoir. A Labrador retriever running over the grass with Khaled's lung slopping from its mouth.

The prickling she felt yesterday was back, but clearer, better than before.

"Um, maybe I'll just browse. Is there anything you want?"

It was their deal; half the reason Kay came shopping with her. She tolerated Emily and was rewarded by Emily buying her items. They left Gap and went to a department store. The streets were November streets, not yet Christmas ones. Everyone was bundled in jeans and warm anoraks and the coffee shops were standing room only.

Emily hung back and watched Kay go at it. This was her territory. She understood shops the way Emily understood mortuaries. The other reason Kay shopped with her was that she liked the creativity of it. The challenge of turning her into someone who didn't just buy beige things from Gap. And she was good. Mostly people wanted to turn her into someone who looked like them, only worse. Kay wasn't like that. Emily relied on her.

She shuffled through racks, holding clothes up against her, discarding most and retaining some. Emily tried to play her part. Really tried. She gave it steady, focused thought, but she never knew what she was doing. After a while, Kay had found three things she wanted her to try on. Emily found one, a blue dress that she picked more or less at random.

She looked at Emily's offering and, deep in thought, said, "Mmmm," before taking the large size item

Emily had in her hand and replaced it with the same thing, but in her size. "It's a bit safe," she admonished.

Emily tried things on and each time walked out of the changing room, arms stuck out like a ten-year old boy being good for his mum.

"God's sake!" she muttered, plucking and tweaking Emily into shape. "What do you think?" Before Emily could reply, "I don't know," she said something which was, in her view, an insight of staggering genius. "Don't think about what you look like," she told her. "Just imagine the person in the mirror is someone completely different. Someone you're watching on a stakeout or whatever."

Contrary to popular belief, the police didn't have many stakeouts in that area. No men with guns, pint bottles of whisky, and dubious attitudes to police violence. But she knew what Kay meant. And she was right. If Emily tried to figure out whether she liked something for herself, she had no idea at all. She just saw a woman with her arms stuck out like a ten-year old. If she switched the question, detached herself completely from the person in the mirror, it became instantly more simple. She tried everything on. The star of the bunch was a dark grey, woolen suit. Knee-length skirt. Jacket. It was super safe, the sort of refuge clothing she usually bought, but working on the someone completely different principle, she saw beyond that. The suit was sharp. Stylish.

"It's really good," said Kay. "Half sexy secretary, half woman of mystery."

Emily didn't know whether she wanted to be either of those things, but it felt like an extremely bold idea that buying new clothes could make her into something she wasn't before. She wondered if that was why other people shop.

The suit was expensive; more than three hundred pounds, but she bought it anyway; dazed, but in a good way. She ended up spending another £150 on stuff for Kay, who did a little skip of excitement as they left the shop and said, "Fab." Emily hadn't heard that expression in a very long time. It belonged to another time, but still said what it meant, with a forceful emphasis.

Kay was meeting friends in a coffee shop, so they parted company there and Emily went back to the car. She put the shopping bag on the back seat. She doubted she would ever wear the clothes inside, but that was not the point.

Books sometimes thought she was extravagant, but she disagreed. She hardly ever bought clothes, took holidays, or went out. She wasn't even very good at buying the basics: food, cleaning stuff, anything at all. But when she did spend money, she was terrible at calculating her purchases. She didn't have any have any sense of value. Normally, she just picked something up and paid for it. Mostly, it was some awful budget item and sometimes it was totally at the other end of the scale. She didn't often run out of money and when she did, she made do with porridge until payday. Her father would have been appalled, but she was an independent woman.

While they were busy shopping, Books, Webster and Konchesky were hunting for a connection between Khaled and Rose Flowers. A connection that Emily had brought them.

But what was their history?

Khaled could have met Rose Flowers at the Unicorn and they could have had some sex thing that went wrong. But then what? He decided to chop her into pieces (but why?), deposited her in various freezers and outbuildings (but why?), then lived happily for five years until someone decided to take revenge by chopping him into a thousand pieces and leaving his lung bobbing on a grey and empty lake surrounded by toads and slowworms.

The story made a wearisome sort of sense, but fell apart at the seams. Khaled seemed to her to be too sane to be a person-chopper-upper. She knew that no one is too sane to be a murderer, we could all be that, but you've got to be a fairly committed nutter to slice and dice with such happy abandon. That wasn't the worst part of the story, though. The bit that made no sense was the revenge killing. Who took the revenge? Rose Flowers, Rose's mum? Her solicitor husband with the collapsing face? The Flowers had a twenty-three-year-old son who had been more keenly investigated now than would have been the case some years ago. She remembered the beige carpets and the willow tree in the garden. Some families just gave off a choppy-uppy odour. Others didn't. This one didn't.

Which left Emily back with Aftab Khaled. He of the mobile face and the glide-rail know-how. Her head had been too full of Flowers and Mortimer to give Khaled proper attention, and it was time to put that right. She wanted to know him better. There was a way in which police work stopped her doing that, but she had all weekend now. She slipped the car into gear and left the car park. Woman of mystery. Time to use her gift.

-21-

Emily didn't know where to stop first. She was looking for clues, trying to pick up the atmosphere. She wanted to immerse herself and move away from straight-line thinking. Because of the lovely way this enquiry started, because she found her leg, her lovely, lovely head, Rose Flowers felt vibrant and alive. She was singing to Emily. Yet the blunt, objective truth was that Flowers, poor girl, was really too boring to end her life distributed across a number of suburban outbuildings. The cow teeth and the hockey should have won out over the pole dancing. She wasn't, on the face of it, the sort of victim that most attracted men.

Khaled was different. In a way, that displaced, clever, well-connected womanizer should have piqued her interest from the very first. She should have attached to him at least as much as she had to Flowers, yet he was still nothing more to her than a couple of photos and a pathologist's report. It was time to get to know him, and she was starting with the reservoir. That vacant and almost hostile place; empty of water and empty of purpose. Clouds raced fast overhead and there was enough cold in the wind to feel like a threat.

She drifted around, just getting a feel for the place. The fenced-off, empty lake. The rough ground around it. The dog walkers. She thought it would be a good place to die. To lie spread out, under the wind. The prickle she felt yesterday had settled in now and had a feeling of permanence. When she got too cold to stay longer she went back to her car and drove to the dead man's flat. A two-bedroom penthouse down by the bay, valued at around half a million pounds. Half a million was a lot more than a lecturer could afford, but Khaled bought early, when prices were lower, and he did plenty of consultancy work for private sector firms. Overall, there didn't seem to be any huge discrepancy between his incomings and his outgoings.

It was easy enough getting into the building as there were people coming out as she entered. The flat itself was locked. She tried knocking at the door in case there was still any SOCO activity there. She also tried neighbours in case any of them had a key. She ended up having to rouse someone from building maintenance and had to produce her warrant, sign a book and get the key. She would have preferred not to have done that, because Webster would be angry if she learned, but she probably wouldn't learn.

The apartment was all about the emptiness. There was a huge east facing balcony opening onto the bay. The same grey light that Adams had. The same changeless change. Except that Khaled had the city version of this view: the marina, the Assembly building, the patches of muddy green. There was something addictive about the view, but not necessarily in a good way. After all, self-harm is addictive too.

The interior boasted blond wood floors in the kitchen and living room. White was the predominant colour; the walls and the kitchen units, which were topped with a shiny black work surface. One wall was lined with an expensive designer looking wallpaper that had a silky finish, but Emily doubted that Khaled had chosen it. She bet it came with the flat. His own taste seemed timidly restrained to a few choices. A few Moroccan things: tiles, rug, photos, a framed print of some fort or other, and some engineering stuff. There was also a cubic sculpture made of interlocking pieces of machined metals, half curiosity, half art object.

It was hard to find the human in this room. She moved around, changing the position of things, for no reason except to make a mark. The only thing that felt personal or in any way sentimental, was a small wooden sail boat with heart shaped sails cut from white painted metal. It sat in a little alcove with a garland of fairy lights. Its lack of stylishness was almost its best feature, as if he temporarily forgot about being cool, forgot about wanting to impress.

She thought of herself inhabiting the space in her newly purchased expensive outfit. Clicking around in heels. A woman of mystery, she would carry a slim pearl-handled pistol and take secret lovers.

She wondered where Books was and what he may have found.

The bedroom offered more. It was flash, not in a clever way, but in a touchingly crass one. There was a giant bed covered with a white duvet and a purple silk throw. She saw blue and red silk scatter cushions, some expensive clothes. The mirror was large and there were twin mirrored side tables. In the bathroom she found more of the same. The fixtures were all modern, glitzy, posh. But it was those other touches that delighted her. The leather shaving set with the badger-hair brush. The bottles of body lotion. Monogrammed towels. She ran the brush against her cheek, smelled the lotion, felt the towels.

Emily's colleagues, though worthy enough, had neglected this kind of evidence, because it wasn't court-worthy. Because you couldn't photograph it or tabulate or put it into an evidence bag. But it was solid gold, all the same, in her view. There was a packet of condoms in the mirrored cabinet. The whole place was very tidy,

She spent an hour or two just kicking around the apartment, then left, handed back the key and signed out. She knew what she was doing now. She was on the scent. The gift was alive.

Khaled had a female colleague, Jenny Harrison, who was about Emily's age and attractive. One of her colleagues had interviewed her in the normal way and came up with normal answers, which did not surprise Emily in the slightest. She had a pile of paper somewhere that had a mugshot of her and an interview report sheet. She didn't have her address but drove to the university, showed her warrant card and forced an unfortunate receptionist to give it to her.

She found Harrison's house, which was modern, as bland as a shoebox and as functional. She knocked and Jenny Harrison was in. Emily took in her appearance: brown hair, blue eyes, nice eyes, friendly, jeans, boots, jumper and some jewellery. She was every bit as pretty as her photo, maybe prettier. And, after introducing herself, Emily asked the obvious question.

"Six months," she says. "It's our first."

Emily didn't know who the 'our' was but didn't care. They sat down in the kitchen. There were postcards stuck to the fridge and a loaf of bread proving on the worktop.

"Aftab Khaled," she said. "You and him."

"There wasn't really a me and him. And it was ages ago."

"I know."

People were so stupid, Emily pondered. Sweetly, irritatingly stupid. Of course, there was no connection between gentle, pregnant Jenny and whoever danced around the locality scattering Khaled's body parts. But that made her an ideal witness.

Emily nudged her for her story and she told it. It was five years ago. She was fairly new in the department and Khaled was a well-respected lecturer. He was charming to her, very attentive. She knew that he had an agenda, of course. He invited her out one evening, ordered champagne. They ended back at his place.

"Back at his place. Meaning?"

"Well, not that, no. But I did go up there."

"So you must have thought about it? Having sex with him. You wouldn't have gone back there unless you'd thought there was a possibility."

"Yes." Gentle Jenny had a grounded quality that was nice to be around. It made her a steady witness too. "I think I was curious. I wanted to see him in action. Wanted to see his place. And, you know, I was a bit drunk. A tiny bit flattered. New in town and all that. I'm not the one-night stand sort of girl, really, but – well, you're right, I was interested enough to go back with him."

"Did he pressure you? Was there any intimidation involved? Even that creepy sort that hovers in the background but isn't definite enough to put your finger on."

She laughed. She knew what Emily meant.

Jenny says, "No, I mean, there was the champagne, the nice restaurant, the BMW he picked me up in. You can call that "pressure" if you like, but not intimidation. No way."

"And in the apartment? You get up there, and....?"

Emily could see it. The big, expensive view over the bay. Lights set to moody. Mozart on the stereo. More champagne. The place was a shag pad. A single man's idea of every single woman's dream. Gentle Jenny gave the lie to that. She had what most women want: an ordinary house on an ordinary street. A good job, a steady husband. Bread rising on the worktop and a bun in the oven.

"As soon as I got up there, it felt wrong. I mean...." She wrinkled her face. It was a look that managed to be compassionate and patronizing at the same time. "You know, he tried hard. It was quite sweet really. That's almost what made it feel wrong, the trying. I think he wanted me to be something I wasn't. Like he wanted me to be wearing designer perfume and was disappointed when I said I got my stuff on sale or at Boots."

They laughed and shared the female-bonding moment.

She resumed, saying, "I sobered pretty quickly, said sorry, I wasn't ready, and got out of there. He was okay with it. I mean, I think he was."

She wrinkled her face again. The same expression. Emily predicted she would have a wrinkly baby.

"If you'd gone ahead and had sex, did you get any sense that the sex would have been weird in any way?"

"No." She answered too quickly and Emily made her think again and take longer to answer. She still said, "No." "Was there a moment, even a brief one, where you felt threatened, especially when you said you were going?"

"No, definitely not. We kissed goodbye."

"Drugs? Did he offer you anything? A party drug, I mean. A line of coke? Ecstasy?"

"No."

There was more hesitation and Emily broke the quiet. "But you're not that kind of girl, are you?"

"Put it this way, I think if I'd been a different sort of girl, there might have been more exotic fare available. Looking back on it, I think he was anxious. Anxious to score, anxious about what I thought of him. He tried really hard. I don't just mean in a dirty-old-man way, but in general. Working for the department. Getting his consultancy work. Dating women."

Forensics had done the basics on the flat, but drugs were never their principal focus. They'd have been looking for signs of struggle, traces of blood, any DNA. They probably swabbed the toilet cistern in the bathroom as standard procedure, but that's not where Khaled would have snorted his coke. He'd have done it straight from the shiny black worktops in the open-plan kitchen/living room with Mozart playing, the champagne cooling and a woman there to admire it all.

The worktop on the island unit wasn't in one piece. There were two pieces, butted together with some black silicone type material in the join.

"The thing about Aftab," she said, "is he never quite felt like he fitted in. I mean, he did. In reality, he truly did. He was British much more than he was anything else. I don't think anyone treated him differently because he had Moroccan origins. But I think he tried extra hard to compensate. Maybe he'd have done better if he'd been more relaxed about it."

Emily nodded, but also noticed that she said "British." She thought of Khaled's flat. His consultancy work. All that departmental diligence. All that effort, and what he really needed was to belong; to be accepted locally as one of their own. He never understood that you have to be born in a place to actually belong. Ask the Cornish and they'll confirm it.

They talked a bit more, but gentle Jenny didn't have much more to offer. She saw Emily out.

"Look," she said, "can I just ask? I never told anyone about that night with Aftab. It just seemed better to let it go. I know maybe you can't say, but I'd love to know..."

Sweetly stupid.

"He was career minded," Emily said. "He knew not to try it on with students. These days, that would get him fired. But you? You were new, young, pretty; you were fair game. He seems to have been reasonably compulsive where women were concerned. I just wanted to understand his game plane. How he operated."

Jenny nodded, almost blushing. She made a little movement that intrigued Emily: tossing her head back and simultaneously flicking her hair aside with her hand, as though correcting herself. It was like some old-time maiden who'd been caught with her garter loose or an ankle flashing free of her petticoats. Emily tried to read the look in more detail, but it escaped her.

A moment later, the door was closed and she was alone. She went to her car and called forensics, telling them to get someone to re-swab the kitchen on Monday. The silicone join. They agreed to do it.

Emily knew she really ought to write up notes of this interview and get them on the system. But that meant telling Webster what she'd done and she would not be happy at her for going off-piste. Thus, Emily didn't do the write-up. Gentle Jenny hadn't given her evidence that would help her in the courtroom or the police enquiry. She'd just given her a glimpse of Khaled. A chance to get closer.

She leaned back in the car seat, allowing herself to think of Flowers's head. The dripping hair. The clack of the pebble. She tried to picture Khaled, tried to find him, but got nothing apart from that prickle. The Khaled prickle.

There was almost no movement on the street. Down the road from Emily, a fat woman was loading plastic bags into an old red car. She could hear piano scales being practiced indoors somewhere. Soft notes, laid over the hum of traffic.

Emily knew what would happen next, what she needed to do. The gift was rising. It was as if she had lost all feeling in her body and couldn't tell what was happening with her emotions. There was normally a kind of upward spiral thing that happened first, as though her soul was escaping upwards through her head. Emily thought that was why people with out-of-body experiences reported themselves as floating above the room, not peering up as if from below. It was why normal people sometimes called themselves dizzy, or ungrounded, or say they have their head in the clouds. These normal people never went where she went, never experienced what she experienced.

What she had now was a kind of heady uppiness, that was upbeat, even euphoric, and it could be like that at times. But not now. What she had was just a grey, upwards draining. She wasn't scared by it. She didn't have any feelings about it at all.

She did her breathing exercises, because she had drilled herself into doing them, no matter what, but the exercises only helped when she was lost in the foothills. It was too late for that now. She was past the treeline and heading up.

-22-

Home. Bath.

She called Books, not because she wanted to, but because she knew they would have to talk sometime and she didn't trust herself to do it later. They had a short, stupid conversation, and then she finished the call and was alone.

She sent a text to Webster. "DAD SAYS DO I WANT TO COME AND CHAT WITH UNICORN STAFF ON SEMIOFFICIAL BASIS. OK?"

The reply was "OK." It said nothing else, but it was enough for Emily.

She wasn't frightened. She was actually annoyed with herself. She knew she was not worried about physical or sexual safety. It was not as if she was a dainty Victorian flower. She realised that she had long known it was going to come down to this. That first night, in the office, the one with the fireflies and the dead girl's shoes, when she made the call to her father. Did really not know then it would come to this?

It took her time to notice and she had to concentrate hard to figure it out. She put her hand under the cold tap, the hot tap, and back into the bathwater. She used to think her senses just went numb, but it wasn't that. They were still doing their job, diligently reporting their information, presenting their little manila packets of facts and data. But the management staff were all away on leave somewhere. She was like the last person left in corporate HQ desperately trying all the phones and getting no more than a fading crackle and an echo from somewhere sandy. She got out of the bath, and began the process of choosing what to wear. She chose the first dress she came to and moved on to shoes. She knew she should put makeup on too, but all she had were a few disconnected words and phrases like 'eyeliner,' 'lip gloss,' 'mascara' and 'blusher.' There were some things on the bathroom shelf and there were some words in her head. She waited around to see if anything joined them up, but it didn't. She saw a tube of lipstick and made her lips go red. The person in the mirror still looked reasonably normal, she thought, though she wasn't too sure.

Downstairs, the clock on the oven said 21.38.

She spent some time looking for her car keys, then decided that maybe driving wasn't a brilliant idea. She called a taxi and waited for it to arrive, watching the nice green clock on the oven door.

22.18. She wasn't frightened, but didn't know why she was like this.

Outside a car pulled up in front of the house, with its headlights blazing. The doorbell rang. There was a wooden knife rack on the counter containing six knives, at least four of which would have made effective weapons, but she decided the doorbell man was probably the same as the taxi man, so she decided it was safe. She left the knives, answered the door and saw the taxi man.

She was about to walk straight out, when he said, "Don't you want a coat, love? It's freezing."

She went back and got a coat and also remembered that she hadn't got house keys, money, bank cards, phone or bag. When she got in the car, it was nice and warm. She told the man the name of the street, not the name of the place. His car seemed very clean. It smelled like bubble bath. The streets slid by very easily. There was no noise except that his radio talked quietly all the way. The world outside looked like a film of itself.

-23-

Emily stood outside the club, The Virgin & Unicorn. She felt like a wooden toy as the neon glow lifted the street and deposited it somewhere else altogether. New York. Tokyo. Bangkok. Montmartre. She approached the club and two black-suited, black-shirted doormen who stood guard outside.

"Entry for one," she said, because she really didn't know what else to say.

"You know what this is, darling?"

"Yes. I'm joining friends."

They exchanged glances but didn't object. They started to run through the rules. No touching. No photographs. No videos. No fighting. No excessive drinking. No propositioning for sex. The dancers are dancers, not prostitutes. It sounded like some dispatch from a foreign war zone. The doorman who was speaking had a head shaped like a bullet and there were three gold rings on his right hand.

Whenever there was a gap in what he was saying, Emily inserted, "okay." After a bit, she was still saying okay and he wasn't giving her more rules, so she stopped and he allowed her entry. She wondered about an entry fee, but nobody had asked for any money. Inside she found tables with black shiny black tops, chrome seats with black leather seats and backs, dark red walls, low lighting and framed pictures of art house porn. Everything looked sleek and dark and glossy. Leering and acquisitive. Like the sort of men your mother warned you about.

She knew there was music playing, because it created a pressure in her head, but she couldn't tell if it was loud or quiet, or what songs were being played. There were people in the room too, but she couldn't look at them yet. She had fragments – legs, shoes, a man's wrist with intense black hairs and a Rolex-style watch - but she wasn't yet ready to join the pieces. There was a platform, strongly spotlit, at the end of the bar. She sensed it in much the same way as she sensed a headache.

This was Khaled's place. She could feel the energy of it chiming with the energy of him. His apartment and this club: they were the same thing. Different slices from the same loaf. He felt more real to her already. Purple silk. Black marble.

She went to the bar and ordered one of her non-drink drinks. Mineral water, a slice of lime and ice. She didn't care about the lime or the ice, but she just didn't want to look like the out of place person sipping a mineral water. She was out of place enough as it was.

The barman gave her change. A man standing next to her leant in and said something. She didn't hear what he said over the music and the buzzing in her head, but it was a friendly thing. Not hostile. A beery welcome.

And that was all she needed. Something altered in her head, as sudden and complete as flicking a light switch. She was still out of body and still couldn't feel a lighted cigarette pressed up against her arm, but her other senses suddenly intensified.

There were about fifteen customers in the place, including one other woman. The men were dressed well enough. Jackets, dark trousers, shoes that weren't awful. Her newfound clarity allowed her to look at the pole-dancing platform too. It had all the class of a Las Vegas casino personally styled by Donald Trump. There were three poles, three dancers. One of the girls was really pretty, the other two just thin. They were all either big-breasted or, she assumed, had had boob jobs. Also, the big hair, lots of make-up, fake tan. The aesthetic was unashamedly what they would call 'soft porn'. It was as if these women had disassembled themselves into their sexual parts only

She didn't have a moral reaction to this, not then anyway. Those parts of her just were not available. She could dimly feel that the glass in her hand was cold, but only dimly. The music remained just noise. It wasn't just the Unicorn that had made her like this, it was also Khaled.

The thing she was experiencing wasn't the connection she was seeking, but she couldn't pick and choose. She realised she had to take what she was given and this was what he cared to give.

She was confident now. She knew what she was doing. She walked to one of the best seats in the house, close to the dancers. She was aware for the first time of what she was wearing. A gold beaded dress. It was short enough on her, but would have been micro on Kay. Her shoes didn't quite go, but they'd have to do. She exchanged glances with the other woman customer. The unity of the sisterhood, you'd say, except that, in there, the sisterhood served a pretty thin gruel.

When she turned her eyes back, there was a girl in front of her. Blood red shoes, a sequined bikini and nothing else. She wanted to know if Emily wanted her to dance. Emily knew she had to experience what Khaled did. It was part of her gift. No stone unturned, no detail left out. It was twenty quid. The current song was coming to an end. In the gap between songs, she told Emily that she could touch if she wanted to. "Supersexy," she said, in an accent that could have been Polish or Slovenian or Finnish or Dutch. Then the next song started and she started dancing, lips open, eyes half shut. Emily didn't touch her. A couple of times the girl tried to put her hands on her thighs, but Emily moved them away. At the end of the song, she took the twenty quid but her eyes were already on the hunt. That was why she wanted me to touch her. Get the men so aroused they'd buy the next dance.

It wasn't about the dance, but about the hustle. There was an intensity to the sell that she didn't think she had experienced before. Silent. Furious. Unrelenting.

She realised she'd got Rose Flowers wrong too. Not completely wrong, but enough. The core of her was what she'd already seen: the hockey player, the English student, the girl with the sensible mum. But no one worked in a place like this just to earn some extra cash. To work there, you have to have something self-hating. The dancers in front of her slid up and down their poles like marionettes. Drug-fuelled. Drugs or drink.

"The force that through the green fuse drives the flower."

The poem in Rose Flowers' room. How did she get from there to here? Why did she work for one short year, then stop? What brought her here? What drove her away?

Emily didn't know. The picture of her had just grown more complex, more ambiguous. She thought about her mother's sobs, her father's choked numbness. The grief that filled the house.

Emily knew she tended to spend more time thinking about the dead than the living. She bonded easily with Flowers's head, with Khaled's elusive shadow. But there were other victims too. Living ones. Rose Flowers's parents. Her two siblings, Stephanie West, who was not her favourite person, but her life was damaged too. Althea and Tristan whose worlds had never recovered from their father's death and perhaps never would.

And Khaled. Who mourned him?

She didn't have an answer to that, but she did feel Khaled now. Felt him strongly present in this room. There was a lovely unity between his lonely corpse, shredded like some macabre goulash on that empty reservoir, and this place now. Over to her right, the dancer was dancing with another girl right in the face of a man in a black jacket and a dark navy shirt. A man who looked to have all the charm of a car salesman who just made Salesman of the Month. The two girls hardly made eye contact with each other as they were roving for the next target. The next twenty quid.

No touching, no photos, no fighting.

There wasn't a difference there. No exploiter and exploited. The men were governed by their brains in their trousers and the women dragged by their self-destructive lives. The two dancers had finished with the Salesman of the Month, but he had not finished with them. He tucked twenty-pound notes into their bikini bottoms and pulled a fifty note from his wallet. He was on his feet. His mates were clapping him. The place had got more crowded since Emily had entered, and there was a din behind her.

The two girls were leaning in close to his mouth. He was saying something; half shouting, half miming over the music. But the deal was pretty clear. There was a competition for the fifty pounds. The man's mates cheered. One was sent over to get champagne. Or rather, non-label fizz that sold for forty-five pounds the bottle. The pole dancers rested on their poles as the spots were trained on Salesman Man and the two girls. It was a striptease. Sexiest stripper got to go to a private booth with Salesman Man, the fifty pound note and the champagne.

The two girls were good at what they did. It wasn't easy, Emily reflected, to tease with so little to strip. One girl was prettier, more blonde, skinnier and with better features. But the other one, the brunette, had the advantage of technological warfare: hair extensions, pumped up boobs and lips full of collagen.

Blondie seemed too casual, as if she assumed her looks would win, no matter what. There was nothing relaxed in the brunette. She had attitude. If there was a fight on, she'd fight it. War without limits. Emily watched her keenly. Brunette's gestures were big, her miming blatant. For a while Emily thought she had overdone it, but she knew her market. Salesman Man pointed to the brunette.

The two of them walked past Emily with the booze. Salesman Man was living the moment. This was the highlight of his car selling month. Brunette wasn't like that. She was still selling cars. Her face was still doing the spreadsheet, the maths, figuring out those cash in/rent out sums that would tell her if she had enough money left over to feed her habit.

The sight clarified everything for Emily. It had not been a wasted experience. Her gift was paying dividends.

She realised that Khaled knew Flowers. That wasn't a definite fact, but a highly probable one. Khaled came to these clubs often enough to have seen himself as a connoisseur. He'd have wanted to know the talent, so he could appraise it. Flowers's plump white hips might or might not have been his thing, but he'd have known her. When they were back at work on Monday, Salesman Man and his buddies would talk about and dissect every dancer here.

That was not the main thing, though. The main thing was the transaction she had just witnessed. She had thought lap-dancing clubs were about sex and it turned out they were not. They were about cash and addiction and status and anxiety. Khaled's status. His anxiety.

He was a lecturer – good, diligent and well-respected – but on a lecturer's salary, a lecturer's perks. No Lecturer of the Month bonus for him. He had his private sector consultancy money, but how far would that go when bad quality fizz was forty-five pounds a bottle?

What this place told her had to do with Khaled's yearnings. He was a British – Moroccan man. No amazing looks, no inherited wealth. One talent, which had to do with engineering savvy. Or two talents, really: engineering know-how combined with a flair for a certain sort of networking. He had parlayed those talents into his position at the university, where he acted both as lecturer and honeybee. Buzzing around, making connections, fertilizing projections.

But he wanted so much more. He had a half-million-pound apartment and wanted a million-pound one. Had a low-end BMW, wanted a high-end one. Fooled around with lap dancers and pubs and clubs, but wanted more. The same thing, but classier. He wanted the stick-thin model girlfriend, the yacht in the bay, the supercar in the garage. He went out with pretty, skinny Jenny from the office, hoping that she could be his trophy girlfriend, but she let him down. She didn't want to snort coke from his kitchen worktops and she didn't buy designer clothes. The harsh truth was that Khaled didn't have enough to attract the kind of girl he wanted. Not enough of anything. Looks, class, glamour, cash. The only part of that he could change was the cash.

Emily spent another hour in the club.

Her feelings were returning. She could hear music as music, not just as relentless aural pressure. When she went to the Ladies and washed her hands, she could tell the difference between hot and cold. If she pressed her forearm hard against the side of the basin, she could sense the pressure, or almost could. The face in the mirror was the face of a stranger. Gold dress, red lips. Lips that moved in sync with hers. She didn't even try to join up with that face. It wasn't hers.

Back in the club, she spent enough time to be sure she wasn't missing anything, to make certain she was leaving on her own terms. Mostly, though, it was a good discipline for her. Training, learning to reverse that grey, upward draining, bringing herself down from the snow line, toward the trees, and through them down to the valley floor.

No drugs, no doctors, no dramas. Just her.

It helped that Khaled was there too. His energy. His dead presence. That made it easier, but she did not know why. She bought another drink. A white wine spritzer, which was mostly spritz and a splash of wine. She was even feeling confident enough to risk a few sips.

To the barman she said, "if the punters want to spend time with the girls, you know, get to know them, have a kiss and a cuddle, a proper chat....."

He interrupted her. "Not here. Strictly a no no."

"But then where? Is there a place where people go after?"

"Yeah, well, maybe. Different places."

He felt uncomfortable saying what he'd said and she didn't push it.

She left in a taxi and by sheer chance, it was the same taxi driver as before. He said, "Did you have a nice evening?"

Emily replied, "I did."

-24-

Emily went through the nightly routine of undressing, washing and brushing her teeth. She put Kay's dresses back on hangers knowing they would probably never leave again. It was long after midnight. She smiled as she thought that on Planet Books they'd have had sex and fallen asleep by now. On her own planet things were not as simple.

Unable to sleep she went down into the kitchen. She left the lights off because she liked the dark. The streetlights and that friendly green oven clock gave her enough light to find her way around. She swung open the fridge door, wondering whether she had actually eaten anything, but couldn't remember.

Her fridge was more interesting than Books'. It had less food, but there was more happening on the microbiological level. There was a half-eaten nut yoghurt, whose mould had now grown higher than the carton itself. Long filaments of moss-brown hair. She drank some orange juice, then swung the door shut again.

She was barefooted and not tired. She cogitated on the fact that other people got tired predictably. Books, for example, was wired up like some old-fashioned bomb. When the hands of the clock reached a certain point, something triggered unstoppably. By ten, he was yawning. By eleven or eleven thirty he was in bed and fast asleep.

Emily slept well enough most of the time, but she didn't have those rhythms, that predictability.

She got into bed. There were no lights inside the house and the glow of the streetlights through gaps in the curtains provided the only illumination. She imagined lying there with a gun in her hands, barrel pointing straight at the bedroom door. Chest height. Lethal, at that range. The thought game relaxed her.

It was half past one in the morning, when she reached for the phone and called Books.

"Yes?" The voice of a sleepy man.

"I just wondered whether you've checked your smoke alarm recently? Did you know that a working smoke alarm halves your risk of death by fire?"

"Oh bloody hell, Emily."

"In a strikingly high proportion of households, smoke alarms are present but non-functional, because the batteries have either been removed or are dead"

"Look, is this about something or did you just want to chat?"

"Um, we could just chat, if you liked. Since we're both awake."

The call was disconnected from the other end and she smiled to herself. She tried pointing her pretend gun at a pretend person behind the bedroom door again, but this time it didn't do much for her. Then Books called back. Emily knew he would by then have slapped cold water on his face, rinsed his mouth, got himself something to drink.

"Is it tea or whisky?" she asked.

"Tea."

"Good." Whisky indicated that he was having a rough time or she was being extra awful. Tea was good. "How was your day?" she asked, thinking that after one o'clock in the morning people were bad conversationalists. She found they needed warming up. Books sort of answered, but didn't say anything interesting. She tried again but Books was not Mr Sparky no matter how much she tried.

Eventually, he gave up and said, "How was your day?"

"I went to a lap dancing club and bought a dance for twenty quid."

"You did what?"

"She told me I could touch her."

"Well, for twenty quid...."

"And when I was there, I was completely dissociated. When I ran a bath before, I couldn't tell if the water was hot or cold. I couldn't feel a single thing.

"Bloody hell, Em."

He was awake now. She could see him sitting up in bed, gripping the phone. He asked the obvious questions about how long she was dissociated for, how completely and whether there was anyone with her now. She answered his questions. Degree of dissociation: very complete; duration: very short, probably just a few hours; nobody with her at the moment. Then he asked the Big One, the question he was most worried about. "Negative affect? How was your mood?"

"Negative affect?

"You know what I mean. Were you depressed? Did it go dark?"

"Not really."

She tried to explain how it felt, but it was like trying to explain red to a blind man. Or a blind man describing a watermelon to the sighted. You can shuffle partway across the bridge of meaning, do your very best to link hands through the darkness, but in the end, the effort only serves to prove that you're you, and they're them. You might brush fingertips, but you'll never merge, never join.

She knew what he what he was asking though, and why he was asking it. Her thing, her Cotard's, arose when two lethal forces came together. Dissociation plus depression. Dissociation removed her from her feelings. It numbed them. Depression painted the entire world in charcoal greys. Put the two together and you had Emily at varying stages in her life. So far. A young woman who couldn't feel herself existing, who saw the worst and assumed the worst. In herself and in everything. She still dissociated sometimes, but was not depressed these days. She was staying positive. It was very rare that she crept up to the edge of full-blown Cotard's. When she lost touch with her feelings she remained in a reasonable place by staying close to Books. She could keep it together then. She also grew marijuana in her potting shed and had an illegal handgun stashed away in a secret place. She didn't mention the last fact, though.

She asked, "why do you think it happened? I mean, I was okay. I was having a nice day. My version of nice. A bit crazy, but no crazier than normal. Then I realised that the logic of my investigation would take me to a lap-dancing club. For some reason, that did it. I drained away. Emptied out."

Books waited until he was sure she had finished and then asked, "do you think it was the sexual aspect?"

"I don't know."

There was a pause. She didn't know who started it, but she knew why it was there. Cotard's Syndrome, her illness, is the big, ugly mother of all psychological conditions. It's usually lethal. A large majority of those who suffer from it attempt suicide. Many succeed. Forget the logic of it. Why do people who think they're dead need to kill themselves? Just stay with the fact. Cotard's is generally lethal. It is almost always associated with early childhood trauma, but not in Emily's case.

"Em!" Books' voice was warning her, cautioning her.

She didn't feel cautious.

"Okay, let's pretend I'm a copper. Let's just say I might have some expertise in criminal investigation. We normally try to make connections. Sift through piles of data and see if we can make something in Pile A match something in Pile B."

"Yes, and let's just say that my day job involved clinical psychology...."

Emily interrupted. "A girl with Cotard's. You'd probably guess that sexual abuse had been involved somewhere along the line, right? Only a guess, but a pretty damn strong guess, right? Then twenty years later that girl enters a lap-dancing club and experiences a very powerful, temporary increase in her symptoms. Tell me what the other options are, Books!"

"You really want to know?" He was heated now. Not angry exactly, but heated. He said, "You have no idea. You think you do, but you don't. Sexual abuse is one way to screw up a child, yes, but there are others. Neglect, drug addiction, physical abuse, injury to the brain or brain stem, inflammation or infection of the brain or brain stem. You just don't know." He stopped to take breath. He didn't like speaking to her in that way, but had no choice. She had to know. "Oh and yes, you can present as evidence the fact that you had a weird evening tonight. But then again, I could present as evidence the fact that you do not seem to be very screwed up around sex. When we're together, the sex is about the most normal thing about you."

She was about to respond. Pressured speech is the clinical term. Where a speaker is so driven to talk that they can't listen. Can't even get their own sentences out properly. She was there, in that place, and then she wasn't. It was as though she was worn out by the day, the night, the argument. By herself.

So she just said, "Yes."

"Those things cut both ways, you know. You don't know, Em. You really don't."

"Okay."

She wasn't that humble, that submissive, but she knew he was right.

"I think I've always been waiting for The Clue," she said. "I wanted some kind of eureka moment, one that would unlock the past."

"Emily, do you remember Brian? The man with the beard and the acid burns?"

Yes, she remembered Brian. A schizophrenic. He was always having eureka moments. Two or three a day when he was fizzy. He'd lean in, with his bad teeth and stinky breath, and explain his latest vision. One of those visions resulted in him pouring battery acid down his face. Hence the burns.

Books went on talking and she tried to argue, but she knew he was right. The eureka moment wouldn't come. And if it did, it couldn't be trusted. They talked a bit more. Books yawned. Maybe just a yawn, maybe a 'shut up and let me go back to sleep' signal. Either way, Emily was as good as gold, and said, "You sleep well, Books, my love."

"Thank you. You too."

They said good night and hung up. She let the room drift back into silence, raised her nonexistent gun at the nonexistent intruder and fired off six rounds. Two groups of three. Chest and head.

She had many questions dashing around in her head. "Why do I miss having a gun with me? Why does the possibility of violent response to intrusion feel good? Why did my brain go AWOL today?"

Books was right, she knew. You can't trust eureka moments. But that didn't make the questions go away. They were real. Then she called Books back. He mumbled something into the mouthpiece.

"Don't talk, Books. I don't want to wake you up this time. Not really. Just thank you. Thank you for being you. Sweet dreams."

He mumbled a mouthful of nothing and she hung up. The room was full of silence now, the hall full of dead intruders. The streetlights glowed their unprotesting orange. She went to sleep. She knew what she was doing tomorrow.

-25-

Many of our maritime cities, with their links to the slave trade and piracy, are built on corpses. In some, the past blows like rubbish in the air, sags like a collapsing door.

The place Emily wanted, Precision Tools, was down by the docks. Industrial sheds tamped around a rectangle of water. Slate green and restless. She parked. It was Sunday and the place was closed, its gates locked by a padlock on a fat chain. Wind, rain, and cold. She had gloves but her coat wasn't particularly warm and she didn't fancy getting out of her car in order to jangle uselessly at the chain. Nevertheless, that is what she did, just to satisfy herself that she couldn't open it. The cold from the padlock repaid her by penetrating her gloves within seconds.

Some people, Books for example, would have known exactly what to do. He had an almost instant intuition. She supposed it was a product of his youth spent roaming London as a pickpocket, scraping a life as best he could against the odds. He would look at the padlock and say something like "See what the silly buggers have done? All we need to do is slip the split pin out of the O-socket, then bend the hasp back – no, the other way - and the hinges should just lift off, like so." Intuition, well-honed street cunning and that unfussed masculine strength. All Emily could see was a tangle of cold metal that hurt her hands.

She returned to her car and noticed a black and yellow sign on the fence which gave the name and number of a security company. She called it and said she was the police and was responding to reports of a break in. The phone operator, apparently overwhelmed with boredom, said she would send someone.

She waited. There was enough wind that she could hear it whistling in the fence, over the roof of her car. This northern climate is hostile to life, she thought. If you fell in the water, how long before you died?

She made a call to Rhys Jordan..

"Hi, Rhys, are you okay after Friday night?" She didn't wait for his answer. "Look, funny question. But a few years back, where did the girls go at the end of their shift? To get something to eat, have a chat, whatever they did to end the evening off?"

"Oh, well, the club finishes around four in the morning. A lot of the girls go straight home."

"Right, but if they do stick around? Have a smoke. Get something to eat?"

"There's nowhere really good anymore. A few years back, the big place was Macca's. An all-night café. It opened early for the truckers and the market traders and people. But we used to pour in about four fifteen, four thirty, whatever."

He started laughing and told her a story, the gist of which had to do with a trucker getting a full strip from two of the girls in return for a plate of egg, chips and beans. The place was closed now, but he gave her the name of the person who used to run it, a man called Gavin Watson.

She thanked him and disconnected.

The wind still chattered in the fence. She wondered if she could pick the padlock, convinced herself that she could, but remembered she didn't have the tools with her. Instead she listened to music. Radio 2. Classic FM. She settled on Brahms. Unhappy violins and plenty of them.

Then the security man came. He had a proper coat, she noticed, warm, rainproof, and covered in fluorescent strips in case she had difficulty seeing him.

She showed him her warrant card. "It's probably bollocks," she said, trying to use language that he might relate to, "but I need to take a look around."

He nodded; bored. He had a dog in the back of his van that wanted either to come out and play or eat Emily. The guard unlocked the gate and they drove through to Precision Tools. There was a blue shed, fairly new, and large, possibly ten thousand square feet or more. A stock-holding yard and security cameras.

The guard had keys to the unit but needed to call to get the codes for the alarm. More waiting and then they were in. They flipped some lights on. There some thinly partitioned offices at the front of the building, but the main space was a factory. It contained some fancy machines, steel gantries, forklifts. The place was orderly, tidy.

There was no sign of a break in and the guard looked at her. She said, "Look, can you just take a look around the perimeter? I'll check around in here. Meet you outside in five minutes?"

He walked off. She spent a bit of time in the factory, and ran her hands over complex metal objects. Things she didn't even know how to describe. Compressor blades, cylinder heads, turbofans. She didn't know what those things were, but for all she knew she was surrounded by them now. Rods and bars of speciality metals. Tungsten, copper, low-density steels.

Mark Mortimer knew about this stuff and so did Khaled. They were both dead.

She liked factories, but it wasn't the factory she needed, so she went back to the offices, which just looked like ordinary offices. Holiday calendars, a coffee machine, grey invoice files, red swivel chairs and mouse pads with adverts on.

The executive suite wasn't much either. An office with glass windows that looked out only to the reception area. It just had a fancier type of desk lamp. She went inside. It was all weirdly normal; neither thronged with the spirits of the dead nor even particularly bland. Not obviously hiding anything. It just was what it was. A not very smart office inside a middle sized engineering company located in a decaying port town in an unimportant part of the United Kingdom.

She crawled under the desk on the burgundy nylon carpet tiles. She noticed the particular smell that comes from electric wires and office carpets. She fiddled around at the back of the computer, pulling at various cables until she worked out which one belonged to the keyboard. She chided herself for not bringing a torch and pulled out the lead. She took a thing like a memory stick from her pocket and fitted the keyboard lead into one end of it. The other end went into the keyboard port of the PC. She shoved the computer back to where it had been, using marks on the carpet as a guide. Satisfied, she got up.

Everything was the same as it was, except that her gadget now sat between keyboard and computer. A keystroke recorder, bought for thirty pounds from Amazon and so simple to use that even an IT Queen like Emily could use it.

It didn't collect mouse clicks, store images, record web addresses or e-mails or copy files. But it did collect keystrokes. And people use keystrokes to enter passwords. Companies use those gadgets to monitor staff and ensure business usage only and seek out inappropriate use of the system. She rooted around until she found a stash of stationery and took a few envelopes, found a memory stick and took that too.

Outside, she asked the guard about the perimeter fence. He shrugged and she returned the gesture. She pretended to call the office while he reset the alarms. Then they left, the gate again locked and padlocked. The guard went back to wherever he ought to have been. Emily didn't leave straightaway. She wound down the windows and got cold. It sharpened her and she felt good. She sent a text to Webster, telling her about Gavin Watson and the place called Macca's.

Aftab Khaled liked sex with pretty girls, but she thought he was also desperately concerned about his status. He wanted money, the better apartment, the girl with cool and style. She didn't know where Mark Mortimer came into that, but she hoped her little keystroke recorder was about to tell her.

She was feeling good, but not quite satisfied. She and Books were due to spend the evening together and a couple of his friends were coming to dinner. These normal boyfriend-girlfriend days used to terrify her. She assumed that the effort of playing normal for many consecutive hours would blow a fuse somewhere. Yet that hadn't been her experience. She felt the whole thing a challenge, like the way yachtsmen must feel about crossing the Great Southern Ocean. Not a voyage to undertake lightly, but one which mostly repays the commitment.

She was in the car, driving slowly, windows still down, heater on full blast but the air still cold. She hugged the coast instead of scooting down the motorway, wanting to see the seas as much as possible. Slate-green water and Atlantic winds. The waves foam-topped, with that foam that's never really white. When the Ice Age comes, it'll start like this, she thought. She was driving to connect with Rose Flowers, seek out her old haunts. Places where she lived as a student, cafes they knew she frequented. She ended up down by the sea, in the blast of the wind.

Five years ago Rose Flowers left a party and walked away to her death. A few days ago, Aftab Khaled walked out of a coffee shop, out of CCTV range, and also ended up dead. The two corpses strewn across the locality in a muddy unity.

Last night's insight still seemed more true to her now. The two of them knew each other, were more than strangers. She didn't know where these reflections were taking her, but she knew enough that these things can't be rushed. She felt like she was getting to know them, though.

When she was too cold to brave the seafront anymore, she zipped back to the office, sat at her desk and turned the computer on.   She   typed   in   her father's name and waited. There was an unusual silence until "Access Denied" appeared on the screen. She toyed with the idea of entering Ray Quinn's name, but cowardice and common sense prevailed. She knew enough not to go any further and closed down, but she also knew that even that dead end was informative in its own way.

The phone burbled. "You're late," was all Books said.

"On my way," she said in return.

And she was. On her way for an afternoon of high intensity girl-friending. An afternoon during which she wouldn't think or talk about work at all. All in all, the perfect woman and the perfect lover. She aimed to be both. Just for Books. The thought sparked a familiar warm and moist glow.

-26-

Monday. Webster the Great was briefing for Operation Takeaway. An event which used to be daily and was now only twice weekly, with additional helpings of Websterian sunshine served as required. The 'persons of interest' board now had 275 names. It was there to focus minds, to eliminate gradually, but all it had done was to provide space for ever more names to be added. More interest, you could say. Progress? Who knew. Stagnation? Ever more likely.

But that morning Webster was in the closest thing to a good mood as she ever got. It wasn't that she cracked a smile or anything anatomically dangerous like that, just that she ejected nails and they flew out at slightly lower velocities than usual and weren't always aimed at the eyes.

Good mood should mean good news, so the crowd was expectant as it awaited the starting pistol. Intensive enquiries over Sunday afternoon and evening succeeded in tracing one of the waitresses from Gavin Watson's now defunct greasy spoon café. The waitress, one Sandrine Cooper, currently working as a server in her uncle's fish and chip shop, was shown eight photos of different women, including Rose Flowers and another dancer who worked at the Unicorn over the relevant period. Cooper picked out both girls immediately, and correctly named them both. She also picked, from a group of eight photos, a picture of Khaled. She didn't know his surname, but named him correctly as 'Aftab.' She thought that he and Rose had a relationship of sorts, but she wasn't sure. She knew they 'hung out a bit,' but didn't know any more than that.

It wasn't much, but enough. Webster finally had her connection. To any copper, a connection like that was like a point of weakness in a fortification, a vulnerable angle on an unguarded wall. It was where you trained your artillery. Where you concentrated your fire.

Webster must have known that the Khaled-Flowers connection brought as many questions as answers, but she redeployed the manpower she had to focus aggressively on this new line of attack. She wanted people who saw Flowers and Khaled together. Anyone connected with the two of them. They had done some work on that in the past, but had never brought all their resources to bear on that single question. The enquiry had found its centre.

Webster started to dole out assignments and interview schedules. Emily vaguely noticed that Webster didn't mention it was her text to her that gave them the Sandrine Cooper connection. She didn't really care, but it was another breach of senior officer etiquette. They were meant to give patronizing little public accolades to their baby detectives when they managed to do something a tiny bit right. Emily consoled herself with the thought that she could have the woman banged up in the Tower of London with one phone call.

But that wasn't what concerned her most. What concerned her more was the question of what happened next?

What happened next was that people were paired up and given targets. Books and Jon Breakell would be interviewing or re-interviewing current club employees. Bev Rowland, Jane Alexander, Jamie Donaldson and Angela Yorke were going to re-interview as many dancers as they could find – not the current generation of dancers, obviously, but those who were working five years ago. For the first time in what seemed like ages, there was a stir in the room, a sense of excitement. A fire trying to fan itself back into life.

Emily waited for her name to be read out. She was relieved to hear she wasn't with Jamie Donaldson, but sorry that she wasn't to work with Bev Rowland. Then the meeting ended and she realised she had been excluded completely. Kicked off the whole damn operation. Her eyes widened with indignation. The normal charge for the coffee machine passed her by and she didn't even take the opportunity to say something pointlessly offensive.

She was still standing there, appalled, when she realised Webster was at her elbow.

"My office," she said.

She walked away and Emily followed, thinking of Beefeaters, ravens and the Tower. On the way upstairs her phone rang, but she didn't answer it. A couple of moments later, a text came through and she didn't look at it.

They got to Webster's office and Emily closed the door behind her and sat down without invitation. They faced each other over the desk. Storm grey eyes from Webster and an 'up yours' face from Emily. Lines of battle.

"Okay," she said.

"Okay what?" Emily replied.

"Your semi-official conversation. Who, where, when what?"

"I spoke to some of the bar staff, without gaining any real information. I subsequently called Rhys Jordan and asked him if there was a place where dancers used to hang out after hours."

"And it was Jordan who told you?"

"Yes."

"Have you made a note of that conversation for the records?"

"No."

"Do so. You should have done so immediately."

Emily nodded.

Webster needed something on the system to document how the enquiry came to bang on Sandrine Cooper's door. Like every good copper, Webster had an eye on how an eventual prosecution would play out in court.

"Right. Now this Flowers connection. I understand your father simply volunteered the information without prompting."

"Correct."

"Correct, meaning that what I have been told is correct, or meaning that is what in fact happened?"

Emily was tempted to fudge the issue, but didn't. A sudden burst of honesty found her saying, "I nudged my father for information, yes. Not directly, but via a trusted colleague of his. What my father did with that nudge was up to him."

"You didn't offer any kind of protection or amnesty?"

Emily's mouth fell open at that. If Webster was asking that question, it would be because the entire high command of the area force was uncertain about Emily's ultimate loyalties. She was genuinely astonished and hoped she looked it.

"That would be beyond my pay grade!"

"It would be a very long way beyond your pay grade."

"I offered my father nothing. The day after we went to interview Rhys Jordan, my father asked me if there would be any comeback. I assume he had in mind any tax irregularities. I said I didn't think there would be an issue. That was the entire extent of our conversation."

Webster did her storm-grey thing at Emily, who just stared back. Eventually Webster saw what she needed to see, or just moved on. Either way, she gave a sharp nod.

"If the Unicorn is involved in this case in any way, I can't have you connected with it. Not that aspect of it."

"My father isn't," Emily began, feeling angry again.

Emily knew Webster was taking her information from the file, but she knew exactly what her father's file contained, because they had written it together in the planning stage of the operation. His prosecutions comprised two armed robberies, one possession of a firearm with intent, and one each of kidnap and arson. A well balanced portfolio if you asked Emily. The crimes of he was suspected but for which he was never tried would have made a vastly longer list. Handling stolen goods was, as far as she recalled, picturing the exact page, his particular forte.

Emily had to play along, so she consoled herself again with thoughts of Webster and Beefeaters, ravens and the Tower. It had obviously worked as Webster had been taken in completely. Her father would have been tickled pink to witness the scene.

The file was in fact currently weighing down the bottom drawer of Emily's desk and she felt its tug, its undertow.

She knew Webster was right. Their investigation had to be whiter than white. If the Unicorn became central to a prosecution case, she needed to be nowhere close to it. She knew it may come to that, but nevertheless felt angry and disappointed.

"I don't want to leave the case," she blurted out, knowing that was the required reaction. She wasn't being strategic, not figuring out how best to get what she wanted. It was just the truth. She said, "Rose Flowers, Aftab Khaled. I feel I know them and I don't want to be reassigned."

"I'm not reassigning you."

"You're not?"

Emily was stunned. If she was still on the case, then what was the problem? Her look must have revealed her confusion.

"I need you off the Flowers – Khaled connection, that's all." Webster said almost gently.

Her version of gentle: one that left the skull intact.

"Okay."

"I wasn't asking for your permission," she stabbed.

"No?"

"I'm guessing there are aspects of the case you have an interest in exploring?"

"Yes." Then, as she glared at her, Emily added, "I think there continues to be merit in exploring Khaled's engineering connections. The nature of any connection between Flowers and Khaled remains very unclear. Even if he killed her, his own death is completely unexplained. He did know Mortimer, who died violently. There is a consensus among Mortimer's family, friends and colleagues that he was not a drug-smuggling type. Also, why does anyone kill anyone, if it's not just a pub brawl type thing? It always comes down to sex or money, doesn't it? And there is money floating at the edges of all this. Mortimer's drug smuggling, Khaled's work for the university, those private sector consultancies, his taste for the expensive."

Webster nodded. "I agree."

She didn't seem to be angry with Emily now, which felt weird. Webster nodded again and something happened to her lower face which could have been a muscle spasm or an attempt at a smile. She was about to say something when her phone rang and Emily's phone vibrated again with a text. She answered her phone, only to say that she wasn't taking calls. Emily used the interruption to look at her phone. When Webster turned back to her, she was ready to restart from where they were.

Emily was not ready and showed Webster her phone. The text, the second one, was from the duty medical officer at Dartmoor Prison. It was about Jon Johnson. He had been attacked and was in hospital asking for Emily.

-27-

Emily remembered hospital as being wheeled beds squeaking on over-polished vinyl floors and the smell of medication and bedpans, with nurses in starched uniforms and sensible shoes. It proved to be an inaccurate memory. She found floors that didn't appear to have been polished at all, and there were no beadpans in sight. The nurses' uniforms lacked the starch of yesteryear and had been worn all the way from home on the bus or whatever, and no doubt carried all sorts of killer bugs. Sensible shoes had given way to whatever turns you on.

Johnston was in a bed by a window, looking out. She found him in good mood.

"I could see my wing from here," he said, "if it wasn't so many beautiful miles away."

Emily didn't look at his imaginary landscape. She preferred the light beyond the city. She liked the way it reminded her that the universe is huge and that we humans dance on its surface, briefly, and without sound.

Johnston's head was swathed in bandages, which had been recently done, because blood hadn't yet had time to soil the nice white linens. He hadn't shaved for a day or so, and he was one of those men who look almost instantly grizzly.

"Making friends, then?" She asked.

He grinned. "Yeah. In prison, everyone loves a copper."

She sat down on a squeaky leatherette chair that was designed to be comfortable for long visits, but was too big for her. The synthetic fabric immediately started gluing itself to her legs.

"DI Webster is outside."

"Webster? I get a visit from the Ice Queen herself, eh?"

He chuckled at that. For him, being out of prison was as good as a trip to the seaside, even if the local tourist attractions involved the A&E department and the scariest detective for miles around. But it was almost information. DIs didn't chase around after every lead. The fact that Webster had chosen to come was partly police solidarity as Johnston was a former officer, even if also a convicted criminal, but mostly because Webster didn't have complete confidence in the Flowers-Khaled connection, or, indeed, complete confidence in Emily.

"She's off checking your records with the head nurse. Wants to know if you'll live." Emily looked hard into his eyes. "And you will, will you? You're okay?"

"I'm grand. It's nice to be back in the saddle, actually. I've never minded taking some knocks." He gave her a twisted grin. It's odd the way people work; maybe a near death experience was what he needed.

On a sudden impulse, she said, "Before you went to London, when you were still a copper, who was the best officer you worked with? The best detective, I mean."

"Why?"

"Just let me have this one. I can't tell you why."

He gave her some names. She didn't recognise most of them, or, if she did, she discarded them because they were too long retired or because their careers took them in different directions from the one she wanted. But one name worked for her. DCI Jack Yorath. He had spent his whole career in the CID, and retired only a few years ago. He had specialized in organized crime.

"Yorath," she said. "He was good, was he? You'd trust him?"

Mischief hovered around Johnston's mouth, but didn't quite take possession. He said simply, "I'd trust Jack anywhere. He's got brains, guts, and integrity. A good copper."

A good copper: the ultimate police compliment.

"Thanks, that's helpful."

Webster came in. She was wearing a long coat, a warm one, and Emily suddenly remembered that she'd meant to get herself a proper winter coat when she went shopping with Kay, but had herself an expensive and unnecessary suit instead. Ah, well.

Webster struggled to find the right tone with Johnston. She couldn't be horrible to him, because he didn't have to talk to her, because he wasn't a copper anymore, and because he'd got a gash in his skull so bad that he was rushed to hospital, given a blood transfusion, and was being held for observation. At the same time, he was a former police officer serving a prison sentence, so Webster couldn't quite bring herself to be nice.

"Mr. Johnston. DI Webster." She gave a stiff semi-bow from the neck.

"Yeah, nice to meet you. How's Gethin these days?"

Gethin: DCI Gethin Matthews. Johnston was only using the name to remind Webster that he knew some of her more senior colleagues. Those little power plays were more or less compulsive with him.

"I'm sure he's fine. I understand that at the request of my colleague here, you were making preliminary enquiries into the suicide of Mark Mortimer?"

"Preliminary inquiries, you say? There must have been an inquest, surely. I don't think my inquiries were preliminary in nature."

Webster wasn't enjoying this at all, but there wasn't a lot she could do about it. What could she threaten? That she'd throw him in jail? Crack his skull open?

"Maybe you could just tell us what happened?"

"Of course, but be a love, would you and fetch me a cup of tea? I'm parched, I am."

Webster glared at him, then at Emily thinking she was colluding, but she could see she wouldn't get an answer unless she submitted to his crap, so off she went to hunt down a cup of tea.

As soon as she had gone, Emily looked at Johnston and laughed.

"I'll send it back if it's too weak," he grinned.

"Did you learn anything?"

"No. Somebody just hit me from behind with a brick. Lots of blood, because it was a head wound, but it looks worse than it is really. I'm not even sure who did it. I mean, I might have a guess, but I'm not too sure I want to. Ignorance is bliss sometimes."

"But the attack was definitely connected with Mortimer?"

"Yes. I asked around. People knew I was asking. I wasn't trying to keep it especially quiet, because in prison you never really know who knows what. I wanted to get word out."

Johnston shrugged. There was something sad in his face for the first time. For all his macho posturing, it couldn't have been that easy being a policeman in jail. Not that much fun being half-murdered just because you've been doing a favour for a friend.

She put out her hand and rubbed his upper arm. He gave her grateful eyes, then added, "After I was hit, I was down on the floor, with blood in my eyes. Someone kicked me in the ribs and said right up close, 'keep away from things that have nothing to do with you.' Then he kicked me again. Then after a bit he stopped. End of story."

"That's not proof positive."

"I haven't been asking about anything else. And it's not the kind of jail where people get beaten up for no reason."

She nodded. She believed him, but it was Webster who would need convincing. Just then she came back with a cup of tea. There was tightness all around her mouth and anger lines above her eyes. Emily thought it amusing that there was a man who'd been violently beaten while serving a four- year sentence and a woman with a good income and a respected job, who had been asked to fetch a cup of tea. One was happy, the other really wasn't.

Johnston took the cup, peered at it all disappointed, and said, "Oh sorry, I should have said..."

Emily had her hand out to take the tea before he could even finish his pointlessly needling comment. She took the cup and left the two of them alone together. Johnston would end up telling her what he told me, he'd just make sure he annoyed her all the while.

Emily didn't do anything with the tea. She just found a window with a view towards the prison miles away on Dartmoor and then the sea. And a pale blue light that had no limits.

When Webster finally came out, she looked grim and said just two words. "Let's go."

-28-

The frigid green water threatened in the dock. A cold northern wind had forced a floating throng of industrial refuse up against the concrete walls. Discarded plastics, chunks of polystyrene, broken pallets. Because it was no longer the weekend, there were no locked gates at the entrance to the property. Webster parked her BMW in a free space overlooking the dock and Emily parked next to her. They had come in two cars, so Webster could get away quickly and Emily could stay on if need be. Getting out, they heard the slap of water against the dock, the moan of wind. Precision Tools's blue shed rose like a tent against the elements.

"Nice place," Emily said, "pretty."

Webster opened her mouth and closed it again primly. They marched across the car park to reception where they were signed in, offered 'refreshments', and taken through to Jim Dunbar, Barry's chief executive. He was short, strong, dark-haired. Give him a few acres of upland field and he'd look the part right away. Here, in suit and tie, he was trying to look all executive and still smelled of the farm.

Webster did the intro. Double murder. Drug deals. A prison suicide. One of the murder victims known to have had close connections with Dunbar's former employee. Dunbar took it in with composure, but he was also careful, vigilant. After speaking for no more than two or three minutes, Webster shut up and let Emily get on with her questions.

Mortimer's dates of employment, his speciality, his job performance, Dunbar's impressions of him as an employee, Mortimer's reputation within the work force. Any notably close connections with clients or suppliers? Any previous evidence of drug habits?

Dunbar dealt with some of those questions smoothly and easily. Mortimer had been with the firm six years. He was a skilled engineer. Well respected, internally and by clients. Never known to be a drug user. Never known to have had drug issues.

When she got to the questions she was most interested in, though, Dunbar slowed down and was markedly more careful.

"Did Mortimer cause you any managerial problems?"

"No. No, I wouldn't say problems. Mark was a careful man. He had high standards. But we're a precision engineering company, so we trade off high standards, and I don't have a problem with that."

"But...?"

"Well, in some ways I think Mark forgot he worked for a commercial enterprise. It sometimes felt like he wanted to work in a research institute or university. Working here, you work. You have to hustle. If a client wants something, it's your job to deliver it, not find reasons why the client shouldn't want it."

There was a sudden emptiness in the room. Big enough that she found herself glancing at Webster who was simultaneously glancing at her. It was the same emptiness that she had felt at the university with Macintosh, but bigger. And closer.

Emily pushed away at the silence. "Can you give me an example of Mortimer not wanting to deliver on a job?"

She brought her chair as close to the desk as she could. Partly she wanted to see his face close up, but she also wanted him to feel pressured. In addition, she wanted to get her leg into a tangle of computer wire.

Dunbar stared at her. He was teetering on the edge of telling her something. Teetering, but then pulled back.

"He tended to get into dialogue with clients. They'd ask us to make something to such and such a specification. He'd want to know how they evolved those specs. Sometimes he'd end up persuading them they could achieve the same performance with an off the shelf solution. Which wasn't exactly good for our sales."

"Did he have ethical issues with your clients?"

"Ethical? Mark would have had ethical issues with a roomful of bishops."

"Which made him not exactly your run of the mill drug smuggler."

"No, but he did bring five kilos of cocaine into the country. I've no idea how he argued that one to himself, but I'm sure he found a way."

"Yes."

Emily looked at Webster. She felt this thing Emily was feeling. A DI is the most senior active field rank in the CID. Go any higher, and you start to be a desk jockey. Marshalling paper, not interviewing suspects. Webster was a field officer, not a bureaucrat, and she felt the withholding too. Nothing that was necessarily criminal, but an intriguing lack of openness. And Johnston in hospital with an ugly skull wound.

There was something awry and they both knew it.

She said, "Mr. Dunbar, could you just give me a couple of moments with my colleague?"

Dunbar looked briefly surprised at being ejected from his own office, but he shrugged and left us. He went out to talk with his secretary on the other side of the internal window. Emily rolled back from the desk. Her foot had become caught in his computer wires and she'd pulled out a couple of leads.

Webster pointed, unsmiling, to the tangle around her foot. Emily got down on hands and knees, repaired the damage. As she did so, she pulled the keyboard from her keystroke recorder, put the recorder into her pocket and replaced the lead. She emerged, bum first, from the desk. The way every girl liked to be seen by her boss.

"He's not telling us something," she said, as she rose to the surface.

"I agree."

"And nothing about Mortimer makes him sound like a drug importer."

"Mortimer pleaded guilty. Didn't even offer a defence."

"Which could cut both ways."

If you don't offer defence, it's because you're either very guilty or very innocent.

Webster nodded. "Yes. Quite. Are you happy conducting further interviews here on your own?"

"Yes."

She called Dunbar back in, explained that Emily would be staying around for a bit. There was a bit of sorting out to be done. When was over, she walked back to the car park with Webster. No reason really. It just seemed natural. It was cold and windy and she had left her coat inside. Her eyes started tearing up with the cold.

Webster was saying something. She didn't catch the first part of it, but then she did. "well done. Your instincts here have been good."

"It's a family thing. An interest in the criminal justice system."

If only she knew!

Webster's mouth moved at that, but not in a good way.

"Don't push it," she said, making an odd repeated hand gesture as she did so. A choppy, downward gesture, but more nervous than that sounds.

"Of course not."

She gave Emily a look of iron and steel, then relented. "Well then." She attempted a smile, except her face didn't really do smiles, so she just flexed some muscles in the right general area and hoped for the best.

Emily returned her grimace with a peach plucked from her own orchard of smiles. Crinkly eyes, white teeth, plenty of dimply cheek action, and said, "Thank you," which didn't make sense either.

Webster was about to turn away and get into her car, when Emily said, "Khaled's family. I assume you'll be assigning someone to look after them when they're over here?"

"You want to do that?"

"Yes please."

Webster nodded. She turned abruptly and got into her car. She was cold too.

When she got back inside, someone had cleared a tiny conference room for her and an interview rota was being organized. Emily told them who she wanted to see and who could wait. Someone brought tea.

She asked for a few minutes to set up and dragged out her laptop. She booted up and popped her keystroke recorder into the USB port. The laptop detected the new device and offered to import its files. Emily pressed the key and the one file appeared as plain text. It was a complete record of Jim Dunbar's keystrokes from first thing on Monday morning to the moment she had crawled under his desk a few minutes previously. It wasn't a long file. All she needed were the first items of text.

A helpful little guide that came with the recorder informed her that the back pointing arrow was the backspace key. The other one was the enter key.

Dunbar looked like he was in his fifties, so the 57 was probably his birth year. She didn't know what the 'shelby' was. A pet. His mother's maiden name. His wife's maiden name. Her laptop was picking up two available networks, one labelled PrecTools1. That would do. She clicked the connect button and was asked for a password. She guessed at shelby57 and it admitted her to the network. She searched the File Manager and checked what the system had to offer. The answer was everything. Everything she could have wanted, and more. All neatly filed. Accounts, CADCAM, E-mail archive, HR, IT, Facilities, Invoices, Letters, Tenders, Suppliers EU, Suppliers UK, Tech.

She poked around for a few minutes, then started to copy everything that looked even half interesting.

She crammed in six interviews that afternoon. All uninformative, but who cared? Behind her, the laptop was finishing gathering its harvest. Before leaving she copied her lovely new data from her hard drive to the memory stick she had taken when she was there before. She dropped it into an envelope addressed to the station and posted it from the main post office in town. She tootled home feeling happy.

That night, her good mood remained intact. She had been intending to spend some lovely private hours investigating her pilfered stash of documents, but instead decided on an impulse to cook for Books. Properly. Not something found in the fridge and dropped in a saucepan. She announced that she was going to cook a chicken stew, an Italian version, with red wine, tomatoes and anchovies and zoomed out to get ingredients. She zoomed out for a second time when she realised her shopping haul somehow failed to include either chicken or anchovies.

She concentrated hard on the cooking, but somehow it was long past nine-thirty before the food was ready. Books kept wanting to help, but she shood him away. She wouldn't even let him set the table or light candles. She wanted to show him that she could do those things if she put her mind to it. Or rather, she wanted to show herself. Train herself into it.

It was almost ten when they sat down to eat. But Books tasted, smiled, appreciated, and clinked glasses. He would do all that anyway, she knew, but she thought he was doing it for real and she felt a familiar wave of warmth towards of him. Or love. Quite possibly love.

That thought was in itself somewhat stunning, so she was relieved when Books, who had manfully eaten not just seconds, but thirds, pushed his chair back and said, "We'll wash up tomorrow, shall we?" In Books-speak, that sentence had nothing to do with keeping order in the kitchen. It was strictly a question about her appetite for sex. Which was perfectly healthy, so they took her still-stunned brain off to the bedroom, where they found other ways to occupy it.

Afterwards, when Books was snoring and she'd grown bored of playing with his hair, she turned her attention back to that rush of warmth she'd felt as they were eating.

'Is what we have love? He may well feel it for me, the poor fool. But what about me?' She wondered.

She checked he was fast asleep, then spoke to him.

"Books, my beautiful man, I think I'm in love with you."

It didn't feel wrong, so she said it again, only this time without the "I think", and it still didn't feel wrong. But was it the same as it feeling right? Books didn't care. He snored away. The city around them snored away. A cold front rode in from the north and industrial trash thrashed against the walls of an unused dockside.

'Where's Johnston? Still in hospital or returned to prison? And where are Aftab Khaled and Rose Flowers? Where is Mark Mortimer and his secrets? And what was it that DI Webster meant with that odd, repeated chopping gesture when we said goodbye?' All questions that invaded her brain. Lots of questions, not many answers.

Her thoughts turned to her father and Ray Quinn. The criminal underworld is an unstable place. You don't get to the top and stay there without making enemies. Without using your fists, or worse. When she wanted a handgun on the Rattigan case, her father had supplied one with a deftness that was almost breathtaking. Neither Ray nor her father had ever let her down with anything. Their power was breathtaking in its scope and awesome in its capacity to overcome and destroy forces of evil. And she loved them both. And now she was falling in love with a third man. Would he be cut from the same cloth?

She was still sitting up when she fell asleep, left hand thicketed in Books' hair.

-29-

The next day the morning news was full of the coming cold spell. It had been predicted for a while, but the forecasters were now more confident, their prognostications darker. Snow, ice, blizzard and freeze.

Books said, "Do you have an emergency kit in your car?"

Emily started to say she had, thinking of the chocolate and the joints, then realised that he meant things like shovels and torches.

"I'll get you the basics. You ought to have them."

"Thank you."

He didn't approve of her coat either, so she promised to get one.

"Right then," he said.

He had already been for a run, shaved, showered, made breakfast, washed up both his breakfast and their supper from the previous night, was dressed and ready to go into the office. Emily had showered and was sitting around in one of his T-shirts. She hadn't eaten anything and didn't know whether she was going to.

"Right then," she said, echoing him.

Books gave a military nod, they kissed, and he marched out. She knew he wanted her to be more like him, so, by way of experiment, she tried. She didn't do anything drastic, like going for a run, but she did eat something, wash up, get dressed and make the bed. In the same spirit of investigation, she even hoovered the living room, which didn't need it as far as she could tell. She wondered why people hoovered when rooms seemed perfectly clean anyway. By the time she had done all that, she realised she was going to be forty minutes late for work and bolted out of the flat, leaving the hoover in the middle of the floor.

Cold was whitening the streets and she was stuck behind a lorry scattering grit. There was a white-blue sky above, with what looked like frost at its edges. She spent too much time looking up at it and almost ran smack into the back of the gritter when it stopped at the lights. Only the metallic patter of grit against her bonnet alerted her in time.

From the car park to the office, she felt the shift in temperature. Books was right that her coat, which was a blue woolen affair, was too thin to keep out any real cold. Then again, she lived in a world that had doors, walls and central heating, so Books' survivalist anxieties seemed a little out of place.

When she got to her desk, there was not a queue of senior officers angrily demanding explanations for her absence. Indeed, it looked like no one had noticed at all, which didn't say much for her impact on world affairs. She waited for the mail which hadn't yet chugged its way over to her desk. She couldn't quite bring herself to sit prettily and wait, so she made tea and spent ten minutes chatting to Shona, who wanted to know all about her day out with Webster yesterday. Emily lied and said that Webster was lovely to be with.

"Honestly? Oh my God, you are too nice, really!"

She made up for her gossip-failings by agreeing to criticize Webster's cold weather coat, which was a padded green affair and made her look like a pensioner of indeterminate gender. It was meagre fare, but Shona seemed pleased with it.

Then she drifted over to Bev's desk. She's wasn't instantly happy to see Emily, which normally meant that she had some actual work to do. Delightful company as Emily thought herself to be, she didn't always help create a purposeful working atmosphere. This time, though, she was as good as gold.

Bev had been allocated the tedious task of collecting Khaled's bank records from five and six years back and seeing if she could match them against anything that cropped up in Flowers's record.

The Flowers end of things was easier to work with. Because she earned essentially all of her income in cash, her bank records showed a few college related items, such as charges for rent, a parking permit and a bookshop account. They had all been settled by bank card or standing order. Little else showed up. Investigation was also made simple, because they still had the entire data set from the earlier investigation. Everything filed and boxed, nothing missing. Because they were now reaching far back into Khaled's past, the data they had for him was patchier. A tidy-minded engineer, he was pretty good at his record-keeping, but not perfect.

"There's nothing here," Bev complained. "I mean, I've started listing all the places where Aftab spent money, but since Rose hardly ever used her bank card, I don't know why that helps." Bev wasn't normally one to complain, but the spectre of Webster's icy disapproval was making her anxious. She was the only copper Emily knew who always referred to victims by their given names. "Half these places don't even exist anymore."

Emily saw her point. She had tried the Internet for help, but businesses that had changed their name or gone defunct in the last few years were hardly likely to have web pages still operative.

"The library should have some old Yellow Pages," Emily said, and a couple of phone calls proved it.

A prissy-voiced person on the other end of the phone started listing their collection in date order.

"That's wonderful," she interrupted. "My colleague will be over in a few minutes to pick them up."

Prissy voice told her that she couldn't let reference material leave the building. Emily told her she would if they sent a van full of uniformed policemen and seized it. She said something betokening sour surrender and Emily grinned at Bev when she replaced the phone.

"Get the volumes for Cardiff and Swansea," Emily said. "Check any dead businesses against the directories, mark them on a map, and see if any of the places are close to the university or places where we know Flowers or students hung out. You'll get a map of those from the note on the first enquiry."

She scrutinized Bev's list of Khaled's credit card payments. He was always mobile.

"You might want to make sure you get Yellow Pages for the whole of the South West and Midlands, she said. "Better safe than sorry.

Bev nodded. "Thanks, Em."

She started winding herself into so much woolen outerwear that she began to resemble an accident in a knitting factory. The library was a bare ten-minute walk away and the cold front, the real one, had not yet arrived.

"You'll be all right, won't you? You can have my scarf too if you want."

Bev looked puzzled, then anxious, then decided she was joking and laughed. Emily would have gone with her, except that she had spied the lovely internal-mail cart tootling past her desk and wanted to sup of its bounty. Bev left but, instead of going to her desk right away, Emily spent some time studying Khaled's spending habits. Not just the historical data which Bev was interested in, but the more recent stuff too. Dates. Places, figures. Orderly columns that might offer a peep into murder.

They would certainly offer a peep into his personality. Whenever his spending was essentially invisible, he held the purse strings tight. They knew, for example, that he used price comparison websites for his utility supplies, his broadband service, his home and car insurance. He had no private health care. He wasn't mean, but he was careful. And yet, when it came to spending money that people might see, that flashy edge was always there. A spring break in Dubai last year. A week spent in Jordan this year. Designer suits. City breaks to Lausanne, Doha, Vienna, Cairo.

That prickling feeling she'd had off and on recently intensified again. It was a good feeling. A sense of being in the presence of the dead. She printed off all the data that Bev had compiled, then fiddled around on the system until she found his tax returns and printed those as well.

She had started by thinking that Rose Flowers had nothing to do with Khaled. Khaled, however, had, as she saw it, plenty to do with the violent death of Mark Mortimer. She still thought the latter, but was now less sure about the former. The fact that Flowers once danced in a bar where Khaled drank was, as far as she was concerned, the weakest of weak evidence. There must be literally thousands of people in South West Wales who saw Flowers in her tiny bikini. That Khaled was one of them was hardly more remarkable than any other big-city coincidence you could think of: sharing a bus route, having the same postman. But still, it was the angle that Webster was bombarding with her massed artillery. It was the angle that was sending the much bescarved Bev out to do battle with sour voiced librarians. Was it, maybe, the angle that was making her prickle now?

In the incident room, they still had the 275 'persons of interest,' but all the papers in the centre of the board had been moved aside, to be replaced by a photo of Flowers, a photo of Khaled, and a thick black line running between them. Someone had adorned that black line with a little red cutout heart. Mark Mortimer's name wasn't on the board anywhere.

Paper poured from the printer until the output tray overflowed. She grabbed the pile and took it to her desk, where on the top of her regular mess and clutter was a plain manila envelope with a small bulge at one end and a smudged, unreadable postmark. She opened the envelope, removed the memory stick, brought up the documents it contained. She couldn't conceal a grin at the joy of investigating.

She called Webster and told her about her treasure.

Webster arrived and stood beside her, looking at the documents on the screen.

"Someone wants us to know something," she said.

"Yes. Someone does."

Emily wasn't lying. Althea and Tristan. Maybe Khaled. And then there was Rose Flowers. Her, her parents, her brother and sister. She felt the pressure of those people, the living and the dead, clustering around her desk. She felt crowded by them, and Webster's bad-tempered presence didn't make it any easier,

They stared at the list of file names on the screen. An incomprehensible amount of data. A mountain of secrets.

-30-

Police work always moves in circles. The witnesses stay the same, but each time around you drive a little closer to the target.

In one way, the archive from Precision Tools had been disappointing. In another way, it was a game changer. It had been disappointing because it was hard to see anything awry. Neither Emily nor Susan Konchesky, who had been assigned to help her, was an engineer or an accountant, but the material they had looked through so far seemed exactly what they expected from a mid-sized engineering company. Tedious, orderly, baffling.

On the other hand, any real secrets were not going to be blazingly obvious. If, for example, the company had been running drugs from Gibraltar, they'd presumably have ensured that any related documents were encoded in some way. So for all Emily knew, they had been looking at a mountain of incriminating data that they didn't yet know how to interpret.

One thing they had found was that El Saadawi, the Egyptian businessman whose car was on Marine Parade that time, was one of Precision Tools's buyers. That was an interesting fact to Emily, because she knew about the Marine Parade incident and no one else did. Even so, it was elusive. Saadawi was, presumably, visiting Khan. But why shouldn't he? There was nothing wrong or even underhand about a major buyer visiting a company's owner. Emily knew nothing about business, but presumably those sorts of contacts were part of how stuff got done.

In any case, the main thing was that Webster was now certain that there was something there worth investigating. From her point of view, she had three pieces of evidence all pointing in the same direction. In mounting order of importance: that weirdly unproductive interview with Dunbar, the memory stick, the assault on Johnston. She knew the memory stick didn't quite mean what she thought it meant but still: Johnston was assaulted and her little altercation of Marine Parade did take place. There was something there, and Webster knew it.

So committed was she to this new line of enquiry that it was she who ordered the re-interview with Stephanie West. Susan Konchesky and Emily were to conduct it, and tape it. They discussed taking West down to a police station for a formal interview, but instead settled on requisitioning a patrol car so that West's neighbours would see the police presence. It's the sort of non-intimidatory intimidation that can work very well. It can sometimes force disclosures from people who are reluctant talkers, not hardened criminals.

They arrived at the appointed time.

Same kitchen. Same sulky, pretty Stephanie West. She was in a grey pinstripe skirt, boots and a camel coloured polo neck. The police car was visible through the kitchen windows. The kids were not yet back from school yet, but Emily was wearing Althea's shell bracelet just in case. She made coffee, which neither Susan nor Emily wanted or asked for, and banged things around to show how petulant she could be. Which was fairly petulant.

"I've put milk in. There isn't any sugar," she said.

Emily didn't respond directly; just turned the tape recorder on and gave names, place and date. Because Emily had interviewed West before, she led. Konchesky was present so that they could confer if anything unexpected arose.

"Ms. West, are you happy for me to call you that? Or should we call you 'Stephanie?'

"Yes, either."

"We're here in connection with the suicide of your former husband. With his conviction on drugs charges. And with the murder of Aftab Khaled."

She didn't answer, preferring to pull her sleeves down over her hands, tuck her chin into her polo-neck and give eyes that smouldered. If Emily were a man, she thought to herself, she'd probably roll over onto her back and drool with desire. As it was, she wanted to slap her.

Emily continued with the basics. When she met Mark Mortimer. When they married. When he joined Precision Tools. She gave her answers resentfully and briefly. After a while, she said, "I should probably have a lawyer here. Aren't I supposed to have a lawyer?"

"Why? We're not charging you with anything. Do you think you need a lawyer?"

"No."

"And you would be prepared if necessary to swear on oath to that effect?"

"Yes." The reply was mumbled.

"Your former husband. Prior to his arrest on drugs, were you aware that he had any involvement with the drug trade?"

"No."

"Did he seem like the sort of person to be involved with drugs?"

"Well, obviously."

"What do you mean?"

"Well, he was arrested, wasn't he? He pleaded guilty."

Emily wasn't getting the sulky kitten eyes anymore. She was getting a woman's eyes with tears in them.

Better. She felt Susan glancing her way, and gave her a little micro-nod to let her know that she'd observed the same things.

"That's not what I asked. I asked about your impression of him prior to his arrest."

"Then he was arrested and...."

"And everything went to shit. Everything."

The tears were spilling now. West's self-absorption was now exposed. She was not crying for her husband, but for herself. The girl she was, the woman she'd become. It explained something too, this reaction of hers. She must have known her husband was an improbable drug dealer, yet she seemed oddly ready to see him as guilty nevertheless. But in her world he was guilty. Of hurting her. Of spoiling her cocooned little life. Of getting into some dark and dangerous little corner with no regard for the possible consequences. West was still angry at that betrayal. Angry enough that she'd treat him as a drug smuggler, though part of her knew he wasn't that. Angry enough that she'd airbrush him from his children's lives.

"Did he have any concerns regarding his employment at Precision Tools? Concerns about the legitimacy of any aspect of its business?"

Emily got a shrug rather than an answer.

"Stephanie, we need a yes or a no."

"Look, Mark didn't talk to me about any of that. There's a cottage he used to go to. He shared it with his brother and sister. We used to go as a family, in summer mostly. It's a bit...."

She made a face. A face which said, "I'm too precious to deal with anything muddy, or wet, or rustic, or basic."

"The address of the cottage. Please." Emily was all business now. She gave it to her. A place in the Black Mountains.

"He used to work in this cottage?"

"Yes."

"On a project that he kept secret from you but which, to the best of your knowledge, was connected with Precision Tools?"

"Yes." Her answer was so mumbled that she was made to repeat it. Not so much for the tape recorder's benefit, but to remind her she was in the presence of two police officers, who could mess her life up if they so chose.

"That project. Are there papers or computer files connected with it? Yes or no?"

"I don't know. Not here."

"In your former home? In the cottage?"

"Not in my old home, but in the cottage, maybe. I said I don't know."

"We may need access to the cottage."

She shrugged and said nothing. Emily's voice hardened.

"Stephanie, we're asking for permission to enter that cottage. If you say yes, we will go there discreetly and investigate discreetly. If you say no, we apply for a search warrant, in which case we will force entry and we won't attempt to be discreet. It's your call."

"You can look around, I don't care. I don't go there."

They talked about access and Stephanie told them about a key which had been left somewhere. In an outbuilding, she thought. She was either being obstructive or genuinely didn't know.

Outside, Emily saw the kids arrive back from school with their grandmother. They were shepherded into the living room. She asked a few more questions, going back to the issue of whether she, her husband or her children had been threatened. But she'd got the hang of the interview now. Her answers got ever sulkier and briefer and the line of her polo-neck was level with her lips.

But they'd got what they needed. Emily snapped the tape recorder off, conferred briefly with Susan, then said, "Thank you, Ms. West. You've been remarkably helpful."

They didn't leave at once, though. Emily went through to the living room. Tristan and Althea wanted to see her, she could tell. They wanted news. They wanted an answer to Tristan's question: 'Was it a mistake?' They knew their father was dead, of course, but they wanted a hero dad, not a suicide dad or a criminal one.

Emily didn't know if she could deliver the former, but she'd stopped believing in the latter.

She showed Althea the shell bracelet. "We're still trying, we haven't stopped trying," she said.

They said their goodbyes and Konchesky drove. As they passed the Gloucester junction on the M5, Emily said, "It's probably worth taking a look at that cottage in the Black Mountains."

Konchesky shrugged, "I suppose."

-31-

Books had been as good as his word. The back of her car now boasted a snow shovel with a giant red plastic scoop, a torch, a tow rope, a sleeping bag, bottled water, chocolate, biscuits and a spare can of petrol. And some snow chains, which she promised him she would practice putting on before driving anywhere, but which she couldn't see herself using under any circumstances. She had also promised again to buy a proper coat. Also to take gloves and so on, but most of her clothes, including her cold-weather gear, were at home and not Books' flat.

Emily's promises weren't always worth much, she mused uncomfortably. She picked up the shovel and wondered what it would be like to use it. It looked like an object designed by men for men. And in any case, she was standing in a car park with no snow anywhere around. The temperature was chilly, but hardly arctic. Nothing felt real.

She slammed the boot down and got behind the wheel. Her exhaust plumed briefly in the air behind the car. Ahead of her there was a row of leafless trees and the slate water of an Atlantic Wharf. A man dressed in a dark coat over a suit appeared, looked at her, got into a Volvo and drove away. Emily wondered whether his boot was full of giant red snow things.

Just for a moment, she had no idea why she was there, where she was or who she was. It wasn't a disconcerting failure, more a temporary lapse., like an elderly lady mislaying her glasses or a garage mechanic groping for a spanner. And sure enough, she found the missing knowledge before much time passed. She rehearsed a potted history to herself as she prepared to drive.

"I'm Emily. I'm driving up into the mountains to investigate murder. My boyfriend is Books and I was the person who taught him to read. I am working on a murder investigation run by DI Webster and she has the authority for this trip."

She laid these pieces of knowledge in front of her. Some of them made sense, but others didn't. She understood about driving up into the mountains. She understood about the murder and the investigation. She could feel Khaled's chuckling interest in her labours and Mortimer's sad despair. The journey out of the city was fine. No snow. No ice. No multi-vehicle pileups or lines of shivering refugees re-enacting the retreat from Moscow. The radio reported heavy snow in Scotland, Northern Ireland, North Wales and Pembrokeshire. Eight inches of snow over the Pennines. But she didn't live in those places and wasn't going to them either.

She took the motorway to Newport, then turned off to Cwmbran and Pontypool. Scars of coal mining hung over her. Pit explosions and dead miners. Towns built on corpses. Then through the mining belt to Abergavenny and the mountains beyond. Mortimer's cottage was in the Llanthony Valley, the most easterly of the valleys that divide the Black Mountains. Not far past Abergavenny, she made the turn left for Llanthony.

This was a different world. The valley narrowed as it climbed and there were pastures and snippets of woodland on the valley floor. Green fields pasted as high up the mountainsides as technology and climate could take them. The flanks of the hillside were grizzled with the rust-brown of bracken, humped with gorse and hawthorn, slashed with the rocky-white of mountain streams. There wasn't much on the roads. A tractor carrying a roll of hay, an agricultural 4x4 with a couple of sheepdogs panting in the back and an old Rover 25 driving at twenty miles an hour.

Just for once, the pace suited her. She wasn't in a rush. She could feel Khaled and Mortimer, of course, but she thought about Books too. Why, of all the girls in the world, should he choose her? Was he simply making a mistake or did he see things that eluded her? Human relationships weren't her strong point, so she genuinely didn't know the answer to that. And that warmth she felt toward him the other night was with her now. That warmth, glow and, yes, the moist feeling as well. All that nonsense in the boot of her car was placed there by hands of love. She felt grateful and humble and loving all at once.

She thought it was how other people felt. How they felt if they were lucky enough. As lucky as her.

At Capel-y-ffin, the way divided. The main route headed up to the valley head and the passed over the mountains to Hay. Her fork cut to the other side of the stream and ran up a side valley to a dead end. Both roads were real Welsh mountain roads. A car's breadth wide, no more, and hedges almost brushing her on both sides. If she met a vehicle, one of them had to reverse to the mouth of a gate or a field turning. And when the fields ended, the transition to open moorland was abrupt. Exposed and dangerous.

Mortimer's cottage was one of a straggle of houses linked by the dead-end road. Once, she supposed, each house would have been its own tiny farm. A few bony acres yielding a scant living in good times, a starvation diet in times of hardship. These days, the fields were probably all operated from one big mechanized hub farther down the valley. These houses, including Mortimer's, were relics of that earlier age. Adapted now for holiday rentals in the summer, vacation cottages. Dinosaurs.

She drove slowly, searching for the right place. She would have asked someone but there was nobody around. On the far side of the valley, she could see a farmer on one of those quad bikes rounding up the sheep, but he was three miles away though the crystal air.

She got all the way to the farmstead at the end of the road. There were sheep shuffling in a barn and a dog barking somewhere inside, but no one to ask the way. She turned back down the valley and this time saw the entrance to an unpaved track, with a carved wooden board marked Pen-y-Cwm. Her car was a city pool car, poor dear. She pointed its wheels at the alarming slope above her and cautiously, in low gear, started to floor the accelerator. The surface was atrocious. Grey aggregate laid over rock. Streams had formed in the paths of the tyre tracks, washing away any smaller grit and leaving the occasional violent hole in the path. The car's bottom hit rock deafeningly once and there were a couple of other scrapes, but she got to the top in one piece.

Pen-y-Cwm. In English: the end of the valley.

Up there, she could see why it was named this way. The land flowed away from the house in one long liquid scoop. It was closer to the buzzards above than the cluster of houses down valley in Capel-y-ffin. The city felt utterly remote. A myth. A rumour once heard, never believed.

Mortimer's house was built of local stone, hard and grey. No whitewash. No snuggling into the mountainside behind. There is a little stand of rowans, mountain ash, but nothing larger. Nothing offered shelter. A stream poured off the hill behind the house. The crash of water onto rock.

No lights on, no car outside.

She was expecting neither. When she and Konchesky had discussed this visit with Webster, the main question was whether to arrive with a brace of uniforms and a forensic specialist, just in case. They all agreed that didn't make sense. Not yet anyway. They didn't actually know that there was anything there. Susan Konchesky was meant to have come with her, but she never really wanted to, and found an excuse to cry off. Webster let her go on her own, because there wasn't much reason not to. Her job was simply to ascertain if the site held any secrets, if it called for a major deployment of resources. It was the sort of task that would take forty minutes, if that.

She tried the door to see if it was unlocked. It wasn't. She turned, so she was standing with her back to the grey house, looking out at the fall of the hill. Ravens bickered in the valley. The distant farmer had his sheep gathered in a flock and was headed down. She looked out for the black and white dots that must surely have been there too, and finally saw them. Sheepdogs loping in bracken. A friendly sight.

The rowans clustered around a low outbuilding. A pigsty once? A small barn? The key was there, according to Stephanie West, so she got the torch from her car and peered around. There were some gardening tools. A bit of kids' stuff: toboggans, a paddling pool, the limbs of a plastic climbing frame. She heaved junk around looking for the key, without joy, then turned back to the doorway. The wall was rough stone, in poor repair, but there was one stone that looked looser than the rest. Looser and more polished. When she put her hand to it, it slid out easily. Something glimmered in the shadows and she reached and took the key out.

The front door unlocked easily. She wasn't certain that there'd be electricity up there, but there was. The lights flicked on. The place was as cold as a tomb. The main heating was provided by night storage heaters, which meant that by that time tomorrow, the house might be getting warm. In the meantime, she found an oil-filled electric radiator and turned it on, thermostat turned up to maximum. For good measure, she went into the kitchen and turned the electric stove on as well. She was already regretting not having bought that coat.

Silly girl, sensible Books.

But a bit of cold wouldn't kill her. She started to explore.

The living room had a mustard coloured carpet laid over old stone flags. A black wood burning stove, two red sofas, and a non-matching armchair. Some cheap pine bookshelves filled with books. A windfall from past bestseller lists. Some tatty boxed board games. On a windowsill facing down the mountain a pair of binoculars and a bird watching guide.

The kitchen was similar. China and glasses, plentiful but cheap. Some plastic picnic ware. A mismatched assortment of pots and pans, but enough to cook with. The cupboards had some basics; salt, sugar, oil, some candles, a bag of tea, a scrunched up packet holding some penne pasta, a bottle of malt vinegar, but nothing more.

A downstairs toilet smelled of some chemical pine freshener. There was a boot-room for coats and spare wood.

The vibe was comfortable enough, but low budget. Stephanie West's worst nightmare. She messed around for just long enough to get used to the space, but wasn't downstairs where any secrets would lie.

She headed upstairs, where everything was carpeted and felt newer. Three bedrooms, bland and neutral, and a tiny bathroom tiled in blue and white. The bathroom had frosted windows, though the nearest neighbours would have needed a telescope to see anything. That plus a change in the curvature of the earth, because, as far as she could tell, the house was out of sight of everything else. You didn't get much farther from people than this.

The room she was after, however, was none of these. The 'study' that Stephanie West referred to was really little more than an alcove on the landing. A small desk. A laptop. A lamp. Books. Files. There was a little bit of corkboard behind the desk pinned with photos of military hardware. Boys and their toys. Soldier porn. Books didn't keep anything like that. She turned the light on and got the laptop fired up.

Back in the city, Webster had a team exploring the data dump from Precision Tools. She was confident, Emily thought, that it held some answers, but so far as she knew nothing suspicious had yet been found. She wondered if she should have been there instead., but was pleased she wasn't. It was colder upstairs than down, so she rummaged around in the bedrooms until she found a huge Arran wool jumper, man-sized XL, and it hung around her as though a hot air balloon has collapsed and died on her. She was as cold as she was before. She had hiking boots in the car instead of her stupid office boots, but couldn't quite face going to get them.

The laptop was ready for action and she sat in front of it, expecting a torrent of secrets to come pouring forth. The first things she tried yielded nothing, however.

There was no internet connection up there. Mortimer could have brought a mobile dongle with him, perhaps, but the only web browser she could find was years out of date and the pages stored in history didn't seem to be of any special interest. In any case, her phone didn't get a signal up there. Perhaps other networks had coverage, but it was not likely. It wasn't the kind of territory that got phone executives hot and sticky with excitement.

So next, she tried to find any documents stored on the hard drive. There weren't many. Some letters and what looked like some school projects. Althea and Tristan were too young to have authored those. but their cousins, Mark's nieces and nephews, were presumably the right age to have compiled 'reports' on the Tudors, fossils, and the Battle of Britain. A giant history sandwich.

She found something more interesting when she came across some technical documents, but she didn't understand the language involved. The document headers were effectively in code. Not secret-agent-speak, just a combination of engineering- speak and office acronyms. The documents were headed with things like 'MC Shpt 110305.' They contained mostly compilations of technical specifications. Stuff that seemed to Emily as being broadly similar to the data she had abstracted from Precision Tools. Same sub headings, same layout. She should really have brought that other data with her, but she was really expecting something simple, not some arcane technical conundrum.

She wasn't immediately sure what to do, so she went downstairs and filled the kettle and made tea, which, sadly, was not herbal. There was no milk either, so she had to be content with a strong black brew that a builder would have enjoyed. Contrary to her usual habit, she added sugar, to take away the taste of the metallic mountain water, the strongly tannined tea. It tasted like sweetened bog water, but was nevertheless somehow welcome. A comfort against the cold.

As she left the kitchen, for the stairs that rose directly from the living room, she noticed what must have been obvious from the kitchen window. It was snowing. Big, heavy flakes, falling with a calm insistence and a sense of purpose.

Against the grey sky above, the flakes looked black, like imperfectly burned coal ash settling back over a mining village. But the ground below gave the lie to that. It was already covered; sheeted in white while she was at the alcove upstairs. Every field, every hedge, every stroke and line of moor and mountain. The rowans stood black fingered against the white. Farther down the hill, little stands of oak and hawthorn seem to have contracted into two dimensions. Given up colour and volume for purity of shape. The naked essence of tree.

She stood at the window for a while, watching.

Because she was who she was, and because she was where she was, she couldn't help but feel the terrible peacefulness of death. It was as though the world had given up on life, as though the sky was shredding itself and scattering its remains. One giant burial, robed in white.

It wasn't a bad feeling at all. On the contrary. It was calming. Under other circumstances, she would have allowed herself to sink into it. Relish it. For a while she just stood at window and watched the landscape disappear. Cardiff was no longer even a rumour. Abergavenny lay on the outer edge of the world. The storm and fury of Webster's police investigation meant nothing up there. The rules, the files, the tasks, the duties. All that stayed real was that whitening mountainside and the presence of those who died. Rose Flowers. Mark Mortimer. Aftab Khaled. The two halves of the human race joined by this snow. A temporary unity.

She didn't know how long she stared out at the scene, but the untidy realities of the present summoned her back.

It was four in the afternoon and the light was failing. She needed to leave immediately or spend the night there. There was no option really. The lane was already under two inches of snow and the temperature was below freezing. There were steep hills and sharp turns on the road back into Capel-y-ffin, and she didn't trust either herself or her car to navigate them. Still less did she want to attempt it at the onset of more than fifteen hours of darkness.

She left her bucket of tea and bustled around trying to be sensible. Books style sensible. Very cautiously, she turned her car, then took it, skidding, to the bottom of the drive. There was another hideous encounter with a rock about halfway down, but the car still seemed to be in one piece. She was guessing that there would be tractors or four-wheel drives moving in the morning. Once they'd dug out the road for her, she should be able to slide down their tyre tracks into the valley bottom. And if the worst came to the worst, she could always walk. If she allowed enough daylight, she couldn't see herself getting seriously lost.

She checked her phone again so she could text Webster, but there was still no whiff of a signal. It was annoying, but not the end of the world. Books would worry a little, but he would know she was likely to be out of signal.

The next issue was getting through the night as warmly and safely as she could. She changed into hiking boots and grabbed Books' biscuits and chocolate. She ploughed her way back up to the hill to the cottage. Hard work. Not just the steepness of the hill and the uncertainty of the track, but the snow was already thick enough that she could feel it dragging against every movement. She was panting by the time she reached the front door.

The next issue was heating. She was wearing the ridiculous Arran jumper with her coat buttoned over it. The jumper's sleeves were so long that she used them like gloves. There was not a glimmer of warmth from the storage heaters, but they'd presumably start kicking out heat in the morning. The oil radiator was ridiculously underpowered for the size of the property, but she supposed it was only there to top up the storage heating. She did, however, manage to rustle up paper, firelighters, wood, and matches and get a fire burning in the stove.

She thought how little Stephanie West would have liked this way of life. The room was still cold, but between the stove, the radiator, and her unerringly fashionable outfit, she was warm enough. She threw out the tea and made a fresh mug. She brought the laptop down from the alcove, along with a heap of Mortimer's files. Thinking about it, she went up and dragged down a couple of duvets. The only room in this house that was going to be even half warm was the living room, and she could sleep well enough on one of the sofas.

Food was the next puzzle, but one with a refreshingly simple solution. There was nothing to eat except the stuff she had brought up from the car, plus the pasta, oil, and sugar from the kitchen. So she would eat that. She wouldn't starve.

She made a nest of sofa cushions and arranged the duvets around her like some Ottoman sultan. The laptop snuggled with her in the centre of her nest.

She realised that there was something about the way police officers work that was utterly inimical to real investigation; or at least, inimical to the way she liked to work. The office was about institutions and procedures and all the false realities of any large organization. None of that stuff made any sense up there. All she had was words that a dead man had written, there in the place where he wrote them.

She lit a couple of candles and turned the living room lights off. She decided to work by candles, the light of the laptop screen, and the red glow from the stove.

She turned her attention back to Mark Mortimer. Already she knew she was going to find what she had come for.

-32-

Outside the cottage, the early evening darkness hardened into something blacker. Emily could see a single light from her window, from a barn, miles away in the valley. Aside from that: nothing. A black sky, no moon, a million stars.

The cold was intense. It was chilly enough inside the house, with the stove burning non-stop, but she ventured outside a couple of times, simply to see and feel the diamond hardness of the night, and the cold had a physical presence she'd read about but never previously experienced. Waterfalls were being frozen into place, trees stiffened, the air clarified, the ground plated over with iron.

She liked it. It was easier to feel herself at times like these.   When she got hungry, she ate Books' biscuits and when she became hungry again, she cooked the pasta.

Most of the time, though, she spent with the laptop and the files. She knew the answer was there. It was just a case of finding it. She decided to read every piece of paper, examine every computer file. By eleven in the evening, she had more or less accomplished that. No joy. She had a notepad filled with little questions to herself. Things to check later. Things to check when she was in a warm office with access to the internet. But nothing screamingly obvious. Nothing that felt like the secret for which Mortimer died.

She made more tea. She probably hadn't drunk as much caffeine as that in her entire life. It felt okay though. Part of the experience; clear, not buzzy.

Back at the laptop, she was uncertain what to do. She had tried every Word document, every spreadsheet. There weren't many e-mails and those that there were,

were very old and presumably dated from the period before the laptop was brought to this cottage. She didn't really know her way around Powerpoint, and Mortimer didn't quite strike her as slick-presentation man, but she couldn't find any Powerpoint files anyway. She was puzzled by the puzzle.

West's silences virtually confirmed it. Johnston's head wound and the incident on Marine Parade Drive certainly did. But what was the mystery? Had Mortimer hidden some documents somewhere in the house, or the loft, or outbuilding? She spent an hour or so rummaging around everywhere she could think of; examining floorboards for loose nails, that kind of thing. She didn't venture into the outbuilding, because it had no power, and she needed daylight to search it, but mostly she ended her search more certain than ever that the laptop had the answers. Somebody didn't come up there to hide stuff. Just by being there you were hidden anyway. And it wasn't as though Mortimer was on the run from anyone. He wasn't. He lived an ordinary life and had a good, ordinary job. Until things went pear-shaped with his prettily petulant missus, he probably had a regular, happy family life too.

So the computer was the answer. She heaved more logs on the fire, resettled in her nest, and went back to the screen.

File Manager this time. She wanted to make sure she understood where all the files were. As soon as she did so, she realised what she'd been missing. It was a 'doh' moment.' Mortimer was an engineer. Of course he used Microsoft Office from time to time, but that wasn't the centre of things for him. There was a program on the computer called Solid Edge and she opened it. It was a CAD program: computer assisted design. It had heaps of files associated with it. In terms of memory usage on the hard drive, there was almost fifty times more data associated with Solid Edge than with everything else put together.

Here. The answer was here.

She wasn't an engineer, had no training in Solid Edge, and didn't know exactly what she was looking for. But she fooled around learning how to open files, how to look at what they contained. It was slow work, and she was starting to feel tired, hungry and cold, but she got the hang of it.

Shapes appeared from the computer. She found she could revolve them, inspect them. Virtual steel turned by virtual hands. Tubes, rings, flanges, gears. Countless things whose names and uses she didn't know. A mass of associated technical data and computations. There was a kind of beauty in it all. A flowing exactitude.

A lot of it looked like the data she had taken from Precision Tools. She hadn't yet looked at the technical drawings in any detail, but presumably the two datasets had a lot in common. On the other hand, the Precision Tools data was far more copious than this. This was an oldish laptop and its hard drive was barely one third full. This data was carefully selected. Those selection criteria would, she was certain, be key to the riddle, but how to know what they were? How to guess?

Then she realised that Mortimer worked up there. That is, he didn't just examine documents brought from work, he did creative modelling work of his own. By tracking back on the document histories, she could find the documents that he either worked on or created up there. She went through her notes marking the documents that seemed to have had extensive work, and those that didn't. The files divided into two sets. If there was a forged hollow tube in the set of files brought up on disk from Precision Tools, there would be an analogous file created up there. If there was a gear coupling in the Precision Tools dataset, there would be a gear coupling created up there. Pinion rods. Moulded steel.

She understood something else as well. There was no technical data, no calculations. Then it clicked. Mortimer wanted to understand those shapes for himself. He needed to understand them the way any engineer would; through maths and through design. So he rebuilt them from the ground up, reverse engineering the technical data from the shapes.

The Precision Tools dataset was impoverished. It contained pictures, but not the maths. Up there, Mortimer reconstructed the maths. And the maths taught him something which would end up killing him.

At six in the morning she made more tea and took it outside with the rest of the biscuits. The stars were gone. Someone had come along in the night and stolen them. Cloud has rolled in again and it was snowing once more. She had come out in the giant jumper, her coat and a duvet over her shoulders, and it was still cold. She wondered how long her wood would last.

She went back into the cottage. Her eyes needed a rest from the computer screen, so she prowled the house, still wearing everything, including the duvet.

In the living room, she topped up the stove. There was a weak heat starting to come from the night storage heaters. In the kitchen, she boiled a kettle again, not because she wanted more to drink but to create a little heat. In the boot-room, she counted the logs on the pile. There wasn't many there, but if the storage heaters worked properly, she should not be so reliant on the stove during the coming day.

Upstairs, the bathroom was so cold there was ice on the inside of the window. The bedrooms were bland and dull. She was about to go back downstairs again when her eye fell on the alcove.

Tanks. Artillery pieces. Rocket launchers. This was what she had been looking at all night. Weapons. Not the whole assembly, but individual parts. One of the photos was of a tank firing in a desert somewhere. The gun barrel had a distinctive shape. It wasn't a single smooth tube, there were areas of greater thickness, parts that moved. She'd also seen that exact object downstairs, floating in a 3D void. She didn't recognise it because she didn't know what she was looking for. She thought it could be because she was a woman that her mental attic didn't have that kind of stuff kicking around. All the same, there wasn't much doubt in her mind now. Another hour's work and there was no doubt at all.

From the photos pinned to Mortimer's wall, she could identify at least six different weapons parts, plus three other possibilities. That still left numerous files without an obvious link to weapons, but she doubted if she put the whole lot in front of a procurement officer at the Ministry of Defence, she'd learn exactly what those links were. The unlicensed export of weapons is a serious offence. And, though she needed to check, Precision Tools held no export licences, She'd bet her life on it.

Stephanie West's words from that original interview came back to her. 'He had this Saint Mark thing going. Butter wouldn't melt and all that. Then, what is he, really? A drug dealer who was busted and sent to jail.' She couldn't have been more wrong and her children's silent belief in their father couldn't have been more correct.

And this, she bet, was the story. Precision Tools decided that the manufacture and export of weapons parts would be a profitable, if illegal, sideline. Mortimer found out what his employers were up to. He made certain that he was correct before making any accusations. No doubt he discussed the whole thing with Khaled. No doubt, in his patient engineer's way, he became remorseless and obsessive in documenting the entire profitable, lethal scam.

He pissed off his wife. Neglected her. Nudged her just enough to get her started on her path of sulky self-pity. The one ally he might have been able to trust was increasingly lost to him.

His employers somehow found out. Or perhaps he told them. Either way, they decided to destroy his life. And did. Framed him on a drug smuggling charge. Something so clumsy, so crass, that if he had wanted to fight it, he probably could have. But she bet they also threatened him. His wife, his children. Told him that if he didn't accept his time in jail, his family would all be killed or injured.

So he took it. Saint Mark took the drug charge. Lost his job, his wife, his means of making a living. Accepted that he couldn't take the risk of divulging what he knew. A martyr to his own purity of purpose. The suicide, she guessed, was simply the outcome of all that. When your life is completely ruined, what's the point of continuing?

Other parts of the puzzle started clicking into place too. Some clearly. Others dimly. Like water trickling under ice or a weight of snow settling on a roof.

And that was fine. She didn't need the whole thing immediately. She had what she needed. She was still wearing Althea's little bracelet. She touched it and promised her and Tristan, once again, that they were going to drag this whole mess out into the open.

Their father: not a criminal, but a fighter for justice.

How much difference would it make to the children to know that? She thought it would make all the difference in the world. She imagined Tristan's serious dark-eyed little face when she told him that it was all a mistake.

It was past 7 am. And still dark. Nothing had moved on the lane and nothing would until full daylight. The snow was above her boots now., still falling, still beautiful.

She decided to get two or three hours' sleep, then get down the hill early enough so that she could walk if she really had to. She had enjoyed her night up here, but there was almost no food left and not much wood. She was exhausted, she realised. Bone-tired. She pulled her nest closer to the stove, added logs to the fire and was asleep within the minute.

-33-

Emily awoke achy and cold. It was dark and she knew that was wrong. Her watch told her it was early afternoon. She had slept for almost eight hours, which was unusual.

The room was dark because more snow had fallen and the window was occluded. A dim white light filtered. The room was not supposed to be cold, but the stove had gone out long ago. The storage heaters should have been burning the place up but they weren't. A moment's experiment showed that all the electrics were dead. None of the switches had tripped, so it must have been a full-scale power cut. Hardly surprising, she supposed, and, up there, engineers wouldn't be racing to restore power.

She needed to get out of there, but her brain was feeling muddy after too much sleep. There was only half a packet of biscuits left. Otherwise only oil and sugar. She shoved the biscuits into her pocket and trod carefully down the drive to see if her car would start. It was completely buried in snow. The door was frozen shut, and she had to use all her strength to free it from its bonds. She inserted the key and uttered a quick prayer to whichever god protects sporty little cabriolets of dubious mechanical reliability. She turned the key and the engine fired on the second attempt. She muttered a quick thank you to the god in question.

There had been vehicles moving on the lane. There were tyre tracks already partly filled in, but at least they pointed her in the right direction. She was a little uncertain as to whether she'd be able to get her car out of the drive and onto the lane, but she set to work with Books' precious shovel. It was indeed oversized, but needs must when the devil drives. She worked hard until the car stood clear of its snowy curtains. Clear enough, at least, to identify a way through to the lane.

Emily knew she had to chance it. She knew she would have to drive over a little ridge of snow and turn hard through ninety degrees, to avoid ramming the hedge ahead opposite. She knew Books would have an instinctive feel for how to do this. 'Back up a little, Emily. Rock it, don't let the wheel spin. Easy now. No, no, half-lock only. Don't try to force it.' Books would ease that car out onto the road and make it look as easy as pie. My lovely Books, she thought.

Emily's technique was different. She tried easing the car over the ridge, but there was nothing doing. Then she started to panic, revved the engine and gritty snow flew in a gale of fury from her front tyres. The car stalled. She was able to restart it and left it running while she hacked away with the shovel again. She wished Books was with her.

When she considered she had cleared enough of a path she stopped digging. She tried the car again. At first nothing happened, then the car shot forward out of its rut. She turned the wheel, skidded, slid straight into the bank opposite, bounced off and ended up pointing downhill, the right way, square in her tracks. Sheer good luck! She drove a few yards, just to check the car could do it. Her thinking was now completely clear. She went back up to the house, unmade her nest, put the duvets back on the bed, washed anything she had used in the kitchen and dried it. She put everything back in its rightful place. Webster was a stickler for these things. West gave her permission to enter the house, not to eat all the food in the kitchen and sleep there overnight. She didn't want to provoke complaints. For the same reason, she took off her supersized Arran jumper and left it back in the drawer where she'd found it.

She made sure she remembered to take the laptop as it was evidence in relation to a major offence, and she didn't want to run the risk of data being lost. She left the house, returned the key to its resting place and slid back down to her car. She swished she hadn't left it so late. The light was dimming behind thick cloud, but she wasn't too concerned. She planned the route in her mind and decided that if for any reason the car got stuck, and it might, she would simply follow the tyre tracks by foot. It was no more than a few miles down to Capel and probably not even as far as that to the first inhabited house. It was cold but hardly murderous. She had a torch. She planned to walk quickly, and, if that didn't work for any reason, she would spend the night in the car. She had a sleeping bag, water and chocolate. The petrol tank was nearly full, so she could run the engine through the night if necessary. She would get through it. She wasn't worried.

She changed her wet hiking boots for her dry office ones, which were easier to drive in. Proceeding with extreme caution to use police speak, with headlights on full beam, she started to creep down the hill.

34-

She wasn't about to win prizes for extreme cold weather driving. She was going so slowly that when she came to a slight rise in the road she didn't have the speed or traction to ascend. She scolded herself and considered what her lovely Books would do. He'd ramp it up. She reversed up the road as far as she could. The snow was cold enough and hard enough that the existing tyre tracks nudged her back onto the road whenever she started to drift off. She moved forward with more speed and got higher up the hill this time before coming to a stop, wheels spinning uselessly on the ice. She reversed again farther than before. Thus, she moved forward faster. Emily was excited as this time she sailed up the hill with no problem and was so pleased with herself that she had to stop the car to enjoy the moment. In the valley far below, she saw the first lights twinkling through the twilight.

Emily felt a rush of something. It was the familiar warm glow and it was accompanied by happiness, excitement and pride. Books would be proud of her. With that thought, the warm glow turned moist and she allowed herself a few precious moments letting herself feel it. It was also, of course, the computer she had on the back seat. The fact that she was right to explore Mortimer.

She knew she was a good investigator, she expected that of herself, but she had surprised herself with her driving ability in the snow. That was something she had never done and she expected herself to be plain useless. During the last twenty-four hours she'd lit fires, cooked pasta, made tea, kept warm, shoveled her car out, got it out onto the road. That didn't make her Books, she knew, but a girl's got to start somewhere and right now she felt pleased with herself.

She drove on and arrived at a fork in the road. She couldn't recall it being there. One way looked a bit more road-like, but there were tyre tracks, or no recent ones anyway, and the other route looked freshly driven. Peering cautiously down the slope, she saw, joy of joys, a pair of red lights. Lights attached to that thing of beauty: a Land Rover 4x4. Not caring now, she turned down the hill and drove up to the back of the Land Rover. As it saw her coming, it ploughed off into the snow to let her past.

She didn't want to pass it because she preferred to stick close and let it watch her all the way down to the bottom at Capel. So she passed the 4x4 and stopped. Stopped for two reasons. One, to stay close to her saviours, and, secondly because the track ended at a low barn, standing just above the rise of a stream. This wasn't the road; it was a field. It was a dead end.

She cursed softly to herself. She was pretty certain that her sporty little town car wasn't going to have the muscle to climb back up the hill. She had a choice. Either get the Land Rover to tow her or just dump her car and retrieve it later. Silly girl, she thought to herself. Pride before a fall.

She was about to change back into her hiking boots to go and talk to the farmer, when she saw that the farmer had swung his car around, pointing it back up the hill. The Land Rover cut its lights. The two men tramped towards her through the snow, but she couldn't see them. It wasn't fully dark yet, but almost.

One of the men came to the passenger side of the car; the other to the driver's side. She had wound her window down to talk to them, letting the cold air in. They were not, however, a farmer and his mate and they weren't there to rescue her. They were her 'friends' from Marine Parade. Jaw Man and Silent Man. The men who, she'd bet, had killed Khaled.

Fear has a colour. A taste and feel. Cold, mostly. That's what she noticed. The chilly touch of adrenaline finding its way into remote places. The tips of her fingers, the soles of her feet. There was also a cold burning in her ears. The taste was like an absence, she thought, a mouthful of cotton wool, except it was emptier than that. Her mouth felt both choked and as if it was biting down on a vacuum and that same vacuum filled her stomach. She felt scooped out. Empty, like one of those corpses on the pathologists table that look vaguely normal but whose cavities have been filled out with pipe insulation and Sealed Air plastic bags.

These people had come to kill her.

"Evening gents," she said.

Silent Man got into the cramped little back. Jaw Man got into the passenger seat beside her. She let them because she could not stop them. She wasn't sure how they knew she was at the cottage, but then she realised they didn't know. She was sure they, or their employers at Precision Tools, had some kind of hold over Stephanie West. They'd either threatened her or paid her. In any case West must have felt worried enough by her visit to contact them. To mention that she seemed to have an interest in the cottage. That was likely enough the first they knew of the cottage, so they had come there to clean up. When they arrived, they found Emily there too. Two birds with one stone.

When West called whoever it was she called, she probably didn't mean to kill Emily, but she also wouldn't have bothered to think through the possible consequences of her actions.

One loose word, one dead body. Not her concern. Emily could hear her voice in her head now. "I don't want to sound awful. I'm very sorry and everything."

Petulant cow. She should have given that slapping.

But Silent Man and Jaw Man didn't kill her or hurt her. They didn't even seem to want anything from her. They took the laptop and just walked it over to their Land Rover, dropped it on a back seat and sauntered back again. Then they just sat in her car.

On her left was Jaw Man, Scottish. The broken jaw looked both normal and not quite like something was askew, but in the poor light it was hard to see exactly where the problem lay.

Behind Jaw Man was the other man, who hadn't yet said anything audible in her presence. Her car was a three-door convertible and though there was space, it wasn't really the sort of space designed to accommodate reasonably large, reasonably well-padded contract killers. But that was not really her issue.

She waited for them to say anything or start anything, but they didn't.

"This is fun, isn't it?"

No response.

To the Scotsman whose jaw she broke, she said, confidentially, "How's the jaw? Bit sore, maybe?" Since she still got no response, she pushed a bit harder. Turning around to the man in the back, she said, "Did he have to drink through a straw? Or did you have to bottle feed?"

The man in the back chuckled, and said, "Something like that."

He was wearing hat and gloves and so was the other man, but they didn't remove them even though the car was warm. She thought they were being cautious about DNA. She liked to see that in a contract killer. Professionalism. Attention to detail.

"Dunbar," Emily said, "Jim Dunbar at Precision Tools. He's sort of got the motivation, but does he really have the pizzazz? I mean, you're a fairly top-end pair of murderers. I don't think Dunbar is quite in your league."

No response.

"But maybe you don't know about things like that. Why you kill the people you kill. Maybe you're just given a name and a face. Aftab Khaled. He lives here. He looks like this. Go kill."

No response.

"Whose idea was it to copy the Rose Flowers killing?" To Silent Man, she added, "I'm guessing that was you. I think your friend might be a bit stupid, yes?"

There was still no response and the silence was getting tiresome, so she changed the subject. "Okay, shall we play I spy?" There was nothing in the sweep of her headlights except snow and some trees. The barn too, dimly. "I spy with my little eye something beginning with S."

No response.

She gave them two minutes by the dashboard clock to think of something, but they didn't manage it. She gave them the answer. "It was snow. I'm slightly disappointed to be honest, I was trying to start with something easy."

"Ja, I thought of snow." The man in the back. He had an accent of some sort. Not British. Scandinavian, she guessed, and he looked Nordic. His eyes were dancing with amusement. He was enjoying this. His Scottish buddy just glowered at her, or avoided her gaze. She didn't think he liked her.

"I don't know your names and it seems a bit weird doing this without them. You are...?" She asked of the Scottish man, but got no answer. "Ross, is it. Hoots mon and och aye the noo." Her Scottish accent was dreadful. "You know, your jaw looks a bit funny." She turned to the man in the back. "It does look funny, doesn't it? I'm not making it up."

The man in the back shrugged, but it was a gesture. A communication of a sort. His eyes were laughing.

"What shall I call you? Bjorn? Ulf? Sven? Mikel? Olaf? Jakob?" Her well of Scandinavian names was beginning to run dry, but the man rescued her.

"Olaf. We'll go with that"

"Ross and Olaf. Okay. This is nice, isn't it?"

They sat around some more. She switched her lights to sidelights only. The engine was still running and the car was warm.

When she cut her headlights, she sensed, or thought she did, a ripple of alertness from her two silent companions. There was no point in having lights up there, except as a signal. Were they meeting someone here? Now, that was an interesting thought, she mused. If so, she guessed it was Khan. Dunbar could have been a possibility, but what she said to Ross and Olly about him was true. She bet he knew what was going on, but he was too small-time to hire killers. Not enough skin in the game.

Emily said, "Just so you both know, DI Webster knows I'm here and why. So does the entire chain of command. So does, Books and he won't be happy. You need to think long and hard about that. He's not a man to be crossed, believe me. Plus, the connections he has would amaze you. I wouldn't risk that kind of amazement if I were you. Not good for your health."

As she said those words, she felt them. She knew Webster was unaware of what she had found up there in the cottage. She sent her there. She debated sending a team in and decided against it. It was meant to be Emily and Susan Konchesky, but when Susan weaseled out, Webster sent her anyway. Emily agreed with that decision, lobbied for it, but Webster wasn't one to shirk responsibility, legal or moral. If something happened to her, she'd be on the case.

She realised something else too. That she did now belong to the police. To all intents and purposes, she was part of the family. She wasn't the most popular member of that club, but she belonged nevertheless. She was actually more like a wayward daughter, but she also knew something far more significant. If something happened to her, Books would not be lenient. He still had his bolt-cutters, which he kept as a souvenir of the Quentin Legard affair. He wouldn't hesitate to use them either. Also, he had already learned a great deal from Ray Quinn and Frank, and he knew how to deal with these two. Overall if anything happened to her, there truly would be a shit-storm.

She felt a pricking in her eyes. She knew what that pricking meant. Not tears, but whatever came before tears. She had cried once since childhood. This moment wasn't the second time exactly, but it come close. It was the best feeling in the world because dead people can't cry. She bet their eyes don't even prick.

She was sitting there, thinking these things, when she noticed that the lights on the dashboard seemed dimmer than they were.

Olaf said, "You need to turn the engine off and on again."

It seemed logical enough. The starter motor tried its best when she attempted to re-start, but found the task too much. It as an error, she knew.

Olaf, reading her mind, said, "I think there maybe is a small electrical fault with your alternator."

Emily didn't know what an alternator was. She assumed it was the thing that recharged the battery. In any case, it was clear what they'd done. It was they, not the snow, that cut power to the cottage. They wanted to drive her out of there and they did. And at the same time, while she was sleeping, they sabotaged her car. They drove down into this lonely patch of nowhere and kept their tracks fresh enough and deep enough that they could be sure she would follow. How sweet. How beautifully simple.

She tried the engine a couple more times, but each try was weaker than the last. Ross opened the door and the car's temperature dropped immediately. Both men were dressed in heavy boots, down jackets, gloves, hats. They had probably got thermal undies on too, she surmised. Emily, by way of contrast, had a thin blue coat and opaque tights.

Olaf said, "Can I have your coat, please?"

She thought about that. She could fight, of course, but they were prepared for that. There were two of them each was much stronger. She could try running, but couldn't outrun them. Not uphill, not in snow, and not while wearing slipper-soled boots.

So she got out of the car, took off her coat, folded it and handed it to Olaf. He thanked her. She was wearing black trousers that she normally wore to the office. Tights. Wooly socks. A long-sleeved T-shirt with a polo-neck over the top. That's all. The cold was already starting to bite.

"And maybe the pullover."

"That was harder for her to remove. Scarier, but she handed it over and received a polite thanks in return.

She wondered if there was going to be a sexual attack. As a woman, she couldn't help but wonder, even when she was about to die. But, to Emily, this pair seemed too professional for that. They wanted the emergency services to find a hypothermia victim, not a rape victim.

Ross, meantime, was patting down the car. He found the torch and the sleeping bag. The things that might keep her alive. He did something to the torch in the snow and killed its light. There was a brief discussion with Olaf about the sleeping bag, which she gazed on with longing. She couldn't hear their muttered conversation, but it ended with Ross taking the sleeping bag to the Land Rover. She imagined they would take it back up to the cottage and leave it there. Books, the only person who knew that it was in her car, would assume she just forgot it at the house. Typical Emily, he would think. And he would, most of the time, be right to think so.

Poor Books. This would be very hard on him.

"The last part," she said to Olaf. "The very last part. I'd like to be left alone, if that's okay."

He thought about that briefly, but nodded. "Sure." He held eye contact with her. "It's quite fast, you know. And after a while you don't feel much."

He was trying to be nice. "Thanks."

Ross came back. The two men completed their check of the car. They were looking for blankets, tools, anything that might help her out of this. They didn't find anything. The car battery was pretty much dead now. There was a dim spark left in the headlights, but almost nothing.

"Can I get back in?"

"Sure."

We got back in, though Emily's was the only door that was closed. The other one was wide open and a convertible isn't exactly the most heat-proof conveyance at the best of times. A faint breeze, a whisper of air, no more, wandered through the car. It was profoundly cold.

They were sitting in the same configuration as before. Emily on the driver's side, with Ross beside her and Olaf behind. He had her coat and jumper folded on his lap. He took her phone, checked it for signal, which registered zero, null points, forget-about-it. He returned it to Emily.

"You can write texts if you like."

She wrote her last words to Books, her Mum and Dad, Ant and Kay and Ray Quinn. The biggest stones in her jar. She told them she loved them. That they've been her important people. That she wished every good thing in the world for them. None of it was original or clever or witty. Not one word of it. But it was real. Her eyes were pricking again. If she hadn't been so cold she might even have cried.

She loved those people, loved them with all her heart. Nothing else mattered. Not really. She hoped Books and the others knew that and she wished she had more time to communicate. More time to express those thoughts.

She was shivering now. Shaking with cold. As she was completing her texts, her fingers were jittering on the keys. She handed the phone back to Olaf, who wordlessly scrutinized her texts, checking she hadn't said anything about how she came to die there like this. She hadn't. She was too cold to think of anything like that. In any case, that wasn't the most important message for her right now.

Olaf said, "Okay." He got out of the car and walked up the track into the darkness, coming back a few minutes later without the phone.

"They'll find it. I've made sure they'll find it."

"Thank you."

They sat in silence.

These were the minutes in which she would die. Temperature was not a feeling anymore. It wasn't like a spectrum of colour, a range of smells. Cold and pain were the same thing. They'd merged, become one. Colder meant more painful. A pain that expressed itself in every part of her body, which was now compulsively shaking.

"Ross?" She said.

He turned to her. His stupid, gingery, violent face. She shot her right arm out and struck his nose as ferociously as she knew how. With the heel of her hand. He clapped one hand to his face. The other hand wanted to get right on and murder her. He might even have done so except that Olaf physically restrained him.

"To match his jaw," Emily said to Olaf. "Even things up."

Olaf was somewhat amused by that, but mostly pissed off. Emily had broken their lovely little murder in the snow compact. Taken the sweetly amiable edge off it. More to the point, there was blood all over the car and they had to clean up. Olaf released Ross's arm but growled at him not to touch her. There was a fierce authority in his voice.

He ordered her out of the car and guarded her as Ross wiped down the surfaces. But there was a limit to what he could do. There would still be blood in the seams of the leather seats. Blood on her trousers and shirt. They couldn't take those things if they wanted this murder to look like an idiot girl getting lost in the snow and dying of exposure.

Emily didn't know whether anyone would order forensics on this crime scene. Why would they? There was little enough that would look suspicious. It would be totally like her to get stuck in the snow; like her to be underdressed; like her to set out at night in an unsuitable car; like her to forget her sleeping bag. If they came, that spray of blood was a lovely little clue that could lead straight to the murderer, but no one may ever find it.

But maybe not. Webster would be the grim angel of this investigation and she wasn't one to undercook things. She had sent Emily there. She would do it right. And Books. He would be unstoppable. She wished she could see that. There would be no hiding place for these two, and their ending would not be quick. Books was a creative thinker when the mood took him. She knew it would. Not even Ray Quinn or her father would be able to stop him and she knew they would have no reason to try. They would stand aside, wave him on, and smile at their protégé.

They kept her standing there, with just a t-shirt. Practically naked. Punishment. They were long, freezing minutes. The cold was bewildering now. Her feet were burning with the cold. A fire she couldn't step out of. Her hands were the same. But what was worse were the shudders from within. She could feel her body retracting into itself, like the last warm ember in a dying fire. She tried to say something to Olaf and heard herself slurring the words. Her tongue was lolling about in her mouth, useless as whale meat. Any movements she made were gross, clumsy. On the edge of failure.

She didn't know how long she stood there. When she was too cold to stand anymore, she fell over. More minutes passed. She wasn't even shaking now.

Finally, Olaf said, "I think it's time you had your clothes back."

He handed them to Emily, but she couldn't put them on. She wasn't being tactical or obstinate or anything else, she simply couldn't co-ordinate her movements.

She thought there might even have been tears in her eyes by then, but not real ones. Not like when she was thinking of Books and her family. Just eyes watering with the cold.

She found herself being lifted by the two men and bundled into her clothes. Ross held her arms behind her, twisting unkindly, while Olaf fastened the buttons on her coat. They lifted her into the car. She pressed into them as they did so, wanting to snatch any glimmers of warmth from their bodies. They were not returning her clothes to keep her warm. The clothes wouldn't be sufficient to protect her on a night like that, even if she had any body heat left to conserve. They were just setting the scene for this final act.

She didn't object. She preferred having her clothes back. It was close now. Emily's death was close. Olaf was right. It was a kind death in a way. You expect a lot of things from dying. Coldness. Stillness. Silence. Pain. What you don't expect is the great clumsy stupidity she was experiencing. A blanketing idiocy, brought about as blood retreats from the inessential organs, like the brain, to the only two things that ultimately mattered by then. Heart and lungs. She didn't know which of those two things would fail first. She only knew that she would not be conscious when it happened. Any pain she felt was receding now. She was too cold for that. So cold, she could hardly feel the cold anymore.

She said to Olaf, forming her words as carefully as she could, worried that she had already lost the power to form coherent syllables, "Please. Go. Now."

He studied Emily. She assumed he was Swedish or Norwegian. He obviously knew his snow and if he had military experience, which was more than likely in a professional killer, he'd have done plenty of arctic survival training. He knew hypothermia as well and its passage to death. He was looking to make sure that she was on a path from which there could be no return. In his expert eyes, she was on that very path.

He said, "Okay."

He and Ross walked off back to their car. They were leaving her there to die.

-35-

Emily had spent more of her life with death than almost anyone. Not the shoot-bang sort of death. Ray Quinn, her father, Frank, and now Books, all traded in it. Or, at least, in its prevention and revenge; its causes and effects. Her experience with death, however, wasn't external. Not something encountered on the point of a gun, the tip of a blade. It was internal. She didn't confront death, she was dead and lived it. Her illness made sure of that. That doesn't make sense to people who haven't been where she had. To the tiny handful of those that have – well, there's no other way to describe it. They have been dead: lived it and breathed it. Some very few of them even survived it.

You don't encounter something like that and emerge again normal. For long years after it had subsided, after she was no longer officially sick, she still saw death's yellow teeth grinning at her from every corner, every shadow. Those years, in some weird way, were even worse than the ones that came before. She found the struggle for life harder than being dead.

That struggle had abated in the arms of her beloved Books. He had come along and made her know what it was like to live without struggle, sometimes almost without fear. But she never thought she would plant her flag permanently on Planet Normal. That planet was not hers. She hoped to possibly acquire papers permitting residence, even naturalization, but its gravity, its soil and atmosphere, would always be absent. They would never be hers.

She had not thought about it before, but there was no more powerful statement of being alive than the business of dying. Plenty of lifeless things have the power of motion. Crystals grow and viruses replicate. But to die, actually to die, that's an honour only granted to the living. The cost of admission.

She was about to be so honoured. The stupid thing was she felt honoured. In so far as she retained any sensation at all, she had two things in her head. The love she had for Books and her family. Plus, the stunning assurance that she was truly alive, in her moments of death. She thought there were worse ways to die than this. Many worse.

She was too fuddled to think anything quite so clear, but these thoughts hung there in the middle distance like the golden background on a Chinese painting. Gently illuminating. Not interfering.

Which is just as well, because she was not planning to die. She rolled over onto her back in the driver's seat and lashed her booted feet at the window. Not once, repeatedly. She couldn't co-ordinate my movements at all well, but there was something in the abruptness of the action which seemed to work for her. The first few times, she achieved nothing. Then she did. She didn't even realise that she'd broken the window until she lashed out a couple more times and couldn't even find the window. It was gone.

While she was in the position, she groped for the levers that released the bonnet and the petrol cap, and pulled them both. Then she rolled over and forward trying to find a splinter of glass, only to find nothing usable at all. That stupid, stupid window was made of safety glass. It had crumbled, as it was designed to do, into a million tiny granules. None of them were usable as a cutting tool.

She staggered back to the rear of the car. She wasn't thinking anything through. She was just acting out the plan she made as she was standing, dying, in the snow.

It took her several attempts to open the back, but she managed. Books' spare petrol can sat in the way of the little hatch that protected the tyre levers. She heaved the petrol out onto the ground behind, fumbled the hatch open, and groped for the tyre lever. She had to do all this by moonlight because there was no other source of light. She knew by feel where the tyre irons were because they were where she kept her cannabis.

Leaning against the car all the way, she stumbled back to the broken window, felt for the wing mirror and smashed it. The mirror, the little darling, shattered beautifully, long, dangerous shards, reflecting starlight. She took the most dagger like of those shards and started ripping up the seats. Foam rubber burst forth. It was hard getting it out and she kept failing. Her shard broke and she had to find another. There was blood on her hands. Blood everywhere. The stitching on the seat resisted cutting. And everything she was doing was done in a dull soup of stupidity.

Somehow, though, it happened. Beautiful sheets of foam rubber. She got the first out, stuffed it up the inside of her coat. Then, because her technique had improved, she got more from the other seats. Enough to stuff down her back, down her trousers. Anywhere she could, she stuffed it in. She wrapped foam over her head and tied it with the belt from her coat.

None of this would stop her dying, she knew that. The slow leaking of heat from her body was still happening, but not as fast. When Olaf and Ross left, they drove up to the top of the hill, to get back onto the road proper. But they were pros. They wouldn't have left immediately. They would be parked there, looking down.

They'd want to be sure she didn't magic fire from somewhere, didn't summon the airborne cavalry using a micro-transmitter that had been hidden in the sole of her boot. But then once they were confident that she was done for, they would leave. Exit the crime scene as swiftly and noiselessly as they could. Start to build an alibi in some other part of the country altogether. She didn't know how long they would watch her, but she needed to outlast their watching.

When she had done all she could to insulate herself, she forced the car bonnet open. There was still some residual heat in the engine block. Not much, and she lay over it pulling her arms and legs in for whatever warmth she could find. In the old days, drovers caught out in the snow would sometimes get through the night by sheltering in the opened guts of newly dead animals. Forget the smell, feel the warmth. Emily was the same, sheltering in the guts of her car. For the first time in what seemed like an eternity, she could feel her midriff. It was cramping with cold, but that was better than no feeling at all.

She found herself daring to think the unthinkable. She might, just, make it. Only just, but she might. She needed to keep alert. It would be all too easy to drift into unconsciousness.

She tried chanting to stay awake. Counting up to twenty, then back down again. Listing all the people she knew, all the people she loved. Counting the stones in her jar. Some of her words were out loud, but most were said under her breath. Her tongue was made of wood and her cheeks were a wall of bone. She tried to notice whether the engine was still warm, whether it was still giving her any kind of sustenance.

Weirdly, she thought she had an advantage over ordinary people in all this. They were so used to having their sensations arrive in the regular way, they wouldn't know what to do under these extraordinary circumstances. But these cloaked and unreliable feelings were what she was used to, the world she lived in. Figuring out how to manage them, how to make decisions despite the fog, was her own particular expertise. Her sphere of excellence.

She lasted as long on the engine block as she could. When she couldn't any longer count to ten, not even in her head, she knew it was time for the next phase. If Olaf and Ross were still on the hill waiting and watching, she had no chance. She went back to the boot of the car. She was shocked to find that she couldn't walk. Not at all. She had to hit her legs to find out if they were there or not. She had some stupid idea in her head that they'd fallen off. She couldn't feel herself hitting her legs, but somehow her brain caught up with reality and she stopped worrying. In any case, she didn't need to walk; crawling was fine.

She got to the boot. The little tyre lever hatch. She found the little tin that contained her joints and a cigarette lighter. Somehow, on the third or fifth or tenth try she got a joint in her mouth. That was the easy bit. The lighter was harder to use. It was a cheap one, and strong fingers were needed. Emily's were weaker than skimmed milk.

She lost count of the number of times she tried to force a light. She couldn't do it. She summoned all her concentration, all her will, all her effort, but nothing happened. Her movements were too uncontrolled, but she thought her hands were still bleeding from the glass. They were slippery with blood. Her fingers were not strong or adept enough to turn the serrated double wheel of the lighter. She was dying because she couldn't turn that wheel.

Think, Emily. Think, girl.

She changed her grip, pressed the wheel into the fake wool interior of the boot and rolled it along.

Flame. Instantly flame. It excited her so much that she dropped the lighter and it went out immediately. However, she knew what she was doing now and three or four more attempts produced flame. Blue-yellow. Steady. Life-saving. She lit her joint. She wanted to do more than that. Wanted to press her face up against that beautiful steady light. She was in control now.

This time she didn't even try to walk. She just edged around on her knees, leaning up against the side of the car to the petrol cap. It was hard work getting the petrol cap off, but compared with a lighter it was child's play. She took the joint out of her mouth and threw it into the petrol tank.

There was a tiny gap of time in which absolutely nothing happened. One of those relativistic moments, where her body clock was running at warp speed and the rest of the universe seemed to be locked in slow motion. Just Emily, a car, a frozen snowfield, and a hill full of nothing.

Then it changed, with a woof of flame, so hot and intense that she was stunned by its arrival. She jerked instinctively back from the blast, but found that she couldn't. Her cheek had frozen fast to the side of the car. For some seconds, the flame was still not merely pouting from the tank opening, but actually jetting like a flame-thrower. Emily was still wrapped like Michelin Man in foam rubber as it burned back towards her hair. She ripped her frozen cheek from the car. In other circumstances it would have been a painful thing to do, but she felt nothing at all.

She was free, standing in the glorious heat of her burning car. Still utterly hypothermic. Still much more frozen than not. But, for a few magical minutes, she was not getting any colder. She felt the texture of the air change. It became alive, expansive. The torrent of flame was no longer just confined to the petrol tank. The car itself had begun to burn. Seats. Matting. Paint. Lining. She stood much too close to the delirious flame and simply welcomed its presence. Its consuming, destructive, life-giving presence.

She didn't know how long she stood there, but her returning brain kicked into gear. Her hiking boots were still in the back of the car and she tried to rescue them. She made one attempt and was pushed back by the density of the blaze. She tried again and came away with one boot. Her coat was on fire. She wasn't sure how long it had been burning. She fell over and rolled in the snow until it was out. She felt no pain. There was a huge hole in the single best survival garment she had, but she was still winning this particular game.

Or she assumed she was. Emily took a moment to look back up the hill, looking by firelight now as well as moonlight. If Olaf and Ross had seen that, they'd be back for her, but the hill was empty. Emily only had the cold to battle now. Ross and Olly were long gone. She relaxed for a while and explored her burns and embraced the heat. She could feel its crackle changing her skin. Like when you bring your hand close to a grill. Intense, but good. She tried hard not to set herself on fire again and seemed to perform the task without further hiccups.

Her brain was warming up too. She was thinking more freely again. Hypothermia is about core temperature, not surface temperature. Even though she stood close to the blaze, a few glorious minutes was not going to bring her back to life. She was gaining breathing space, nothing more. Nevertheless, she didn't care. Breathing space was all she needed. Emily was going to make it.

She checked repeatedly that she still had her cigarette lighter. Her fingers still couldn't operate it, but they would as they started to warm. There was no rush. She took a little more time to roast in the heat of the car. The gale of the flame from the petrol tank was subsiding now, but everything else was burning beautifully. The flames were starting to shift from the back end of the car to the front. The engine still seemed untouched, but she hoped it would start burning too.

Once Emily was warmed enough to have approximate control of her limbs, she jogged over to the barn. A corrugated iron roof supported on long wooden pillars and trusses. Beneath it she found hay gathered in those big round bales. The barn was two-thirds empty, but that was still one-third full. Winter fodder.

The hay was tightly packed and frozen hard. She could only twitch out a few loose handfuls, but her hope that she could just burrow into a pile of warm hay was a forlorn one. She would have to settle for arson.

Emily jogged back to the car. The engine was on fire now too. She wondered vaguely about the insurance. She was covered for fire damage, but she assumed they would not pay out when she had started the fire herself. She thought that most unreasonable. Maybe they had to if she started the fire to avoid dying. Who knew? Who cared? She could measure the state of her body by the suppleness of her mind. She was warming up. She could think again. Not well, admittedly, but she was beginning to clamber out of that great deathly idiocy that had threatened to bury her.

She spent another few minutes by the car and adjusted her foam rubber padding so that it was as well distributed as possible. Then, when the car blaze was starting to trickle down, she headed back to the barn.

Lighter. Petrol. Hay.

It took her a minute or two to make it work, but she got there. Before long, she had more lovely flames licking up the side of something flammable. The fire would be a big one, a long one. It would burn for long enough to warm her properly. And once she was warmed through, she would jog up the hill, back to the road proper, and follow Olaf and Ross's tyre tracks down to Capel. Their tracks couldn't lead anywhere else. There was only one way out of that place.

A barn fire makes a car fire look like nothing. A child's toy oven next to a catering-scale range. There were flames now reaching the full height of the building. The raging intensity of this heat forced her back, then back again. She spent happy minutes by the blaze. To hell with Olaf, Ross, Khan and the whole lot of them. She would kill them or jail them. They had messed with the wrong girl. And if she didn't or couldn't, they would meet her lovely Books and they would enjoy that a lot less.

She was thinking happy, arrogant thoughts when something struck her from above. She fell sideways onto the ground. She couldn't move. And though the air was warm, the ground was frozen hard. She heard the fire blazing beyond her feet, but felt the heat leaching from her body into the frozen earth. The night was still freezing, with hours to run until dawn.

She tried to move, but couldn't. There was blood on her head. She didn't know what was happening. The last thing she was aware of was a rumble of machinery grinding away and light descending from above.

-36-

She was swaddled like a cartoon character. Bandages on her hands, dressings on her head and arm. She was on a drip. Antibiotics. Painkillers. She was in one piece, even if the piece itself had seen better days.

The thing that knocked her down in the barn was a timber falling from the roof. It struck her on the back of the head and could have been fatal if she'd been standing farther back. She didn't know how long she was lying there, but as it turned out, it didn't matter. The farmer whose barn it was came out in his tractor to see what was going on. He found the wreck of his barn, the loss of his hay and Emily. He hauled her, semi-conscious, into his cab and drove down to his farmhouse. His wife dialed the emergency services while the farmer, whose name was Arthur, as Emily subsequently learned, picked her up, carried her upstairs and dropped her in the bath.

She was in and out of consciousness at this point. She remembered that she kept saying "tepid, tepid," because she was worried that hot water would be bad for her burns, cold water terrible for her hypothermia. Arthur didn't need her instructions. He had hauled enough sheep out of snowdrifts and didn't need any advice from Emily. He dumped her in a bath and kept her there while his wife, Rose, bobbed in and out offering tea and kindness. For some time, she could talk only with extreme slurring and used that slurring to apologise for having burned down his barn. They even, she thought, got into one of those stupid courtesy fights. Emily saying she was a terrible person to burn his barn, whilst he practically told her the damn thing needed destroying.

They couldn't get an ambulance up the hill and any helicopters were in use elsewhere. But a pair of coppers fought their way to her in a police Range Rover, with a paramedic and a case of equipment in the back.

Bouncing down the hill was agony. They took her to the hospital in Abergavenny, where the duty staff took a quick look before rejecting her. Some of her burns were third-degree: that is penetrating all the way through the skin. Abergavenny didn't have the capacity to deal with that, so they sent her straight on to Newport. Lights flashed all the way but they still never crept above fifty on icy roads.

The radio told them that temperatures in the hills were fourteen degrees below zero. T-shirt weather for Emily.

The burns unit at the Royal Gwent enjoyed the clinical conundrum that came gasping in from the Range Rover. It wasn't every day they had to deal with hypothermia and burns on one and the same patient. A junior doctor told Emily with barely concealed delight that he thought some of her toes might have frostbite. The doctor who patched her up told her that on average she was in great shape. Medical humour is a wonderful thing.

It took most of the night for them to repair her. Some skin was removed from her left buttock cheek and grafted onto her left side. There would be some scarring on her bum and she wondered what Books would say. Her side would show some marks, but should be okay. The areas involved weren't huge. No bigger than the palm of her hand. The doctors didn't regard the procedure as especially complex. They just got on with it.

Everyone was very kind. Hospital trolleys and lidocaine. Surgical instruments flashing under lights. Doctors with masks. Nurses with smiles. Surgery was carried out under a twilight anaesthetic, so she was aware of things, but not very. She tried to say that the sensation was like that of advanced hypothermia. Like being curled up on that car engine counting to twenty as stars wheeled in a distant sky. But it wasn't really like that. Here, there were people around her. Friendly ones, creating life, not causing death. In any case, no one could understand her mumbling and they told her, politely, to shut up.

A frozen dawn was greying the sky when she was finally wheeled to her bed. She was staggered at how cold it was, even at sea level in the wash of the Gulf Stream. She had never experienced it as cold in all her life. Part of her brain was still standing in that field, in that snow, handing her coat and jumper to the men who wanted to kill her, wearing a T-shirt, but feeling as naked as starlight.

When she arrived at the hospital, she refused to let anyone notify her family. She didn't want them woken, but it would be time to make that call soon. A nurse came around with a breakfast trolley. Emily hadn't ticked any menu, so she got the hospital default meal. Rubber eggs, sausage, white toast which was both a little burned and a little soggy. It was all delicious. Every morsel. She accepted the offer of more with unconcealed glee. The phone was brought to her and she made the calls to Books, Webster, her father and Ray Quinn. She told Webster not to get there before midday. She wanted time with the others first.

She hadn't slept at all; not a wink. She'd been unconscious at times, but that was different. She could feel a gathering exhaustion, ready to whack her with its great rubber mallet. She would accept that when it came, but her loved ones came first. She needed to see the stones in her glass jar. She wanted to tell them what it said in those texts. Say it face to face. Say it properly.

Books came first. His expression was jaunty when he entered the room, which turned to shock when he saw the scale of the damage.

"Bloody hell, Em."

He wanted to kiss her, but kisses weren't a good idea at that moment. One of her hands was less bad than the other, so he held that. The fingertips. Considerate to a fault.

She told him, through cracked lips, what happened. He got the abridged, expurgated version. Then she said, "Books, when I thought I was dying, I wrote you a text. It said "I love you." It said more than that, in fact, but that was the main thing. When I thought I was dying, I wanted you to know that I love you with all my heart. That was the thing that mattered to me most then. I wanted to say it to you properly now."

Books was profoundly moved. His eyes teared up. Emily's didn't but they did prick again. They stayed there like that, not quite holding hands, not quite crying. There are other ways to be alive, ways other than dying. This was one of them. She was alive now. She was with Books. She could not adequately express how grateful she was that he was there, that he was with her. That he loved her. She could not adequately express these things, but she tried.

She slept a bit with Books beside her at the bed. She knew, deep down with absolute certainty, that Books would deal with what needed to be done. He hadn't even needed to say so, but she knew, and the thought helped her sleep. She almost felt sorry for them. Almost.

She slept only briefly, because it was not long before her family poured loudly through the ward. Frank had brought a mountain of flowers, a basket of fruit wrapped in tissue paper and clear plastic and tied with a ribbon. It would take her a fortnight to eat it all and she didn't particularly like fruit. Mum brought a clucking anxiety, some home-baked brownies and a mild, implicit rebuke that getting stuck in the snow and burning upland Powys to the ground isn't something that nice girls should do. She didn't seem very surprised, though. She made it seem like Emily made a habit of it.

Ant and Kay were both shocked and excited. Kay was worried that she wouldn't get any more rides in Emily's car. Ant half wanted to see under the dressings but was half scared at what she might find there. Books stayed to begin with, then tactfully vanished to fetch hot drinks for everyone.

While he was away, Emily told the story. They were not as good at listening as Books. Her mother kept interrupting and saying, "Well, of course, dear." Her father was better. He cried openly and told her how much he, and they all, loved her. They all held hands, but it wasn't enough for him, so he grabbed Ant and Kay in his giant embrace and pulled them down onto the bed for a group hug.

It was a nice idea and the good thing about third degree burns is that the nerve endings are burned off the skin, so you feel nothing at all. Aren't even meant to. But there were enough other parts of Emily's body that did feel things, and that had been variously cut, bruised, burned, frozen, or surgically removed. She didn't particularly appreciate having three hefty bodies falling on top of them.

She screamed. Everyone leapt off the bed, but the leaping involved more pummeling. A nurse came rushing to see what the commotion was, followed by Books carrying a cardboard tray of drinks. Order gradually returned. Ant and Kay were sent to scrounge seats from around the ward and they had a kind of bedside party, with Emily cast as the Queen of Ward Six. The Bandage Princess.

It was nice for Emily. Noisy, but nice, but after a while she'd had enough and told them all to go. Her father, inevitably, resisted. He had a load of alternatives. He'd just wait in a seating area outside, sit in the car, hire a private ambulance to take her home. His home, he meant. Emily didn't want any of those things. She wanted peace; she wanted sleep. With Books' assistance, they were persuaded to leave.

Just as she was dozing off, she became aware of another figure sitting beside her bed.

"Blood hell, Em."

She recognized the words, but this time it wasn't Books. It was Ray Quinn with a huge grin, pleased at his attempt at imitation.

"I won't stay long, Emily. Just wanted to make sure you'll be ok. I've spoken to Books. I've absolutely no doubt he will do the necessary. I've retired, but I do keep an eye. He's a good man. You're in good hands. They won't be so lucky, though."

He touched her fingertips gently, looked with reassurance into her eyes and bent forward to kiss her tenderly on the brow. She slept and when she awoke he had gone. She couldn't help smiling. A man of few words. An extraordinary man. She was grateful she was on the same side.

A doctor arrived and talked about her skin graft, but she didn't really listen. She trusted he knew what he was talking about and she wanted more sleep. When she awoke again she was once more aware of a figure sitting beside her bed. Webster had finally emerged. She didn't think of her as a good replacement for Ray or Books or any of her previous visitors, but needs must. Webster had her face in her hands, bowed down, showing her grey hair in the grey light.

When Webster became aware of Emily looking at her, she straightened up. There was a lot going on in her face. Worry. Stress. Concern. Other things too, which Emily couldn't identify.

"Emily."

She nodded. "Bit of a mess."

Webster shook her head at that. "I've spoken with the doctors and...."

"I know. I'll be fine. I might lose some bits of toe here and there. They've already done a skin graft."

"Young skin," the surgeon had said, pinching it. "The easiest stuff to work with." Emily didn't say that, though. Not to Webster, not in the grey light.

Webster wasn't in ogre mode, but her other settings were rusty from underuse. She was having difficulty with her range-finding, so Emily helped her.

"There's a bag under the bed. The doctors wanted to throw my clothes away. They looked like trash. They are trash. But they're trash with blood spatters."

She told Webster the whole story. The laptop, the engineering models in Solid Edge, the weapons, what really happened in that field, Olaf and Ross. Webster asked how Emily had managed to survive and she told her that too, except she changed 'joint' to cigarette.

"Does anyone else know this?"

"No."

She spread the coat out until she found some marks. There was plenty of Emily's blood on that coat, but there was some of Ross's too. The forensics people would find both. Emily gave her the Land Rover's registration number as well.

"You think they killed Khaled?"

"Yes."

"Because he knew? Because he was going to spill the secret?"

"Maybe. I suppose so. I'm not sure about that part though. There could be other reasons."

"And the method? The dissection of the corpse? That's..."

Emily shook her head at that. As she always said, the case had always had coincidence at his heart, whichever way you looked at it. If Khaled was killed as some kind of revenge for his murder of Rose Flowers, it was an extraordinary coincidence that his death coincided so neatly with the discovery of Rose Flowers' corpse; a discovery which was essentially random in nature. On the other hand, if Aftab Khaled was being coolly murdered by a pair of contract killers, their decision to scatter his corpse was simply an inspired piece of improvisation suggested by the news spreading on radio and TV.

Webster didn't hide her disagreement. "Why do that? If, as you say, they're professional killers, why not just make a clean disposal of the corpse? Quite likely they've done it before."

Emily wasn't strong enough to argue with her, but Webster was wrong. Scattering Khaled's corpse was exactly the right thing to do. The way they found the corpse sent them chasing after connections between Flowers and Khaled instead of concentrating their firepower where it was most needed. If Khaled had simply gone missing, they'd have been forced to look at his activities in the round. Instead of being obsessed with his sexual and romantic past, they'd have been drilling away at his business contacts, among them Mark Mortimer and Precision Tools. As it was, if it hadn't been for Emily's perverse insistence on following that line of attack, the investigation might never have touched those things.

Even Webster saw the logic. "Of course, it did push the investigation toward the sexual angle. On the other hand, we don't actually know that any of this Precision Tools stuff is connected to Khaled. To Mortimer, yes, but not necessarily to Khaled."

Emily shrugged. She didn't agree with that either. The two men knew each other well. Were buddies. Fellow engineers. Both died violently. What more connection did she want? And if it came to that, the two men who tried to kill Emily did so with a bit of grace. A little flourish of invention and quick thinking. It seemed to her that the same house style was apparent with Khaled's death too.

Webster stared at Emily, who held her gaze. She didn't say so, but Emily could tell she agreed.

"Why try to kill you? That's another question. But presumably they didn't go to the cottage to kill anyone. They learned about the laptop and they went there to retrieve it. Stephanie West must have told them. They found you there. They didn't know how far their operation was compromised, so decided to kill you, take the laptop, hope for the best."

Emily nodded. She agreed but it was odd to be spoken about in that way.

"There's no phone signal up there," Emily added. "They probably figured there was a reasonable chance I hadn't managed to communicate my find to anyone, which indeed I hadn't. If you'd found me dead in a field from hypothermia, you wouldn't necessarily consider foul play. That's why I broke the man's nose. I wanted to leave a clue at least."

"I'd have found it. I'd be sure to have found it." Webster looked severe and authoritative when she said that, but she tried to jam a smile into the expression too. The smile didn't work. It looked clumsily out of place. A child's pink party bow stuck onto a formal business suit.

Emily said, "Yes."

She told Webster that she should get a log of calls to and from Stephanie West's line. She assumed the Olaf, Ross, Dunbar, Khan axis was careful about calling from untraceable numbers, but it was worth a look.

Webster nodded and made a note. "And Mortimer? Any theories on him?"

"I don't know. Perhaps he thought he needed to kill himself to protect Stephanie and his kids. Perhaps he just thought that his life was screwed anyway. Either way, he was pushed into it."

Webster picked up Emily's hand, the one nearest her, and turned it over. There was some blood leaking from the bandage. Her touch was oddly gentle.

"How did you hurt your hands"

"When I was cutting the seats up. I don't know exactly how."

She turned her hand over again, to leave it as it was, but she kept hold. They were hand to hand, fingertip to fingertip, and stayed like that for a time. Emily was not that far from going to sleep again. For a while they just drifted in the silence. But there was something else Webster needed to say.

"We won't get a conviction for what happened last night. Not a chance."

"We might," Emily replied.

"It's all very well having Ross's blood on the coat. That proves that you were in contact at some point. But we've got no way to prove when or where that contact happened. We can't even show that a crime took place. The word of a police officer: that's all. And it's not enough. For a modern jury, under modern rules of evidence, it's not remotely sufficient.

"They're good," Emily said. "They were careful last night. Gloves all the time. Hats. Wiping the car down. They didn't touch me even when I smacked the Scotsman. They'll have been professional about Khaled too. Very clean. Careful about CCTV, number plates, forensics. All that stuff."

Webster nodded. "We'll see."

There wasn't much more to talk about. The world outside was still very grey, very cold. Webster said they were talking about the coldest winter on record.

Emily fell asleep still holding Webster's hand. When she awoke, darkness had fallen and she was on her own.

-37-

A cold world spun. Time organized seconds into minutes, minutes into hours, hours into days. Emily was released from hospital. She went to her parents, because Books needed to be attending to the matters in hand, and because she was still not much good for anything.

She had her old room back, filled with flowers. Frank had ordered special support pillows from a supplier in London and a contraption that fitted under the mattress to raise and lower it like a hospital bed. She laughed at him, but it was nice to have. He put a TV in there too, and, with her mother, she watched recordings of Downton Abbey.

She spent hours with Ant and Kay too. Kay bought her a phone, with most of her savings money. She also collected clothes and her laptop. Her mother went shopping and bought a winter coat for her, which was weirdly similar to Webster's granny coat. Kay took it back and brought her something from Monsoon instead. Fur-trimmed. She also got, at Emily's request, a proper padded coat, the sort of thing people go skiing in. Sort of Michelin Man. It was going to be a while before she walked out under-dressed for the cold again. That wasn't logical: Olaf and Ross would have removed any coat she'd gone out in. But somehow it made sense because even the idea of cold was frightening now.

Ant just liked snuggling with her. She'd worm right in alongside, except that there weren't many bits of Emily that wanted a wriggly thirteen-year-old bumping up against them, so she piled pillows up against her side and let her bump against those instead. They did a school project on herds together and she told Emily about what was happening on Facebook and the music she was into.

Books visited too and they skirted the real subject by discussing office gossip and partaking of some low-intensity kissing. He wanted to know, a bit upset, why she hadn't told him what she had told Webster. He felt that Emily didn't trust him.

She looked at him like he was an idiot. "I didn't. Of course I didn't."

She explained. If Books had known how she came to end up in hospital that morning, he'd have hardly been able to keep his feelings under wraps.

"Em, you know it's okay to have feelings."

"Yes, my dear Books, but your feelings would have ended up letting my father know what happened. You might not have meant it that way, but...."

"You think he'd...?"

"Well, what do you think? How do you honestly think my father would react if he knew someone had tried to kill his daughter? I want them behind bars, not propping up some building or motorway."

Books saw this logic. His mouth fell open with it. To him, a line had been crossed and those who had crossed it would be subject to his special kind of punishment.

"Bloody hell, Em."

It wasn't long ago that she had heard that same expression. She looked at him with love in her eyes, and thoughts rushing in her mind. She thought it must be strange for him, finding himself romantically involved with the daughter of one of the country's most ruthless and shadowy figures, who never forgot or forgave anybody who posed even the merest hint of a threat to his family. A man who was afraid of nobody, now that his mentor and predecessor Ray Quinn had retired and passed the mantle to him.

Books had taken to being one of the anointed inner circle with alacrity, and was now building his own reputation. The accidental chopping of somebody's digits with his bolt cutters, and then his own part in the final demise of Quentin Legard in an earlier adventure, had cemented his place in the scheme of things. Ray Quinn's legacy was being built upon as Frank oversaw the coming of age of Books and now, Emily. It wouldn't have been what he foresaw for himself when he was scraping a living on the mean streets of London not that long ago. How life had changed for him. Not least because he could now read and Emily had walked into his life, along with Ray Quinn and Frank. He had traded his genetic family for a new one. Life's like that: it never serves up what you think it will.

The conversation moved on and they watched a bit of TV and cuddled. After a bit, she wanted to sleep and Books took himself off. It had been a nice, peaceful, contented time.

Emily wasn't ill. She described herself as 'a bit knocked about.' Her burn wounds needed gentle treatment for a few weeks, but her cuts were already healing. The tips of her toes were, in some cases, black, but the cheerful junior doctor at the hospital told her that the rule was 'frostbite in January, amputate in July.' So she knew her toes may need surgery at some stage, or they may not. In any case, there was nothing to stop her working so, when she wasn't watching Downton Abbey or protecting herself from a wriggling younger sister, she worked.

She tried to do two or three hours each day, retreating to the sweet enchantments of Operation Takeaway. She was missing the briefings, and the incident room, inundated with scraps of paper, but she had the intranet and her phone. Webster was now investigating, as well as Flowers and Khaled, the matter of possible illegal arms export, the possible framing of Mark Mortimer, and any threats that may have been made against Stephanie West. Oh yes, and the small matter of the 'attempted murder of DC Emily' on which a team of three was now labouring full-time.

It was clear that the dramas of Capel had revived Takeaway. Interest from senior command had revived and there was a new intensity about the operation. Emily knew part of it was for her sake, and she appreciated that. She got a home visit from none other than DC Kirby, who sat awkwardly on the edge of her bed and praised her for her courage and resourcefulness in the line of duty.

She thought it was seeing one of his young female officers in her nightdress that made him awkward and smiled to herself. She looked at her hands and said, "Thank you."

Webster phoned to ask if she had any suggestions about reviewing those engineering drawings from Precision Tools. Emily knew a man called Stuart Brotherton, an engineering lecturer at the University of Leeds. She knew him when he was a junior research fellow at Cambridge. He was her first ever drug dealer, but Webster didn't need to know that. She told Stuart what they needed and why.

Emily also logged into the secure network and kept up to date with what had been going on while she'd been adventuring. It was less than she hoped. Although Webster's demand for more manpower was now being treated sympathetically by those above her, the cold weather had drained the force of resources.

Officers were managing blocked roads, failed power lines, abandoned vehicles and supporting a programme that aimed to protect the elderly against the cold. Until the weather relented they would be struggling to cover what they needed to do. However, progress was slow rather than absent.

She clicked through to Bev's researches. She had listed, with remarkable neatness and clarity, every payment made on Khaled's bank card, every payment on his credit card. The same for Flowers, though her transaction record was so meagre as to be almost silent.

Bev's work was wonderfully literal. When Khaled bought stuff from Tesco, her notes reported, 'Tesco: large supermarket.' When he spent seventy quid at the Swansea Bay Yacht Club, her notes said, 'Swansea Bay Yacht Club: primarily a yacht club. Also windsurfing and similar recreational/social activities.' She could see why if you were a Webster or a Jackson, you want plenty of Bev Rowlands on your team, not so many Emily's.

But still, Emily had her uses. She spent hours studying Bev's spreadsheets. They were things of beauty. A life photographed in data. The commercial imprint of a man. And these things were strangely informative. She checked some websites, phoned through to the yacht club, called up and studied as many photos of Flowers as she could find.

Her orchard of knowledge grew another apple. Flowers and Khaled. The leg and the lung. Her grinning blonde head rising from its barrel of oil. His freshly scattered parts gleaming in the local mud. She still felt close to Rose Flowers, but she had a better relationship with Khaled now too. That mobile, ambiguous face felt friendly, not just evasive. She realised, also, that she thought of them as a pair, Flowers and Khaled, the way you think about friends who are dating steadily.

Her colleagues were excited because Khaled might have led them to an arms smuggling ring, as though that was where the glamour and excitement really lay. For Emily, all corpses counted the same. One dead body might lead to Precision Tools. Another to nothing more than a love poem lost down the back of a sofa. There was no eminence there, no lowliness. We are all equal under Death's scythe.

She silently apologised to Rose Flowers for her colleagues' mood of indifference and promised her that it was temporary. She admitted to herself that she'd been a little neglectful, in truth. Because she'd had to work hard on Khaled and Mortimer, she hadn't quite given Flowers the attention she deserved.

In the meantime she researched Saadawi. Some of the websites she needed were in Arabic, but the English language Egyptian Gazette had a story which seemed to identify Saadawi as a businessman with trading and construction interests, whose brother was a procurement officer in the Egyptian defence ministry. She thought of it as a smoking gun.

She also researched Precision Tools' other buyers. The company boasted a Libyan buyer. Also Lebanese, Moroccan and Saudi. She couldn't find obvious connections between those names and defence or security services, but there was a limit to what she could do with Google alone, and she hadn't been on the case for long. She mentioned those things to Webster, who told her brusquely that she already had a pair of DCs on the case.

Stuart phoned her back the afternoon after getting her data. It was Emily's third day at home. He told her that she was correct. Precision Tools made bits and pieces for all manner of people, but a sizeable portion of its business appeared to be manufacturing parts that were suitable for weapons. Blast protection equipment for trucks and armoured cars, gun barrels for tanks and, probably, a whole lot more besides. She asked him to send all the details to her in an e-mail.

When it arrived, it was carefully circumspect and didn't contain enough certainties to secure a search warrant. It was reasonable suspicion at best, but she forwarded it to Webster.

Emily then spent more time on Bev's spreadsheets. They spoke to her differently. Four years ago, before Mortimer started having his suspicions, before anything irreversible had happened, Khaled took his holidays in Spain. Later on, Khaled's holidays changed. Dubai, Jordan, Lausanne, Doha, Vienna, Cairo. It only took a few more clicks to figure it out.

She was still grinning when Webster called.

"I'm going to raid Precision Tools tomorrow morning." She briefly spelled out her intentions. Five vehicles. Two dozen coppers. Arrive at 6.30am, an hour before dawn. Gain entry. Seize files. Seize computers. Interview all members of staff. Interview top management under caution.

She asked if Emily wanted to be there. Stupid question.

"Are you alright to move? I don't want..."

"I'm fine. I just won't kick down any doors, if that's okay with you."

Webster responded with her normal lighthearted grace and wit. She wanted to send a car for Emily, but she didn't want that. Instead she said, "Idris Khan owns the company. He lives on Marine Parade in Penarth."

She thought about that, then said, "Okay. We'll take Khan in first." She gave details of where and when they were all meeting.

Emily said, "We'll need to interview him, of course."

"You want to?"

"Yes."

She thought for a moment, before responding. "All right. Mervyn Rogers leads. You support."

Emily nodded, then, because nodding isn't a brilliant telecommunication technique, she said, "Yes."

"And you both stay in close touch with me. No flying solo."

The temptation was too much for Emily. "As if I would!" She continued before Webster could pounce. "Did you know Swansea Bay Yacht Club doesn't do boat hire?"

"What?"

"Nothing."

Webster said something growly and hung up.

Emily got out of bed. Apart from short visits to the bathroom, she had avoided moving around, partly because her healing skin was still fragile and so wanted to be moved as little as possible, but also, bed had been the most comfortable place to be. Since she had not needed to be anywhere else, she hadn't forced herself. It was time for that to change. She pulled off the T-shirt of Kay's that she'd been using for a nightie, and examined herself in the mirror. What she saw was okay, if a little bit bashed around. Walking felt a little strange, because toes turn out to be oddly important when it comes to balance and she still didn't have full feeling anywhere that had been blackened by frost. Nevertheless, she was on her feet and not falling over. She felt achy and sore, but she felt achy and sore in bed too.

She found it odd examining herself like that. When she was staring into a shop mirror with Kay, she couldn't connect with her own visual image. She seldom could. Now, however, she had no difficulty with that at all. Her face didn't seem particularly to belong to her, but the rest of what she saw prompted a feeling of belonging, of recognition. This was Emily. This petrol-scorched, frostbitten, snow-burned, glass-lacerated body was hers. She felt a kind of kinship with the thing in the mirror and the brain in her head. When she moved, the mirror beast moved and it made sense. It all made sense. She stared at the mirror until not just the body but the room behind started to blur.

She ran the taps and went through a normal soap and water routine. She chomped some Aspirin and then got her mother upstairs to help change her dressings. She dug through the clothes that Kay had brought her, and opted for leggings and a jumper, and boots. She didn't recognise herself in the mirror, though. She called her beloved Books. They indulged in something close to phone sex for a while and then he promised to pick her up once he'd done at work. She was back in the saddle and it felt good.

-38-

Long before dawn the next morning it was still astonishingly cold and snowy. Her alarm went off at four fifteen and Emily peeped through the curtain. She was expecting to see polar bears. Emily liked the virginal whiteness of it. It had the added bonus that she was not being left to die in it. The rendezvous was at the station at five thirty. Because of the snow, they couldn't just scream along in a blaze of sirens. They needed to creep there and, because Webster was in charge, no one dared be late.

Books got up, showered and dressed. He chose the sort of clothes you'd want if you were about to see real action. Boots, thick trousers, ski jacket, combat wear. It was hardly necessary, of course. They were not expecting armed resistance. Indeed, they were not expecting anything beyond an empty building and some unguarded computers. But still, the drama of a dawn raid seizes the imagination. Even for Books, who had kicked down a door or two in his time. London doors, with scarier things behind them than anything they were likely to find. But the mood was contagious and, instead of lying in bed and saying annoying things, Emily got up too. She didn't shower, but cleaned herself with a flannel and did something to her hair so that it looked like she'd done something to her hair. Books was in the kitchen, singing to himself and making a fry up. Bacon and eggs and probably a heap of other things besides.

Emily got stuck in the bedroom wondering what to wear. She wasn't normally girly about that sort of thing. She usually just chose something and wore it. She never bought anything complicated, so the choices were easy. However, she already had a reputation in the office of being a bit wild, a bit strange. Her mountaintop adventure was always more likely to happen to her than anyone else, so she wanted to downplay it, make it seem smaller than it was. She wanted to diminish the gossip, not inflate it.

Books appeared to see where she'd got stuck, and she explained her dilemma.

"You could wear that new outfit of yours."

"What new outfit?"

She couldn't remember anything. He reminded her there was a bag in her car. He took it out when he loaded the back with snow shovels and sleeping bags. It was now in the corner of her wardrobe.

"You could wear that," he said.

She blinked. She hadn't really expected to wear it at all, if she was honest, but nothing says 'I'm not the almost victim of a hypothermic contract killing' like a three- hundred- pound suit. Strangely enough, it wasn't a bad choice. It was loose over the parts of her that welcomed looseness. It was also comfortable enough to wear and chic enough to deflect attention from the way she had spent her weekend.

She put it on.   Her face had some minor burn marks and there was still some abraded skin where she pulled her cheek from the frozen car panel, but she played around with makeup until she looked presentable.

"Bloody hell, Em, you look gorgeous!"

He got a kiss for that, despite his tone of surprise. A kiss, but not a long one, because they had a fry up to eat and a raid to attend. He cleared away, while Emily put on socks and boots, coat, hat, scarves and gloves. It was a cold world and she didn't want to feel it.

The rendezvous at the station was a thing of headlights and car exhausts. Men in black jackets and knitted hats and feet stamping on icy pavements. The dirty grey brown of city snow lay in heaps along the side of the road. Darkness overhead battled streetlights for control of the city. Webster, in her granny coat, bustled in and out of view. She was good at these things; certain and in command. There were six vehicles now, and more than two dozen officers.

They left the station before dawn and drove across the bay. Emily was in a Transit van with Webster and two uniforms whom she knew by sight and by name, but no more than that. There wasn't much conversation When they came to the end of the bay, their vehicle and a patrol car turned off. The other four vehicles continued straight on. They crept down the frozen roads into the sleeping town with their headlights shining off ice. An occasional breeze sent a scurry of ice crystals across the road. Between the tyre tracks there was a hard ramp of snow and ice. Cold waves nagged at cold sand and cold rocks. It was six fifteen when they pulled back from the road, a graveled driveway in front.

They swept straight in. Their headlights shone full beam on the front door, partly for lighting, but mostly to disconcert and frighten the occupants. There were six of them all told. Four in uniform, Emily and Webster. The knocker was a big heavy cast iron thing; a lion's head, or something like it. One of the uniforms smashed down on it. Not once but repeatedly. A din that, briefly, became the centre of the world. The only thing that mattered.

Webster stood back. She was on the phone to the leader of the other team. They'd gained entry to Precision Tools. Bolt cutters had been used to cut the chain guarding the property, then a steel ram used to gain access to Precision Tools itself. The uniforms were having another go with the knocker and beginning to yell "Police" and flash torch beams around, when the hall lights went on. The front door opened. Idris Khan stood there. Emily recognized him from the photos she had studied. He was in a dressing gown and half asleep, but was also composed. A kind of silvery indignation.

The uniforms didn't put cuffs on him. They would if they had to, but for now they were not making arrests. If Khan went voluntarily, that would be good enough. They had a search warrant too and they were determined to enforce that.   Webster flashed her warrant card. Khan took it, stepped inside, put the porch light on, studied the card and returned it. He didn't care about the card, though. He was just staging a little show for them. The Idris Khan I'm not flustered show. He was about five foot eleven, lean and tanned. Emily thought he was handsome too, though she didn't see him that way. She wanted him in jail.

A uniformed officer escorted him upstairs, where he was allowed to dress. He wasn't left alone for a minute, not even to pee. Khan's wife, Millie, appeared briefly on an upstairs landing. She was frightened, pretty, wifely. That's what money buys you. The kind of woman who plays the part of loving wife so fully, she's forgotten it's all a part. Above her, one floor up, two moon shapes appeared, peering over the banisters. Khan's kids, Emily assumed. He was twice married and this was his second brood.

There was odour of fear in the house. Webster didn't notice any of this, or if she did, she didn't care. The remaining officers were ordered to search the house from top to bottom, including attic and outbuildings. Almost immediately, they located two mobile phones, an iPad, a couple of laptops, a desktop, some box files, a games console, but all those things were left hanging around in plain sight, in the sort of place they expected. Khan might have been stupid enough to leave incriminating materials there, but he might not. Webster snappishly supervised the operation. Emily was left out of things. Possibly because Webster knew she was still in a fairly delicate state, but more likely because she thought Emily wouldn't be much use anyway.

Khan was dressed by now and downstairs again. Grey suit, pale blue shirt. No tie. Webster had a search warrant and ordered the removal of the electronics and the papers. The standard play for someone in Khan's position is to argue with the warrant, demand a lawyer, start negotiating over precisely what is being removed and what not. He did none of those things. Just said, with a half-smile, "I suppose I can use the coffee machine?"

He was allowed into his gleaming kitchen, with its polished wooden boards and hand fired cream tiles. Coffee for six. Him, his wife, the four of them. Tiny white espresso cups with a blue pattern on the lip. Millie Khan wore a bathrobe over a long cotton nightdress and kept flitting in and out of the room. Emily wasn't sure if it was to look after the kids or to stress over whether the uniforms were grinding dirty snow into the pure wool carpets on her living room floor.

Webster downed her coffee in a single blast. The woman had a throat made of fireboard. She left to supervise the removal of Khan's effects. Emily was left in the kitchen guarding him. He looked at her with as much interest as he'd look at a new secretary at work. A vague sexual curiosity. Nothing else. She looked at him like he was an arms dealer who murdered Aftab Khaled, caused the suicide of Mark Mortimer, and who had almost murdered her. A cold sense of anger. Nothing else.

He looked at his watch and sighed. Emily's anger was tempered with uncertainty. She strongly doubted that Khan was innocent of arms smuggling, but what happened to her? She tried asking whether this man ordered her death. It seemed highly probable that his firm, his arms department, sent Ross and Olaf up into the hills to find that laptop. Given his choice of messenger, the murder of any police officer they happened to encounter probably lay well within their rules of engagement. But her question was more specific than that. What precisely took place? Was there an explicit instruction, a phone call, from this man to Ross and Olaf, saying 'kill the copper?' And if so, did he make that call with the same calm demeanour, wearing the same elegant suit, the same air of impatience? Was that, in fact, how arms dealers conduct their business?

It was a side issue, really. His arms department had created plenty of corpses already. Not in the UK, but abroad. Egypt, Libya, Syria, Iran. How much blood was there in his impeccable kitchen? How many bones beneath these polished floors?

He said, "Will this take much longer?"

Emily didn't answer. It would take as long as necessary. There was a minor commotion out in the hallway. Emily stood where she could see and listen better. One of the uniforms had just found a stack of boxed up mobile phones in the wardrobe of an upstairs bedroom. Eight boxes. All unopened. Eight cheapie phones.

Webster marched from the living room to view the haul. She reached for her phone, summoned another six officers. Then she did a thing which only Emily had seen her do. A kind of 180- degree rotation of the head, stare fixed outward, like a steel spike aimed at anything in her path. The steel gaze stopped when it reached her. She jabbed her chin in Emily's direction, her hand at Khan. "Station," she said, and Emily nodded.

-40-

They agreed the need to wait until Khan had his lawyer. For form's sake, Rogers and another DS put in shifts, one hour on, one hour off, asking the same battery of questions. There was no evidentiary purpose in doing so and they knew he would reveal nothing. They also did it just to piss him off. Both good reasons to keep at it. Rogers didn't need Emily for the time being, and she knew it wouldn't be much fun sitting opposite her probable would be murderer, unless she was sure of nailing him. They were a long way short of that.

"You could always go down to Precision Tools," Rogers said.

Emily found a patrol car going down there and hitched a lift. A civilian vehicle, an Astra, entered the car park at the same time. The woman who got out of the Astra wore a red and white bobble hat and said she was an Export Manager. She didn't look like a dealer in illegal arms, but Emily wondered whether she even knew that's what she was. Or maybe arms dealers liked to wear Christmassy bobble hats.

They escorted her into the building, which had grown mountains of computers, wires, printers, laptops and phones, all in boxes stacked. Yellow police stickers markers with reference numbers abounded. Every item was logged and signed for. It didn't stop at electronics as there were boxes and boxes of paperwork too. Personnel records, employment contracts, bank records, invoices, technical drawings, visitor sign-in books. Everything.

It wasn't just a question of lugging the stuff out. CID IT specialists wanted to map the network architecture, whatever that meant. Potentially they had hours of fiddling around before they could carry away any booty. Whatever excitement there must have been when they forced entry earlier in the morning had long gone. It was now a massive furniture removal project, with lots of data complications and the risk of massive legal liabilities if they messed up. The mood was simultaneously tense and frustrated.

DI Ken Hughes, who led the Barry raid, was overseeing interviews with the bad-tempered snappishness that was native to him. There was a swirl of confused surprise around his desk as employees were paired up with officers. Emily noted that it was surprise rather than fear. It was as though their presence was like the snow. Unexpected. A disturbance of the normal order, but somehow also accepted, a freak of the climate. An IT man helped their CID specialist with the network architecture. Someone showed an officer how to get the coffee machine to produce hot chocolate. There was no end their ingenuity.

Webster was in with Dunbar, giving him the third degree. Emily was sure that she would be a good interviewer. Naturally scary. Dunbar had a lawyer sitting in with him, but Dunbar's budget didn't run to some highflyer from London. His man was local; a cheap grey pinstripe and a voice that was higher pitched than Webster's.

Emily greeted DI Hughes and offered her services. He didn't much like her, which made for a neatly symmetrical relationship, as she felt the same. He assigned her to a spotty boy from sales, who looked eighteen but claimed to be nearer her age. The kid knew nothing. He kept asking, "How are we going to do our work?"

Emily was very tempted to give him the benefit of her wisdom. "Not my problem, matey, if you want to work, you probably shouldn't have started dealing in illegal arms. Shouldn't have framed Mark Mortimer, shouldn't have killed Khaled, shouldn't have left me to die in a bloody snowfield." She refrained though and acted like a copper out of a training video. "We'll keep any disruption to a minimum, sir. We do have a warrant to impound items that may be required for our inquiry."

The kid looked at her blankly with eyes the colour of peat water. She ran her recorder and wrote her notes. She finished and then did another. There was a flavour missing, she realised. Fear.

She thought of Tristan and Althea. Tristan's question asking whether it was a mistake struck home. Yes, Tristan, it damn well was. The atmosphere tasted like potatoes boiled without salt. The lads who, earlier that morning, had broken open a door with a steel battering ram were now reduced to figuring out schedules for the return of property. The vending machine ran out of coffee and a couple of uniformed coppers were dispatched to deal with that most important of situations.

Webster took a rest from the business of throwing hostile questions at Jim Dunbar. She went for a prowl so she could blast anyone who offended her. By this point, Emily wasn't doing anything at all. She didn't think the interviews were helpful, and had therefore ceased. She didn't want to load paperwork into boxes and also didn't want to become involved in the whole logistical mess of figuring out what stuff Precision Tools needed to continue in business and how soon it could be returned to them. As far as she was concerned, they should take everything, without apology or excuse, keep what they needed and dump the rest in Cardiff Bay.

She drifted around, made stupid jokes, and tried to stop other people from working. She was sitting on a desk chatting with a couple of uniformed officers when

Webster hove into view. She lasered a couple of people, just to demonstrate her weapons were in order, then rolled over to Emily. Webster issued the glare and did that circular jaw action thing that was becoming a trademark. The uniformed cops didn't know her well enough to be terrified, but that jaw action was normally a prelude to launch. A countdown to detonation. Emily gave her a sunshiny smile, all tropical beaches and swaying palms.

"How are you feeling?" Webster asked.

"Fine. Mending up."

She nodded and made a half gesture at Emily's outfit. "You're looking smart."

"Thank you," Emily said, hardly believing her ears.

Webster made some incoherent noise in the back of her throat which was like a glitch in her missile ignition system and then trundled away without remembering to reprimand them for existing. Emily turned to her two workmates with a grin, but they weren't impressed They didn't know how close they had come to incineration.

Emily grew bored after a while. She quite liked the factory hall itself. The incomprehensively complex machines. The manufactured parts and works in progress. The precision of surfaces whose form and function was entirely beyond her to fathom. Aside from that, though, the place was alien. The offices at the front of the building were poky and lightless, even worse than theirs. They were there, barreled up in a metal shed, close by the black water seething in the docks, the ice hardening its grip on walls and roads and ironwork, and they saw none of it.

She needed to get out, but had no car. She thought about bothering Books, but his car was at the station and he was busy being a good and dutiful copper. She called Jon Breakell in the office, but drew a blank. She would normally have tried Mervyn Rogers, because he quite liked her and because his attitude to work wasn't always rigorous either, but she wanted to avoid getting sucked back into interviewing Khan. Instead, she tried Bev, and was instantly in luck. Webster had her driving around the various businesses that Khaled patronised all those years ago. Not the large ones, of course, but those small and personal enough that they just might remember a repeat customer. Webster's hope was that if Bev flashed photos of Khaled and Flowers in front of enough people, she might just jog a memory or two. It wasn't even clear how that would assist the investigation, but Webster was remorseless. She'd keep going until there was nothing more to do. Emily liked that about her. Bev was in Penarth, just up the coast, feeling anxious that she was doing something wrong, and Emily persuaded her to pick her up.

Emily was no longer bored. Althea and Tristan. Aftab Khaled. Rose Flowers and her grieving family. Different victims, different remedies. It felt good to act.

-41-

"The yacht club?" Bev sounded dubious. "In this weather?"

Emily knew what she meant. The Swansea Bay Yacht Club was hardly likely to be humming with life, but it wouldn't be closed either.

Bev was wearing a padded coat in sky blue. She had unnaturally blue eyes and a clear complexion. The weather gave her the clarity and perfection of a china doll. When she blinked, she looked like Bambi in pursuit of a butterfly.

"Wouldn't it be better to work more systematically? Go back to Penarth, finish up there, then do Barry?" Bev was worried that she had made an error in going to get Emily. She wanted Emily in Penarth with her because she thought it might help protect her from any Websterian rage. Now she worried that Emily was going to lure her off-piste and end up brining that rage down upon her.

Emily said, "Bev, did Webster specifically ask you to start in Penarth?"

"No, I just thought it would be logical to."

"Then trust me. Let's go to the Mumbles in Swansea Bay. Start at the yacht club. If we don't have any luck there, we'll do it whichever way you like. And Webster won't be pissed off with you or anybody. I'll tell her it was all my idea."

"Okay then." Bev sounded uncertain, but compliant, which was all Emily needed.

She was sitting in the passenger seat next to Bev. Like her, she still had her coat on, but her hat, gloves and scarf now lay in a woolly pile on her lap. Reaching a round for the seatbelt was difficult. Emily didn't want to stress the skin that was starting to grow back on her burn, but there was a moment when a small gasp of pain escaped her.

"Are you sure you're okay?"

"Yes." Emily tried to sound nonchalant.

"I thought you were going to be more, I don't know, more..."

"Chargrilled? Crispy?"

Bev was shocked at her flippancy, but also reassured. She gave Emily a smile, put the car into gear, and drove cautiously out of the snowy car park. The roads eased as they journeyed. Channels of brown slush gouged into banks of dirty snow. Cars drove with their lights on. Snow doesn't just whiten a landscape, it quietens it. Sounds are deadened, speeds reduced. Bev drove sitting forward, hands on the wheel in the ten-to-two position. When she became confident with the driving, she started asking Emily about what happened up in the mountains. Emily gave her the expurgated version.

"Goodness gracious, Emily."

That was just about as close as Bambi ever came to swearing, so Emily worked bit harder to tone things down. She thought it must have worked because Bev ended up saying, "You do look okay. Really fine actually."

"Hey, thanks."

"No, I didn't mean it like that."

They shifted the subject to the weather. Emily resolved that when she saw Shona, she'd give her the same low key version of events, and with a bit of luck her weekend adventures wouldn't have added too much to her my reputation. Funnily enough, she thought, my lovely Books was right. The suit was helping.

The landscape looked like some town in Norway, remade with local road signs. The sea chafed all along the seafront in a contest of salt and ice. The yacht club was disappointing. Emily was expecting it to have a little moneyed swagger to it, but no. It lived in one of those buildings created when grey was the only colour and rectangles the only shape.   A white iron balcony daggered with icicles. Single glazed windows in iron frames. From the roof, a row of flags stuck frozen to their poles. In the yard next door, boats sat on metal trailers, each one swaddled in its winter tarpaulin.

There was only one person inside the clubhouse, an older man repinning notices to a corkboard. They introduced themselves. He was Gwilyam Jenkins and he was happy to help. He asked if they wanted tea. Bev started to say no, because she was still worried about not having achieved enough for the day; not having ticked enough rows on her spreadsheet.   Emily accepted the offer because she wanted the man to relax and confide. He made tea, very slowly, but he found them chairs and handled the china with a courtesy that amounted almost to chivalry. When they were all done, sitting at a Formica table by a radiator, Bev laid out her photos. She started to ask her questions.

"Are you able to identify either of these people? Did either of them use the facilities here?"

Emily interrupted. "Gwilyam, these two are Rose Flowers and Aftab Khaled. We think they took out a joint membership in March 2003. She was murdered a few months later."

"Good heavens. Well, I'll certainly take a look...."

He went to fetch some records, his footsteps soft on the wooden floors. Bev gave Emily Bambi eyes, so she answered her unspoken question.

"Bev, it was your data that gave us the clue. According to your spreadsheet, Khaled spent seventy pounds here. Seventy pounds exactly. That doesn't sound like a drinks bill. It's too large and too exact. It's not for boat hire, because they don't hire boats. So it seemed to me like it had to be some kind of membership fee. I called the club here and asked them about their prices. The prices have changed since, but back then the charge for a double membership of the club was seventy pounds. The price for a single was forty-five. For a family it was ninety."

Bev's mouth dropped open and her eyes, if possible, widened. They didn't, of course, know that Khaled was necessarily buying the membership for himself and Flowers, but the dates would fit with everything else they knew about them. In addition, Rose Flowers looked fit and tanned that spring in the photos they had. An outdoorsy sort of tan, that didn't reach to the neck. The sort of tan you'd get, almost inadvertently, on a boat out on Swansea Bay. That wasn't how she looked in her year of exotic dancing.

Gwilym returned with a membership ledger and leafed through the years. He found the right year, the right month. There were only three new memberships that March. The first of them belonged to Flowers and Khaled. Two signatures side by side on the page. Evidence at last. Bev was awed and relieved in equal measure. Relieved because she'd escaped the wrath of Webster and awed because she credited Emily with some sort of divine inspiration.

Emily said, "Gwilym, we're not sure how often Aftab came here, but I'm guessing that you don't have a huge North African membership."

"No. Not huge." He phoned a colleague and they heard him talking about a 'brown gentleman.' The colleague said she'd come over.

Daphne was forty something and knew everything and remembered more. Aftab Khaled never owned a boat, but he used to borrow one from a Swansea based friend of his. He and Rose Flowers used to come every weekend or so, 'for a while,' Then less often. Then not at all. Khaled and Flowers were definitely a couple. "Oh, they were quite sweet on each other," Daphne told them. "He was a terrible sailor, to be honest. And she wasn't any better. They'd get into trouble if there was any breeze up."

She recounted a hard to follow story about a time when the pair of them brought their boat back with a spinnaker only, after lowering the mainsail because the wind was too much for them. That sounded sensible to Emily, and to Bev, but Daphne and Gwilym were laughing hard.

Emily asked, "Do you think they stopped coming because they weren't cut out for the water. Or because their relationship ended?"

Neither could give an answer with any certainty. They didn't really need to take a statement, but Bev wanted to get all the main points in writing and Emily left her to do just that while she went to get a glass of water from the kitchen and swallowed a couple of aspirin. While she was still in the warm, Emily found a number for Marr-Phillips's office and called it. She arranged an interview. Then she walked outside and over the road. There was a little car park, with a clutter of food and tourist kiosks which might have been busy in season but were now deserted. A concrete ramp, thickly armoured in plates of snow and ice, sloped down into the water. Emily avoided the obvious danger and walked instead to the end of a little pier to the right. It boasted blue iron balustrades and an orange lifebuoy.

She tried to feel Khaled and Flowers there. The lecturer and the student. He, a little uncertain; an immigrant who never quite settled, who never quite realised the uncertainty he felt didn't come from others, but from within. He kept on trying to prove himself because he never quite had the confidence to be himself.

Rose Flowers was different. Emily didn't know what made her turn to exotic dancing, but the spring that she spent sailing with Khaled was surely the time when she turned things around. Quit the clubs, stopped dancing. Remembered that she was a middle-class English kid who rode horses, chased hockey balls and wrote essays about Dylan Thomas. Out there, by these grey waters and chattering halliards, those spangly mini-skirted nights must have seemed a million miles away.

It could be thought that Khaled's was the relationship which saved her life; rescued it from that adventure into darkness, except that, except that within a few months Flowers was dead. Not much of a rescue if your leg ends up in a freezer, your arms in a plumbers' merchant's roof and your head in a barrel of lawn mower oil.

Emily had been missing Flowers, she realised suddenly. She liked the thought of her and Khaled together. It was like when two people who are special to you shyly tell you they've been on a date, that it went well, that they're seeing each other again.

Emily wanted to reward her with the only gifts she had to offer. Investigation, arrest, prosecution and conviction. The girl who chased hockey balls and was crap at sailing. She was smiling at that thought when she heard Bev walking over the yard towards her. She turned to her, still smiling.

"Got what you need?"

She nodded, and waved her notebook contentedly. They drove back to Cardiff and night had fallen long before they arrived. It has been a long day for her tired body, and she asked Bev to drive her all the way home. Bev dropped her at the door and Emily was relieved when Bev refused the offer of a cup of tea. She was also relieved to be alone.

The game was at an end. Flowers, Khaled and Mortimer. Their ghosts were bustling now. Restless. Their satisfaction rested with the living. Emily made herself a cup of peppermint tea and drank it in her dark kitchen. The lights and the heating were off. She was still in her warm clothes. She crunched some aspirin with the last of her tea. This was the end, she knew. She had scores to settle.

-42-

The night was a strange one. Books wanted her to spend the night at his place, but her parents wanted her to go back there. She knew she needed to be on her own. Needed it for many reasons.

One, she wanted a joint. The last time she even had a joint between her lips was the moment just before she threw it into a tank of petrol. There was some strange way in which she needed a long uncluttered smoke to vanquish the memory of the blaze that followed. She could handle the memory itself, but she needed to soften its edges. Smudge it into something a little less than real. There were probably better ways of doing that, but marijuana was her way.

Two, and on a related point, the cold weather wasn't any good for her marijuana plants. The poor things had been trying to get by with heat lamps set to come on for just twelve hours a day. They'd need more than that in these temperatures. She went to her potting shed, checked water Lennyels, adjusted the timers on the heat lamps, and helped herself to a little cube of hash by way of reward. The plants weren't too happy with her, but they weren't at death's door either. They would survive.

Three, she needed space. Needed to feel herself in control and alone. It was thinking time, but it was also being time. Being constantly with other people placed a pressure of normality on her that she couldn't always. When she was alone, she could be her version of ordinary.

And finally, that night, she could feel the clamour of the dead. The restless ghosts and they must be given their proper share of her attention. The living could wait.

She crumbled plenty of resin on a sparse amount of tobacco. She'd smoke only one joint that night, but it would be a rich one. Rich and fat. She put the lights on, turned the heating up and started running a bath. She talked to Books on the phone. He knew she needed time alone, but wanted to know she was okay. Books always looked after her, she knew, and the familiar warm and moist feelings began. Lovely Books. Next time, she would take him into her bath. She smiled at the thought. She knew he would be gallant about who would have the plug end. He told her that Webster was angrier than anyone had seen her after interviewing Khan. The man had brought not one, but two solicitors up from London. Two glossy solicitors from some magic circle law firm. Suits with money. They both seemed to have been well briefed, long in advance of the raid.

"Apparently they're going to sue us if we don't have everything back at Precision Tools within forty-eight hours."

Removing data takes much longer than that if it's done properly, recording where it's come from and how it fits together. Even a week would be good going.

"They'll lose if they sue us," Emily said.

"Yes, but we'd still be sued."

Books was right. If they're sued and lose some portion of the case, or are adjudged faulty on some narrow technical point, they may. end up having to pay costs. Legal costs can quickly rip holes in budgets. A couple of stories in the local press about overzealous cops recklessly placing Welsh jobs at risk could be a career wrecker for Webster.

Books chuckled. Emily didn't They talked for twenty minutes more, affectionate nonsense mostly, and then disconnected. Her bath had grown cold, so she ran half out of it and had started refilling it with hot water, when her phone rang again. Not Books. Not Mum or Dad. Webster.

Emily turned off the tap.

"Emily. It's Rhoda."

Emily was taken aback by the use of first names, but passed no comment. In any case, Webster had news. Nothing about Khan. Nothing about Dunbar. This was about Ross.

"The blood on your coat. We've got a DNA match," she says. "No address, but we've got a name and a picture."

Emily knew what Webster wanted to know, so she told her. "I'm happy to look at photos."

"The light can't have been great."

"It wasn't. But we had lights on inside the car most of the time." Before they faded, that was. Faded into the night she was never meant to leave. "I'm certain I can identify him. If the photo is even halfway like him."

"It's a 2005 photo. He's been on the run since then."

Webster was deliberately not telling her much. It would have been easy to nudge her in the right direction. Give her enough information so that she could be sure to pick the right candidate from a parade of photos. But Webster wasn't that kind of copper. Emily repeated that she was sure to be able to identify him. Webster had already told her to expect the photo of a man looking five years younger than the man whose nose she broke. Emily was tempted to ask about facial hair. The Ross she had seen sported a beard, but might not always have done so. She decided not to ask.

Webster said, "Good. Is eight-thirty tomorrow too early?"

"No."

"Good. Then come down to the interview rooms first thing. Don't go to your desk first."

"Okay."

If she went to her desk first, the office grapevine might have found a way to prime her with the name or the face the moment she arrived. Webster wanted it clean. They may or may not be able to secure a conviction for what happened to Emily on the mountainside, but it was still better to do these things and to do them properly.

"I've checked West's call log. She received a call from a mobile, pay as you go, used once, then apparently discarded."

"They're good. They're very careful."

It was sort of nice to know that they called Stephanie, not vice versa. West needed a slapping, maybe, but not necessarily jail time.

"Yes. Look, I've been having words with my SIO, Robert Kirby." Webster sounded stressed, but Emily already knew what she was going to be told. That the team tasked with investigating her attempted murder was coming up with no meaningful leads. That Kirby wanted to shift resources away to Takeaway proper.

Emily said, "I don't care. I mean, I want the men arrested and jailed. But we're more likely to get them for the Khaled killing. We've got more to go on there."

"Yes."

"We can't even prove a crime took place."

"I've told Kirby to give me time. He's agreed." She paused in case Emily wanted to say thank you, but she resisted the temptation. Then, "I appreciated your help today."

"I didn't really help. I mostly sat around."

There was a moment's silence. One of those shared telephone silences that seem to expand forever. As though you have your ear pressed up against some instrument that lets you listen directly to the emptiness of space. A background crackle that reminds you how little you can truly hear.

Then she says, "You can help tomorrow." There was a line of steel in her voice when she said that. Websterian steel. They rang off.

Emily finally got into her bath. She was still wearing dressings but it didn't matter if they got wet. The hot water was painful on her more battered surfaces, but good overall. She took a moment to adjust, then started to relax. She was about to light her joint, but changed her mind. Someone, Mum she thought, gave her a scented vanilla candle in a glass jar, and she had put it by her bath because she didn't know where else to place it. She lit it, got out of the bath, dripping, and turned the overhead lamp off. Only then did she light her joint.

She called Books and said, "We should have some candles by your bath. We could take baths together."

"I don't have a bath, remember? I only have a shower."

"Oh yes. I'd forgotten that. "Well, maybe we should get one."

"Maybe we should."

They said goodnight again and she finished her joint.

She finished her bath and went hunting in the kitchen. Slim pickings, but she had a jar of pesto sauce and some crackers. She put pesto on the crackers and ate until she couldn't be bothered to eat anymore. The she cleared up, did her teeth like a good little girl and went to bed. She slept easily for once. The bath and the joint probably helped. That, plus a long day in pursuit of a short night. She slept easily and without dreams.

Then, after maybe two or three hours, something woke her abruptly. The sudden, jolting wakefulness arrived with a wash of adrenaline. Of fear. At first she didn't do anything at all, just listened into the silence, seeing if she could detect the thing that woke her in the first place. She couldn't. Aside from the candle that was still burning in the bathroom, there was no light on anywhere in the house. A street light outside beyond curtained windows. She could see the shape of the windows. A glimmer of mirror. She breathed through her mouth, not moving a muscle.

There was someone in the room with me. Someone there now. She didn't know where they were. She didn't know how they woke her, but there was someone there, and she was terrified. She didn't sleep with a gun anymore. She'd have liked to, of course, but part of her be more normal project involved hiding her gun in a Pembrokeshire sheepfold. The 460 bullets she had in a locked drawer of the ops room were as useless as tinsel.

Whoever was there wasn't moving. He was being very silent. Perhaps she made a sound when she woke up. Perhaps he was waiting for her to move. She wasn't fond of waiting games. Although she gave up her gun, she hadn't left herself defenceless. In a holster made of sellotape and kitchen towel behind the brass bars at the head of her bed, there was a knife. The knife was originally an ordinary kitchen knife. A paring knife with a four-inch blade. Black handled. Not particularly expensive.

But there were a couple of gypsies who knocked on doors around the vicinity from time to time. They had a grinding wheel in the back of their van and sharpened stuff for cash. Pruning hooks, lawn mower blades and knives. She had got them to sharpen her knife until it had the devil's own edge, the devil's own point. She got, from a place online, a rubber finger loop that allowed her to attach the knife to a finger, so even if she lost her grip on the handle in the course of a fight, she wouldn't drop it. It remained attached. Ready.

So she slid her bare arm through the bars of the bed to reach the knife, found the handle and found the finger loop. She came back with the knife in a fighting grip, ready for whatever follows. She remembered Lenny's words. 'Don't trust the stab.' The blade isn't long enough to do reliable damage, and in any case, the heart is trickier to reach than you think. Shielded. You have to go in at the right place and angle to stand a chance.

'Rely on the slashing movement.' The face or the neck ideally, but really it's okay to land the stroke anywhere. 'Draw blood.' Stay out of reach. Let the bleeding do your work. You need a lot of blood. Much more than you think. A person contains four or five litres of blood and you might need a litre of that splattering your home furnishings before your antagonist is seriously weakened. So be patient, take your time, wait for the moment. Emily did just that. She held, as far as possible, her original sleeping position, her original posture. She kept her striking arm clear of the bedclothes, as she listened and watched. She watched emptiness.

There was something strange about the silence. She was completely certain that there was someone there, but silence of that intensity is unnatural. There was no creak of a floorboard, no suppressed breathing. The energy in the room felt weird too, as though the space had acquired a chilly pressing quality. A solidification of the emptiness. A cold incandescence. She didn't know how long passed, because when you watch with that intensity, each second seems to stretch forever. Then she realised. Realised and laughed.   Her laughter was silent and she didn't let go of her knife, but she understood what was going on. Yes, there was someone present in the room, but the person in question was a dead one. Khaled. It was his spirit that she was feeling. If her first response was relief, her second was terror. It came to her as sharp and fierce as she had known it. Sharper and more fierce than anything she felt up on that snowy mountainside.

It was not fear of the dead. Far from it. She liked the dead. She was comfortable in their presence. Rather, it was a fear of my own head. A fear of craziness.

Ghosts and dead presences don't exist. What she had wasn't a spirit from the other side, it was psychosis. Madness. And that madness, the sort she had earlier in life, killed her, pretty literally killed her for two years. She was terrified that the illness was returning, and that, if it was, she wasn't strong enough to stop it.

For a few minutes she lay trapped in her own alarm. Was her Cotard's returning? Was she going mad? Then logic, the sweet cold stream of reason, started to wash those fears away. When it happened before, she lost all bodily sensation. She couldn't really feel her heart beat except as some repetitive tapping from an adjoining room. She never felt her feet. Never. They didn't belong to her at all. Some sufferers with Cotard's report 'seeing' their flesh crawl with maggots. She never had that, but she used to turn her hand over again and again, scared she would find that seething crawl of decomposition.

It wasn't like that now. She felt like she always did. Maybe even a bit sharper, a bit clearer. That might not be very sharp or clear by the standards of others, but she was who she was, and, as far as she was concerned, things were okay. She felt her heart beat, felt the knife in her hand. When she moved her feet, she felt them too.

Khaled was still there. She felt the cold intensification. His chuckling laugh, the pressure of his gaze. Felt it too much, too intensely. This wasn't real. It was illusion. It was psychosis. In her bathroom cabinet, she had a bottle containing about a hundred and fifty 100-milligram tablets of Amisulpride. A second generation antipsychotic. It was the only thing she had any time for. It didn't conquer her illness, but perhaps it took the edge off it. She had kept them as a safety precaution and then bought more from an Indian pharmacy on the internet when it first became possible to do things like that. She hadn't touched them in years, but she knew exactly where they were. She carried some in her bag, and if she travelled, she took a bottle.

She could take a pill, maybe two, and watch Khaled fade away. Drive away the flash of craziness. Let the world return to normal. She put her knife back, sat up in bed and breathed deeply. She reached down and massaged her feet, until she was sure she could feel them properly. Her cuts and burns and bruises helped. The process, the breathing, the massaging, the movement, drove away her fear. For the moment she didn't have to touch those pills. Perhaps if the psychosis got worse, if Khaled started speaking, if she started to see him, she would change my mind. She didn't have a stupid pride about such things; survival was all that mattered. But for now, she was okay. She was a kooky detective with an unreliable brain. If a corpse wanted to come and visit her in the night, he was welcome to do so.

She grinned at Khaled, welcoming him for the first time. He grinned back. The room trembled with laughter.

It reminded her of that lovely moment she had with Flowers's head. That lovely, spacious moment. That black and gaping mouth, The feel of bone. Time passed. She felt comfortable. With Khaled. With her crazy brain.

She realised too that the particular psychosis wasn't as new as she first thought. In a way, she had always connected too much with the dead. Felt them too much. Felt them in a way that runs far beyond reality. Strangely, that thought settled her, she felt herself welcoming them all. Rose Flowers, Mark Mortimer, Aftab Khaled. And others too. In particular, Quentin Legard. That cold, loathsome psychopath who met his end high over the Atlantic Ocean as her beloved Books watched from the door of the plane, strapped tightly in to prevent being pulled out as well. Only Legard wasn't pulled out by air pressure. He was pushed by her lovely Books on the orders of Ray Quinn. And good riddance too.

She got up and went to the bathroom. She fashioned another joint, lighting it from the burning candle. Then she went to bed. She plumped up the pillows and sat there smiling in the company of the dead.

The chuckling quality in the room faded to something quieter and more peaceful. But it was a good sort of peace. A special one; the sort you only get from the dead. She wondered what Khaled wanted from her, but the truth was she already knew. He wanted to be with her. He wanted her to complete her acts of justice on the men who killed him. And he wanted her to do right by Rose Flowers. The only girl he ever truly loved. Emily wanted those things too. They grinned at each other, enjoying the communication. At some stage, she must have fallen asleep. When her alarm went off in the middle of a grisly December dawn, she was still sitting up, aching like hell and she was all alone in her room.

-43-

She didn't make it in by eight thirty. Some of her wounds needed their dressings changed and it took longer than she expected. She sent a text to Webster to tell her she'd be late and did the job properly. One of the cuts on her hand opened up any time she moved it too much, so there was fresh blood on the bandage by the time she'd finished. She fairly sure that even the Websterian Handbook of Personnel Management prohibited the ripping off of someone's head when they were newly wounded in the line of duty.

Emily dressed with more formality than normal. Skirt, shirt, jacket. Not posh, but still, it was all part of her strategy to suppress gossip. She put a handful of aspirin in her jacket pocket and a couple of Amisulpride tablets as well, just in case.

She was with Webster in the interview room by eight fifty. She glowered, but didn't give Emily a bollocking. The room was bare. There was a camera, a computer screen, a table and a couple of chairs. The place ought to have looked like the movies, where everything is painted battleship grey and the maverick cops beat the life out of suspects, but mostly it just looked like the sort of thing you have in local government. Budget cuts and equipment compromises.

A technician whose name might have been Michael hovered around until Webster shood him away.

"When you're ready," she said to Emily, who nodded.

Webster turned the camera on and gave place, time and names. She was a little senior-officer awkward about such things. It would have been a routine part of her job once, but the rules and the camera had changed since then. She was only doing it no because violence against a police officer is treated more seriously than violence against anyone else.

Emily looked at the photos on-screen. Sequentially, not simultaneously. The evidence you collect is stronger that way, less prone to challenge. If, for example, you identify photograph number three from a group, where you haven't seen the later photos, it's strong proof that you're picking the right person, not merely the person who's the best fitting candidate from the ones on offer. She didn't react to the first three photos. Ross was dark haired. The first three didn't even come close. She just said no decisively and moved on.

The video camera makes a difference. You're always aware of it. You act for it. Auditioning for the courtroom drama which may one day follow. She needed to look at number four twice. He was bearded and there was something about his face shape which was approximately correct. But the eyes were wrong. The face was wrong. She said, "No."

Number five was Ross all right. Younger. Longer haired. But Ross without doubt.

She said, "This is one of the two men who tried to kill me. When I saw him on November 27th, his hair was shorter than in this photograph. Additionally, since this photograph was taken, his jaw appears to have been broken and badly reset. At any rate, there is some disturbance to the jawline not depicted in this photo. On that night of the twenty-seventh, I struck this man in the face and I believe, but cannot be certain, that I broke his nose. I would expect his nose to retain some sign of the injury, but cannot be confident of this. I am, however, completely certain of my identification. I do not need to see any further photographs to confirm my opinion."

Webster showed her more photographs anyway. Ten more. Emily said no to them all. She showed her Ross again, a different photo this time. Emily repeated her identification.

Webster nodded. "Good." Turned off the recording equipment. "Then, I take it that you are sure?"

"Yes. No question. His jaw has been injured since that picture. I'm not sure about the nose, but I thought it worth mentioning."

Emily took care to do so as it would bring courtroom brownie points if she was right, but wouldn't lose anything much if she was wrong.

Anyway, Webster was satisfied. She told Emily what she wanted to know. "His real name is Callum McCormack. He's got a conviction for armed robbery and he's wanted for an assault on a police officer in Aberdeen. But he's been on the wanted list for five years now, so we have to assume a new identity."

She passed a wodge of paper to Emily. McCormack's record as it appeared on the system. There were a couple more photos. Foster homes or institutions for much of his childhood. Joined the Army aged seventeen. Served three years. Then a drink related assault and battery incident, for which he served time and was discharged from the Army. Then in and out of trouble, until the Aberdeen assault, at which point he dropped off the radar completely. No mention of any Scandinavian partners in crime.

"The car registration number," said Webster. "The plates were stolen from a car in Glasgow a week ago.

She didn't spell out the rest because she didn't have to. McCormack and the man Emily still had to call Olaf would have stolen the plates off a car locally, but driven to South Wales with their own legitimate registration showing, because the stolen ones would have instantly been flagged by cameras and passing police cars. Once they were deep into the Llanthony Valley, beyond the reach of police surveillance, they'd have switched to the stolen plates. Then if any local had noticed any abnormal activity, they'd have only the wrong plates to report.

"Where in Glasgow?" I ask.

Webster gave her an address. Drumchapel. The name didn't mean anything to Emily. It was a dead end. Her killers were professionals who had successfully protected their identities for five years. She was certain they killed Khaled, but they did not have not a shred of evidence to prove it. Although she knew damn well that McCormack tried to kill her, they had no evidence that any crime even took place.

A dead end. Yet she couldn't help but smile like an idiot. She could feel Khaled's laughter in the room with her now. So she sat in the interview room, alone with Webster the Badge and the chuckling spirit of Aftab Khaled. And she smiled.

Webster, she imagined, didn't realise she was in there with Khaled, so she probably assumed she was there with an idiot. She smiled awkwardly, then said, "I hear you and Beverley Rowlands made a breakthrough yesterday."

For a second or so, all Emily could remember was the snowy pier jutting out into an empty sea, the breaking of waves and a hover of gulls. She couldn't remember what the breakthrough was.

Then she did. "The yacht club, the two of them signed up together."

"Rowlands tells me that you knew beforehand. I gather she wanted to start in Penarth and work her way west."

"They were her spreadsheets. I just made one phone call. And I didn't know. We were lucky. I suppose."

Webster made a noise at that. Not a noise with words, just a noise.

Emily said, "Khaled took a holiday in Dubai. Spring 2009."

"Yes?"

"And a holiday in Jordan, May 2010."

"Your point being?"

"He used to go to Spain. His holiday destination changed."

Webster's face said 'so what?' She was on the edge of angry, but her tents are never pitched far from that fierce edge.

"Maybe it wasn't Dubai he was interested in. Maybe they weren't holidays." Webster didn't do or say anything much, so Emily carried on. "Dubai is just down the road from Abu Dhabi. And his holiday dates happened to coincide with IDEX 2009. That's the International Defence Exhibition. The biggest arms fair in the Middle East."

Webster found her voice now. "And Jordan?"

"SOFEX. The Special Operations Forces Exhibition. The dates match. He also travelled to Doha, the scene of another major arms fair. The dates for that trip didn't coincide with the fair, but presumably the city remained a good place to meet the middlemen and buyers. I'd guess that Lausanne, Vienna, and Cairo see their share of Middle Eastern arms traders too."

"So your theory is that Mortimer wanted to expose illegal arms trading, but Khaled wanted to indulge in it?

Mortimer was framed for a drug bust as a way to shut him up. Khaled simply set about building his own contacts. He wanted to do what Precision Tools was doing, but take the profits for himself?"

"It's a theory, yes. Khaled had everything he needed: the technical expertise to replicate anything that Precision was doing. Engineering contacts all over the UK. Fluent Arabic. He'd have been perfect. Better than Precision Tools, in fact. They attracted Mortimer's suspicions because so much of what they made was dual use. In the end, there, was no innocent explanation available."

Webster thought about this and drew the same conclusions.

Emily nodded, "If I'd been him, I'd have placed one order here, another one there, a third one there. Not even all in the UK, necessarily. He had dealings with manufacturers from further afield too. Perhaps he was hoping to build his own virtual arms company. Anyone looking at the output of any virtual arms company would never have identified the trade that was taking place. But from the end user's point of view, what's not to like? British and European engineered components with all the hassle removed."

"That's speculation."

"Yes, but verifiable."

And easy to verify. They simply tracked every firm on Khaled's contact list and asked if he was involved in any recent orders. They got the data on all such orders and passed on the orders looking suitable for armaments, then their current speculation would turn to solid fact.

Webster made some notes. "Good. That's easily done. I'll get that actioned immediately."

Emily said something neutral. Her theory remained to be proven, but she'd be surprised if she had it wrong. Good Saint Mark came to his engineering buddy Aftab worried about an illicit trade. The bad man Khaled thought he saw a route to making his fortune. Neither of them realised the dangers they were getting into. Clever fools, the pair of them.

And it was odd. She liked Khaled as a corpse, got on with him very well. But she'd have detested him when he was alive. Loathed him. He was no better than Khan. Selling guns to dictators, because he wanted a more expensive car.

Webster's thoughts turned back to the murder itself. "Let's assume your idea proves to be correct. You think that when Precision Tools discovered what was going on, he had Khaled killed?"

"Maybe. Yes, I don't know."

Khaled was in competition with Precision Tools, certainly, but he was also in competition with Saadawi and his peers. Either of those forces might have ordered the killing. Or the two of them acting together. Or something else. They may never know. Webster nodded as she traced through the logic of this.

"But Khan did have eight mobile phones," Emily pointed out. "There's no way he's just an innocent businessman."

"And Dunbar? Khaled's other colleagues and contacts?"

Dunbar, Emily thought, was not the cleverest man alive. As for Khaled's other contacts, she doubted if any of them knew much. Perhaps Macintosh guessed something, but she doubted if he knew the whole thing. Emily didn't think he knew about gunrunning or murder. His wasn't that's sort of silence.

Webster nodded again. She had been sitting on the tale while they talked. Now she got up. She was wearing a pinstriped jacket, trousers, and a shirt in some kind of aubergine colour. Some sort of shiny fabric, which might look nice, but only if it was worn by somebody completely else in some completely other way. She preferred Webster when she was fierce and monochrome.

She said, "That's very good work."

She said more than that too. Words of praise. Emily nodded and looked down at her hands. It was what she did when she was getting a bollocking, but the technique was adaptable. It worked both ways. Eventually Webster stopped and changed tack. She told Emily that Khaled's mother was coming to Cardiff soon, and asked if she still wanted to see her? Then she said, "How long have you been with us?"

That was one of those tricky questions. She didn't answer because she wanted Webster to come to the point and she didn't want to risk things that she wasn't supposed to know.

"You'll be taking your Detective Sergeant exams when you can, I imagine?"

Another tricky one. Emily just frowned and made no verbal response.

"You ought to," she persisted, ignoring Emily's non-verbal signals.

"Yes," Emily managed, and wished she'd leave it alone.

"Have you discussed your career with anyone? At a senior level, I mean?"

"No." Emily was restricting herself to monosyllabic answers in the hope that the penny dropped.

"Well, we ought to do it. Lunch maybe? Are you free today?"

"Yes."

"Good. If you come by at twelve thirty, we'll go somewhere."

Emily nodded. She seemed to be doing a lot of that. "Okay. Thank you."

Webster gestured at the bandage on her hand. "You're healing up?"

"Yes."

"Good. Well, I'll see you later then."

She stomped off. She probably had to be extra horrible to someone, to make up for being nice to Emily. She left Emily with the bundle of paper on McCormack. There was nothing very useful there, but she took it anyway. Emily fingered the pills in her pocket. Crunched up an aspirin and checked that the Amisulprides were there.

Khaled's presence hadn't gone exactly, but he wasn't not there the way he was. She remembered the time on the stairwell at the Engineering Faculty when she stumbled and wondered about morning sickness. It wasn't that. It was Khaled. The first jostling manifestation of his presence. He didn't need to jostle now. He was just tagging along.

This psychosis: this presence of corpses. She realised she always had it. Certainly ever since she got better from Cotard's. She knew a student who committed suicide. She'd bumped into him occasionally, but wouldn't say she knew him well. There was some way in which she felt it easier to relate to him dead than him afterwards. Having Khaled's presence come barging into her room at midnight wasn't really so different from that. It was craziness, for sure, but not new craziness. Just Emily being herself.

She went to find Shona, to start her gossip suppression campaign. Emily showed her the dressing on her right hand, but made it seem that it was the worst of her injuries. Shona didn't even hide her disappointment.

"They were saying you almost died out there," she said. contemptuously.

"Well, the hospital was worried about tetanus," Emily replied. "I needed two injections."

Shona looked at her hand again, but her disgust was evident. Quite soon they were discussing whether Owen Dunwoody was going to be headhunted for the Gwent Police and whether Jane Alexander was pregnant again.

After Shona, she went looking for Bev, but she, bless her cotton socks, was going to every other business listed on her spreadsheet. There was a note from her on Emily's desk, saying she looked for her earlier in case she wanted to come. Emily was at work, but no one was giving her anything to do, because they were not quite sure whether she was well enough to work or not.

She chewed another aspirin. Her bum hurt where they took the skin graft. The wound on her hand has opened up again. She could feel the trickle of blood under the bandage.

Callum McCormack stole some car number plates in a place called Drumchapel and the Strathclyde police wouldn't find him because they've been trying for five years already. They didn't know who Olaf was. Although they seemed to have busted an arms-smuggling ring, not only were they not rolling over and playing dead, they were threatening to sue, which was not a welcome behavioural trait in criminals.

And Idris Khan, who had been collecting his fat little dividends from Precision Tools's murderous endeavours, was still a free man of unblemished reputation despite the fact that he very likely sought to have Emily killed. Which was not a welcome behavioural trait in anyone.

She got her phone out and sent a text to Lenny.

It said, 'DON'T KNOW IF YOU'RE INTERESTED BUT I MIGHT HAVE A JOB FOR YOU. EM.'

Sometimes she heard back quickly. Other times she didn't hear back at all. She didn't even know if Lenny had a home, but she assumed not. She didn't even know how much time he spent in the UK. He once spent three weeks on her sofa, smoking weed and listening to twentieth century Russian music, all sweeping strings and self-created sorrow. Then he vanished and she didn't see him again for eight months.

She poked around on the network. Bev's spreadsheets were now things of beauty, with items underlined and coloured according to some runic coding which Emily couldn't be bothered to fathom.

There was a mass of data coming in from the raid on Precision Tools, but it was way too early to see what they'd got. Nothing more from Stuart Brotherton and it was too soon to start hassling him. She needed to know more about pruning techniques. She needed to check that she was right in remembering a cherry tree on Elsie Williams's drive. That and other things. She got stuck into her research and these things were always more interesting than you think.

She was six and a half minutes late for Webster, and she hadn't heard back from Lenny.

-44-

Lunch didn't start well. Emily was late. Webster shivered on the brink of something nuclear; perhaps only the tactical battlefield version of nuclear, because six and a half minutes late is only six and a half minutes, even in Webster land. Nevertheless, she was still on the brink of detonation. Emily muttered something and Webster worked her jaw, managing to squeeze out a 'never mind.' She had added a gauzy scarf in pale blue to her outfit, which didn't suit her. Chain mail would have been better.

Anyway, they tramped around outside and headed out. She asked if Emily liked Italian food. She replied in the affirmative. It was still ridiculously cold. They didn't talk about the case. It was as though Webster had been on some weekend course in Being Nice to Humans. She had all the tricks: the gauzy scarf, the small talk, the asking where they should eat, but she had missed the somewhat essential element of actually being nice.

This new Webster disconcerted her. She liked Webster best when she was most up and at it. Disguising fair nature with hard-favoured rage. At least you knew where you stood. They got to the restaurant intact.

Breadsticks. Ciabata. A little tiny dish of olive oil and some fancy vinegar. A bottle of water.

Webster said, "Still or sparkling?"

Emily didn't care and was sure Webster didn't either. "Sparkling then," she took a managerial decision of the greatest magnitude. Such moments sort the high flyer from the also rans.

The waitress nodded and left. She returned with water, and asked if they were ready to order. Webster said something about how to cook scallops and Emily nodded, without really listening. Then she said something about how to cook tuna and Emily nodded again, also without really listening. She was thinking of Flowers' head. Khaled's lung. She tried to concentrate on her breathing. It wasn't going well.

Webster said, "Look, Emily, I did want to talk to you about your career. I mean, you have talent. You must know that. But I also wanted to......look, I think it's time we spoke about our feelings for each other. Not as law officers, but as......." She didn't finish her sentence. Just lunged across the table and took Emily's un-bandaged hand in hers. She was bright with emotion and her eyes were full. The lips moved but nothing came out.

Emily was lost for words. She had no idea how to react or what to say. She was keeping hold of that image of Flowers' head rising up through the oil, the twilight lustre of her scalp. The sudden weight and the dripping hair and the pebble clacking against her teeth.

Back in the real world, she tried to keep her feet on the floor. She counted her breaths.

Webster said, "Have I got this wrong?"

Emily nodded. Humbled. Embarrassed. She had no idea this was coming. Webster's face was a mixture of everything in the world. There was love and pain and anger and, Emily thought, shame. It was the last of those that made her uncomfortable.

Emily said, "I'm sorry. I wasn't....I'm not...."

"Are you with someone?"

Emily nodded. Webster obviously didn't know about Books. They hadn't made a big deal of their relationship, But Webster wasn't almost everyone. She was too scary, too senior, too driven. She was probably less connected to the office gossip than anyone in the entire building.

"I thought. I just thought..." she said.

Emily knew what she thought. She messed around with her because she gave Emily a bollocking, gave her a physical compliment, which probably no one had done for twenty years. Then went on doing it, deliberately keeping her off balance, and entering her space, giving her compliments, for no reason at all except that Emily was feeling scratchy.

"In the hospital, when I held your hand.....I assumed you'd pull it away, but you didn't. You did the opposite."

"It was nice actually. I liked it."

"And that suit you wore. Almost identical to mine. I thought you were signalling something. And this morning, in the interview room, you seemed so....so..."

So happy, Emily finished the thought for her. She had been happy then because Khaled was there with her, and because she realised something about how her crazy brain operated and because she felt comfortable, at last, with that knowledge.

"I'm an idiot," Emily told her. "You need to know that. Everyone else does. The safest thing, honestly, is to ignore me completely. I'm good at detective work. That's about all. Actual life is not my forte."

She half smiled at that. She was the same. "Can I ask? Your current partner...?"

"It's a man. Books. I assumed you'd know."

Webster looked grim and she looked hurt, but more like the Webster Emily used to know. She knew she was confusing to people. It wasn't the first time somebody had misread her signals. But she knew which way she swayed. Webster cried then. Briefly and with embarrassment, but it seemed like a clean thing to do. Truthful. And after a while, something changed. Things felt easier and lighter. The waitress came with food, messed around with the cutlery, and asked if they had everything they needed.

Webster said, "I'm not very good at the dating game."

"You can't be worse than me," Emily replied. Empathy cost nothing. "You should be more confident. Oh, and you should throw away that horrible little scarf. Forget the shiny aubergine shirts. Just be yourself."

Somewhere, somehow, all the nonsense just dropped away. They didn't judge themselves or each other. They were just normal. Webster allowed herself to be what she was: a fierce old dyke who would welcome companionship. Emily let herself be who she was: a half-crazy intelligence officer, part of an elite secret team, deeply embedded in a local police force to root out corruption and solve murders and arms smuggling, all at the same time. Multi-tasking that suited her many personalities and oddball way of thinking. Ray Quinn said it was her "gift' and she should treasure and nurture it. Oh, and she quite liked scary old dykes and definitely enjoyed the release from the narrow confines of office conventions. Emily imagine she still fancied her, but it didn't bother her if she didn't.

Over pudding, she tried to talk to Emily about becoming a Detective Sergeant, but she shook her head. Webster was obviously completely unaware of Emily's real status and power. One word in the right ear and Webster could be removed completely in the blink of an eye, but Emily contented herself with, "some other time."

Webster nodded. She wanted Emily to call her Rhoda. Emily didn't want to encourage such closeness but couldn't seem rude. At the same time, she needed to maintain her cover, but she drew the line at calling her ma'am. Webster had obviously been looking at her file, because she said, "I see you put your name down for the undercover course."

Emily laughed inwardly because she could run the course herself if needed. Nevertheless, she was pleased that her file, her legend, had not revealed anything it shouldn't have, even under her trained and hawk-like eye. It had been Books who created the file. Beautiful Books. When she met him he couldn't even read, but he had blossomed since then into the newest member of their little gang. She didn't know how many they were in number, but Books and her were the latest incomers as far as she knew. What she was sure of was that none of them, however many they were, would dare to even think of opposing Frank or, worse still, Ray Quinn. He may be retired officially, but they all knew he would step in to solve a problem and it wouldn't remain a problem for very long at all, whether it was a human issue or another kind.

"Just dipping my toe in the water, really," Emily said, being deliberately vague. Books would approve.

"Is that all? Some officers get addicted to danger, you know. The thrill of it. I wouldn't want to see that happen to you."

Emily said the right things. That she was not addicted to danger, that she'd much prefer to stay out of harm's way, that she wanted to build her professional skillset. Webster accepted it, maybe, but Emily had been made to sit a psychometric test for the course recently. Sixty questions to be completed and an hour to do them. No right or wrong: they just wanted to find out what kind of person she was. Emily was prepared, of course. Thoroughly prepared by Books and Frank.

She knew that if she responded honestly, she wouldn't have a prayer of getting on the course, so she just selected which personality she was going to be and adapted her answers accordingly. It wasn't hard. It was probably easier for her to do that, than it was for other people to take the test and respond as they should.

Webster listened to Emily for a while, then changed the subject. She said, "I got Kirby to speak to Strathclyde. We want them to make McCormack a priority target."

"Thanks."

"It might work, you know. If Strathclyde aren't completely useless."

"Yes, but they've sort of had their chance, haven't they? They've been looking for five years."

"He wasn't wanted for the attempted murder of a police officer. And they didn't have a DS demanding regular progress updates."

"Right, but how much of our resources would we put into this if things were the other way around? No leads. No recent photos. No address. If the man does something stupid, they'll pick him up. If not, they won't. On the other hand, there are other ways to catch people."

"Meaning."

Webster glared at Emily. The ferocity of her look made her laugh. She was being herself. She couldn't know how wide of the mark she was. Frank, her father, was more deeply undercover than Emily herself!

"I can find people to ask. Not policemen. Not criminals. Just there may be an alternative to waiting for Strathclyde."

Webster didn't understand what Emily meant, but she nodded. She didn't approve, didn't like it, but didn't rip her head off.

"If they've been careful about DNA," she said.

"It may not do us any good even if we do locate them, but we can't not look," Emily replied.

"Yes." Webster's face moved in a way Emily couldn't interpret. "It's a strange sort of justice, isn't it? Khaled kills Flowers and does that to her corpse. And then, years later, he gets the exact same treatment from McCormack."

She'd expand on all this, except that Emily was shaking her head.

"You don't agree. Clearly." She was laughing at Emily.

"He loved her. Khaled and Flowers. He never stopped loving her. That's what we've been investigating here. A love story."

"A love story that happens to be accompanied by two murders"

"Well, yes." That didn't seem like an interesting objection to Emily. The murders only made the love that bit more real, the flame that bit brighter. "In his apartment. Khaled's. There was a sailing boat lit with fairy lights. It was the only really sentimental thing he had. If I had to guess, I'd say she was the love of his life."

"When did you go to his apartment?" Webster, typically, remembered that Emily was never detailed to go there.

"I wanted to see it," Emily shrugged, and the evasion was accepted. She then added, "and, as it happens, I think he turned out to be the love of Flowers' life too. That wasn't how it was meant to be, not for her. She was moving on. She'd presumably have found someone else, settled down and lived the kind of life she was always meant to lead. But the way I see it, he set her on the path to that new future. Took her from a world that was destroying her. Given that she never reached her future, Khaled was the best thing she ever had."

Emily wanted to say that she was pleased Khaled was chopped to shreds and scattered around. Him and her, united at last. But the happy atmosphere of their session might have buckled at that particular insight, so she kept it to herself. Webster, she knew, didn't necessarily agree. She saw this the way any police officer would. They had a link between Flowers and Khaled. They suspected that she moved on, but he didn't. On Webster's reading of events, it was quite possible that he hassled Flowers. Demanded to see her. Wanted to restart things. She refused and there was a struggle. Then it was either a deliberate killing or a gruesome accident. Either way, he killed her and in some kind of weird, angry ritual scattered her parts across a part of the area they once had made their own. The case began with two victims and a million suspects. Khaled now looked like being the one in a million. The man who did it. Nothing Emily said would convince Webster otherwise, and indeed she did realise that Webster might be correct. At this stage, they were all still speculating. But as she signaled for the bill, Emily realised that the truth suddenly felt closer; a golden apple glimmering in the darkness. She had the strange thought that she knew who killed Rose Flowers. She didn't have a name or even a theory. But it was as though she knew she had all the pieces required, that she'd seen the pattern, just hadn't known that she'd seen it.

"There is a cherry tree at Elsie Williams's house," Emily announced.

"What?"

"And those fruit trees, the ones trained to grow flat against a wall, they're clipped in summer."

"What are you talking about?"

"Rose Flowers," Emily said. "If Khaled didn't kill her, then someone did. Probably one of our two hundred and whatever people of interest. I'm just trying to....." She had nothing, she realised. Nothing tangible. Nothing even that got as far as a theory. So she ended, "trying to think laterally."

In the restaurant around her, she felt Khaled's spirit bubble with joy. She couldn't help but smile with him.

Webster smiled too. "It's a shame you're not a lesbian," she told Emily. "You'd make some girl very happy."

"You too," Emily said. "You just need to get out more."

She nodded. "I'll try. I really will."

"A bit of confidence. That's all you need."

"I'll give it a go."

"There are websites, you know."

She nodded again. When they went outside, sunshine blazed over snow and ice. The streets were almost happy.

Emily said, "Rhoda," and she stopped. She looked at Emily with that twisted expression of hers. Emily teased the scarf from her neck and dropped it in a municipal rubbish bin. She smiled at Emily and mouthed, "thank you."

They walked back to the office as Khaled whooped above them in the frozen air. Emily told herself she was going to find out who killed Rose Flowers, going to find justice for Khaled. Things would turn out well. All would be well.

She was struck by a sudden recollection from long ago. "All shall be well, and all shall be well, and all manner of things shall be well." This referred to Julian of Norwich who was an anchoress, a woman who set herself apart for God and lived isolated in a cell. The similarity with Webster increased the more she recalled the story. She appealed for three things. Firstly, a stronger understanding of passion, then she appealed for a sickness which would last until her death so that she could be allowed to experience all that a body and soul experience in death but without actual death itself. Finally, she longed for three 'wounds', comprising absolute contrition, kind compassion and steadfast longing.

It seemed her unusual prayer was being answered. Julian had indeed become deathly ill. Everyone around her despaired of her life. She also believed she was dying. The last rites were administered to her. Then a wonderful thing happened: Julian experienced what a future generation might describe as a near-death experience. At the crisis of her sickness, between four and nine one afternoon, she received fifteen "showings," or revelations. She reported that heaven opened to her, she beheld Christ in his glory, and she saw the meaning and power of his sufferings. She also saw Christ's mother, Rose, exalted and beloved.

In her thirteenth showing, Julian received a comforting answer to a question that had long troubled her: "In my folly, before this time I often wondered why, by the great foreseeing wisdom of God, the onset of sin was not prevented: for then, I thought, all should have been well. This impulse [of thought] was much to be avoided, but nevertheless I mourned and sorrowed because of it, without reason and discretion. But Jesus, who in this vision informed me of all that is needed by me, answered with these words and said: 'It was necessary that there should be sin; but all shall be well, and all shall be well, and all manner of things shall be well.'

"These words were said most tenderly, showing no manner of blame to me nor to any who shall be saved."

In this she recognized the compassion she had prayed for. She was impressed with her need to be joyful in all circumstances, however adverse, and for no particular reason, except this: that all things will ultimately be put right by Christ. She came to such a sense of the awfulness of sin that she reckoned the pains of hell were to be chosen in preference to it. Indeed, to one who recognized the horror of sin, sin itself was hell. "And to me was shown no harder hell than sin. For a kind soul has no hell but sin."

The following night Julian received a final, sixteenth showing while she slept. In it Satan and his hosts assailed her, but God gave her grace, and she fixed her eyes on the crucified Christ and trusted that because of his suffering and victory over sin he could protect her, and he delivered her from the demonic jeers and mutterings. She recovered to live thirty-three years longer. Soon after her recovery, Julian recorded a short account of her revelations. Twenty years after her visions, having meditated long upon them, she added more thoughts as to their meaning. Both the short and the long accounts were disseminated in manuscript form and, after the invention of the printing press, published in many editions. Centuries later, Christians still read her Showings with interest and wonder to what extent Julian of Norwich actually penetrated the mysteries of the unseen world.

Emily knew it would all end well. She had confidence that they would solve the riddles involved in this case. It wasn't just a feeling. It was a deep, complete knowing. Was this part of what people called her 'gift?' That is something she didn't know.

-45-

The week ended. Warmer weather returned. The polar bears left the town centre. Except where the ploughs had left banks of coarse brown snow, the streets and pavements were mostly clear again. Dirty water gurgled into a million drains and gutters. The gritty salt remained.

There was no sunshine, just the pre-Christmas city they had always known. Cloudy, chill, threatening rain. The sun set at 4 pm. They had a meagre eight hours of daylight and those hours are seldom bright. Emily's body gradually recovered. Her cuts were sore, but her skin grafts were doing fine.

Books and Emily spent plenty of time together. She wasn't up for any very energetic sex, but Books had an impressive variety of gentler alternatives. They told each other that they loved each other. She knew she had said that before, in hospital, but it was different saying it now, without the drama of calamity. And when she said it, she tried to figure out what she felt. Was this love? Did she feel as a person ought to when they are in love? And if she did, did that mean that Books and her were forever? That they needed to get married, have children, buy a nice house in a pleasant district, and, in general, that she needed to model myself on Gentle Jenny with bread on the worktop and a bun in the oven?

Those thoughts made her feel dizzy. And some problems didn't need immediate solution. Books, she hoped, knew her well enough not to force the issue. She hadn't told him, or anyone, about her lunch with Webster. Khaled's mother did come to Cardiff. She guessed there were forms to sign and things to organise, but she spoke almost no English. She picked her up from Heathrow along with a police interpreter. The mother,

Fatima, was veiled and wore sandals over bare feet. Emily doubted she'd ever seen a northern winter. Her face was lined with the sort of wrinkles that go beyond age into some kind of other state altogether.

When they crossed the Severn Bridge into Wales, her eyes stared out over the estuary, with anxiety, or sadness, or astonishment, or maybe something else altogether. She was with Fatima about two days all told. She was with her as she entered her dead son's apartment. With her as they went to the Muslim graveyard, where the graves lay perpendicular to Mecca and the headstones were as simple as possible, because orthodox Islam frowns on excess adornment. They had a bunch of flowers bought from a local garage. Carnations, a mixture of white, pink and yellow. Fatima laid them reverentially. They stood by the grave for about fifteen minutes, until the cold drove them away.

She tried to have a conversation with her but didn't get far. At first she thought it was a failure on her part. Only later did she realise that it was possibly what Fatima needed. To spend these days in silence. A pilgrim visiting the monuments of her son's lost life. On the afternoon of the last day with her, Emily drove her down to the yacht club. The grey, uneasy sea.

"He used to go sailing here. With a girl he liked. They were happy together," Emily told her.

The interpreter translated. Fatima said nothing, but she gazed out to sea, the fringes of her headscarf pulling in the breeze. As they got in the car to drive away, she patted Emily's hand, then squeezed it. Her brown eyes found Emily's. She said, in English, "Thank you." Then again, "Thank you."

Emily hugged her. That evening, when she dropped her at her cheapie hotel, Emily said it would be someone else looking after her the next day. She tried to say thank you again, but she couldn't, and this time there were tears in her eyes.

When Emily was back at work, she made a call she had been putting off. One she was slightly scared of. She phoned Jack Yorath, the DCI whose name Johnston gave her. Trustworthy Jack, Jon Johnston's pick of the old-timers.

Emily gave her name and asked if she could meet him for a drink.

"Emily? The Emily? Frank's girl?"

"That's me, yes. It's my father I wanted to talk about."

"Bloody hell. Okay, yes, I'd be happy to talk."

They agreed to meet that evening at his house, because it was more private than a pub. Emily asked him not to mention it to anyone. Not even any former colleagues. Not for any reason at all. He agreed.

They met that same evening. Yorath lived just outside Caerphilly, a nice house, nicely looked after. They sat in a little snug come office off a tiled hall. From a room somewhere behind them, someone played scales on a piano, interrupted now and again by a snatch of briskly delivered Bach. Yorath offered whisky or tea. Emily asked for water while he got himself a large whisky.

"Blood hell, Emily," he said.

Emily let him inspect her as she thought to herself that a lot of people seemed to be using that phrase. He thought what everyone thought: that she didn't look much like her father. Emily wanted to trust someone. Maybe he could be that person.

She said as much. "Chief Inspector…"

"Jack. It's Jack. Please."

He was sitting in a green leather chair. Emily was perched on some kind of upholstered bench, which was surprisingly comfortable. The room had low lighting, some lever arch files, plenty of books. "I don't know if you can guess why I'm here."

"Not exactly. But a daughter of Frank in the CID? That's not exactly your standard police background." Shrewd, but nowhere near the whole truth.

"No."

Professional interrogators, as Yorath and Emily were, didn't get uncomfortable with silence; they let it work for them. The empty moments could be as revealing as everything else. He sipped from his whisky, while Bach skittered behind them.

"You probably know I was adopted," she said.

Of course he did. The adoption process created plenty of paperwork. All that ended up in police records, and Yorath's career was spent combating serious crime. He could hardly not have known. Another example of the creative magic of her lovely Books. Once he'd learned to read, there had been no end to his talents. Quite likely part of his curiosity in seeing Emily was to find out what she looked like.

"I know my father had his contacts with the police, to put it mildly, but he was a good father to me. He and Mum, both of them."

"I don't doubt that."

"I need to know where I came from. Dad's story had to do with me appearing mysteriously one Sunday, just found sitting in his car."

"Outside chapel," added Yorath, smiling at the thought of her father in the house of the Lord.

"I don't believe that story. I think Dad knows much more than he lets on. I can't ask him direct, or if I do he'll just give me his standard patter. If I ask any of his old friends, they might be helpful, but they'd always let Dad know I'm asking. And if Dad hears I'm digging, my chances of finding anything out will disappear completely."

Yorath nodded. "You haven't been in the job that long, not yet. But when you have been, when you've put in the years, you get to know your quarry. Your dad was the most talented man I ever knew. It wasn't just his organisation, though that was always amazing, it was the way his associates were totally loyal to him. Those things go beyond discipline. It was a kind of love he inspired. Funny word to use, that, but I'm sure I'm right. I think people loved him."

Emily nodded. They did. She was sure they did.

"So I'm here to ask if you have any thoughts at all."

She stopped there, not wanting to lead him by the hand, but impatience got the better of her. "I'm twenty-six now. I was maybe two and a half when I was found." Yorath's face starts to do the maths. Yorath's face was a mask, but a mask that concealed thought. He was still for a moment or two, then put aside his whisky, grabbed a pen and swivelled the light.

"Nineteen-eighty-six. Everything from hard truth to wild expectation. Okay?"

"Okay." Emily knew all about her father, of course, but wanted to find out what was known outside their elite circle. She knew that whatever she was about to be told, would be a legend. A detailed and amazing legend, put together by her more amazing Books. She was testing it.

"His car business: buying and selling dodgy vehicles. Turnover of about five million. Rumours of an inner circle, but never any names. Probably people you know. He always kept them close."

Emily supressed a smile.

"There was one man who was thought to be special."

That would be Ray Quinn, Emily thought. "Name?" she asked.

"You must be joking!" he responded. I don't know and I don't want to know. Legend has it that people have become terminally ill after discovering such details."

"Then the sidelines. Drugs? It'd be the obvious thing. It was always assumed there had been some kind of drugs activity and I think there was. Ecstasy? Possibly. The drug scene was just starting to become big then. Your dad would have had the infrastructure needed to distribute it. But no links to anything harder than that."

Books had certainly been dutiful in his attention to detail.

"Dad hates hard drugs. He wouldn't have touched them. Mum would have killed him if he had." Emily felt the need to lighten things.

Yorath laughed again.

"Okay. But I'm going to say your dad did one or two big deals at least. If someone approached him needing to offload a big supply of cannabis coming in, I don't think he'd have refused."

Emily nodded. "You're right. He wouldn't have said no."

"Okay, so you want to know names. Associates, the inner circle? Same as before. But then there'd have been the international end of things too. He probably didn't know the distributors elsewhere. The way the international sellers operate, they don't want their buyers to know each other. Turnover involved? I don't know.

Let's say two or three big deals, worth a million or two each. Profits on those things maybe fifty percent of turnover."

Emily nodded yet again, but thoughtfully. Her father was not short of money, but his legend made it much larger than it really was. Well done, my lovely Books. "Construction. Municipal contracts. Development permits. Prostitution? We drew a blank."

Emily agreed with that. "Mum would have killed him. She almost killed him when he opened the lap-dancing clubs."

"Handling stolen goods? Definitely. Any fence in Cardiff would have needed your father's say so to operate. Frank saw Cardiff as his turf. If people didn't go via your dad for that sort of thing, they'd have regretted it."

"Yes." It seemed strange, sitting with Yorath, in this comfortable room, talking about her father in this way. There was a question sitting alongside them now, one that she had to ask. "In terms of really serious stuff, I mean the worst things..."

"That wasn't his style. There were rumours. But that was the point in a way. No one ever told stories against him.

"Meaning?"

"Meaning exactly that. The effect your father has had is that Cardiff is controlled. He seems to be cleaning up the place and we haven't been able to find out why or, in detail, how. He has drawn evil people in and dealt with them. For all I know, he may be still at work. Perhaps, even, supported by people powerful enough to be working for our elders and betters. I've sometimes wondered whether the establishment is somehow behind what he does. Now that is a thought!"

Emily smiled. She had tested the effectiveness of her father's legend, as constructed by Books. It had been a necessary thing to do. But he was unwittingly close to the truth.

Yorath and Emily talked for another ninety minutes and at the end, she blundered out onto the street. There were crusted ridges of snow still but mostly the town looked like it always looked at that time of year. A new weirdness this, the weirdness of the normal. Even though Emily had no tangible fact to walk away with, she felt like she had really started. Begun an investigation whose target was her. She drove away certain that her father's secrets were her own. That he knew her biological father, knew her biological mother. That he knew, or guessed, the reason for her illness.

Perhaps he had been a better father for that knowledge. More protective. More loving. More strategic and more thoughtful. She wasn't angry with her father. His secrets were hers too. She belonged. She thought of the team as a family. Ray Quinn, Frank, Books and Emily. Heaven help anybody who opposed or upset them. It was the nicest feeling in the world.

-46-

Takeaway trundled on. When she got back into the swing of the morning's briefings, she found things had changed. Kirby was there every single time, adding the senior officer gloss to Webster's parade ground bark.

The 'people of interest' had been swept away into a single corner of the noticeboards, all 288 of them. The photos of Khaled and Flowers still dominated. The red love heart too. But now there was a whole slew of material being generated by the Precision investigation. More names, data files, lists of statements and interviews. The operation now had a third full time data officer.

Some key facts were pouring in. The biggest: Stuart Brotherton had sent a preliminary report which confirmed that Precision Tools was, beyond doubt, manufacturing arms. Not entire weapons systems, but spare parts for other people's systems. Gun barrels for heavy artillery. Firing pins. The gears and calibration equipment needed for range adjustment. Laser cut ballistic grade steel of the sort used for tank armour. IED blast protection gear. Suspension and chassis systems built to the kind of specifications you'd need for an armoured car. The hydraulic gear needed to raise a multiple rocket launch system to its firing position. Anti-blast screens that just happened to fit the multiple rocket launch systems in most widespread use across the Middle East.

There were still a handful of suspect items where Brotherton hadn't been able to track down their likely use, but his investigations continued. Equally, in some cases, it seemed that the items sold would have needed some modest re-engineering to make them fully functional as weapons-parts, but the sophisticated work had already been done.

By Precision Tools. Which had no export licence.

Webster had also had a trio of DCs investigating the firm's buyers, who existed all across North Africa and the Middle East. Its biggest customer was Saadawi, whose eldest brother bought weapons for the Egyptian military. And whose family owned a slew of construction and trading interests, primarily in Egypt, but operating across the entire Middle East.

Numerous other buyers also looked as dodgy as hell. The Libyan buyer was an affiliate of the state owned Libyan oil company. Its purchases were theoretically all drilling equipment related, but Brotherton said at least fifty percent of the items bought had clear military use.

The Lebanese buyer: a trading company with links to the Syrian regime. The Saudi buyer: a probable intermediary for a putative Yemeni end buyer.

Her hunch about Aftab Khaled was also proving to be right. Webster had officers contact every firm on Khaled's sizeable Rolodex. They'd sought information about what he talked to them about. In particular, any orders he helped arrange for them.

It was slow work, but the indications were that Khaled was indeed building a virtual arms manufacturing network. They'd know more once they had more data and once Brotherton had a chance to analyse it, but it was already pretty clear what the answer would be. Emily regretted that, in a way. She'd got on so well with the corpse of Khaled, it was sad to find how much she'd detested him in real life. His little enterprise was no more ethical than Idris Khan's. Some people are better as corpses. They're easier to like.

It was not just the Precision Tools end of things where they were making progress. They were making progress on the Flowers-Khaled link too. They knew for certain now that they had a relationship. It wasn't just Swansea Bay Yacht Club that confirmed it. The couple also went boating on the reservoir before it was emptied. A man who used to work there, renting boats, was able to recognise the pair.

Re-interviews of Flowers old friends and a new analysis of material generated by the original enquiry all tended to confirm their general suspicion. That Flowers, for whatever reason, got herself into a bad place when she started pole dancing and waitressing. The dancing was both an effect of that bad head space, but also a perpetuating factor. Flowers was spiralling down. Then, her friends seemed to agree, she got happier. Though she kept quiet about the details, it was assumed she had a man. She stopped dancing. Drank less. Got healthier.

As her old life got back on track, she no longer needed that rescue relationship. Again, they couldn't be sure, but it did seem like she was the one who ended it, not him. Some of these things weren't beyond doubt, but most things were. They worked in a world of competing uncertainties. But for the first time since the enquiry started, it felt like all their effort was paying off. They were moving towards arrests, prosecutions, convictions.

Emily's role in the hubbub was nicely ambiguous for a change. Partly because of that lunch and partly because of her little adventure on the hill, Webster gave her considerable discretion in what she did. As far as Emily was concerned, it was time that Rose Flowers had more attention. It was partly that she was intrigued by the testimony of the boat man. Previously, it was assumed that any normal girl leaving a party early and wanting to return to town would simply walk direct from the party to the station and await her train. She'd have had no reason, in failing light, to detour to a largely deserted reservoir.

Only, if you had recent romantic associations with that spot, mightn't you do just that? Mightn't, in fact, it be part of the reason why you left the party early, so you could commune with the spirit of your ex? Your past happiness?

Emily piled her desk with printouts and started to work. When Elsie Williams thrust her walking stick into a small boy's bike, it was August 2007. She checked against her daughter and son-in-law's travel dates. They were visiting that summer. They were there when Elsie did it. Emily checked weather records. When they sent an officer to caution the old lady, it was a hot day. Sitting outside weather. Bee-buzzingly, heat-shimmeringly, summer-lawn beckoningly hot. There was a door at the back of the garage, so if the front was open, anybody could simply have walked from the street, through the garage, into the garden. Or, of course, vice versa.

The officer concerned was away on holiday, which was frustrating because she wanted to talk to him now. But that wasn't the main thing, not by any means. She felt herself convalescing, working more slowly than she normally would. The pace was unimportant. It was the outcome that mattered. Rose Flowers had waited so long, another week or two wouldn't bother her. Her leg was in a freezer, her head in motor oil, her thumb in vegetable oil, and a bit of leg was packed in salt. Her arms were packed in polythene, but hadn't deteriorated as much as they should.

Emily clicked around on the internet for a bit and discovered that supermarket salads are bagged up in nitrogen. The exclusion of oxygen preserves the food that much longer. She also found that she could buy a nitrogen cylinder on eBay relatively cheaply as well as helium. But who would want to do that?

Mervyn Rogers and Emily went down to David Marr-Phillips's glitzy waterfront office to interview him about his arrangement with Khan. He had a copy of the shareholder agreement waiting for them: the one that gave him a slice of Precision Tools and Khan a slice of some of Marr-Phillips's property assets. Also, a report from an accountant stating that the valuations had been determined at fair market value. Some stuff on tax treatment. Accounts for the property companies. Financial data on Precision Tools. And so on.

Marr-Phillips was completely open with them and visibly irritated at the time they were consuming. Neither Mervyn nor Emily really knew how to play things. Mervyn was best at frightening the tough but stupid criminals they spent most of their lives chasing, and they both felt out of their depth interviewing Marr-Phillips. They ended up asking repetitive, circular questions for twenty minutes, then let themselves be escorted politely from the office.

They gave Webster a full report of everything. She too didn't know what to do with the Marr-Phillips, Khan connection. They decided not to pursue it. If they could nail Khan, other things may start to emerge. But maybe not. It didn't look to Emily like Marr-Phillips had done anything much wrong. Nailing Khan seemed well within their grasp. Dunbar too. Webster and Emily shared a grim determination to see both men destroyed. Emily had a personal preference to see how much they'd enjoy a prison in Libya. Or taste the pleasure of Bashar Assad's hospitality in an Aleppo jail. Smashed ankles and screams that echoed forever.

That wouldn't happen, of course, but she'd have been happy enough if they did a long stint in Cardiff Prison. They may or may not get Khan on murder, but there was a maximum ten-year reward for weapons export offences. That was twenty years too short, in Emily's humble opinion. She thought about Althea and Tristan. What did it do to children to learn that their father was a criminal and a suicide? What kind of abandonment was that? The jailing of Khan might seem like redemption of the best sort.

These things ran slowly, however. Precision Tools' lawyers were working to impede the investigation at every turn, claiming unreasonable interference with the operation of their business. So far the Chief Constable and the county court had swatted aside every objection. Emily didn't think the lawyers expected anything else. She thought their strategy relied on pushing up the cost of their investigation to a point at which they'd have to start scaling back their effort. But Webster had the total support of top management. She thought, like Emily, that they would secure their conviction.

Slow was okay, it was the outcome that mattered. One week ended and another began. It was now two weeks before Christmas and the station started to feel a little Christmassy cheer. Secretaries wore tinsel earrings. Jon Breakell attended the morning briefing in an elf hat. Jamie Donaldson went out to lunch at twelve fifteen and returned four hours later, barely able to focus. A fake memo was circulated seeking the apprehension of a well-known criminal, thought to operate an unlicensed flying vehicle, to be in breach of multiple immigration regulations, and to force nocturnal entry to millions of homes. Believed to operate out of Lapland. Aliases included Saint Nick, Santa Claus, Father Christmas etc.

Tuesday was usually Emily's night, which meant, in theory, an opportunity to clean and iron things. In practice, it meant an opportunity to smoke a joint without worrying that Books was going to find her. An opportunity to moon around her own house, in her own way. On most nights that she spent on her own, Khaled came to see her. He wasn't always chuckling. He had a sadder side. There was something unsustainable in his earlier mood. Something skittish, excitable.

She liked his visits. If this was the form her psychotic side would take, she welcomed it. Better the occasional visit from a corpse than for herself to become one of their number. She didn't take her Amisulpride. The pills went back to the bathroom cabinet. One Tuesday night, she came home from the office at six thirty and, as she let herself in, she heard someone moving about upstairs. There was a black bag on the landing. She shouted up a greeting, but got nothing back. She went to the kitchen and put the kettle on and fetched some weed from the potting shed.

She started rolling joints. She hadn't left the house unlocked but some people don't need keys. There wasn't much in the fridge, but there was probably enough because Lenny was like Emily. He ate randomly. She made peppermint tea for herself and put black tea out ready.

Then Lenny appeared. The unremarkable Lenny. Old jeans and a jumper. Brown eyes like a spaniel's. They didn't kiss, hug or shake hands. She made Lenny's tea and they lit a joint each. Emily had never asked Lenny much about his life. She used to, but realised he either said nothing or made stuff up, so she stopped asking. He would talk when he wanted to. Emily told him her news. About Books. About Flowers and Khaled. She told him about Precision Tools: how a small Welsh engineering firm figured out it could make big money by exporting weapons parts on the pretext that they had innocent industrial purposes.

"This company is where?"

"Down on the coast, just beyond the city."

Lenny's face was dark. He'd been in war zones. He knew what modern weaponry could do.

"Okay," he said, meaning 'go on.'

She told him about Ross and Olaf. About being made to stand outside in the snow, wearing nothing more than trousers and a T-shirt. About how she escaped and how she almost didn't.

Lenny muttered something in what might have been Russian but could be Lithuanian. Then he said, "you know these people?"

"We've identified the Scottish man." She gave Lenny his name, photo and the fact that he stole a number plate in Drumchapel. "There's money in the drawer," Emily said. "Books asked me to give it to you." She had put three thousand pounds in cash in the kitchen drawer. It was clever of Books, she thought, to use Lenny. Good use of resources, and easily deniable. He took the documents, studied them briefly, then he said, "You want me to find him? Or what?"

Emily didn't know how far Lenny would go, but she wanted to meet those two again. "No, just find him. I need an address, that's all."

"Okay."

He nodded. Not much more to say on the matter. The result was inevitable. They talked about other things. Smoked and drank tea. Lenny decided to take a shower.

Emily was perfectly comfortable with it. Books was her love and nothing would disturb that. Lenny came down. His hair was wet and his t-shirt stuck to his to his back and chest because he hadn't dried himself properly. Bare feet.

And then they weren't alone. In the opening to the living room, Books appeared. There were storm clouds rolling around his head and he had a deep bladed anger between his eyes. Emily had never seen him like this. Ray and Frank had and it had convinced them that he was ready. Ready to be part of their elite and highly secretive, team. That side of Books scared Emily, she had to admit, but it was a side of him that Ray and Frank viewed as a good thing.

He called around from time to time, even on her nights off. He never stayed and only dropped by if he was in the area, but there was no rule that said he wasn't allowed there. Emily was sure he'd have knocked before using his key, because he was a polite man and because he knew Emily liked her space. Lenny's eyes were watchful, but they always were. He was completely calm, but he always was.

Books studied Lenny and the evidence of a recent shower. Emily recognised an ugly biology in the room. The biology of rutting stags. Silverback gorillas battling over harems. Wolves snarling for supremacy.

She knew what Books was thinking. He was figuring that he was taller, stronger, younger, fitter. That he could give Lenny a kicking. Emily was unsure, but didn't want to find out. She followed the template of her own biology and stood up.

"Books, no. This isn't what you think it is. Books, this isn't anything." How trite did she sound? She could hear her own voice high and shrill. Too high and way too shrill.

Books stepped up close to Lenny. Emily didn't think he was going to hit him, but he was certainly not getting up close for a kiss. Lenny looked into Books' eyes, held the gaze evenly, and took one pace, only one, back. It was to give himself room. Emily danced around being uselessly feminine but this wasn't about anything she said or didn't say. The male hormones needed to find their balance first.

Lenny said softly, "Please be a little careful and we can all talk like respectable people."

Then he stepped away another pace, but only a small one. Emily babbled. "Books, I smoke dope. Not often, but I do. This is Lenny. He's a friend. My martial arts teacher, or used to be. He's just taken a shower. That's all. We have never had sex. Never. Not once and I've known him for six years now."

They tiptoed back from the precipice. Books looked at Lenny with different eyes, wondering what kind of man this was who could resist such temptation. Emily wondered whether this would change his opinion of her. Would he look at her through different eyes?

Her colleagues at the station loved to tease her about a couple of incidents in the past. A man whose knee she dislocated and whose testicle she ruptured. Another man whom she kicked in the head and threw off a cliff. It was assumed that she achieved those things by accident almost, that a petite woman of no great strength or fitness could do these things only by fluke. Some fleeting combination of time and circumstance.

Emily said, "Can we talk? Can we all just sit and talk?"

Her voice sounded unreal, even to herself. Lenny ignored her and talked to Books. "Come."

He took Books outside, showed him the potting shed, the marijuana plants, the heat lamps, Emily's bag of weed, her cubes of resin and the little seedbank which allowed her to grow the sweetest weed. Emily stayed put, sitting at the kitchen table wondering if she still had a boyfriend. When Books came back, his eyes were filled with questions.

Emily began the explanation.

"When I was in recovery, half in Cotard's half not, marijuana was one of the few things I could rely on to calm my mind. I don't smoke very often these days. Maybe once a week. Two or three times if I feel my head is in a bad place. And one day, maybe, I'll give up completely. But for now, I still need this. Maybe I always will."

"So it's medicinal?"

Books' voice was hoarse, as if he'd lost it in an attic somewhere, and had only just found it, rusty and cobwebbed, like an old key.

"Well, not always, obviously." She gestured at the table. At Lenny. "It can be social too. But not often. I grow my own so I don't have to buy it. And I never sell it."

"You could have told me."

"Really? Do you really think I could have done?

Books didn't answer. He was no idiot, but in the last few minutes he'd uncovered an assumed infidelity, discovered that his girlfriend was a drug user and was now starting to wonder just how much violence his possible future wife was capable of. This was not the gentle Emily he wanted her to be. The possible future mother of his possible future children stood waiting to hear their father's verdict.

It didn't come. Lenny said, "You are Books, yes?"

"Yes." The same rust and cobwebs.

"Mr. Books, I think we go to the pub now. You and me."

And all of a sudden the biology flipped again. To a place she had not thought possible. She was standing in the room, not two yards from either man, and she wasn't there at all. There was some male to male thing being exchanged which bypassed her completely. She thought Books was trying to make sense of Lenny, and Lenny was figuring out Books. And she didn't appear to be there at all. She said something, but her voice was without sound. It did not register. Unimportant.

Books said, "okay." He extended a hand and Lenny shook it. Their eyes were still hard, but it was that masculine hardness which carried no personal implication. Books, remembering that Emily existed, half turned to her and said, "you'll be okay?" It was not a question and her nod wasn't an answer. The men left and Emily, tidied up. She put on Annie Lennox, because that would drive them nuts, she hoped.

They were still not back. How long can it take to drink a pint of brown liquid? She was bored enough and agitated enough to clean the kitchen and hoover the living room. She found herself dusting, for heaven's sake, but decided to stop cleaning in case she turned into a dutiful housewife. She started to text Books, but cancelled without sending. What on earth could they be talking about? She thought about ironing, but removed limescale from the shower screen instead. She plucked her eyebrows, walked downstairs, then walked back up again.

This was not going well. She was having feelings, but she didn't know what they were. She had exercises for times like this, breathing exercises, mindfulness, but she was too agitated to do them. She was just walking downstairs to fetch the hoover when she heard Lenny and Books outside. She sat on the stairs waiting for the door to open, the possible mother of Books' possible future children.

-47-

When they came in, they were best buddies. Backslaps and beery in Books' case; quiet but emphatic in Lenny's. They arrived back hungry and she'd thrown most of the food away. She made the best of what was left. She cooked chips and laid out some tinned mackerel, a jar of korma sauce, some stale mini-pretzels, a tube of tomato paste, some crackers she managed to rescue from the bin, and some more bendy carrots. Lenny inspected the feast and said solemnly to Books, "You're a lucky man."

Emily was relieved to sense that it felt okay. She did, however, want them to leave. She wanted them out of her house with an urgency she didn't dare express.

Luckily, Lenny understood. He knew what it was like to have problems with your head and he didn't need Emily to tell him. After a while, he just got his things, took a couple of bags of weed, and left. Emily waved a weak goodbye from the kitchen table.

"I will send you a text," he said.

Books wanted to take Emily back to his place for a vigorous sexual workout. He needed to assert his own proprietorship, and Emily wanted that too, she needed space and said so. She put her arms around his lovely neck, found the muscles of his lovely back, and promised that tomorrow there would be no holding back. Emily hoped he understood and was relieved when he agreed to wait. Emily asked whether he was alright emotionally and about their relationship. She also meant the weed on the kitchen table and the cannabis plantation in the potting shed. But Books just said, "You might have told me the man was Spetsnaz."

Spetsnaz: the umbrella term given to the Russian special forces. Books had found out that Lenny worked in their Vympel counter terrorist unit, first as an operative, then as a trainer. He had got that information before he found the bottom of the first pint. Emily suddenly thought that Ray Quinn knew as well and probably even had dealings with him. She looked at her lovely Books, who was smiling indulgently at her. Smiling. Comfortable in their relationship, comfortable in the knowledge all was well and would be well. There was much that Emily had not been told and it was better that way. The team was working well. Emily's special gift was being allowed the room to flourish and develop.

Emily said, "you didn't give me much of a chance."

"No."

And then they kissed. And then kissing wasn't enough. And then Books carried her upstairs, dumped her on the bed and before very many seconds was getting started on a vigorous sexual workout a day earlier than agreed. Emily responded and, she hoped, reciprocated in a way likely to generate few complaints.

Afterwards, they lay panting beside each other.

"Any more secrets?" Books asked.

She thought about the hidden gun, the knife behind the bed. She considered her special relationship with Webster, the visits from Aftab Khaled, the Amisulpride in the bathroom cabinet. She brought to mind the full story about McCormack's jaw and the data leak from Precision Tools, and all the other details that could matter a lot to people like Books. But none of that stuff seemed very significant. Not at that moment.

"I haven't yet got you a Christmas present," she said.

He had his hand on her stomach. Emily drifted happily. She knew that her lovely Books was a fit lad and he ate his greens. She knew, with joyous recall, that he had been known to recharge, reload, and fire, two or even three or even (once) four times in the same night. She could see him wondering whether tonight might be one of those nights.

But it wasn't. She needed her space and said so. After Books left the house was empty, and when silence returned to the kitchen and crept like moonlight over the garden and stole upstairs like the last breath leaving a body, she became aware of her mind finding its peace. She didn't smoke any more. She had already had enough, so she took a shower, resenting the soapy water washing away the lingering presence of her lovely Books. She darkened the house and drank peppermint tea. She sat upright in bed, castled in pillows.

She expected Khaled to come, but all she sensed of him was a prickle of energy. The same sensation she first felt that night in the station with her, Books, Webster and Konchesky. She hadn't known what it was then, but it was Khaled making contact. She would miss him, of course, but she couldn't hang on. They grow up so fast. She wished she'd got closer to Rose Flowers. She would have, but chasing after two murders limited the time she could give to either. She regretted that, but was sure she would be forgiven. The dead are always forgiving, and Emily would give her what she needed.

She didn't know whether she slept or not. All she knew was that she was still sitting up when dawn arrived to reclaim the streets. The peppermint tea site was empty beside her, and her paring knife was in her hand. Her finger was through the loop and its blade pointed upward and outward at the lightening sky.

-48-

Later that same morning, Webster came by Emily's desk. She was in a severe dark suit, rumpled white shirt. Her iron grey hair had been recently cut and Emily liked her look. She wanted to smile, but didn't.

"Emily."

"Yes." Still no "ma'am" from Emily.

"I wanted to update you. The investigation into your attempted murder. We're not getting very far."

She delivered her update brusquely. Number plate recognition: nothing helpful. Forensics: nothing at all. Eyewitnesses: less than nothing.

"As you thought, it's going to be all but impossible to bring this to court, even if we find the perpetrators."

"I know."

"And we haven't found them."

Emily didn't know what to say to that. She moved her hands and face, just so it looked like she was doing her bit.

"The team I've had looking into things. They're on standby. They're available if anything comes up. But otherwise..."

Kirby has had his way. The troops were being redeployed. Emily admitted to herself that she would have done the same.

But Webster wasn't finished. "The other day. You mentioned there might be ways of finding McCormack."

"There might be. Yes." Emily stopped, because she wasn't sure why Webster was asking and then carefully, she said, "I'm making enquiries. I don't yet have anything concrete."

"Yes. I see." She rapped on Emily's desk with her knuckles. She moved a yellow notepad which wasn't in anyone's way and glared over Emily's shoulder at the grey stones of the Crown Court across the street. Then she came to a decision. She pulled something from her pocket. It was a small clear polythene evidence bag. "This is material attached to the Khaled enquiry. Would you please return it to the forensics lab? It shouldn't have been removed."

She handed it over. There were three hairs in the bag. Body hairs, from a hand or leg or chest. Specks of skin at the root.

"Yes."

She was about to say something else, but thought better of it and said nothing. She turned abruptly and stalked away. She was swallowed by the glass door that led to the lifts. A swinging monochrome reflection was all that remained. That, and those three hairs. Perversion of the course of justice, if looked at one way, justice itself, if you looked at it another. She put the bag in her pocket. Nobody needed to know about this.

When she looked that morning, there was only two grand left in her kitchen drawer.

The cold weather returned. First the cold, then the snow. There were satellite photos shown on the news. Britain re-created in ice. A white island floating on a sea that was dark teal close to the shore and a deep, inky aquamarine farther out. There were close ups of south Wales too, shown on local news and reproduced in local papers. The Bristol Channel was its usual dirty brown. The forests were white, but pricked through with evergreen. Holly and ice. Emily had never seen anything like it. Nor had anyone else. Temperature records tumbled again. Night after night she revisited that field above Capel in her dreams. Trousers and a T-shirt, worn under starlight.

Her father didn't quite accept that she was well on the road to health, and kept putting pressure on her to go back and live with him and mum, "at least until after Christmas, love. You don't want to worry about cooking and that." Emily told him, truthfully, that she didn't spend much of her time worrying about cooking, but compromised by spending more time at home than usual. Mum spoiled them with huge meals. Kay had boyfriend troubles and wafted around, wearing black, an iPhone always glowing at her palm. Ant was on the verge of being a proper teenager, but her natural sweetness kept popping out to overwhelm any incipient moodiness. Her Christmas list was already two pages long.

One evening, after they had eaten, as the family started to scatter, mum and Ant to watch TV, Kay to nurse her woes upstairs, her father scooped her up and took her through to his lair, his giant, cluttered studio. He clinked around with glasses, because he liked the whole palaver of the lead crystal tumblers and the heavy decanters, but neither of them drank very much. When she had something peaty and expensive in her glass, he showed her his latest toy. It was a chunk of rock, a meteorite supposedly.

"Three and a half kilos," he said with awe. "Just imagine where that's come from, how many miles it travelled to get here." He whirled the lump of rock through the air to show her how a meteorite travelled. She had no idea whether the item was genuine or not, or how much you'd have to pay to get a three and a half kilo chunk of space rock sitting lumpenly on your coffee table. If the rock was for real, then it was an extraordinary thing.

Then he turned serious. Worried, even.

"Listen, love, I should probably tell you."

He composed his features, but she interrupted. She thought she knew what he was about to say.

"About Capel?"

He nodded.

"It wasn't an accident," Emily said. "They were professionals. I was unlucky to get caught. None of us had any reason to suppose there was a risk. But I was lucky to get away, so it all evened out."

Dad was sitting by a heavily shaded lamp. His face intersected the angle of the light, so his face was a jigsaw of shadows.

"You shouldn't have been there alone," he said.

"No, I shouldn't really. There's an internal enquiry into whether we judged the risks appropriately. Someone was supposed to come with me. At the last minute, she couldn't come. I chose to go anyway. No one made me go."

"Love..." he began.

"Really, Dad? Really? You're going to say I should have told you that first day in the hospital. When you were most worried about me. Most likely to act on impulse. Let's say I had told you. That day. Or the next. The first time we were alone together. If I'd said, "Hey, dad, two professional killers did this to me and I'm lucky to be alive," you tell me: what would you have done?"

"Give me some credit. I don't just do the first thing that comes into my head."

He moved his face out of the light. It darkened, but simplified. He hadn't touched his drink.

"I don't know. I'd have made some calls. Have you located the people?"

She shook her head.

"Do you need our help?"

Emily knew who he meant.

"No. I'll deal with it. They will be found."

His face flickered with a smile. "It's what you do if you manage to catch them."

She smiled right back. "Oh, I think they'll regret their actions."

For a moment their smiles hung in the air together, pushing at each other. A flickering contest, then a truce.

"They're not local. One of them is Scottish, one of them Scandinavian," she added.

"I know," he said.

Emily looked at him.

"Let me do it," she said. "I need to do this myself. Don't forget, I'm not alone. I have Books. They won't want to meet him."

"I know," her father added. "You haven't mentioned Lenny."

Emily should not have been surprised. "Let's put it this way," she said, "whoever finds them, they will not be a happy pair."

Frank recognized her use of understatement. She was definitely growing as a member of the team. They chatted for a while, but she didn't volunteer any information. She didn't mention Drumchapel and didn't give McCormack's name. She knew one phone call from her father, to Ray Quinn, would settle the matter within one hour, and the result would be that she would not come face to face with the two men again. They didn't deserve such mercy.

She wore her woman of mystery suit into the office and got loads of compliments. Aside from the frostbitten spots on her toes, which would be there for some time, her skin was returning to normal. She hardly ever needed aspirin now.

She still lived in a world where Books' current and actual girlfriend and actual mother of his possible future children might be one and the same person. And so far, Books seemed to be okay with that. On one memorable evening she cooked him a meal and got all the ingredients just right and the cooking just right and the candles just right and everything just right. They even sat down to eat on the right side of nine o'clock.

Such occasions were necessarily rare. They still had work to do. They had investigated Idris Khan's stack of mobile phones. None of them had been used but, an interesting tidbit this, they didn't know that the whole lot were purchased as part of a batch of fifteen from an internet retailer. One of the phone numbers sold as part of that transaction received a call from the Capel area on the day of her almost murder. That wasn't remotely strong enough to secure a conviction for anything, but as far as Emily and Webster were concerned, it largely eliminated doubt that Idris Khan issued the order to kill me. Ross and Olaf asked for instructions. Khan told them to kill the copper. They drove back up the hill and tried to do just that. She wanted to see them with a passion that took her by surprise.

Her flame of anger burned brightly for Rose Flowers too. She wanted her killer too. And now, at last, she thought she was getting closer. The officer, Dai Beynon, came back from his time away and told her that he remembered the day concerned. He'd rung the front door bell and got no answer. But the doors to the garage had been open. Both doors: the big one at the front, the small one at the back. "So I walked straight through," he said. "They were all there."

Emily nodded. The garden furniture was stored in the Williams's garage. It would have been easier taking it in and out via the large front opening, and it would have been natural to leave the door up. Natural too for Beynon to stroll through the garage into the garden. See if he could find his quarry there.

"And they were all there? Elsie Williams? Her daughter and son in law?"

"That's it," said Beynon.

"Did you stop in the garage for any reason? Move things around? Make a noise?"

Beynon shrugged. There were limits to memory. He didn't say exactly, but he sort of did. He stood at her desk answering her questions, lifting her stapler and tapping the surface of her desk with it. And that too was an answer of a sort. The fidgety PC David Beynon. Moving through the garage, banging things around, because he was the banging around type. She didn't have proof, or anything that resembled it, but she did have a theory.

She got on the phone, trying to locate the firm that built Elsie Williams's conservatory. It took sixteen calls, but then she located a builder in Llanishen who said he did the job. Ewan Jenkins was his name.

"I need to know how you were paid. If you were paid in cash, if you fiddled your VAT, I don't care. There will be no repercussions. Just tell me how you were paid."

"Yes, well, I do sometimes take cash. I mean, I wouldn't normally, but like I say....."

"I don't really care. I'm not a VAT person. You can do what you like as far as I'm concerned. I need to know who paid you, Owen. Who physically gave you the cash?"

"It would have been the old lady, Mrs. Williams. But there was a young man there too. Her son in law maybe. I think it was his money. I'm not sure. It felt like there was a bit of an atmosphere. Like there had been a row or something. The job had been okay, actually. The conservatory went up pretty well, considering, and there wasn't a problem in getting paid, exactly. But I didn't like it. There was something funny there. You know. Not just one thing. But other, little things."

"Go on."

She was holding the phone so hard she could feel it creak in her grip.

"Well, like I had to take tools and everything off site all the time. I've got a lock up, so that's not a problem, like. But normally, I'd just use the garage. Keep it tidy, obviously, but....."

Jenkins went on talking, but Emily was only half listening.

Gotcha!

She told Jenkins that they'd need him to come in and make a statement at some point and reassured him again about the VAT before hanging up. And then, because she wanted a conviction, not just a story, she researched things. Always an illuminating process. SNAXPO, for example. An entire conference in Arizona, just to discuss the humble snack. If you didn't know those things existed, you'd never guess. Not just one conference, dozens of them. Interpack 2011. Or who would believe that there was even something called the International Cheese Technology Expo? That delightful event takes place in Wisconsin, but I bet the UK turns out to have its own thriving equivalents.

Which is all good. She checked some dates and made some calls. She could be smiley and nice when she needed to be. That, plus she offered a load of money which she was never going to pay. While she was working on her laptop, Books looked over her shoulder and said, "What are you doing?"

"I've decided to move into PR,"

"No, really. What are you doing?" he persisted.

"I'm catching murderers," She replied.

"No, really. I mean what are you doing?"

She smacked the laptop closed and gave him a kiss long enough that he stopped asking boring questions to which she had already given two perfectly accurate answers.

Other things went well too.

Stuart Brotherton submitted his completed report on Precision Tools. It was lethally comprehensive and utterly devastating. They handed over six files to the Crown Prosecution Service along with six files of additional evidence. Brotherton listed 188 counts of weapons export. Whether it was judged by the number of offences or the value of the items shipped, this was the UK's biggest ever arms smuggling case. Webster, Kirby, Dunwoody, Jones, and a couple of other senior officers went out for a celebratory lunch. They came back drunk.

Emily sent Idris Khan a homemade Christmas card with a picture of a prison in the snow. Bleak and unforgiving. Inside she wrote, "10 years. Home in 6."

Emily visited Jon Johnston a couple of times. He was okay. Head down, doing his time. He asked how she'd been getting on with Mortimer. She told him she couldn't say much now, but things were going well. After she'd seen Johnston, she didn't run straight out of the prison. She lingered, feeling the walls, the cells, the bars, the keys. It wasn't a comfortable sensation, but it was not insupportable either. She was coping.

She wondered if she might be getting more normal, but ran from that thought. She thought the answer was probably no. But for the first time in her ridiculous life, she had a small but increasing pile of evidence to the contrary.

She had a stable relationship with a proper boyfriend; she had a good job and was respected by colleagues, even if not always liked; she could sometimes cook an edible meal in less than seven hours; she had been known, if not often, to clean, dust and hoover; she went clothes shopping with her sister and sometimes wore the clothes that she bought and she'd even plucked her eyebrows.

It's not, now that she thought about it, the most impressive list of achievements, but you can't measure impressive from the height of the wall alone. You have to consider the depth of the hole you started with.

She was sometimes scared by how much progress she'd made.

And then she heard from Lenny. Nothing much. Just an address and a name. The address was of a flat, in an area just outside Drumchapel. The name, she assumed, was the one McCormack was using.: Callum Fraser.

She checked the place on Google Maps. Then Street View. The building was five storeys high. Unpainted stucco. Flat roof. Either council housing or ex-council. Net curtains in most of the windows. Some washing on lines. Concrete balconies and plastic garden chairs. Skies the colour of stucco.

No visible contract killers, but Lenny didn't get such things wrong. Emily had what she wanted, but she didn't know what to do next. Her most obvious option, the one any half normal police officer would take without a moment's thoughts, was to call Strathclyde Police and give them McCormack's current location. Wait for them to do the rest. That's what she ought to do. The correct option.

And yet she knew if she took that option she'd never see him again. The Strathclyde Police wouldn't maintain surveillance for long. If he was alert enough to check his surroundings for two men waiting around in a car all day, he'd be sure to wait them out, or just move on under cover of darkness. And that would be that. He'd never come back. Also, the Strathclyde Police did not have in their possession three body hairs taken from a corpse.

The truth was that she had got only one option. She told Books she'd be away for the weekend. She hadn't yet replaced her car, so she bought one for cash. It was a wreck really, but it worked. She didn't tell anyone she'd bought it. She parked it a mile and a half from her house and did not insure it.

There were a few other bits and pieces she needed, but she had most of them already. A couple of things to practice, but she was reasonably practiced already.

Oddly, she was quite relaxed. She didn't have big anxieties over what she was about to do. She did bits and bobs at work without getting herself into trouble. She spent time with Books and her family and it all felt pleasingly ordinary. The snow remained. The latest satellite picture showed an ice bound island, waiting for something to break.

-49-

Glasgow felt appropriate in the cold. A northern city, chained in ice. There was something industrial about the way they handled the cold up there. The gritters and snow-ploughs had a dirty, yellow used look to them. A clanking brutishness in nursery yellow.

She arrived after dark, which is to say after four in the afternoon. She hadn't had a good drive up and was in a foul mood. The GPS on her phone guided her straight to the block of flats, as awkward and graceless in real life as it was on Street View. Four apartments on each floor. Her man, Frasier McCormack was in Flat 5B, so on the top storey.

She rang his bell, got an answer, mumbled an apology for pressing the wrong button, then went back to her car to sit and wait.

Buying a cheap car had its drawbacks. It didn't have much of a sound system. She tried listening to Classic FM, but the radio picked up two signals simultaneously: Classic FM's own tedious repertoire and some strange Nordic station, all folk music and improbable, excessive laughter. She switched off. Stayed gazing at the front door of the building. On McCormack's floor, there were two apartments with lights on, two without. She was parked as far as possible from any streetlight.

Time went by.

She had the engine off, sat back, out of sight. She didn't know how alert McCormack was likely to be, but she didn't want to do anything that could attract attention. At least she was wrapped up warm.

Two kids passed her car. One of them rapped on her window. She wound it down and heard something in an accent so thick she couldn't understand it. She didn't bother trying because someone left the apartment block at that moment. It wasn't McCormack. It was past six o'clock and Emily wondered how long people could take that freezing city, that darkness, before they were driven to the boozer?

Another forty-three minutes, it turned out.

The lights went off on a remaining top floor apartment. A minute or so later, a shape entered the lobby. Then the door opened and McCormack was briefly visible under the outside light. He was wearing a woolen hat and a padded coat: the same ones, she thought, as he was wearing when he tried to kill her. There wasn't much of him to see. But everything fitted. The clothes, the way he moved, the brief view she caught of his face. It was him.

She felt a cold spill of excitement. Capillaries opening up to adrenaline and fingertips were awakening. But was brief, the feeling. She was there to do a job and was not looking for hassle and not expecting any. The adrenaline drained away. The fingertips closed down.

McCormack walked off up the street. She waited ten minutes, then left the car. She had some cigarettes with her, bought specially, because she hardly ever smoked tobacco. She hung around outside the apartment smoking. After a while, a couple of people approached the block. One of them was dredging keys out of her bag. Emily threw her cigarette away and followed them in. There was a lift and stairs. The people she had followed took the stairs but Emily chose the lift. It carried her stutteringly to the top floor, together with a faint smell of urine. The landing had a low energy bulb restrained behind thickly frosted plastic. A single paned glass window stared blankly over the city. A silent rectangle of lights, darkness, cold. The floor is some kind of composite stone. Cheap and durable. Metal railings led downstairs but she wasn't heading down. There was a bag of rubbish sitting outside one of the apartments, but not McCormack's.

She put on an elastic hair cover, the sort of thing they use in food preparation. Also latex gloves. Then she got tools out of her bag. She rummaged around for a set of lock-picks which she'd bought off the internet along with a few practice locks. She also watched some YouTube videos on how to use the picks. She practiced on her own locks and any others that came her way. She became reasonably adept, reasonably swift, then shoved the tools away in a bottom drawer. She hadn't forgotten about them exactly, but they weren't top of her lists of things to worry about.

She turned her attention to McCormack's lock. Her tools were probably good for about 90 per cent of the locks in the UK, maybe more, but they were good for all the cheap ones. And these were cheap. Probably five pin. Easy. The light was poor, but in a way that helped as lock-picking is all about feel.

She slotted a torque wrench into the lower part of the lock, the part where the shaft of the key would normally fit. Worked it in both directions until she figured out which way the lock normally turned, then placed a little pressure on it. Inside the lock, the pins would be pressed tight against a ridge in the locking barrel. That was the way she wanted them.

She took a raking tool, something whose business end looked not unlike the grippy half of a hairclip, and slotted that into the lock above the torque wrench. She jiggled it in and out, applying upward pressure all the time. She couldn't exactly feel any pins releasing, but there was a little give in the torque wrench, so she thought she'd probably scored a couple of successes already.

Then she started the more detailed work with her picks. She'd chosen a fairly basic pick, because she didn't think this particular would have any real complexity. And sure enough, it wasn't long before she felt the first definite pin-release. She worked a little more, then felt the second one go. She raked the lock again, looking for an easy win, but didn't get it. After trying a couple of different picks on the remaining pin the torque wrench moved all the way around. She turned the handle, opened the door and walked in.

Emily wasn't sure what she was expecting to find, but was struck by how ordinary it was. Vinyl flooring in the little kitchen, tacky underfoot from poor quality cleaning. Beige carpet in the living room and bedrooms. Charity shop furnishings. A big TV. There were curtains in the flat; thin, unlined things in orange and red, but McCormack hadn't drawn them, so his windows offered more empty rectangles. Darkness, streetlamps, snow. Red tail lights, moving slowly.

The interior didn't offer much. There were some bottles kicking around. Whisky, vodka. Some DVD's, action movies mostly. A bathroom which could do with a good clean.

She started to probe the apartment more closely. It was all very well finding Ross, but she wanted Olaf too. Ross would have his phone with him, most likely, and she didn't see a computer. But still. People commit things to paper too, even now.

She started opening the drawers, searching the desk. She didn't find anything much. She noticed how it was strangely hard searching like this while wearing latex gloves. They didn't grip properly on paper and she couldn't use saliva to moisten them, so she was obliged to work slowly.

She found things like utility bills and grocery receipts. Not filed, just shoved away in a drawer. She looked through the receipts, but found nothing interesting there. She did, however, find a postcard mailed from Norway. A village tucked away somewhere in the mountains. Wooden houses, painted rust brown and ochre. Forested slopes sweeping right down to the huddle of green fields. On the back, *Greetings from Norway!* Nothing else, except Ross's own address. There was a postmark, but it wasn't decipherable. The slogan on the card said, in English, *Experience Norway.*

She wanted to take the card, but thought better of it. She looked behind one door, to find a junk room. A small boxy room, with an old bed, a sleeping bag, a heap of clothes. Not a lot. She had the same impulse that she had experienced in Khaled's apartment. An impulse to make a mess of everything. Play loud music. Open the windows. Not a good idea.

She went into Ross's bedroom. He had a built in wardrobe with a wonky door and an old pine chest of drawers. The wardrobe has some shirts, a coat, a couple of casual jackets, a suit and there were some shoes kicking around on the floor. There was a smell of something indefinable; a smell which probably what happens when a mouldering apartment got too little cleaning for years on end.

Emily looked at the shoes and shirts closely. The shoes were not overly clean, the shirts not overly new. There were marks which could quite well have been bloodstains, but could equally well have been curry sauce or motor oil or Glaswegian mud. They were just marks.

The chest of drawers was altogether. Socks and underwear. T-shirts. Trousers. Jumpers and sweat shirts. A plastic grocery bag containing a boiler suit. Also leather gloves. Also some socks and boots. The boiler suit looked washed but had plenty of stains

Khaled's blood, she bet herself a million pounds. Quite likely other people's blood too. These looked to her like Ross's work clothes. What he wore when he was on a job. A messy job, that is. Killing a girl in a snowfield should have been nice and clean.

DNA is normally destroyed by washing. Not one hundred percent guaranteed, but most of the time. If a commercial washer was used, or particularly if a high chlorine washing powder was used, the chances of usable DNA surviving, even in a seam or zip, are pretty much nil.

That might rule out the boiler suit as evidence, but it's very hard to clean boots well enough. You only need one drop of blood in a line of stitching or soaked into the leather and that'll be enough for the forensic bods. If Ross had dunked his boots in bleach, or microwaved them, or boil-washed them, they'd be clean but unusable as footwear. And these were usable. Thus, the betting was that McCormack had left enough evidence here for us to secure a conviction. But that's all it was: a bet.

She had Webster's evidence bag in her pocket. That and a dilemma. All she needed to do, to make certain of her target, was to drop those three body hairs in that bag. Secrete them in a fold of clothing. Close the bag. Close the drawer. Walk away.

Then just wait. Let McCormack come back to his apartment. Wait for him to go to bed, go to sleep. Then call Strathclyde. Tell them where to find him. Watch for long enough to make sure they don't cock it all up. Let the forensics people find those hairs.

Justice.

She felt myself watched by an invisible gallery of spectators. Althea, Tristan, Webster. Watching to see her choose. She found that she couldn't quite do it. Perversion of the course of justice. In a way, she was amazed at her own scruples. After all, there was no doubt that McCormack was a killer. He did, after all, try to kill Emily! She didn't need a court to tell her that. And the blood on this clothing might not be Khaled's. It might not be blood. If she didn't plant this evidence, she might be waving farewell to her only chance of securing a conviction.

But, although she hung over that damn boiler suit with her latexed fingers holding Webster's evidence bag above it, the bag stayed closed. The body hairs encased in their little plastic prison. She couldn't do it. She just closed the bag, closed the drawer, put the evidence bag back in her pocket. It felt strange. Not bad strange or out of body strange, or any of those other versions of strange that had wandered through her life. It just felt weird to be in the apartment of a man who tried to kill her. To be there and not to plant those hairs. She wondered vaguely if this was Books' influence, turning her into the sort of woman he wanted her to be.

The blank window rectangles opened onto the night and gave her no answer. They did, however, give her a view down onto the path that cut through the snow to the road above the apartment building. A path down which two men were walking. One of the pair was, she was pretty sure, Ross.

God! Whoever heard of a Scotsman returning so early from a pub? Do killers have no drinker's pride these days? She watched them until they stepped out of sight beneath her. What now? She could try to bolt for it, but she didn't know whether to use stairs or lift and she certainly didn't want to deal with two men at once. She hesitated a little, trying to decide what to do, but because she did so, she ran out of options. At least it meant she knew what to do.

She went out onto the landing, take the bag of rubbish and emptied it out, kicking bits down the steps. If Ross wasn't a total slob, he'd pick it up.

She went back into his flat and got out her picks. A good locksmith would probably have been able to lock that door in fifteen seconds. She wasn't as good as that, but she wasn't awful either, and in about thirty seconds she'd locked the door from the inside. She heard the wheezing of the lift, so she could probably have just walked down the stairs. Hindsight is a wonderful thing.

Ah well. She took one of the bottles from the back of Ross's stash. A bottle of rum, mostly full. She went into the junk room and rolled under the bed. She had her knife with her, the one she normally had behind her bed, and she got it out, just in case. She wasn't in knifey sort of mood, though.

Ross was obviously a tidy soul, because it took a while before the apartment door opened. She heard him talking to someone. Presumably the man she saw him walking with. She was curious to see what followed. Was it possible Ross was gay? That his current companion was a partner picked up for the night?

She didn't know why, but the thought tickled her. Prompted a silent chuckle. But she doubted it. She heard gruff voices. Someone using the toilet, the fridge opening and closing. Then the TV coming on loud.

That's all she heard for a while. Some kind of action thing, all chases and shootouts. The apartment walls were as soundproof as damp cardboard, so she heard every squeal of tyres, every beat of dialogue. She followed it for a while, but wasn't really interested. She drifted off. Not asleep by any means, but as if in a trance. She should have brought something to eat. Sandwiches or something. But she had nothing at all, so she just lay there, staring up at the bed, knife in her right hand, bottle by her left.

Time passed. She remembered lying on the car engine beneath the starlight, wondering if she was dying.

That place felt very remote from her now. Other people, she thought, would have feelings like anger or revenge. Maybe if she was more whole as a person, she'd have those feelings too. But she didn't. She wasn't kidding when she Books that she hadn't got him a Christmas present. Him or anyone else. So she lay there figuring out who should get what. She decided she should cook Books a big festive meal and tried to think of a menu that would feel Christmassy but would still still be simple enough for her not to cock up.

At around nine-thirty the movie ended and the TV switched to boxing. She'd studied fighting, obviously. Indeed, she had learned from, she thought, one of the world's leading authorities on that unkindly subject. But her interest was purely practical. She had never watched boxing. She disliked the whole aesthetic of it. The shiny shorts, the giant belts, the boasting.

It had gone eleven before the damn TV turned off. It had given her a headache. Ross and his buddy stomped around a bit before the front door was opened and closed. Ross remained behind. He had a heavy tread. Thuggish. He crashed through to the bedroom. There was thump and a swearword, which were both good news. The drunker he was, the better.

Emily rolled out from under the bed. She was stiff, so it was nice to be able to stretch and roll her shoulders. Ease the knots. He went from the bedroom to the bathroom. She heard the shower run, and stood outside the bathroom door, where she would be concealed as it opened. There was a tune in her head. Adele's 'Chasing Pavements.' She didn't know why and it was all she could do to stop herself singing it.

She was in a pretty good mood, she noticed. Was this happiness? It could have been, but she couldn't absolutely tell. She often needed to concentrate to figure those things out, and right then she needed her attention for other things.

The shower stopped. A tap ran. Toothbrushing.

He seemed to take a long time in the bathroom. Longer than her, she thought, and she was half-minded to go in there and tell him to get on with it, but she didn't have to. Ross, finally, was ready for her. He stepped, naked, out of the bathroom.

She allowed herself a second, a half second actually, to be present in this moment. To enjoy the sensation of being alive, there and then, in a place she wanted to be. It wasn't an ideal moment, though. She studied the side of his skull. Somewhat above, and forward from, his ear. The pterion, is what doctors call it. What Lenny called it, in his darkly accented English. It lies at the join of four bones. A major artery lies beneath. The skull wall is thinner there than anywhere else. God's little joke, as it's known. A spot so weak that blows to other parts of the skull often end up causing fractures here.

She marked the spot.

"Hi, Ross."

As he turned she hit him as hard as she could with the bottle of rum. He dropped, almost silently, to the floor.

-50-

He wasn't dead, but it wouldn't have massively bothered her if he had drawn his last breath there and then.

She saw some duct tape in a desk drawer; one of your contract killer basics, she supposed, so she taped his hands and forearms together. She didn't do half measures. She circled his arms about twenty times. She lost count, but was satisfied with the result as she cut the tape with a knife, not her teeth as she was still DNA conscious. Next, carefully, she taped over his mouth. Then, more confidently, taped around his ankles and knees. Because there was still spare tape on the roll, and it was a shame to have wasted it, she lashed his ankles to the sofa leg and stood back to admire her handiwork.

He wasn't going anywhere and he still had a pulse. There was some blood oozing from his temple, but not copious amounts as you sometimes get with a skull wound. Good enough. Emily was satisfied. She rolled him into the recovery position as she didn't want the bastard swallowing his tongue. He was going to need that to talk with. But even as she rolled him, he started to wake up. His eyes groggily searched the room. She waited until he was alert enough to make sense of the world, then bent down so he could see her face.

"Evening," She said.

His mouth said nothing, but his eyes did. She walked around and kicked him hard in the coccyx. No particular reason why. She supposed she wanted to see what she would feel, kicking the man who had tried to kill her. But the answer was: not much. It was just a kick. It felt right and good to have that part of things tidied away, but she didn't feel much personal triumph.

Also, Ross seemed amazingly naked. There was something about their situation which somehow emphasized that he was wearing nothing but duct tape and an air of hatred. She covered up his disappointingly small manhood with a bathroom towel, reflecting that a small flannel would have sufficed. His nose was crooked, which meant she did break it that night in the car.

Now that she had time, she could go through the apartment at more leisure. She didn't find anything more than she had the first time, except that she now had Ross's phone, if she wanted it. She did want it, but decided not to take it. Strathclyde would have access to technical specialists who could get through any password protection he may have. And the phone may yield evidence that was wanted in court. Plus, she'd be able to access anything that Strathclyde gathered. So logic won out and she left the phone.

It was time to clean up. It had already been reported that Ross had been in recent contact with her, so any small particles of her DNA that were found would likely be consistent with that contact. On the other hand, she didn't want it to look like she was physically in the apartment at any point, so she wanted to erase any significant traces of her presence. She set to work with a hoover, cleaning the area under the bed where she had lain all through the evening. Although she had kept on clothes, gloves, and hair protection, it would have been impossible to remain that long in one place and leave no trace.

After hoovering, she mixed half a bucket of water with a whole bottle of bleach and rinsed down anything that worried her. Bleach doesn't guarantee destruction of DNA but it does a pretty good job. She thought it would be more than enough.

She told Ross she was going and he gave her angry eyes, so she gave him another kick. Basic stuff, but still communication. Human contact.

She doused the parts she'd kicked with bleach just to be on the safe side. She hoped it might sting more than a little. Next, she went to the bathroom, took the showerhead off its stand and dropped it on the floor. She turned the cold tap on to maximum and water started to spray out.

She helped herself to the Norwegian postcard. If Strathclyde wanted it, well, that's tough. Emily took the hoover as well. She left the apartment door open and took the lift down. She trudged wearily to her car, thinking it wasn't beating the crap out of people that takes it out of you; it's the waiting beforehand, the cleaning up afterwards. You should be able to get support staff for that sort of thing.

She drove south to Lancaster. That would normally be two and a half hours, but it took four because of the weather. At a service station on the way, she found one of those big commercial waste bins and dumped the hoover. She was so tired that her eyes kept glassing over. She almost nodded off, repeatedly, and needed the vibration of the car tyres hitting the icy roadside snow to wake her. No lane warning alarm in this car.

At Lancaster railway station, she parked the car and bought a ticket for cash. She waited for a train to take her south; first to Crewe and then on to Cardiff. When the train had pulled few minutes out of Lancaster, she threw her car keys out of the window. They disappeared down an embankment into a blackthorn bush. There would be loads of her DNA in the car if anyone were to choose to swab it. But they wouldn't. It was just a car. Bought for cash, never registered, then abandoned. In a few weeks' time, it'll be towed by the police and destroyed.

She slept until Crewe, then waited on a cold platform until the Cardiff train came in. She felt home already as she heard the ticket inspector's lilting voice.

She rehearsed her Christmas cooking as the train trundled along. She'd do a roast chicken with all the trimmings, roast tatties, bacon, gravy, two veg, cranberry sauce. Probably cheat and buy a ready-made pudding. She promised herself a practice cook with Mum with all the timings being noted down just to make sure.

On Monday morning, Webster phoned. Ordered her up to her office. She greeted her and said, "I don't know if you've heard. Strathclyde Police think they've got McCormack."

"Oh, that's good."

She told Emily the news. Water pouring from an upstairs bathroom brought down the ceiling in the flat below. Then, because that flat was unoccupied, the ceiling one storey down was next to follow. The occupants of that flat called the landlord, then went up to investigate. Found the door unlocked. Called the police, assuming theft.

"McCormack was found with a severe blow to the skull, but no long term damage. He had been secured with duct tape, apparently. Swaddled like an Egyptian mummy.

"Or baby Jesus," Emily offered, trying to be seasonal.

Webster didn't answer right away, maybe because she wasn't very Christmassy, so Emily took the evidence bag out of her pocket. The one with the body hairs.

"I'm sorry, but I forgot to return these to the lab. What do you want me to do with them?"

She took the bag. She seemed moved. Moved and grateful. She took the bag, half closing her eyes as she did so. Nodding to herself. "Thank you, Emily. Thank you."

It was strange to hear her like this. Perhaps she had never in her life knowingly contravened rules of evidence, or any of the other laws that govern investigations. By returning the bag to her, Emily had kept her one hundred per cent record intact. She realised how much it must have taken for Webster to have given her the bag in the first place.

"If they've got McCormack, I probably don't need to pursue my enquiries."

"No. No, you don't."

"Good. That's all good." Emily thought Webster had said everything she wanted to say, but she wasn't being told to go.

"Have you gone on any of those websites yet?" Emily asked.

"Yes." She nodded. She didn't have full control over her voice, which was half husky, half whispering. "I was going to ask, if you wouldn't mind, sometime....."

"We could take a look at your profile together. Make sure you're presenting yourself right. I'd like that."

Webster nodded. She was red. Scarlet. Webster the Ice Queen in a puddle at Emily's feet. Real friendship, or it could become one. They were as awkward as hell now, but that would pass. Her eyes say the opposite of McCormack's. No need to give anyone an extra kick.

Emily smiled and said, "See you soon," as she went downstairs to start her day.

-51-

Humans want endings. Perhaps we need them. Tidy finishes. Christmas wrapping paper and a big red bow. We don't get them, though, except perhaps at Christmas. Maybe that's why the festival endures. Maybe it's not only children who need the myth.

That Christmas on our frozen island was a spectacular one. Hoarfrost was so thick, there was as much as an inch lying on branches and twigs. Icicles four feet long hung from gutters and balconies. Books told Emily that he'd seen icicles that he measured at over six feet, and he, unlike her, always told the truth about such things.

Christmas Eve was sunny. Emily wasn't working that day and Books was, so she used the freedom to drive, in Frank's Range Rover, away from the coast, up into the hills. A range Rover which wasn't going to get stuck anywhere. It flew over icy roads with a certainty altogether lacking in her late and still lamented Peugeot. She hadn't intended to go all the way, but she did. Up to Mortimer's cottage. Then to the field where she almost died. She wanted to see it again.

The place was piercingly beautiful. White hills and infinite light. A bird of prey sharpened its wings on the air overhead. The barn that she burned down was still charred and black, but its remaining timbers were jeweled with diamonds. The stream in the little dip beyond the barn chuckled at her presence. A line of fox footprints marked little blue dimples up the slope of the hill.

Tonight, Christmas Eve, they were forecasting temperatures of minus sixteen degrees, which meant minus eighteen or colder up there. That was colder than it was when she was there last, but not much. Either way, it wasn't T-shirt weather.

When the Ice Age last covered Britain, these mountains lay on its fringes. Glaciated, but only just. These old red rocks, the sandstones and the siltstones, were scraped clean by moving ice. To them, this weather was just a reminder of things past.

She stayed in that field awhile. The sun stared down without comment. The air flashed with cold fire. The bird above me disappeared and then returned.

Eventually, she didn't need to be there anymore. It was gone. The whole car death cold thing had slipped from one place to another. From something that was still injuring her in the present to some other place where it no longer hurt. The past still happened, but she didn't have to live there. She didn't have to worry. The barn would get rebuilt. Her skin grafts were increasingly looking like ordinary skin.

She drove down to the farm below. Arthur was in a barn, scattering feed for his sheep. Rose came out of the kitchen when she saw her. Emily had presents for them both. A huge bottle of whisky for him. A bunch of Flowers for her. Nice ones. They seemed genuinely touched, as was Emily herself by their surprise, their smiles.

They invited her in, but she declined. They stood for a while on the stone yard, looking out at the snow, and agreed that it was cold, beautiful and that they'd never had a Christmas like it.   Emily asked Arthur how his insurance claim was going. He said fine. She told him that she distinctly recalled the barn being at least three quarters full of hay. She'd already phoned him to say that, but she repeated it. He shook her hand with a grip so strong, she could feel bones starting to fuse in her hand.

And then she left. Her father's Range Rover driving on ice like it was diddling over a suburban street. And McCormack in prison.

His boiler suit yielded no useful forensic evidence, but his boots did. And his gloves. And the plastic bag that housed them all. Khaled's blood. Also, the blood of a Scottish man who disappeared two years ago, with suspected gambling debts. Also, the blood of a third individual who had not yet been identified.

McCormack's phone use linked him to Cardiff Bay on the night of Khaled's murder. McCormack's car, the one they used the night they tried to kill me, could be tracked via the ANPR database to both Cardiff Bay and then, later, Llanishen. Strathclyde Police told them that they had a strong murder case for the gambling debt man too. In short, McCormack is cornered. He'd spend the rest of his life in jail, near as dammit.

Emily didn't think about him often now. He was history.

Webster wanted to add her attempted killing to the list of charges, but the CPS told them they had nowhere near enough evidence to secure a conviction. Webster tried to argue them round, but Emily told them to leave it; she didn't want the publicity or the hassle. A long as McCormack went to jail, she'd be satisfied.

There was more good news too. McCormack's phone was unlocked by Strathclyde's technical staff. The call log contained outbound and inbound calls from a pay as you go phone purchased in Denmark. That phone showed use in Glasgow, London, Bristol, Copenhagen, Oslo. And also in parts of rural Norway.

Emily contacted the company that produced the 'Experience Norway' card she'd taken from McCormack's flat. They told her that the picture was taken from a valley in the mountains about thirty miles south of Trondheim. The village in question had a population of just six hundred people. If she included everyone within a ten-mile radius, that still only gave her about fifteen hundred. And Norway, bless it, had a compulsory national register of all residents. The sort of thing you associate with the Stasi, but somehow an idea that's taken root in this little Nordic paradise too.

She sifted her list of possible names to exclude women, children, and anyone outside an age range of twenty five to forty five. All male Norwegians are obliged to perform military service, but she had a strong suspicion that Olaf would have done more than the minimum. These people usually did. If you like violence, have an aptitude for it, you're drawn by the glamour of warfare. The training, the guns, the toughness. The Norwegian armed forces have a veterans' administration which keeps information on one hundred thousand ex-service personnel. Emily asked it about veterans of the right age registered to the area she was interested in. The agency was initially reluctant to divulge its data, but pressure was quietly applied from behind the scenes. Emily knew its origin and smiled. They never failed, she thought to herself. The data was promised for the new year, which was fine by her.

She was back in Cardiff by four in the afternoon. Books was supposed to be spending Christmas Day with his family in London, as he hadn't seen them since leaving for pastures new, and Emily was scheduled to be with her family. That evening, therefore, they were having their own private celebration. She had everything she needed. She had done her practice cook, supervised by Mum, and had written down all the timings.

Those timings didn't just apply to the chicken. They applied to her too. She wanted to do everything right. Clean hair. New dress. Proper makeup. Sexy underwear. Though her dress wasn't exactly new, it was one that Books hadn't seen. She couldn't tell if it looked nice or not, but knew it was passable. Most of Kay's dresses didn't fit Emily brilliantly, because of their height difference, but she liked her dresses short and some of them suited Emily well. This one looked okay, she thought. The mirror didn't say 'woman of mystery,' but it did say 'girl looking nice for a special date.'

Inevitably, she didn't get her timings absolutely right. She was aiming to have dinner served by seven thirty, but it was going to be more like eight fifteen. That didn't matter too much. Books had strict instructions not to show up until she texted him. He was out at the pub with a bunch of people from the office, so he was fine.

And then she was ready and sent the text to tell him he could show up at quarter past. There were candles on the table. Wine. The table was laid. Everything was either cooked or just approaching perfection.

She wanted to be a domestic goddess for him that night and she was a skitter of nerves. She'd put her posh shoes on much too early, so her feet were already killing her, but she bumbled around checking things she'd already checked. She looked at her watch five times in twelve minutes. Checked herself in the mirror three times.

And then Books arrived. Her stomach flipped, as though it was the first time she'd ever seen him. She felt ridiculously anxious and didn't know why.

He was about to say, "Bloody hell, Em," because that's what he usually says when she was making a visible effort. But then he didn't. He just kissed her carefully and said, "Happy Christmas, love." Emily said, "Happy Christmas," too, but her voice was croaked and hoarse, like Webster's was when she asked her to help with the dating sites.

They ate dinner. The potatoes were crispy, the chicken cooked enough to be non-lethal, but not so much that it was black. The gravy tasted good and there was plenty of it. The veg was fine too. She got the right sort of wine. They clinked glasses and said, "I love you," and that felt like a real thing to do, not a TV movie thing. All of it did; the whole thing.

She was still nervous, but no longer skittering. For all she knew, she even appeared reasonably calm. When it became time to serve pudding, she realised that it was frozen hard. Her list didn't have an entry that read, "Remove pudding from freezer, you numpty," so she hadn't. Not even thought about it.

Books, her lovely saviour Books, took the pudding out of its wrapper and put it into the microwave to defrost, then twenty-five minutes to heat in the oven.

"I wonder if we can think of a way to pass the time for forty minutes," He said.

But he wasn't allowed that. Not yet.

They sat on the living room floor and gave each other presents. She gave him a jumper that he looked really nice in. She also gave him a hockey stick with rave reviews on the hockey websites. This one was made of some special composite that was meant to be much better than the knackered old wooden one he used. It cost two hundred pounds. She was a bit worried that he'd have some manly attachment to his wooden one, but he didn't, or at least, he said, "Bloody hell, Em, that's fantastic," in a way that made her think he meant it. She gave him some other things too. Nice things. Things she took care about when she bought them.

She had almost no money left in her account, or anywhere else for that matter. And that was fine. She wasn't very good with money, but she didn't starve.

Books gave her presents too. Girl things mostly, but she liked that he thought of her that way. Someone who wanted scented candles, a cute little jacket from Oasis. She lit a candle and tried on the jacket and still didn't feel like a TV movie person. Giddy, but okay.

He also gave her a small box and she had a sudden terror that it might be jewellery. It was, but a necklace, not a ring, and she felt a surge of relief. She loved this man, but wasn't ready to take that step yet. She didn't know if she ever would be, but more things are possible in this life than ever she thought likely.

"Are you okay, love?"

She nodded. Smiled. Put the necklace on.

"It's lovely," She said. "I love it."

They had used the word 'love' or 'lovely' three time in the space of nine words, and it didn't feel excessive.

Books took the pudding out of the microwave and put it into the oven. He did some other things in the kitchen too. Probably things she'd forgotten. She wasn't looking at her list anymore.

When Books came back, she gave him her final present. A small box, wrapped, with a red bow.

"This is a funny present, really," she told him. "It's not something for you to keep. It's something for you to destroy."

He opened it, smiling. The box was full of seeds, like green lentils, only paler. Some speckled, with tones of buff and slate and pale grey.

"What are they, sweetheart?"

"They're my cannabis seeds," she told him. "The next generation. My seedbank."

"Emily, That's amazing." He hesitated. "I mean, technically, giving an industrial quantity of Class B drugs to a police officer isn't amazing, it's criminal, but...."

She interrupted him. "I'm not saying I'm giving up. I'm not even promising that I will give up. I don't know if I can. But I am promising to try. I want you to know I will try."

He was speechless. Then his freckles moved in for a long kiss. His lovely freckles on his lovely nose.

They ate some pudding, but though there was cheese to follow, they didn't touch it. They headed through to the bedroom and did what they did best. Then there was a muddle of showering and washing up and watching a bit of rubbish on the telly and cuddling up close as possible. And eventually bed. Books said, "Happy Christmas" once more. Emily said the same to him, but it wasn't Christmas yet, only Christmas Eve.

Before the church bells tolled the midnight, Books was asleep beside her. She had her hand on his chest so she could feel him breathing. Then, when that got boring, she tickled the hairs in his nose to make him snuffle and shake his head.

She tickled his ears too, but that didn't work as well.

Time passed.

As soon as Webster told Emily that Strathclyde forensics had found Khaled's blood in McCormack's apartment, as soon as, that was, they knew for certain he would be going to jail, she asked Webster for permission to request an appeal against Mortimer's conviction. She nodded and instituted the necessary proceedings right away. There's a time lag for these things, but they'd get what they wanted, she was certain.

She borrowed a patrol car and drove, with Susan Konchesky again, up to Solihull. Got Stephanie West, her mother, the two kids into one room together. Told them formally that Mark Mortimer had been wrongly convicted. Said that they were working to get his conviction reversed. Told them that, because of their father, a major criminal conspiracy had been uncovered. Said that the first man was under arrest and heading for prison.

She thanked each personally, Stephanie West, Althea, Tristan, for their help. Althea and Tristan cried buckets. Stephanie West cried too. Emily didn't know if she'd given the children what they needed, but she'd done all she could. Given them a father to be proud of. Not a criminal, a hero.

She'd still like to have given their mother a good slapping, but she couldn't have everything.

Afterwards, as they were driving back again, Susan said, "Back there. You were amazing. I just wanted you to know."

She was at the wheel and had her eyes fixed on the snowbound motorway, but Emily thanked her and meant it.

She didn't think Mark Mortimer was a hero, not quite. It was brave of him to look into the arms dealing. It was stupid of him not to alert the police. A courageous idiot: that would be closer to the truth, but his kids didn't need the truth. They needed their father back.

Somewhere beyond their window, a bell tolled midnight.

Books snored his even, deep, masculine rumbles.

She'd like to find Khaled, or Flowers, or even Mortimer, but their spirits were silent. Perhaps that was a good thing. Something a bit like peace.

The weapons systems that left Precision Tools factory filtered out across some of the world's nastier regimes. Egypt. Libya. Tunisia. Syria. Yemen and Somalia. Who knew how far those weapons travelled? In whose hands they ended up? The only thing that was for certain was that none of them were destined for the hands of democratically accountable governments, because if they had been, the firm could simply have applied for and applied export licences.

Precision's weapons may never have been fired. The firm made parts for heavy weaponry and armoured vehicles. Artillery pieces and tanks, not small arms. It was quite possible that few or none of those weapons were fired in anger. Yet the burden of guilt was horrendous all the same. Those armaments protected regimes against their peoples. The dictator's ultimate recourse. Precision Tools, Jim Dunbar and Idris Khan played their toxic little part in keeping those regimes intact.

She'd wanted to find the souls of those victims. To make contact, however dimly or however briefly. To touch hands with them, feel their existence.

She couldn't do that, though. Perhaps there were just too many of them. Or they were perhaps too distant. Maybe you can only feel the dead when you know them a little, the way she knew Khaled.

A pity.

But even if you can't feel the dead, you can think about them. Make them a gift of your time and care. So she did. As the bells of Cardiff counted towards the first light of this frozen Christmas, and as Books snored beside her, his nose hairs now unmolested, she spent time with the dead. The countless, nameless, uncomplaining dead.

Books rolled in his sleep, allowing her to kiss the back of his neck, which was beautiful.

Outside, the great freeze endured, tightening its hold. Ice thickened. In a snowy field somewhere above Capel, a burned out barn flashed diamonds at the moon, while owls hooted in the solitary woods.

And sometime before dawn on Christmas Day, Emily fell asleep.

-52-

The Norwegian veterans' administration came back to her with names. There were five people in her target area who spent significant time in the armed forces. One of those was a naval officer, an improbable career choice for Olaf, she thought. One of the others was just twenty-six, and Emily was pretty sure Olaf was older. Of the three others, one served for seven years, most of that time in the Brigade Nord, based in the far north of Norway. A place where you'd learn all about snow. About hypothermia.

She checked out all five names. It was hard. Armies like regimental photos. Ski teams. Biathlon contests. Those things need teasing out, but they're not private. She posed as a documentary maker researching a series on winter warfare and got all the co-operation she could ask for. She got photos. She got a photo of Olaf.

His real name was Jan-Erik Fjerstad. He was thirty-five. He was, indeed, my man from the Brigade Nord. He represented them in long distance cross country skiing competition, before an ankle injury ended all that. He was registered to an address outside a remote hamlet in the mountains of middle Norway.

Olaf didn't sound like a person she'd like to tangle with one-on-one. Ross was just as tough, just as strong, but he was stupider. Not as careful. And Ross's arrest would have put Olaf on his guard.

So she texted Lenny, asking him if he fancied a trip to Scandinavia. She didn't hear back from him for a while, but when she did, it was a yes. They set a date for March. In the meantime there was work. Lots of it.

She had been working with a team of two on Khaled's little adventures in the arms trade. They could track thirteen separate orders split across seven different firms, all of which appeared to be for weapons parts. There were a further eighteen suspect orders, either commissioned or planned, which probably related to weaponry too. There was no use, however, in detailing these things beyond a certain point. Khaled was dead and couldn't be jailed. Emily drew up a report presenting their conclusions, and then they were assigned to other things.

Precision Tools itself was where the action was, and the battle with the firm is turning into a minefield of lawyers. Like Stalingrad, only with legal arguments in place of mud, snow, and tank manoeuvres. But Emily believed they had miscalculated. If they wanted to sap their resolve or budgetary capacity, they had actually done the opposite. The Chief Officers and the top decision makers at the CPS were determined to proceed. There was a rare institutional unanimity in pursuing the case, and pursuing it hard.

Plus, Kirby and Webster, it turned out, were superb at this sort of thing. Kirby was wonderful at the politics, the lawyer stuff. Webster was relentless in her accumulation of evidence; presenting it in a way guaranteed to break down any opposition, to destroy any counter argument. At the same time, she was scrupulous about conducting every aspect of her investigation to the proper standards. Every procedure followed, every box ticked.

Precision Tools's lawyers were still snapping away, but so far they had accomplished nothing at all. They were snapping on air.

Dunbar and Khan were going to prison. Once a week, on a random day and using different stationery every time, Emily sent Khan a card. A picture of Cardiff jail. No message.

Idris Khan made his money in private equity. Paid UK tax at a rate of 18%, but kept most of his business interests offshore, so his effective tax rate was well under 10 per cent. Emily said as much to Books, who said, cheerfully, "Well. We must be mugs then," and went to work, being a mug.

Except they were not mugs. They did a good, honest job at a fair rate of pay. That wasn't stupid; it was responsible. It was an attitude response for every good thing in society. And though there was nothing illegal about the way Khan paid his taxes, for someone to make that much money, and to pay that little tax, and then to make more money by selling weapons to dictators and to compound all that by giving, calm as you like, the order to kill Emily because she might, just might, put an end to your stream of profits, well, there was breathtaking arrogance in that approach to life. Something so stunning and patronizing that, as far as Emily was concerned, ten years in jail was never enough.

She hoped Webster a judge would award the maximum sentence and that Khan had a horrible time in prison. And she hoped it would all happen soon. Though she did admit to herself that she might be biased.

But first things first. Rose Flowers had waited too long already. Five years, poor lass, almost five and a half. Time enough.

On Monday 3rd January, Emily went to see Webster. She was deep in paperwork, but waved Emily into her office. She had gone back to her monochromes, but was less rumpled somehow. She didn't know if she'd bought new stuff, or if she'd lost a few pounds, or what it was, but she looked better. She still looked fierce, but the human sometimes peeped out anyway.

They had done some work on her website profile. Picked a photo that made her look nice, nice in a scary way, admittedly, but nice. Rewritten her profile so it didn't sound like a two-page report for some corporate HR department. She was about to set up her first date.

"Do you have a moment?"

She did. Emily brought coffee for her, a mug of peppermint tea for herself.

"Rose Flowers," Emily began. "I've been looking at the case notes again."

Webster rubbed her face. The Flowers investigation bothered her, Emily knew. It was two failures for her, not one. The first five years back. The second now. And she was not used to failure.

But she was friendlier these days. Webster friendly, anyway. "Yes?"

"I know who killed her."

Webster raised her eyebrows. Not angry eyebrows. Just prove-it eyebrows.

So Emily told her. Who did it and how she knew. She connected up the bits and pieces. Elsie Williams's insomnia. The garage. The conservatory. The hot summer's day when PC Benyon gave the old lady her caution. She talked about the old woman's vendettas: the kids on bikes, people lighting garden bonfires. Stupid things, summer things. She also talked about the man stuff. Car mechanics and pressure washing.

Webster listened intently. Nothing Emily said amounted to a single grain of proof. Nothing that would remotely stand up in court. But the hypothesis almost always comes first. The proof comes after.

"You're right," said Webster. "He's our man. It's him."

Emily was sure and so was Webster. But our man didn't live in Britain, or even a European country which would respond to a European Arrest Warrant. They would need to show 'reasonable grounds' for suspicion. Emily's pruning manuals and theories about bird droppings made for pretty evidence.

It wasn't just that he could fight extradition and probably win, it was that they would lose all their advantages of surprise. Really, with a man like that, you want to yank him off the street, run him straight to an interview room, and give him a good hard interrogation before he's had time to think through his strategies. Even if he gets lawyered up straight away, and these days that's hard to avoid, their chances of success would go up dramatically if they hit hard and early.

Webster was thinking these things through. The light in her office had gone back to ordinary Cardiff light. No snow. No frost. No mounds of gritty snow or fistfuls of diamonds. Just low voltage overhead lights. Nylon carpet and slatted blinds. And outside, that subdued January light that was never far from a wash of rain.

The frozen December island had already vanished into myth. Like something briefly escaped from the time of fairytale, when unicorns stalked the land.

Webster was saying something. Emily wasn't sure what. She interrupted Webster.

"He's coming to the UK tomorrow week. There's an industry conference where he'll be a guest speaker."

Emily gave her details of the relevant website.

"You're sure it's him?"

"Yes."

Emily didn't say so, but of course, she was sure. It was Emily that booked him. She set herself up as a PR agent. Paid two hundred pounds for a cheapie website. Got an associated e-mail address. Bought a disposable phone. Invited their man to a big industry conference as guest speaker. Offered to pay business class travel in both directions. And accommodation. And a generous speaking fee. He haggled over the fee, so she said yes to his highest demand. Then contacted the conference organisers and said that this man was going to be in the UK during their conference. Would they like him to come and speak? There'd be no fee attached, because he was in the area anyway. They said yes. And that was that. Job done. She would need to pull the website and ditch the phone, but not until he was actually in the air.

"Do you know what plane he's on?"

Emily said no, which wasn't true, because he e-mailed her his itinerary, but it wasn't hard getting passenger information.

Webster's smile started in her eyes, flickered at the corners of her mouth, then ignited to reveal a full set of teeth,

"Do you want to be there?"

Stupid question.

-53-

Bath. They travelled there, Bev and Emily, in the rain. Emily was driving her new car. It wasn't a convertible, this one. Though she loved her little Peugeot and though it was hardly her fault that she almost died inside her, she needed to move on. Her first thought was to play safe. Get something less flippant, more German. She thought about a VW Golf, perhaps. An Audi A1. But then she was seduced by the South. By an Alfa Romeo Guilietta, all moody curves and sulky power.

It still had that new car smell. Plastic and leather. New carpets. Volatile organic compounds created a sweetly heady mix, only a shade off toxic.

"It's lovely," says Bev, who couldn't afford anything like it.

Emily's father bought the car as a Christmas present. She knew he would and he did. She told him that she would give him the insurance money when it came through. But Frank also, she discovered, put five thousand pounds in cash in the glove box. She kept the car and the cash and deflected Bev's unspoken interest in her financial affairs.

There was a light rain falling again. Wipers like a metronome. She normally drove quickly on the motorway, but because Bev was in the car she stayed at a steady seventy. Sidelights on and indicating when she changed lane.

Bev was wearing the dark jacket that she lent Emily when she made this journey three months ago. Emily was wearing her new suit. It was dark enough, formal enough, for this visit.

Webster was right the first time, when she saw her jeans and didn't approve. There are times when clothes matter. When it matters what they signal.

They rolled down the long hill into Bath. The day was drawing to its close. The city was a darkening bowl beneath them. The western sky was violet and orange. A lament for the departed. For the violently lost.

"They're expecting us, are they?"

She'd already asked that. Emily said, "Yes. They're nice. They'll be okay. I mean, okay given everything."

"I've got Kleenex in my bag,"

"It'll be fine."

The traffic was clogged. Jerky. Bev was talking about her parents' comical new puppy and Emily felt jabs of annoyance as she talked.

Then they'd arrived. A magnolia tree in a front garden. A middle class street full of middle class lives. A black cat trotted away from them under a garden door.

They parked. Emily said, "we won't go in yet. I want to tell you what I think has happened before we talk to them. I want to rehearse."

So she began her saga.

"You know why we're here," Emily began. "We now know a lot about how Rose died. We have arrested the man who killed her. He will be spending the rest of his life in jail. I also need to tell you that this story isn't a pretty one. It's as we thought, as you feared. She was almost certainly raped before she died. She may well have been physically hurt as well. There's a lot that we can't say for sure, but we can make some very good guesses."

She stopped there, trying to get the measure of her audience. She didn't always have good sensors in these situations, but she could trust Bev's and looked at her for guidance. Her face told Emily that she was doing okay, so she carried on. She told the story.

"Almost six years ago, Rose Flowers was coming out of the most important relationship of her life. We don't know why it ended, or even really why it started. But the relationship in a strange way both saved her life and ended it. First, it saved her. From the drink and the stripping. From that self-destructive path glazed with black marble and red leather. She found love. She found something strong enough and bright enough to change the course of her life. Her new course led her to the sailing clubs of Swansea Bay and Llanishen. She went back to her studies. She had never exactly terminated them, but during those strip club months her commitment had dwindled to almost nothing. She found her way back to the life path that was first mapped out for her in these confident Bath streets.

I don't know why it didn't work out with Khaled. Probably just two people with too many differences. Any case, they stopped seeing each other, but Rose still liked to haunt the places she had known with him. The Mumbles on Swansea Bay. Llanishen. Places that reminded her of those times. She left that unfortunate party early because she wanted to see the reservoir again, in the last of the light. Which, as mischance would have it, was a bad idea."

Emily paused to see what effect the way she was telling the story was having. Satisfied, she carried on.

"It was a bad idea because Karen Johnston, Elsie Williams's daughter, used to visit her mother for two or three weeks each summer. Her husband, Derek, accompanied her. When they were over here, Karen and Elsie did whatever a mother and daughter do. Derek attended to those household chores that never get done by elderly widows living alone. He hired a pressure washer to rinse cherry-coloured bird poo off the driveway. He went down to Dick Hertford, the plumbers' merchant, to buy parts necessary for whatever plumbing job needed doing. He took his mother in law's car to the garage for its MOT and service.

But Derek wasn't a nice man. He was a rapist and a killer. Walking in the area one evening, he came across Rose, who had come to sit by the moonlit waters. She was young, pretty, defenceless and alone. He raped her. Raped her, then, I imagine, killed her to escape the consequences of his crime.

That left him with a dead body to dispose of. And which might, under normal circumstances, be a little tricky for a man vacationing with his mother in law."

Another pause.

"Option one, presumably the first thing that occurred to him, was simply to drag Rose into the woods, throw some soil over her and hope for the best. But the area around the reservoirs is a mecca for joggers and dog walkers, and Johnston must have felt, rightly, that the chances of discovery were way too high. Her body would have contained his semen. Most likely his blood and skin would have been under his nails too. He couldn't afford the risk. I'm sorry to be so graphic, but I think it right that you are told everything. Anyway, to continue, he took Rose's corpse back to his mother in law's house. To the garage. There were garden tools there, easily sufficient to hack up a corpse. Also a big chest freezer: an easy place to stash the body parts until a more permanent solution could be arranged. There was even a hose and water supply, assuming that he wanted to wash down the garage floor.

Here the story becomes very speculative, but I feel confident all the same. The old woman was an insomniac. Had sleeping issues. The doctor gave her pills, but those things don't always work, as I know well myself. I guess that, on the night of poor Rose's death, the old lady heard noises coming from the garage. Went to investigate and found her son in law ankle deep in blood and body parts.

That's how I picture it, but perhaps she heard everything, stayed in bed, and investigated quietly the next morning, when Johnston was out doing something else.

Whatever, he murdered Rose, brought her home. Elsie Williams found out. With most in laws, that kind of thing would be a problem. Fortunately for Derek Johnston, however, his mother in law was a vicious woman. Not a murderer, but a quarrelsome, vindictive woman of nasty mind and nasty temper. Not the sort of person to let a good corpse go to waste, and she didn't.

It was from about that point that Williams started to receive supplementary income from the Johnstons. It was a year after that she got her new conservatory, paid for by Derek Johnston. The loathsome old woman apparently didn't mind too much that her son in law was a killer. Not if she could wangle some extra income and a house upgrade.

I'm sorry, but we haven't yet found all of Rose. I'm guessing Johnston disposed of the other half the way you might. Chunks of corpse wrapped up in polythene, weighted with a brick, dropped in some remote lake up in the hills. But he didn't have much time. Flowers's death took place just thirty-six hours before the two Johnston's were on a flight back to Oz. Assuming that Karen didn't know anything, he'd have been limited in what he could do. Throw in the time needed to clean down the garage, come to some accommodation with his mother in law, plus the time needed to pack up and generally act like everything was fine, and I think he flew away the next evening, leaving plenty of Rose in Elsie Williams's freezer.

And then? Well, criminals generally feel panicky and upset in the first day or two following a killing. But soon, if police action doesn't seem to be catching up with them, those feelings often mutate. Serial killers almost never start out intending to kill multiple victims. The first one happens almost by accident. Thereafter, they start to feel a kind of superhuman untouchability. It's that feeling which creates the repeat offender.

Johnston went back to Australia. No visits from the police. No alarms coming from South Wales. Everything normal.

A year passed.

Johnston, I suspect, returned to Wales intending to finish the job of disposing of the corpse. But he didn't. I think Elsie Williams wanted to keep the corpse as a way to keep the blackmail money coming in. She needed that corpse, or felt that she did.

But as well as that, I think the pair of them had a nasty pleasure in knowing that in the garage freezer, next to the bits of pork and the apple compotes, there was half a dead girl as well. Did they talk about getting rid of it? Did Johnston try to dispose of it? I don't know. Invulnerability does strange things to rational thinking.

Then, the following summer, Elsie Williams tumbled a small boy off his bike. A hot day. The family out in the garden. The garage door lifted. Beynon would have come in via the garage. Might have banged around in there. Certainly emerged into the garden from the garage.

That moment would have terrified Johnston. He'd have realised, suddenly, how thin his skin of protection truly was. If he went back to Australia, if his mother in law did anything stupid, or if, in a moment of senility, she started to babble about the corpse in the freezer, he was done for.

He no longer felt safe. His mother in law didn't want to release the corpse because her hold over Johnston would disappear if she let that happen, but he needed some way to protect himself.

The plan they cooked up was something that could only have occurred to the mentally unbalanced, yet it had a strange kind of logic to it too. The plan was to distribute the body so widely that it would be impossible to pin the blame on any one owner.

So Derek started to distribute the corpse. To anyone who had offended him or offended his mother in law. His target were the people he interacted with on his various maintenance chores. The pressure washers, the garage mans, the plumbers' merchants. Maybe they pissed him off in some obscure way. Or maybe he was just a bastard.

Elsie's targets were more capricious. Arthur Price, who burned his garden rubbish. His plot was mostly devoted to vegetables, so there wasn't much rubbish to burn. But espaliered fruit trees need pruning in summer. Either while the Johnstons were making their annual visit or just before. So the old lady's rage would have been burning at its brightest just when Derek was on hand to satisfy it. It was the same story elsewhere. The church warden's bicycling children, for example, would have been busiest in spring and summer, offending the spiteful old widow with their youth and their shirtlessness. No doubt she found reasons to be furious with people in autumn and winter too, but they weren't top of her summertime hate list.

The combination of summertime targets and household maintenance targets first alerted me to Derek

Johnston. What clinched it was the weird way the Flowers body parts were found. In freezers. In barrels of lawn mower oil. In jam jars of vegetable oil. The forensics bods were puzzled, but pretty consistent in their belief that none of this stuff had been decomposing for the full five years. And even if you date the degradation from Benyon's house visit in 2007, the rate of decomposition looked puzzling. In particular, the polythene wrapped arms in Ryan Humphry's roof had degraded less than their apparent age would suggest, even if you take 2007 as the date.

But that was a clue in itself. These days, any bag of salad is packed in nitrogen. It's done like that to exclude the oxygen which would accelerate deterioration. Nitrogen isn't a hard gas to get hold of. Any welder will have it. Other inert gases, notably helium, are even simpler and cheaper to procure. My guess is that Johnston packed those arms in helium to make them last longer.

That's speculation, admittedly, but what isn't is Derek Johnston's background. He worked in food processing. A little investigation told me that he was a food technologist, senior enough to be on the conference circuit, talking about the latest advances in packing technologies and the like. His day job involved preserving foods, including meat. I think he saw Rose Flowers's corpse the same way. A dark joke, if you're kind. A personality disorder with schizoid elements, if you're not.

In any case, Johnston was reluctant to let his trophy wither and decompose. So he made efforts, however basic, to preserve the pieces. That was part of the reason I never really bought into the linkages between Flowers's death and Khaled's one. One corpse was preserved, the other one scattered. That always said two murders to me, not one.

It came to our attention that Johnston was going to be travelling to the UK on business. When he came to immigration control, we detained him. The flight had got into Heathrow late. It had come via Singapore, been diverted by a mechanical problem en-route, and had finally discharged its cargo of exhausted, cramped, and smelly passenger around four hours later than scheduled.

There was a long queue at immigration and we let Johnston get to the head of it. As soon as he did, he was asked to step aside to answer some questions for Border Control. We had him ushered to one of those small white bureaucratic rooms. So cheap and small and standardized that any sane person would want to kick the walls in after about twenty minutes.

We left him on his own for two hours, with a small plastic cup of coffee that we'd allowed to go cold.

Then we got an Asian-British immigration officer to spend thirty minutes asking him pointless questions about his paperwork and punching buttons on a computer keyboard, while we watched proceedings from behind a one-way mirror. Me. Webster. Mervyn Rogers. Our man looked pissed off and shattered. Just how we like our suspects.

Then we made our move. We entered the room.

Webster first told him that he being placed under arrest for the murder of Rose Flowers. Rogers put the handcuffs on, none to gently.

Then we battered him. Not physically, alas, but with one of those hostile interviews that Rogers is so good at. He made it seem like we knew everything. That we were only after various final confirmations.

For an hour or so, I thought we were going to swing it. Rogers led the interview. Webster launched occasional rocket attacks of her own. I interjected when I needed to, which was seldom. The pair of them were scary. Relentless, well informed, in control.

Most people would have crumbled. Johnston almost did. English law doesn't allow us to give suspects the full Guantanamo treatment, but give or take some orange jumpsuits, a Sydney to London flight comes remarkably close on the sleep deprivation and general craziness front. Johnston almost gave way, just so he could get himself to a shower.

But he didn't. At about the seventy-five minute mark, he said, "Sod it," pushed back his crappy little cushionless chair, and said nothing more. Our tape recorder picked up the background chatter of flight announcements but not a further word from him.

They wouldn't necessarily have been defeated even then.

Part of the problem with Takeaway all along was that we never really knew where to focus. Now that we did, we'd already got the lab men looking to link all the various parts back to Elsie Williams's garage. They'd already got one positive hit. The jam jar that held the thumb and the vegetable oil contained in the seal of its lid particles of ceramic dust that appear to match a broken vase on Williams's tool shelves. Further work of that sort may help us to build a case that was viable in court. Owen Jenkins's statement that he wasn't allowed to store tools in the garage was persuasive evidence that Williams and Johnston knew parts of Rose Flowers were still in there. The financial data which showed that Elsie Williams's income suddenly took a hike after Flowers's death. All the other little bits and pieces.

But perhaps we won't bother.

Because we are not now the only people with an interest in Johnston.

Our arrest of Johnston was notified automatically to Interpol. And, as luck would have it, while Johnston was in the air over the Indian Ocean, the New South Wales police received an anonymous phone call from a young woman alleging violent sexual assault by Johnston. The woman might or might not have had a Welsh accent, and who might or might not have been calling from her very sexy new Alfa Romeo.

The Aussie police obtained a search warrant. Forcing entry to the property, they found two dismembered female corpses stored, frozen, in a garden outbuilding. The corpses were incomplete, suggesting distribution had already begun. Although the house itself appeared normal in every respect, the outbuilding contained the dismembered, preserved remains of countless wild animals and even a few domestic ones. Items had been pickled, salted, dried, frozen, desiccated, vacuum sealed, and tinned. There were fax paws in nitrogen, a human hand packed in potassium nitrate.

No one, Karen Johnston said, was ever allowed access to the building, which had no windows and a triple lock on the door. The police, so far, believe her.

Intensive enquiries are ongoing.

Our own preliminary psychiatric investigation of Johnston has revealed a withdrawn individual of low affect. In the words of the summary, "His mood is neutral or even blank. He shows emotional activity only when asked about the reasons for his arrest and incarceration, a subject which confuses him. He gives conflicting reports of his previous mental history, but some episodes of psychosis or hallucination cannot be ruled out."

Emily stopped.

"You're not going to go through all that with them, surely?" Bev said.

"No, of course not, but they deserve to know as much as they need. We'll know as we go along."

Rosemary Flowers, Rose's mother, answered the door, wearing a navy jumper and a charcoal skirt. Her husband hovered behind in his dark grey suit, home early from work.

They went inside to the kitchen. Tea was made. Neither Emily nor Bev wanted tea but it was part of the ritual. What law abiding people do when they have police officers in the house.

Then they were all at table. A clock ticked somewhere in the hall. Through French doors at the back, Emily could see the long tresses of the willow tree and the same black cat motionless underneath.

She thought back to the low-key Swansea psychologist. The man was pretty much bang on the money from the word go. If Johnston had lived in the UK, they'd have got him much faster, but you can't go to foreign police services on a hunch and nothing more, and they didn't even have a hunch. There had been 288 people of interest and not a clue.

"The good news is," Emily began, "is that we have your daughter's killer. He will receive a life sentence. I doubt if he will ever walk free again. He will certainly never injure anyone again. What I don't know is whether we have enough evidence to convict him here. If you want us to, we will try. We'll keep him detained as we build our case. If the CPS, the Crown Prosecution Service...."

But the husband, John, interrupted her. He cleared his throat, with the hoarsness of scraping rocks.

"No." There's no need. As long as he does his time."

His wife was crying then. Tears like sand. But also nodding. "I don't want him," she says. "I don't want him...."

She couldn't complete her sentence, but they all knew what she meant. She and her husband wanted the man in jail. But they didn't want the trauma of a trial. They didn't want the trauma of a trial that might go wrong. If the police in New South Wales would take care of everything, and if he served his jail time on the other side of the world, so much the better. The moons of Saturn wouldn't be too far, as long as this pair are concerned.

Bev and Emily had accomplished their mission. A mission to save their own police force and the British taxpayer some unwanted costs. Emily, however, didn't have any sense that they'd pushed this pair into a decision that they didn't want to make. It felt like the right outcome. A good one.

"I'm so pleased you've got him," said Rosemary Flowers, "so pleased." As her tears still fell.

They didn't rush off. To start with they assumed they were intruders in the grief, but then they realised something different. The opposite was closer to the truth. They were actors, essential for this stage of things, as necessary as the vicar, the counsellor or the mumsy neighbour.

So they took their time.

"Her body," said John. "I assume we can have it now? For cremation, I mean."

"Yes. There'll be one or two last formalities, I'm sorry to say, but we'll get those done as soon as we can. I'm sorry it's been so long."

They were almost finished when Emily asked, "would it be possible for me to see Rose's room? One last time. I feel I've got to know her a little. I want to pay my respects."

Emily was unsure how the request was received, but was, nevertheless, taken upstairs. The willow tree. The beige carpets. But the room was not the same. The duvet had changed. The poster was no longer on the wall. The wardrobe was empty.

Her look must have expressed her surprise.

"After you came last time, you and Mrs. Webster, John and I realised it was time to move on. We shouldn't still hold on to it all. We've kept everything precious. The photographs, of course, we could never throw those away."

For a moment, she was on the brink of more tears. But it had been five years and even tears must have an end. Emily sat on the bed. There was a box of junk. Stuff that looked like it was for throwing away, not keeping. There's a small plastic model sailing boat and Emily picked it up.

"Your husband mentioned that you'll cremate Rose's remains. Do you know what you'll do with the ashes? Will you inter them or....?

"We'll scatter them. She liked her freedom. And she didn't have long enough to explore the world. Maybe on the Gower somewhere, she liked her time there."

"Swansea Bay," Emily said, with too much speed and certainty. "She loved it there. You should scatter her ashes on the waters of the bay."

"Maybe. Maybe, yes."

Rose's mother gave Emily a look that questioned her right to have any opinion on the subject. All Emily could see was Rose, the daughter and her mother with the same name. like they were one and the same person. The hockey playing girl merging with this Bath housewife. For a moment she couldn't quite tell whose world she was in. They seemed equally present; equally real.

There was some more conversation between them, but Emily was a bit lost. She wasn't sure what either of them was saying. When they got up to go back downstairs, Emily saw that she was still holding the boat.

"Were you going to throw this out?"

She was.

"May I keep it?"

"Yes."

They went downstairs. Bev was telling John about the final processes with the coroner and the forensic people. Her tone was professional, sympathetic, competent and Emily saw how bad she herself could be at times. They drove back in silence and darkness and the windscreen wipers kept the beat all the way.

-54-

Oslo felt much as Emily expected. An enormous sky with the sun fixed low against a pale horizon. Darkness welled up at street level as lights came on. The buildings were solid, blocky, a northern twist on classical. They could exist anywhere, almost, except for those muted Nordic tones. Lichen green, rust brown. ochre yellow and, always, at the ends of streets, a glimpse of sea and the scrape of salt.

She was due to meet Lenny at a city hotel. A bland business type place. Unremarkable. She booked in under her own name and made a mental note that she would be paying in cash. She hired a black Toyota Land Cruiser at the airport; boxy and basic. Lenny asked her to get a car. He didn't say what sort, but it seemed about right.

She checked in, dumped her bag, stayed just long enough in her room to get annoyed with it and then went downstairs so that she could start getting annoyed with the whole of downtown Oslo.

As she stepped out of the lift, she saw Lenny entering the hotel. He looked like he always did, but with a gym bag over his shoulder. He checked himself in. Emily didn't see what name he used, but she knew he used a few identities. He told her to go upstairs as he had to go and see about some stuff. He took her car keys and said he'd find her later.

She didn't know what he meant, and didn't want to be copped up just waiting, so she went out to explore. She walked down to the seafront to watch the boats and the waves. She thought it resembled Cardiff, except for those extra few degrees of latitude that crept in everywhere she looked. They were farther north than any part of mainland Britain, on a parallel with Orkney and Saint Petersburg. The sea has a grey blue seriousness it lacks in Wales. It is fed by meltwater running off granite and calving glaciers. A sea that booms with the sound of beluga whales foraging under ice.

The buildings lining the front were treble glazed, thickly insulated. Cold stones set by an icy sea.

The Precision Tools case was shot. The whole thing. If their battle was for Stalingrad, it turned out that they were playing the part of the German Sixth Army. Webster was their General Paulus: surrounded, starved, frozen, tricked, destroyed. They thought that the multiple waves of legal attacks launched by Precision Tools were there to bleed their resources, slow the enquiry to the point of stalling. They were wrong. It was a blind, a diversion.

Khan, it turned out, spent the winter chasing up his connections. A rich, well-connected businessman murmuring in his buddies' rich and well-connected ears. Ivor Harris stood up in Parliament, denouncing their pending case, though no charges had yet been brought, calling for ministers to intervene on behalf of "this fine local firm." Initially, his speech appeared no more than empty showmanship. He was speaking to an almost empty Chamber. Any response he got was evasive and placatory.

Except that soon it wasn't. A senior civil servant at the Ministry of Defence issued a paper 'clarifying' the regulations on the licensing procedures for weapons export. The paper referred obliquely to 'persistent misunderstandings arising from inadequate MOD guidance.' It launched a consultation paper aiming at an intended regulatory reform. The document was bullshit. The original regulations were crystal in their clarity and Precision Tools was in breach. But following the 'clarifications', the UK Trade and Investment and Security

Organisation called Precision Tools in for meetings, the upshot of which was that Precision Tools signed a Memorandum of Understanding which made certain representations as to its future conduct. A small contribution was made to charity by way of recognizing possible past infractions, without admission of liability. A junior minister issued an apology for poor communication.

A junior minister at the MOD and a more senior one at the Foreign Office had lunch with the Director of Public Prosecutions. Emily didn't know what happened at that lunch, what threats, what lies, what blandishments, but, after a DPP ordered 'review,' the CPS said that it could no longer be certain that any prosecution would be successful or that any such prosecution would be in the public interest. They wimped out, backed down, surrendered, gave up.

Emily and Webster: alone in the ruins. No boots, no ammo, nothing to eat but the rats, and Soviet armies surrounding them on every side. They couldn't launch a prosecution on their own. So, like Paulus, they flew the white flag. Dropped the while damn case.

Far from injuring Precision, they had helped it. The UKTI DSO had taken the firm under its wing. Helped it secure new contracts. The firm now planned to sell openly at the IDEX arms fair. At SOFEX. At others too. Farnborough in the UK. Defexpo in India. Defence Services Asia. The firm was expanding, negotiating for new industrial space to replace its existing facility. Idris Khan's only mistake was to have gone undercover in the first place. If he'd just had the wit to ask the British government for its specialist Selling-Guns-to-Dictators marketing support, he'd have got it. The whole nine yards. He wouldn't even have had to frame Mark

Mortimer. Aftab Khaled, silly sod, could have won himself a knighthood for export services, instead of getting himself chopped to pieces and scattered throughout his favourite beauty spot.

Webster tried to cheer Emily up. McCormack was certainly heading for a life sentence. Johnston too. But she wasn't cheered. Johnston was a nut. A sadistic dangerous nut, who deserved jail and would get it. It was their job to put people like him away and they had done their job. Nothing more. As for Olaf and Ross: they were trivial. Units moved around the battlefield by a distant field marshal. What those two did was wrong, but you still want to hang the general, not shoot the infantryman.

She was starting to think she was playing a game whose rules had been tampered with. The opposition was winning. Perhaps they always did. Except that the game wasn't quite over. One part was still in play. Olaf. Idris Khan either directly ordered the Khaled killing or was involved in it. Emily couldn't prove that, but they did know that one of Khan's phones received a call from Capel the night she was almost murdered. They had very strong evidence to suggest that Khan's employee, Mark Mortimer, was framed for a drug deal as a way to silence him. It would seem remarkable, to say the least, if Khan had not also authorized, or at least assented to, the Khaled murder. And, if so, Olaf was their one remaining chance to prove it.

She hung around on the seafront long enough to get chilly, then bought a sausage and mustard hot dog from a fast food place and ate it standing up.

When she couldn't think of anything else to do she drifted back to the hotel. No Lenny. She lay on her back and read an airport paperback until it annoyed her. The process took all of seven pages.

At half past eight, she got hungry again and ate a sandwich from the bar downstairs. At half past nine, Lenny came to find her. He tapped lightly at her door and walked straight on in. He had hash, rolling tobacco, and cigarette papers. They threw the window up, even though there was a light frost outside, and smoked. There was nothing much else to do. At midnight, Lenny said, "Okay. We leave now."

Emily stared at him. Was he serious?"

He was. Emily didn't argue. They drove out of the underground car park with Emily at the wheel. They picked up the signs to Trondheim and stuck to the E6 most of the way. It was six and a half hours according to her telephone satnav. She could have cut the time if she had been willing to speed.

Emily drove and Lenny slept. The road was unlike any British motorway. It had one lane in each direction. Tarmac creasing where the land had moved. There was water and ice on the road and flashing stems of silver birches. Snow. Grey rock wall and a million whispering pines. The roads were all but empty.

At three in the morning, they had a comfort break. There were stars overhead, more numerous than you ever see in Cardiff. A million stars. More stars than people. Emily spent a few minutes stretching. As she was doing that, she was surprised to find Lenny beside her. He stretched too, but briefly, before rummaging in the back of the car and pulling out a rifle and a couple of handguns.

Emily didn't think they had come with the car hire.

She said, "We're not here to shoot anyone."

"I know," Lenny's voice and gaze were level.

"I just want a clean capture. Nothing messy. Nothing...." She gestured at the guns.

"I know." He gave her one of the handguns, the smaller one. "That's why you need this. So no one wants to be silly. Here, try this. Is for little hands."

She fired a few rounds at a tree trunk. Lenny adjusted her grip and stance. He nodded. "Okay." He wanted her to go on firing, though, so she did. Fifty rounds. Concentrating. Waiting for the weapon to stop feeling alive. She knew she'd have gunshot residue all over her wrists, so was rather hoping no one was going to be swabbing them.

Meanwhile, Lenny tinkered around with his rifle. He was firing from behind the car at a tree trunk caught in its headlights. Each time he fired, he checked the shot through the telescopic sights, then adjusted the calibration. He checks the settings until he was satisfied, then blazed off ten shots in rapid succession and checked the target again. He fired a few rounds with his handgun, but doesn't bother with any calibration.

He reloaded the guns and put them back in the car.

"Accuracy International," he said. "Arctic Warfare type."

She didn't know what that meant but didn't ask. They had made a real mess of a couple of trees, and there was a litter of cartridges on the ground. But who cared? Norway's a big place. It could afford a couple of messed up trees.

She drove on while Lenny slept. The din of their shooting was still echoing in her ears. For the first time, she wondered whether she'd made the right call in coming there. She felt afraid.

The road unspooled under her wheels. Trees, rocks and stars. The car felt different now that she knew there were guns in the back. Heavier. More purposeful. After a while, it was time to turn off the E6. She glanced at Lenny, wondering whether to wake him, but found that he was already awake.

"Okay. I drive."

They swapped over. It was colder up there than it was in Oslo. Partly the night. Partly being higher and out of the city. But also these accumulating northerly miles. They were in late March now. It wasn't spring as she'd ever known it, but it was what passed for spring up there. Although everything was hard frozen, she could see the streaks and marks where ice had melted during the day. When they stopped in the middle of the night, some of the snow had that granular, crystalline quality you get when snow softens during the day and refreezes at night.

Lenny said, "You want him alive, yes?"

"Yes."

Emily wanted more than that. She wanted evidence. His phone, his laptop, his papers. Anything that might expose the line that linked Khaled's corpse to Khan's silky arrogance. Olaf might well be cautious enough not to retain anything that might connect him to murder, but perhaps not. Out here, on the very edge of the habitable world, he might figure that keeping a mobile phone wouldn't prove disastrous.

Lenny drove on. It wasn't yet sunrise, but there was a softening of the darkness. When they were ten miles away, Lenny stopped. He drank from a thermos of black tea. Also something else. She didn't know what, but thought it could have been ethanol or something of that sort. To reduce muscle tremors. She knew marksmen use it.

The guns in the back seem huge. She was scared now. Not so much for herself, not with Lenny next to her, but because of the scale of these choices she was making.

Going to Glasgow didn't strike her as a big deal at the time. She hadn't expected to encounter Ross, but was reasonably confident of managing him if she did. Likewise, the other little things she'd done off-piste in this case. But now? She had in her head a picture of what ought to happen. Her vision was: surprise Olaf in his sleep, tie him up, search the house, locate all incriminating items and place them where the Norwegian police will surely find them. Then leave. Back to Oslo. An anonymous phone call to the local cops. Let the ordinary processes of justice do their stuff.

But a picture in her head was one thing. Reality was another. She hadn't driven up to Glasgow with a carful of guns. They could still turn back. She almost said something, but when she opened her mouth no words come out.

She didn't know what she was doing. Lenny did, though. He drove with alertness. She'd never seen him like that. In hunting mode, not training mode. When the satnav said they were five miles from their target, Lenny flicked his headlights off and the road became a channel of dark grey through ribbons of snow. They rode uphill. Rocks on both sides of us. Grey cliffs blotting out the stars. When the road forked, they took the one that was unpaved. A rough track, leading up.

As they got to the top, Lenny travelled slower, searching for the crest. He drove like a man who knew the landscape, even though she didn't think he'd been there before. Homework with Google Earth, perhaps.

He came to a halt, just before the final rise and they got Lenny shoved his handgun into his coat pocket, then took his rifle. He checked the wind. It was still earlier, when they had stopped in the night. It was not windy now, but there was a whisper of breeze running down the valley. Lenny felt the wind and made a small adjustment to his sights. Emily took her handgun, feeling like a girl in pigtails. Her first day at school.

They walked to the top of the hill, but didn't stop. Lenny didn't want us silhouetted against the light.

They started descending. The track was worse on that side. Exposed rock wherever water had washed away the surface. It was gently freezing. Their breaths made steam ghosts in the air that hung a moment, then dispersed. Pines whispered to each other in Old Norse.

There was only one dwelling visible below them. A rust-red wooden house. Not big. Single-storey. Huddled against the cold. There was a single out building, a log store perhaps. A patch of dirt with a parked four by four.

Beyond the house, the valley flattened into silver. The river coming down from the mountains widened out to a kind of lake, before narrowing again, bolting through a gap in cliffs that walled off the valley end. The lake was ice. The slopes on the far side forested and steep. It was getting lighter all the time. They worked their way farther downhill, until Lenny stopped them. He pulled out some binoculars. Night vision things, she assumed. He scoped things out. There was no light in the house, no smoke in the chimney, no dog in the yard.

As he did his stuff, Emily started to feel better. Almost relaxed, as though this stupid plan might actually work. And because she was relaxed, she didn't notice that Lenny wasn't.

He passed her the glasses.

"There," he said, "Also there, there, and there."

To start with, she couldn't find what he was pointing her towards. Then she could. Dots that glowed a bright green through the glasses, that were otherwise all but invisible in the frost.

She didn't know what they were.

"Is surveillance device. All around the house."

Then she did feel fear. The real thing. A wash of cold that pricked open every capillary. She looked at Lenny, because this was his world, not hers.

He shrugged. "We leave. We kill. We try to capture." Lenny offered her three options, like a waiter offering a choice of soups. Tomato. Chicken. Minestrone.

"I don't know. I mean, isn't there some way to.....?"

"Disable or evade device? Yes, is no problem. Give me six men. Counterterrorist training. Also arctic experience. Easy."

He looked at me, waiting for an answer.

"Let me think."

It felt weird standing out there, in the three quarter dark, the surveillance cameras in front of them, a professional killer in the house below. A gun in her hand and Lenny tooled up beside her.

She asked, "If we go in, what are our chances of making a clean capture? No shooting, no blood?"

"Twenty prozent. Maybe ten. I don't know this man." Lenny used the German word *prozent,* instead of *percent.* The odds were terrible in either language. "If we continue, is better to start now." Lenny gestures up at the sky. He didn't want it to get any brighter.

Her mouth said, "we can't leave."

She heard the words. She understood why someone would think that way. Jan-Fjeistad was a professional killer. Leaving him untouched meant allowing him to continuing his bloody trade. If they drove away from there now, someone would pay for that decision with their life.

But Emily didn't move. She was a motionless thing in a motionless world.

Lenny made a tiny gesture, asking her to commit. And this time, she said, "We can't leave." Not just her mouth; all of her. She gave a little nod of decision.

"Okay," said Lenny. "So we try to capture. Otherwise kill."

Minestrone it is. If they're out of minestrone, they would go for the chicken.

She nodded. "Okay."

Her voice sounded like it belonged to somebody else completely. Nothing there felt real.

"Wait here. When I say, you go there." He pointed, off the track, to a boulder partway down the slope. "Don't run. Just walk. Gun please. Safety off. If you have to fire, aim with both hand and shoot slow."

She nodded, despite having understood nothing. Lenny was already off. Down the hill. Dancing really. Rock to rock. Tree to tree. A shadow dancing through the half-light.

After a while, he stopped against a tree. She was about to follow him, when she realised he hadn't yet given the instruction to move. So she stayed put. Lenny checked his binoculars again, then his scope, then the binoculars.

Somewhere around them the colours shifted a millionth of a shade as dawn strengthens its grip.

Then Lenny signaled and she walked down the hill. The house they were approaching had only a single window facing them. Lenny had his rifle fixed on the window. He didn't acknowledge her as she walked past not ten yards from him. She could see the nearest one, a small black box on a rickety fencepost. Wires too, presumably, but she didn't see them.

Then she was behind her rock and Lenny moved again. He pointed at a new rock. She walked quickly toward it and smeared herself into its shadow.

Lenny's turn. As he passed her, there was a sound from the house. She heard the detonation and it took her half a second to realise the shot had come from Olaf. She didn't see where the bullet struck, but Lenny hadn't stopped moving. He got to a thin rise of ground, now just 150 metres from the house. He settled into a firing position. Lying on his belly, legs slightly spread and to the side. Fires.

She couldn't see where the bullet went. She didn't know what Lenny was trying to do. He turned, beckoned her toward him, made a gesture to indicate she needed to come slowly, then rolled back onto his belly and fired another shot. He fired three more times as she descended.

When she got next to Lenny, the house felt very close indeed. She could see Olaf's gun now, a thin metal line against the angle of the open casement.

Without taking his eye off his rifle scope, Lenny filled her in.

"Okay, Fjerstad has rifle, not just shotgun. From this range, very good shot can hit us, so be careful. But this rifle" – Lenny indicates his own – "is for snipers, not just for hitting big stupid animal. Also, bullet can go through wall, no problem. Fjerstad maybe knows this.

Anyway, is worried." His voice adjusts and turns posh and English. "Right now Mr. Fjerstad is shitting himself.

She nodded, as though this was all normal.

Nodded, and saw as she did that there was smoke beginning to rise from the house's only chimney. That was either because Olaf was starting to prepare himself a nice grilled breakfast, or because he was in the business of destroying evidence.

Emily said, "he's burning evidence."

"Naughty man. Is not allowed. I think we ask him to leave the house."

Lenny swung his rifle through ten degrees and aimed at the big green oil tank up against the wall of the house. He put two bullets into the tank, waited for a spill of oil, then shot another round onto the tank's concrete base.

Bullet. Concrete. Spark. Flame.

The oil tank disappeared in a fireball. Intense orange and black. Oily clouds circled down around the updraught. She could feel the heat as the house started to blaze.   While she was admiring the flame, Lenny put five bullets through the timber walls in a kind of hurry up to Olaf, as though having an oil tank explode outside wasn't enough.

Then Lenny was moving again. Running for the corner of the house. She didn't know what she was supposed to do, so she followed him. She still had her gun in her hand. Still haven't fired it. The ground was rocky and sloping, but she ran the way Lenny did. By instinct; letting her feet find their own placement.

Lenny was twenty yards ahead of her. He was fixed, she thought, on gaining access to the front of the house, to get a clear sweep of the terrain there. If he could get to the front corner of the house, his superior weaponry and his vastly superior superior skills would give him command of the battlefield. But there was a stand of trees and low bushes between the house and the track leading back up the hill. The trees blocked Lenny's view. Because Emily was farther back, they didn't block hers. The upper branches of the trees were already starting to singe and crackle with the flame.

Olaf wasn't in the house anymore. He wasn't trying to defend his turf. He was trying to get the hell away. He was at the door of his Land Rover Defender. In an instant, he was inside, gunning his engine and heading up the hill.

She screamed to Lenny, but her feet were travelling faster than her brain. She burst out onto the track. Olaf was forty yards away, thirty.

He'd happily run her down. She'd happily shoot him dead.

The car was accelerating towards her as fast as it could, given the adverse slope and the uneven terrain. She saw Olaf's face, tense and white at the wheel.

She found a shooting stance. Fired. Feet planted. Hands out. Squeezed the trigger. Fire, fire, fire, fire. The windscreen ahead of her was shattered glass. The vehicle hit a pothole and instead of adjusting course, slewed up the bank and almost overturned. The front right tyre was exposed now and, aiming as carefully as she could, she emptied the rest of her magazine into it.

The Land Rover didn't move. Then Lenny was next to me.

"Are you okay?"

He didn't wait for her answer, just patted her down, checking her. It turned she was okay, but she only knew that when he told her.

She didn't know where Olaf was. She kept thinking that Lenny was being an idiot, standing there in the open. She was fumbling for a spare magazine, trying to alert Lenny to the danger.

He changed the magazine for her. "You hit him in shoulder. He's going the other way now."

Lenny took her to the front of the house, from where they could see Olaf heading down to the frozen lake. He was moving purposefully, but not running. He had a small backpack, slung over one shoulder only. A ski pole in one hand, his rifle in the other. He was good on skis, she remembered, but he wasn't looking too mobile now. There was something about the way he moved which confirmed that he was wounded.

"He's getting away," Emily said, stating the obvious. Her head was ringing with the gunfire. She felt slow, shocked and stupid.

"No, I don't think."

Lenny laid himself on the ground. His rifle had a stand made of two little folding legs. Lenny opened those out, took a moment to sight himself, then fired a single shot.

Olaf falls instantly.

Emily stared at Lenny, amazed and furious. She knew the whole idea of a clean capture had turned to shit, but since when did Lenny think it was okay to kill the man without even asking her? She had shot at the man too, but in that case it was him or her. She was acting in something approaching self defence.

Lenny disregarded her look. Simply folded his gun stand and says, "ankle."

Sure enough, they saw Olaf righting himself, flinging us a furious look, and staggering on. But not far and not fast. He was on the rocks by the lake shore now.

He moved clumsily. Stones glazed with ice and an ankle shot to hell. If they wanted to pick him up later, they'd be able to do it at a stroll. But they had things to do before that. The house was ablaze. Any evidence they might want was rapidly disappearing, if it hadn't gone already,

Lenny ran to the house, with Emily close behind. The front door was open. Scorching air poured out, as from an oven door. The interior was strangely lit. Nordic dawn and fireball heat, like some carefully constructed palette of beige and grey and violet has been ram-raided with tinfuls of orange, red, and black. That, plus incredible heat.

She went inside.

A strip of dirty cotton hung over the door window. She ripped it off and Lenny knifed it into two. They held the material over their mouths and kept their heads low. The house was small. Just one large living space, then presumably bedroom and bathroom leading off from doors at the end.

They made for the stove. The door was open and there was stuff burning inside. Olaf was probably still feeding the fire when the corner of his house blew up and bullets poured in through his walls. A small ash shovel stood by the stove. Emily used it to shovel everything out. There were some papers, a phone, a laptop. A load of crumpled up newspapers and handfuls of firelighters. Fire and smoke everywhere. She burned her hand on the laptop, trying to get it free of the firelighters.

The wooden building was burning fast now. They needed to get out. She hurt her hand a second time trying to pick up the laptop, but Lenny was ahead of her. He brought a cushion from the sofa, knifed open the top and ripped out the pad. They used the cushion pad like an oven glove to bundle all the items from the stove into the cushion cover. Laptop, phone. Whatever papers they could rescue.

They ran out of the house, lungs screaming. They'd probably wasted their time. Emily doubted if Olaf wrote much on paper, and the electronics look knackered.

The valley suddenly seemed amazingly clear and cold and bright.

Above the lake, a rocky hummock rose from the fields. Lenny got there before Emily. He lay out on the ground and set up his rifle. Olaf was four hundred yards from them now. Crossing the frozen water. Moving slowly.

Lenny sighted up just for the sake of it. But there was no hurry now. No hurry at all.

Emily pulled the laptop out of the cushion bag. The surface was hot, but no longer scorching. She tried to open the screen, but the whole machine was buckled. There was a mess where the battery leaked.

Lenny looks at it solemnly. "Is fucked," he says.

"Yes."

The phone was in worse shape.

"Is also fucked," says my electronics guru.

"Yes."

She looked through the papers, but they looked like trash to me. Literally. Stuff that Olaf pulled from the dustbin so he could get a fire burning more quickly. If they couldn't salvage data from the electronics, she doubted if they'd have anything useful at all.

The smoke which was leaking from the house was billowing now. A latticework of rafters outlined in black.

Lenny had his sights fixed on Olaf's back. He adjusted his posture by infinitesimal amounts. Either to keep pace with Olaf's movements or to move his aim onto different targets. Head. Chest. Leg.

Olaf, as though feeling that invisible pressure, turned and looked at them. Motionless. A black figure against the white. She didn't know what they looked like to him. Didn't know what his thoughts were as he saw his house ablaze, his possessions gone, his cover blown.

What do you think when you're in that position? What do you think as you turn back to face your direction of travel and see your future? A frozen lake. A facing slope of rock, snow, and pines. On the run for ever, uphill and alone, shoulder wounded and ankle smashed. And a rifle bead tightening on your body.

Emily recalled that when she was alone in the snow, she hadn't felt alone. She felt her family. Most of all she felt the wonderful presence of her lovely Books.

"Leave him," she said to Lenny.

"Leave? Really?"

"Yes."

"If there's salvageable data from the electronics, we've got it. If not, it's gone forever. And we've done enough to debar Fjerstad from his current career. A shoulder can be fixed, perhaps. The ankle, possibly not. But the physical side of things is only half of it. We've made a thorough-going mess of his home. His car is riddled with bullets. There are bullet casings everywhere. The Norwegian police will have to investigate hard. As they do, I'll find a way to allege, anonymously, on the internet that Fjerstad is a contract killer. I'll link him to Khaled, to McCormack. Publish photos, his army resume, his address details, everything.

Contract killers need darkness to operate in. By the time we've finished his face will be on every newspaper in Norway. On the radar of every police service in the world. He won't do to others what he did to Khaled. What he tried to do to me."

As she was explaining this to Lenny, he didn't listen. He just laid down the gun and rummaged in his pocket, got out a joint, lit it, took a puff and offered it to Emily.

She shook her head. Her attention was all with Olaf, who is moving differently now. Slowly and with a sudden terrible vigilance.

She turned to Lenny, not sure what was going on.

Lenny said, "Is not lake. Is river."

He traced the line of the river's flow with his finger. Emily saw it. There was a bluishness in the ice. A difference in the way it carried the snow.

Olaf was moving with acute care now. With fear. She saw him jolt. His boot had gone through the ice. He recovered and carried on.

And she didn't want him to. All of a sudden, she didn't want this anymore. She wanted him to retrace his steps. To share a smoke, shake hands, forget about all this. If he could give her anything on Khan or Saadawi, she would take it. And if not, well, they would shake hands anyway.

But Olaf didn't know what she was thinking. Didn't know and didn't care. He went on. Stumbled once more and recovered. Then another stumble, and he was gone. The grey ice field suddenly darkened as water blackened it. Olaf's head and hat were visible above the ice. His arms. He was trying to roll his weight out of the water and back onto the ice. But each time he tried it, the ice shelf crumbled beneath him. He was too far now for them to see his movements in any detail. He was a fly struggling against glass.

It didn't take long. They were too distant to witness the final choreography in any detail. They just saw that, one moment, there was a head above the water, and the next moment, only a level silence. Black, silver, white. And moving water. A glimpse of moving water.

Half a minute passed without sign of further movement.

Lenny offered her the joint again and she took it.

"This first time for you, I think."

"No. the second," she said automatically, because it happened to be the truth. But there were different possible truths and she'd chosen the wrong one. So she corrected herself, "The second time I've killed someone, but it feels like the first. The one before went very fast. I didn't have the time to notice anything."

"You are okay?"

"Yes."

Lenny laughed at that, took the joint from her and drew hard on it. "Stupid question.

Olaf's house was pouring with flame now. The roof was mostly gone. She could see the roof joists still, spiderlike through the fire. They wouldn't last. The walls were still largely intact, but they'd completely gone too.

She didn't know how much information there might have been there, but they would not find out. Olaf's property was rapidly reuniting with its owner. Entering the same dark house by different routes.

Fire and ice.

Ross was a thug. Unprincipled and brutal. Olaf too. But he wasn't only that. In another world, another life, she could imagine sharing a drink with him. Enjoying an evening in his company. As it was, she'd spent one evening with him and one morning. The latter resulted in his death. The former, almost, in her own.

Emily said, "I think I knew. I was just pretending I didn't."

Lenny gave her a questioning look.

"I had this picture in my head," she said, "that we would stroll into Olaf's house at dawn, catch him unawares, locate all the evidence we could possibly need. But in truth, I think I knew that was always an outside bet. I think I knew we might have to use force."

"Always better to have gun." Lenny shrugs.

"Tomato. Chicken. Minestrone. I guess I knew I'd be eating chicken."

Lenny looked at her with those eternal brown eyes of his. He didn't know what she was talking about. Doesn't care. He finished the joint and flicked it away into the snow. Emily picked it up.

"DNA on the saliva," she explained.

They walked back up the hill and down the other side to the car. Lenny took the wheel for the drive back to Oslo. It was twenty minutes before they passed anyone at all and seventy minutes before they saw a CCTV camera.

The Norwegian cops would find the evidence of their shootout, all right, but they wouldn't be able to place their car at the scene or have any reason to guess that a kooky Welsh cop and her screwed-up Spetsnaz buddy are the ones they needed to interview.

Somewhere along the way, they stopped for food. Lenny filled his plate with cheese and sausage. She couldn't face any of that. She took a bowl of muesli, but didn't make much of a dent in it.

Olaf was alive and now he was dead. That was a pencil mark of a kind. When they got back to Oslo, Emily went straight to bed. When she woke up, Lenny was still around, but the car had no weapons in it. And last night never happened.

-55-

Three days later, back in England, Emily took the laptop and phone to a commercial data-recovery outfit that did work for the MOD, among others. She showed Olaf's phone and laptop to a technician, but even before she had them properly out of her bag, he said, "You are joking, right?" Three minutes later, she was leaving the premises, with Lenny's diagnosis amply confirmed.

Just like their case against Precision Tools. Against Idris Khan.

She wouldn't leave it there, of course. The man was an arms smuggler who tried to have her killed. But she would leave it there for now. She had no other option.

The Flowers family did, finally, hold a funeral service for their daughter. It was a private service, so Emily didn't go, though she'd have liked to. But they also held a memorial service at a little grey church. A lot of Rose's student friends come along, not that they were students anymore. A group of people about Emily's age.

Rosemary and John Flowers were there, of course. They recognized her. They seemed surprised to see her, but not unhappy. Emily didn't usually get a lot from church services, because she didn't think Christianity understood dead people very well. She thought it seemed embarrassed by them. But it was a good service. Dignified and sad and celebratory and uplifting. Some people cried. Emily didn't, but she felt something. Perhaps her view was changing.

Webster came along too. She slipped in at the back, after it started. Emily was pleased she came.

After the service, everyone trooped down to the seashore. Rosemary Flowers scattered her daughter's ashes onto a west wind and the west wind blew the fine grey dust far out to sea. People clapped and some cheered. It was a good parting. The right way to finish.

Emily didn't hear from Aftab Khaled anymore, but she bet he was there then, overhead, in the wind, in the unreliable sunshine, in the scream of the gulls. Following Rose's ashes as they spread out on the glittering water. It was a good ending for them both. Emily found herself praying for them both. She caught the significance of the change.

Khaled both saved Flowers's life and, by accident, helped to end it. But by a strange twist of events, his death ended up mirroring hers. Two men who killed for money needed a way to dispose of a corpse. Because Emily happened to report the discovery of a corpse, Olaf – she bet it was him – thought to use that discovery to throw a nice fat red herring their way. A red herring that, to a large extent, succeeded in subverting the whole enquiry.

And yet every circle closes in the end. Khaled never quite found unity with Flowers in life. But he did in death. Operation Takeaway: their own macabre wedding celebration. It was hard for her not to feel a sorrowful sense of completion. Like something satisfied.

As they crunched back up the beach towards the cars, Webster walked alongside her. She said, "Are you able to stay a little or do you have to rush off?"

"I can stay."

"Good," she said. "That's good, because there's someone I'd like you to meet."

Webster's eyes had the luminous excitement of young love. Was it the first stone in her jar?

"I'd like that; I'd like that very much." Emily replied.

In her pocket, Emily had a little plastic boat. Around her neck, she had the necklace that Books gave her at Christmas. On her wrist, she had the little shell bracelet that a little girl gave her. Emily's jar was filling nicely.